When He Was Mine

MJ Masucci

This book is a work of fiction. Any resemblance to actual persons, living or dead, or actual events is entirely coincidental. Although every precaution has been taken to verify the accuracy of the information contained herein, the author and publisher assume no responsibility for any errors or omissions. No liability is assumed for damages that may result from the use of information contained within.

ISBN 978-1-950175-63-5

Chapter 1

I woke from a deep, dreamless sleep, my arm instinctively reaching out to find the bed beside me empty. The last thing I remembered was Oliver's voice, sharp and angry, carrying from the other room as he spoke on the phone. I had drifted off before I could grasp the details.

"Oliver?" I called out, my voice still groggy.

"Yes, sweetheart?" His response was immediate. My heart swelled as his handsome face appeared in the doorway, his sandy hair damp from a recent shower.

"Why didn't you wake me?" I asked, sitting up and rubbing my eyes.

"You were exhausted," he said, leaning against the doorframe. "Probably from all the travel."

“Or maybe because you keep me up,” I teased, a playful smirk tugging at my lips.

His eyes sparkled with mischief. “I keep you up? You’re not exactly innocent in that department. It’s not always me who starts things.”

“You know what I mean,” I replied, raising an eyebrow. “I might need to go back to sleeping at my apartment one night a week just to catch up on rest.”

“Why would you do that?” he asked, crossing the room to sit beside me. “We’re doing great together.”

“So I can sleep,” I said, poking his arm.

He chuckled softly. “Admit it, you sleep better with me next to you.”

I sighed, knowing he was right. Since my father’s murder, nightmares had haunted me, but with Oliver beside me, they had mostly subsided. “Yes, I do.”

“What's on the agenda today?” I asked, pushing the plush white quilt off me. The bed at Hotel SW Los Angeles was so comfortable it felt like sleeping on a cloud.

“We’re meeting one of the developers and touring the property. It’s a mess, so no heels today,” he instructed.

“That’s all I brought, except for my sneakers,” I protested.

“Then wear those,” he said, matter-of-factly.

"With a business suit?" I said with a raised aeyebrow.

Oliver rolled his eyes. "Ryleigh, lots of women wear sneakers with business wear. Trust me, you don't want to be stuck in heels on a construction site."

"If I wear heels, you'll just have to carry me," I teased.

He laughed, shaking his head. "That might be fun, but definitely unprofessional. Sneakers, please."

I stuck my tongue out at him, and he chuckled. "Didn't anyone tell you not to stick your tongue out unless you plan to use it?"

"Come here, and I will," I purred.

"Tempting, but we've got an hour to get ready. Go shower. Breakfast is waiting."

I grumbled as I stood up, opening the thick white terry robe Oliver had wrapped me in the night before. For good measure, I let it slip off my shoulders, hoping to entice him into joining me in the shower like he had the night before. But Oliver just smiled and turned away, leaving me to wash alone, my desire unquenched but the promise of a busy day ahead.

When I emerged from the bathroom, Oliver was already dressed, looking effortlessly dapper in a sharp graphite suit, a crisp white shirt, and a black tie. As handsome as he was naked, clothed he was breathtaking. The tailored suit highlighted his muscular, lean frame, and his jacket sleeves strained slightly against his biceps as he moved, a sight I never grew tired of.

He sipped his coffee, engrossed in a report. On the table next to him was an almost empty plate, the remnants of his breakfast, and a small silver dome covering my meal. I lifted it to reveal a perfectly cooked cheddar cheese omelet, a side of fresh fruit salad, and crispy bacon. He knew me so well.

“Thank you,” I said, settling into the chair opposite him.

“For?” He glanced up, his eyes warm and curious.

“For breakfast. For the job. For you... just everything.”

God, I sounded like an idiot. I was gushing about him like a little girl with her first crush.

He smiled, a genuine, heart-melting smile. “You don’t have to thank me for any of it. You earned the job. As for me, you claimed my heart the minute I saw you in that graduation line. I love you, Ryleigh.”

“How did I get so lucky?” I murmured, marveling at the way he looked at me.

Oliver put down the report, his gaze intense. “It’s me who’s lucky. I waited thirty-six years for you. Honestly, I never thought I would marry.”

“I still can’t believe none of those gorgeous women you dated ever captured your heart,” I said, shaking my head.

“My heart was open, but it was waiting for you. None of those women ever meant anything compared to you,” he replied, his voice earnest and sincere.

Before I could respond, his phone rang. He excused himself and took the call in the bedroom. I picked up the report he had been reading, delving into the details of the real estate project as I ate breakfast. By the time he returned, I had finished my meal and had about half an hour to get dressed.

"Everything alright?" I asked, noticing a slight tension in his posture.

"Yes, fine. Just some loose ends at the office. It was Henri," he replied, taking a seat.

"Why don't I ever see the other two assistants?" I asked, my curiosity piqued.

"Because Henri is their boss. He handles everything directly with me and delegates the rest to them. They're quite capable," he explained.

"What are their names?"

"Anna and Melissa," he answered, raising an eyebrow. "Why the sudden interest?"

"Just curious. Where do they sit?"

"In the cubicle area," he said, a hint of amusement in his voice. "Is this what you want to discuss this morning? The assistants?"

"I'm just curious," I repeated, shrugging.

He chuckled, reaching across the table to take my hand. "Let's focus on getting ready. We have a big day ahead."

. . .

I headed to the bedroom while Oliver answered the knock at the door. Our security team was here, stationed in rooms on either side of us. Vlad, the supervisor, was a man built like a brick wall with beady dark eyes. He rarely spoke to me, and I never engaged him in conversation when he drove me places without Oliver.

Quickly, I dressed in a black business suit and a sleeveless white blouse, opting for my sneakers instead of the matching black heels I preferred. I pulled my mahogany hair into a ponytail, applied a light layer of makeup, and finished with a soft pink lipstick. When I exited the bedroom, Oliver noticed my sneakers and smiled.

“Good girl.”

“Don’t patronize me,” I whispered, frowning.

“I’m sorry.”

The project site was near the ocean, a group of rotting buildings that needed to be torn down and redeveloped. The limo felt crowded despite its size. Our security team, consisting of Vlad, Trevor, Jamal, and Brenda—the only woman—sat on the two bench seats opposite each other. I’d never had a full conversation with any of them.

“Are you okay?” Oliver asked, his voice low and concerned.

“I’m fine. Why wouldn’t I be?” I replied, trying to sound

confident despite the knot of nerves tightening in my stomach. This project was huge, and I didn't want to make a fool of myself by saying something stupid.

"You seemed a bit tense back at the hotel."

"I'm not a child, Oliver. I might be fourteen years younger than you, but I'm an adult," I snapped, my voice sharper than intended.

"I only commented on your sneakers."

"You called me a girl."

He pressed a firm kiss to my cheek and whispered in my ear. "I think you need some sex."

"We had sex last night in the shower. That's not the issue," I whispered back, feeling a mix of frustration and amusement. The truth was, I was cranky this morning. My period was still two days from ending, and not having the freedom to make love wherever we wanted was adding to my irritation.

I turned to look out the window, watching the shoulder of the highway blur by. Oliver curled his hand around mine, giving it a reassuring squeeze. I smiled a little, though he couldn't see it since I was facing the glass.

The ride continued in silence, punctuated only by the hum of the engine and the occasional murmur from the security team. As we neared the site, my anxiety began to ebb, replaced by a growing determination. This project was crucial, and I was ready to prove myself.

Oliver's hand tightened around mine, pulling me back from my thoughts. "We've got this," he said softly, his confidence steadying me.

I nodded, squeezing his hand back. Together, we were unstoppable.

A half-hour later, we arrived at the job site. The limo rolled into the cracked concrete parking lot, drawing the attention of a group of men. They waited as our security team exited first. I was the last to step out, following Oliver as he led me toward the men, all dressed in nearly identical navy-blue striped suits, white shirts, and various red ties.

Two of the men were young, probably a year or two younger than Finley's age of twenty-seven. Their eyes lingered on me a bit too long, but Oliver, a few steps ahead, didn't notice. When we reached the group, introductions were made, and handshakes exchanged.

The men were all related: James and Callan Ryder, the older men, were brothers, and Dillon and Rick, the younger ones, were their sons. Oliver took the lead with James and Callan, discussing business details, leaving me with Dillon and Rick. They quickly engaged me in conversation.

"Are you enjoying Los Angeles?" Rick asked, his eyes studying me.

"It's nice. The weather's cooler in New York, so I welcome the heat," I replied, offering a polite smile.

"It can get pretty hot here during September. Have you had a chance to see the city?" Dillon inquired, his tone friendly.

"Not really. We just arrived yesterday evening."

"You should come out with us, leave the old guys to handle the details," Rick suggested with a playful grin.

"Oliver isn't old," I retorted, a touch defensively.

"He's older than us and much older than you. He's your boss. You don't want to hang out with him. Come out with us tonight. We'll show you a good time."

Dillon chimed in, eager to back up Rick's offer. "Yeah, you'll have a blast with us."

I could just imagine what kind of "good time" they had in mind—probably getting me drunk and trying to take me to bed.

"No, thank you," I said politely even though I was seething.

Rick smirked. "What are you going to do, sit around your hotel room all night?"

"First off, I'm engaged," I said, holding up my hand, the diamond ring glinting in the sunlight.

Dillion snorted. “So? Does that mean you’re strapped to your fiancé? You have a mind of your own, don’t you?”

“You didn’t let me finish. Second of all, that old guy talking with your fathers is my fiancé, and I’d rather spend my night in the hotel with him. Thank you for the offer.”

I left them standing there, jaws agape. What a couple of assholes. They reminded me of the entitled guys I’d encountered at Columbia, used to getting everything they wanted. I stuck close to Oliver, absorbing everything he said to James and Callan.

When it was time to leave, I gave a curt goodbye to the men and slipped into the limo, where our security team was already seated. As the limo pulled away, I stared out the window, trying to shake off my irritation.

“That was rude,” Oliver said, breaking the silence.

“Rude how?” I asked, genuinely puzzled.

“You could’ve offered your hand.”

“Not to those assholes,” I hissed.

His brow furrowed. “James and Callan? You know them?”

“No, their sons. They called you old and wanted to take me to a club, probably to get me drunk and have sex.”

“What exactly did they say to you?” Oliver’s tone darkened, his protective side surfacing.

"They said you were too old and that I shouldn't want to hang out with you. They invited me out, implying I should ditch you for a good time."

Oliver's jaw clenched. "I'll handle it."

I shook my head. "No need. I shut them down pretty effectively."

"I don't like them disrespecting you—or me," he said, his voice tight with anger.

I squeezed his hand. "I handled it. Let's focus on the project. Those guys aren't worth our time."

Oliver nodded, his grip on my hand tightening. "You're right. But if they bother you again, tell me immediately."

"Of course," I assured him. "But for now, let's get back to the hotel. We have a lot to discuss about the project."

As we rode back, the tension slowly ebbed away, replaced by a shared determination to make the project a success and to enjoy each other's company, free from the distractions of entitled brats.

Upstairs in our room, I slipped into a pair of light pink shorts with "Columbia" stamped on the posterior in white block lettering and a matching short t-shirt without a bra. It was just us in the hotel room, and I didn't feel the need for one.

Oliver paced around the living area, phone pressed to his ear. He had discarded his jacket but still wore his dress shirt and slacks. I grabbed a bottle of water from the small refrigerator and plopped onto the couch, picking green grapes from the complimentary gift basket.

"Don't eat too many of those," Oliver said, glancing my way as he loosened his tie and unbuttoned his sleeves.

"Why? Are we going out?" I asked, raising an eyebrow.

"Not right away. I thought we'd order lunch soon. It's almost twelve. We have a conference call at 1:30 and another at 2:30." He paused, his eyes roaming over me. "You're not wearing a bra, are you?"

I grinned. "No. Why do I need to wear a bra?"

"You don't, though you're very enticing without one."

He sat down next to me, his fingers tracing the outline of my breast through the thin fabric. My nipples hardened instantly. Oliver's mouth followed his fingers, sucking gently through my t-shirt. My belly clenched as I pushed his head away.

I let out a frustrated breath. "Don't."

"Why not?" he asked, his voice low and husky.

"Period, remember?"

Oliver's brow furrowed. "I don't give a shit. It doesn't bother me."

"It will make a mess," I protested.

"Want to take a shower together?"

"I wanted you this morning," I admitted, my voice tinged with desire.

Oliver raised his head, his sapphire blue eyes locking onto mine. "You didn't say anything."

"I didn't think I had to. I practically pranced around the bedroom naked."

He quirked an eyebrow. "That's what that was?"

Oliver removed his tie, seductively slipping it through his collar before he started to unbutton his shirt.

"Oliver, sometimes you are so unaware."

He chuckled, his fingers brushing a stray hair from my face. "I hope you know once the house on our island is built, I'll want you naked the entire time we're there."

My brow furrowed. "What about the security staff? It would be embarrassing if they saw me."

"I'm having a secondary residence built for them. They won't be with us."

I wrinkled my nose. "But I can't walk around naked outside. They'll see me."

Oliver smirked. "Let me figure out the details. I want you in as little clothing as possible. Maybe we can take our honeymoon there."

"Honeymoon? We haven't even picked a date," I protested.

He leaned back. “I spoke to Sebastian Wyatt, and the garden room at the SW in New York is ours.”

“What if there’s another event on the date we want? He can’t just bump them.”

Oliver smirked, stretching his arms on the back of the couch. “Sebastian owes me a favor. If we pick a date, that garden room is ours, no questions asked.”

I raised an eyebrow, intrigued. “How do you have that kind of pull?”

“Let’s just say it’s good to have powerful friends. So, when do you want to get married?”

“I’m not sure I’m comfortable with that arrangement. I wouldn’t want to be bumped from my dream venue. Can’t we just find a date they have an opening?” I asked, a hint of worry in my voice.

“They have nothing for the next two years, and I’m not waiting that long to make you my wife,” Oliver said firmly.

“At this point, why don’t we just elope? Find some little chapel and get married right away.”

“Ryleigh, don’t give me that option,” he warned, his eyes gleaming with a mixture of mischief and sincerity.

“Why?” I asked innocently.

“Because I’ll take you right now to get married.”

“Even braless?” I teased, a playful smile tugging at my lips.

"Even braless," he replied, without missing a beat. "Pick a date for our wedding and Sebastian will see that it's taken care of."

"It has to be next year. I have so much to do. I have no idea what type of wedding dress I want or cake flavor to choose."

"We'll hire someone to handle decorations and schedules. We just need to choose food, cake, music, and a few other items. The wedding planner can help us with all that. As for your dress, Rachel and Rigo Vicaria are friends of mine. I'm sure they would be happy to make you the dress of your dreams."

I squealed, "You know Rachel Vicaria? I just read an article about her in the New York Times. She's probably booked solid."

"They'll make room for your dress," Oliver said with a confident smile.

I stared at him, amazed. "You really have connections everywhere, don't you?"

"It's all for you, Ryleigh. I want you to have everything you've ever dreamed of."

I threw my arms around him, burying my face in his chest. "I don't need a fancy dress or a perfect venue. I just need you."

Oliver kissed the top of my head. "And you have me, now and forever. But I want you to have the wedding of your dreams too."

I looked up at him, my eyes shimmering with tears. "Thank you, Oliver. For everything."

"Anything for you, my love. Now, let's figure out a date so we can start planning our perfect day."

"I want the summer, but we can't go to the island during that season," I said, contemplating.

"Why not?" Oliver asked, curious.

"Hurricanes. I'm afraid," I admitted, a hint of anxiety in my voice.

"Don't worry. If there's one approaching, we get out of there. I have my own jet, remember?" Oliver reassured me.

"What about getting off the island?" I asked, wanting to cover all my bases.

"We'll have a boat at our disposal. I can navigate one. I prefer not to."

I was satisfied with his explanation and had to decide on a date.

"How about July thirtieth?"

"The day before your birthday?" Oliver raised an eyebrow.

"It's a Saturday next year."

"Then that will allow me to celebrate you twice in a row," he said with a smile.

I laughed. “Yes, it will. Can we eat lunch?”

“You sure you don’t want to take a shower with me?” Oliver teased, a mischievous glint in his eyes.

“If I take a shower with you, we won’t be eating lunch.”

“Hmm, maybe later then. Let me change—you look at the menu.”

After we ate lunch, we got busy with phone calls and a few emails that needed Oliver’s attention. Any chance of my plan to head to the pool was slipping away as the sun got lower in the sky, heading toward early evening.

Feeling bored waiting for him to finish, I decided to stretch out on the comfortable champagne-colored couch and take a nap. I must have dozed off, as I woke later to the sensation of Oliver’s kisses. My eyes fluttered open as he knelt next to me, his lips leaving a searing trail down my neck. I moaned softly, feeling my nipples once again harden under his touch.

“Do you want to go to the pool?” Oliver whispered against my skin.

“No. I just want you to keep doing what you’re doing,” I murmured, lost in the sensation of his touch.

He continued to lavish attention on me, his lips trailing down to my breasts, his thumb teasing my nipples. My body responded eagerly, but then a sudden realization hit me—I couldn’t.

“I... I can’t,” I whispered, feeling a pang of disappointment.

“Stop it,” I whispered.

“Stop what?” he asked.

“Seducing me. I can’t have sex.”

His brows knitted together. “I told you I don’t give a shit. It doesn’t bother me.”

“The shower is the only place we can do it.”

“Then let’s go because I can’t wait until you’re finished.”

"Oliver," I moaned, the sound muffled by the steam-filled shower.

He was fucking me so hard, my body pressed against the condensation coated glass as he pounded into me from behind. It felt incredible, each thrust sending waves of pleasure coursing through me. When he reached around and started rubbing my clit, it sent me over the edge.

"You're so snug, I love it," he grunted, his voice rough with desire.

"I'm gonna come," I gasped, my breath hitching with anticipation.

"Come on, baby, come for me," Oliver groaned, his movements becoming more urgent.

With a guttural moan, I surrendered to the ecstasy, my orgasm crashing over me like a tidal wave. I clung to the cool glass, my body trembling with pleasure as Oliver continued to thrust, his own release imminent.

As my climax subsided, Oliver pulled out and guided me to the bench seat, his strong arms supporting me. Despite my initial reluctance, I couldn't deny how much I needed this release.

Leaning against the tiled wall, I caught my breath, the steam swirling around us like a veil. Oliver stroked my wet hair away from my face, planting tender kisses on my cheeks as we basked in the aftermath of our passion.

"I love you so much, Ryleigh." His voice was soft, filled with warmth.

Oliver was unlike any man I'd dated before and it wasn't his financial means, it was how he looked at me when he said he loved me. It was genuine and when I heard the words, it felt like a comforting embrace.

"I love you, too," I replied with a yawn, stretching my arms above my head.

He smirked, raising an eyebrow. "Am I boring you?"

I stifled another yawn. "Not in the least," I said, shaking my head. "I'm just so tired lately."

Concern flashed across his face. "Are you feeling okay?"

"It's just from my period. I always get tired during it. Nothing to worry about."

Relief relaxed his features. "I'm glad to hear it. I guess it's too late to go to the pool."

I glanced at the clock on the wall and nodded. "I would think so. Maybe tomorrow?"

"It's a lighter day, though we have to speak with another developer," he reminded me, leaning back against the wall.

"For the same project?" I asked, curiosity piqued.

"No, this is another building," he clarified, running a hand through his hair.

"Why don't you just handle the project yourself? You certainly can afford it," I pointed out, giving him a puzzled look.

He sighed, a thoughtful expression crossing his face. "I want the projects, but I don't want the financial burden. It wouldn't be prudent to devote a good chunk of funds to two projects. Working with other developers allows me to diversify in other areas."

I nodded slowly in understanding. "That makes sense."

"Yes, it does," he agreed, a hint of pride in his voice. "I've done this for years. It helps to develop positive relationships with those in the same field. I don't want to be hated or deemed greedy."

"Does that worry you?" I asked, tilting my head slightly.

"That I'll be hated?" He paused, considering. "Yes. I thought someone with your wealth wouldn't care."

"Some of the companies I've worked with have needed a helping hand. I don't mind offering it. I had help when I was coming up, and I'm simply paying it forward. I'm respected as a businessman. There are others whose business practices are despicable. I don't want to be grouped in that category," he explained, his tone serious.

I reached out, taking his hand in mine. "That's why I love you. You're not just a businessman. You're a good man."

Oliver grinned wickedly. "Am I?"

"A pervert in bed but a decent man in the office."

"Pervert? Take that back."

"What will you do? I'm already wet and naked."

"I'll think of something. Let's get finished so we can rest."

We washed each other and a few minutes later, we were wrapped in the thick white terry cloth robes supplied by the hotel. We went over a few things for tomorrow before Oliver called it quits.

"Do you want to get dressed and have dinner out?" he asked.

I yawned again, not interested in getting dressed to go out. "No. I prefer to stay inside if you don't mind."

“I don’t mind. We can order dinner whenever you want.”

I reclined on the couch. “In a little while.”

“Fine. I want to call Sebastian about the date.”

Oliver went into the bedroom, closing the door while I sat on the couch and turned on the television. I must have fallen asleep because Oliver woke me as he stroked my cheek with his knuckles.

“How did it go?” I asked sleepily.

“We have our date without bumping anyone, as long as you don’t mind having a night wedding.”

“I don’t mind... But how late are we talking?”

“Five to whenever.”

“Oh, it’ll still be light out in July at that hour. I’m fine with that.”

Excitement curled in my belly. This was becoming real. We had a date and a venue. Everything was happening so quickly.

“I’m glad. Sebastian has a wedding planner you can work with. I’ll call Rachel and Rigo when we get back to New York.”

My fiancé was making this easy. When I was a girl, I always thought of how my wedding would be and all the work it would take to create the perfect day. But with Oliver, it was coming together with little effort at all.

"Now we just need to decide on the honeymoon," I said, looking over the wedding plans.

"I said the island," he replied, a determined glint in his eyes.

"You only have ten months to build an entire place," I reminded him, eyebrows raised.

"Do you underestimate me?" He crossed his arms, a playful challenge in his tone.

"No, but it's pretty tight," I admitted, leaning back in my chair.

He leaned in closer, confidence radiating from him. "I can do anything with the right amount of motivation and employees. It will be done."

Before I could respond, he plopped down next to me and pulled me onto his lap, cupping my breast through the terry cloth of my robe.

"Hey, unhand me," I protested, swatting at his hand.

"It's hard to concentrate knowing you're naked under this robe," he said, a mischievous grin spreading across his face.

"Control yourself," I said, trying to sound stern but failing miserably.

"I'll try, but it's never easy with you around," he murmured, his voice dropping to a husky whisper.

"I'm glad I'm so irresistible," I teased, a smile tugging at my lips.

"I'm glad no one else finds you as irresistible," he said, his tone suddenly serious.

"Maybe they do," I replied, my voice light but my heart pounding.

"Who?" he demanded, eyes narrowing.

"I don't know," I lied, avoiding his gaze. I did know. Ty was in love with me and wanted what I had with Oliver, but I would never tell my fiancé that piece of information.

"Whoever is out there can't have you. You're mine," he declared, his grip tightening slightly.

"Possessive asshole," I murmured under my breath.

"You seriously did not just call me that," he said with a smirk, eyes twinkling with amusement.

"Maybe I did," I said, challenging him with a grin of my own.

Oliver chuckled and put me back on the couch next to him.

~

We spent the next few days bouncing between meetings and lunches, never quite making it to the pool. By the time we returned to New York, I was relieved to be back home. We had one more day of work before we could finally rest for the weekend.

Oliver decided to work with both developers we had met, each for different projects. It was a smart move, diversifying our efforts and resources.

I was especially glad we never saw the younger Ryder men again. Their presence had made me uneasy, and I was worried they might do something in front of Oliver that would create a problem. Their behavior had been borderline inappropriate, and I knew I would need to develop a tougher skin and become more assertive if I wanted to succeed in a business dominated by men.

As I reflected on the past week, I realized how important it was for me to assert myself and stand my ground. The world of business was challenging, and I couldn't afford to be seen as weak or easily intimidated. I would have to learn to navigate these situations with confidence and poise if I wanted to make my mark.

Chapter 2

“I have to leave early today,” I said to Oliver as we went over a spreadsheet in his office.

“Why?” His voice was laced with concern, his brow furrowing.

“Doctor’s appointment.” I tried to sound nonchalant.

He put the spreadsheet we were looking at on the table so he could focus his attention fully on me. “Are you sick?”

“No. This is for my yearly check-up.”

“What kind of check-up? I could come with you.” He leaned back in his chair, eyes searching mine.

“To the gynecologist?” I raised an eyebrow, trying to suppress a smile.

"Oh." He looked momentarily flustered. "You can join me if you like."

"No, thank you. I'll save those visits for when you're pregnant."

"That could be a while away." I told myself to shut up because I really didn't have a doctor's appointment.

What I needed time to do was prepare for Oliver's birthday the next day. He had kept me so occupied and busy since we got back from Los Angeles that I hadn't had time to purchase a gift or plan anything. I wanted to make his first birthday with me special.

"I think I'll pass. I have a conference call at four. What time is your appointment?"

"1:30," I said, glancing at the clock.

Oliver looked at his watch and saw it was noon. "You could've told me this sooner."

"I'm sorry. I forgot about it and just got an alert."

"Don't they usually call the day before?" he asked.

"They did, and I didn't listen to my voicemail. Does it matter?" I tried to keep my voice steady, but I could see the skepticism in his eyes.

He narrowed his eyes. "Are you sure you have an appointment?"

I fidgeted in my seat and laced my fingers in my lap.

"What are you implying?" I asked, feigning offense.

"That you're up to something since tomorrow is my birthday."

"Birthday? I thought tomorrow was just another ordinary October fifth," I teased, trying to lighten the mood.

"Uh huh," he said, clearly unconvinced.

"I really do have a doctor's appointment," I insisted, hoping he wouldn't see through my lie.

"Let Vlad take you. I don't want you out on your own," he said, his tone softening but still firm.

"Fine. It's just a quick appointment."

He sighed, rubbing the back of his neck. "Text me when you get there and when you leave. I worry about you."

"I will," I promised. "Thank you."

I couldn't help but feel a pang of guilt for lying to him, but I knew it would be worth it when he saw what I had planned for his birthday.

"I love you," he said.

"I know."

He raised his eyebrows. "So confident."

"You said I have you wrapped around my little finger. That's why I'm confident."

I pressed a hard kiss to his lips as I rose from my chair.

"You're wrapped around my whole body. You own my heart and soul."

"I love you, Oliver," I said as I put my hand on the door handle to leave his office.

"I know," he returned.

"Vlad, please take me to Schering Jewelers."

"Yes, Miss Stewart."

I ground my teeth. I had asked him to call me by my first name several times but he ignored me.

"You can just call me Ryleigh."

"I prefer to call you Miss Stewart."

"Uh, okay."

Vlad didn't give me an explanation but I was used to his silence. He rarely engaged me in conversation. I had searched for the perfect gift for Oliver that would show him my commitment to our relationship. I was already wearing his ring, but I wanted to return the favor. I spent my leisure time when I wasn't with Oliver, searching for the perfect gift.

I found a gold wedding band with a thin ring of sapphires encircling the entire band. Inside, I had it inscribed with the words: *My love, my life, I love you with all my heart, Ryleigh.* I knew this ring would stir up his emotions.

He was stoic and solid when it came to business, but when we were in private, I got the best of him. It was expensive, and I had to dip into my inheritance, but it was well worth the cost. Oliver was well worth the cost.

From there, I had Vlad take me to a party store where I got several balloons, a card, candles, and a gift bag with tissue paper. Afterward, he took me home. I had ordered a cake, and Vlad would pick it up for me the next day before he got us from work. The other security members had entry to the penthouse, and I recruited Brenda to bring all the items there before we arrived.

Oliver wouldn't be out of work for another hour, so I went to Boudoir Fashions to look at some lingerie. I usually slept in a short t-shirt and panties or nothing at all, but I wanted to surprise him. He had mentioned to me before that he would like to see me in lingerie.

I spent a half hour picking out a couple of see-through baby dolls in light blue and black. The sheer fabric left nothing to the imagination, but I was sure he would appreciate the effort. Maybe I would wear them to bed tomorrow since it was a Friday.

After I paid for my purchases and waited for Vlad to bring the car around, I noticed a dark-haired, stocky man staring at me with black, brooding eyes. He seemed familiar, but I couldn't place him. I looked away and was glad when Vlad double-parked and helped me with my bag.

The man continued to stare as we drove by. I decided not to mention it to Oliver. It could be that this man saw me on the news or the internet and was just curious. I called my fiancé on my way home.

"How did the doctor go?" I could hear the smile in his voice.

"It went fine. You'll be happy to know I'm healthy down there."

"I know you are."

"I should be at your place in a little while. Vlad might be late picking you up," I said, trying to keep my tone light as I juggled the party supplies in the backseat.

"That's okay. I have a last-minute call I need to take at 6 p.m.," Oliver replied.

"For what?" I asked, curiosity piqued.

"It doesn't concern anything you've been working on."

"So, you don't want to tell me?" I challenged, my frustration seeping through.

He sighed heavily. "Do you want to have a full discussion about business right now? We can talk when I get home for dinner."

"Perfect," I said sarcastically, rolling my eyes.

"Ryleigh, don't be upset. Not all things concern you."

"You want me to learn your business, right?" I shot back. "Isn't this part of it?"

"Yes and no. We can talk later. I'll see you at the penthouse."

Anger started to well up in me. He was treating me like a little girl. "Maybe I won't be at the penthouse. I haven't spent much time with Sadie in the past two weeks. We could spend the night apart."

"No," he growled. "I want you with me."

"Possessive asshole," I mumbled under my breath.

"I heard that."

"You were supposed to," I said, hearing him sigh deeply.

"This conversation is getting nowhere," Oliver huffed.

"Then I'll see you later, maybe."

"If you want to have a tantrum, then it's better you stay at your place."

He was giving me an ultimatum and I would take that challenge. Some time away would give me a chance to figure out everything for his birthday. Right now, it wouldn't be good for us to be together. I was afraid I would lash out and say something I shouldn't, ruining his birthday celebration.

"Good, I will." I hung up on him and powered down my phone, fuming. I stared out the window at the bustling pedestrian traffic below, trying to calm my racing thoughts.

Vlad's cell phone rang, breaking the silence. He answered and then handed the phone back to me. "Mr. Fox is on the line."

"Tell Mr. Fox I don't want to talk to him right now," I said icily, pushing the phone back to Vlad.

He relayed my message just as we pulled up to my apartment. I stepped out, dragging the balloons, bag of lingerie, and party supplies from the car before Vlad could even open my door. If I knew Oliver, he would try to have Vlad take me straight to the penthouse instead.

"Miss Stewart, will I be waiting for you?" Vlad asked, concern evident in his voice.

I shook my head. "No. I'm staying here tonight."

"You should have security with you."

"I don't need it. I'm fine."

"Mr. Fox insists," Vlad said.

"Tell him I don't need his help right now." I slammed the door and hurried to the lobby as fast as I could with the packages and balloons.

The concierge, a light-haired woman with an elfin face, nodded at me and smirked when she saw the balloons. I almost lost one of them as the elevator doors closed but managed to pull it inside.

It had been a few days since I'd last seen Sadie. With as little free time as my brother, Finley, had, she was spending most nights with him. Their relationship was real, and I was positive they were in love even though they had only been dating for a short time. I wondered if they had more than just a few romps together over the years.

As the elevator ascended, I sighed, leaning back against the wall. The tension with Oliver gnawed at me, but I pushed it aside. Tonight was about planning his birthday, not stewing over our argument. I'd make his birthday special, no matter how stubborn he could be. The doors slid open, and I stepped into the hall, heading to my apartment.

I fumbled for my keys from my purse, juggling the packages I had in my hand. The key stuck, and I had to wiggle it to fit in the lock. It was odd because I never had trouble before. When I finally pushed the door open, what I saw made me drop everything I held.

My apartment was ransacked. Pictures on the wall were topsy-turvy, cushions and pillows littered the floor, and papers were strewn about. And that was only the living room. I dreaded to think what the bedrooms looked like. My heart pounded as I backed out, abandoning all the packages and the balloons floating aimlessly around the entryway.

I jammed my finger on the elevator button several times, tears leaking from my eyes. When the doors finally opened, I dashed inside and pressed the lobby button repeatedly, willing the elevator to move faster.

In the lobby, I rushed to the concierge desk. "Call the police," I gasped, my voice trembling. Without waiting for a response, I dialed Oliver. He answered immediately.

“Over your tantrum?” Oliver’s voice was strained with exasperation.

“Someone broke into my apartment,” I blurted out, my voice quivering.

“What?!” he screamed. I heard him directing someone in the background before he came back on the line. “Where are you?”

“In the lobby. I told the concierge to call the police.”

“Stay there, I’m on my way.”

“I’m afraid,” I whispered, tears welling up in my eyes.

“Don’t be. You’re safe. Brenda should be there in two minutes.”

Where was she that she would be here so quick? Sure enough, Brenda walked out of the fire stairs less than two minutes later. Did Oliver have her living here? I quickly recounted what happened, and she sat me down in one of the mustard-colored upholstered chairs in the lobby. Brenda, a pretty, petite woman with dark chocolate skin and close-cropped hair, soothed me while we waited for the police to arrive.

"Was there anyone in the apartment?" she asked, her voice calm and reassuring.

"Not that I could see," I replied, my hands trembling in my lap.

Brenda noticed and placed one of her hands over mine. Her touch was reassuring, and I began to calm down until the police arrived. Then, my anxiety surged, and I became hysterical. Two officers went upstairs to check my place while a detective questioned me. Oliver arrived a few minutes after the officers. Brenda got up so he could comfort me.

He put his arm around my shoulders and reached into the pocket of his gray pinstriped jacket for a handkerchief. I dabbed at my eyes while the officer spoke with me. The two uniformed policemen came downstairs to report that the apartment was empty and my jewelry, some cash, and other valuables were still there.

I breathed a sigh of relief, thinking of the gold bracelet my father gave me before he was murdered. It held immense sentimental value. After the officers left, Oliver, Vlad, and Brenda escorted me up to my apartment. The sight of my bedroom was even worse than the living room. It was a mess, and pillows were sliced open, more than likely with a knife.

“What the hell were they looking for?” I muttered, surveying the destruction. “And how did they get up here without being seen by the concierge?”

Oliver’s jaw tightened. “We’ll find out,” he said, his voice resolute. “This won’t go unanswered.”

Vlad was already on his phone, likely coordinating with additional security. Brenda started tidying up the living room, moving with efficient precision.

I sat on the edge of my bed, feeling the shredded pillows beneath me. The chaos around me was overwhelming, but Oliver’s presence was a steady anchor.

"This is why you can't stay here," Oliver said, his voice a mix of concern and frustration as he surveyed the wreckage.

"Obviously. I don’t want to stay here. Who would do this?" I demanded, my voice trembling with both fear and anger.

"Let the police figure that out." He turned to me, his eyes softening. "Do you have some things you want to take to the penthouse? You're not staying here until we catch this person."

"Then I might never come back. What about Sadie? I have to call her." I walked to her bedroom, pulling out my phone and dialing her number.

She answered on the second ring, the noise of my brother, Finley, evident in the background. "Hey, stranger."

"Someone ransacked our apartment," I said, trying to keep my voice steady.

"Oh my God! When?" she yelled.

I exhaled loudly. "Today, sometime. I came here, and it was a mess. I called the police."

"What did they say? Was anything stolen? Are you all right?"

"Our apartment is a disaster. They sliced open pillows in my bedroom."

"Did you look in my room?"

I glanced around her room, which looked relatively untouched. "It's not as bad as my room. Oliver doesn't want me to stay here."

I hadn't told Sadie about the threat against me that Oliver had discovered. If I did, my whole family would know, and I didn't want to worry them.

"I don't want to stay there alone if someone broke in. I don't feel comfortable."

"Maybe we should let this place go. You're always with Finley, and I'm always at Oliver's."

She sighed, and I heard her footsteps as she walked into another room. "I can't ask Finley if I can move in."

"Sadie, bullshit. Put him on, and I'll ask him. You can't stay here alone."

I heard her footsteps as she walked back out, and hand the phone over to Finley. "What happened? Someone broke into your apartment?" he asked, his voice tense.

"It's ransacked. The police took a report, and Oliver doesn't want me to stay here."

"I don't want Sadie staying there by herself," Finley said firmly.

"She can't afford to stay in a hotel, and most of our friends live in Westchester or Long Island," I reasoned.

"Who said she should go to a hotel? She can stay with me."

"Thank you, Finley," I said, relief flooding through me.

"You don't have to thank me. I think I love her," he said quietly.

"You're saying that right in front of her?" I asked, surprised.

"She went to the bathroom."

"We should have dinner together sometime."

I missed my brother and I barely saw Sadie ever since I got involved with Oliver.

"That sounds good. The next two weeks are busy for me. I have a couple of deadlines I need to meet. After that, I might have some time."

"Sounds good. I'm happy for you. Put Sadie back on."

A moment later, Sadie came back on the line. "I heard. I guess I'm moving in with Finley," she said with a mix of excitement and nervousness.

"Yes, you are. And I'm moving in with Oliver for now. We'll figure out the rest later."

I spoke to Sadie at length while I sat on her bed. When I came out, my living room was straightened as well as the pictures on the walls. Vlad, Oliver and Brenda had put the shredded pillows in my bedroom in a garbage bag and fixed my dresser as well as my bed. I felt violated that someone would go through my things let alone a stranger. I wanted to get out of here as quick as possible.

“Are you okay?” Oliver asked.

“I just want to get out of here.”

“Let's pack a suitcase. We can come back if you need anything further.”

Oliver helped me pack and when we walked out to the entry, he commented about the balloons that were now floating freely.

“Were these for me?”

I nodded. “Yes. It was supposed to be a surprise, now it’s ruined. I’m sorry.”

He stroked my hair. “Sweetheart, it’s not your fault. Let’s go home.”

Oliver carried my suitcase and Brenda helped me gather the bags and balloons while Vlad went to retrieve the car.

“Do you feel better?” Oliver asked softly, pulling me closer to him as we cuddled in his bed. It was barely 9:00 p.m. but the events of earlier in the evening took a toll on me. I wanted to tell Oliver about the man I saw when I came out of the store but I was hesitant.

I sat on the edge of the bed, my voice barely a whisper. "A little."

Oliver held me tighter. "You’re safe here. I won’t let anything happen to you."

I looked up at him, my eyes searching his face. "Oliver, where does Brenda live?"

"I got her an apartment in your building," he replied, his tone calm and reassuring.

"But why? I’m not there much."

"It’s a home base for when you are," he explained, a slight smile tugging at his lips.

It didn't surprise me. Since we started dating, Oliver had become increasingly protective, and with the break-in, his concern had only intensified.

"I won't be for a while, if ever," I admitted, my voice tinged with uncertainty.

"Does that mean you're moving in with me?" Oliver asked, a hint of hope in his eyes.

"I want to, but I should talk to my parents first," I said, glancing away.

"Ryleigh, you're an adult and we're engaged," he reminded me, gently lifting my chin so our eyes met.

"Don't you think it's better if I discuss it rather than spring it on them? You wouldn't understand because you're older," I replied, trying to make him see my perspective.

"And I have no parents," he said softly, a shadow passing over his face.

"I wasn't going to say that," I protested, but guilt twisted in my stomach.

"But you thought it, didn't you?" Oliver's voice was steady, but I could see the hurt in his eyes.

He was right; I had. My parents' opinions mattered to me, but given the circumstances, moving in with Oliver felt like the best option.

. . .

"I didn't, and I'm sorry if you thought I did. I want my parents to be proud of me," I said, my voice earnest.

"They are proud. How could they not be when you're so wonderful?" Oliver replied, his eyes softening.

"You're just saying that because you love me," I said, a small smile playing on my lips.

"You don't think you're wonderful?"

"It's not for me to think. It's for others to think," I said with a shrug.

"I've already got compliments from other employees at work about you," Oliver said, a note of pride in his voice.

"By a bunch of ass-kissing employees?" I retorted, raising an eyebrow.

"That's ridiculous. Why would my employees compliment you? You think because I'm the boss they need to stroke my ego about my choice for a mentee?" Oliver asked, a hint of frustration creeping into his voice.

"And because one day I might help you run your company. I highly doubt they would want to get on my bad side," I replied, crossing my arms.

"You will help me run my company. I'd be more than willing to share the duties," he assured me.

"I want to discuss what happened between us before I got to my apartment," I said, my tone shifting to serious.

"I can't teach you everything at once. I'm sorry if I upset you. The call didn't concern anything we've dealt with so far," Oliver explained, his brow furrowing.

"But I want to know everything," I insisted.

"In due time. I haven't even touched the tip of the iceberg with you. You've seen my real estate business, but I have so many more," Oliver said, his voice full of promise.

"I know about you Oliver. I've read about the areas your company is in. You have software, green energy, healthcare, you own a string of upscale bars, a beef farm and thousands of acres of property in the Midwest. And that's only in this country."

"I underestimated you."

"I'm well versed in what's under the Fox umbrella. Don't treat me like I'm stupid."

"I could never. You're brilliant. It's one of the many things about you I love."

"So, you didn't fall for me because of my beautiful face and hot body?" I teased, a playful glint in my eye.

Oliver chuckled, shaking his head. "Is that a joke? Of course I did. I was mesmerized as you approached me on stage. My mind was going in a thousand directions about how to score a date with you."

I snorted. "Are you serious? All you had to do was ask."

"I wanted to get to know you first," he said, his voice softening.

"Oliver, I was wondering, when did you love me?" I asked seriously.

"At first sight."

"Don't be ridiculous."

He pressed a kiss to my neck. "I'm not. I saw you walking from your seat and my heart jumped in my chest."

"Then why didn't you find me? Suppose we didn't work in the same building?"

He kept his lips against my skin, nuzzling my ear. "I thought about it, but wouldn't you consider that a bit creepy? I didn't want to seem like a stalker."

"There was a man watching me when I came out of the lingerie store," I blurted out.

He withdrew and his soft expression changed instantly. He let me go and pulled me to my back so he could look at me directly. "When? Was Vlad with you?"

"It was only for a few seconds. He was staring at me."

"You're not to go in stores by yourself from now on. Brenda will go with you."

"I don't want to be babysat," I protested.

Oliver looked down at me with his brow furrowed. "It's for your own good. I won't risk some lunatic hurting you or worse."

"What about the threat you said was made against me?"

He shook his head. "It turned out to be nothing."

I pursed my lips. "Nothing or you won't tell me the truth?"

"Nothing. Just some crackpot who saw your picture on the internet."

Oliver pulled me against his chest, and I almost knew he was lying to me.

"I'm tired," I yawned.

"Go to sleep then. I have a few things I need to take care of before I come to bed. Will you be all right by yourself?"

"I think so," I mumbled.

Oliver planted a tender kiss on my forehead, lingering for a moment before slipping out of bed. He was only wearing a pair of black silk pajama pants, and I couldn't help but admire the way his muscles rippled in his back as he walked out of the bedroom door. The sight was both comforting and disconcerting, a reminder of his strength and the intensity that lay beneath his calm exterior.

I turned onto my stomach, snuggling into my pillow. The warmth of his kiss lingered, lulling me into a sense of security as I drifted off to sleep.

But my sleep was anything but peaceful. My dreams were filled with vivid, unsettling images—shadows lurking in corners, whispered threats, and the sensation of being watched. I snapped awake, my heart racing, just a half hour later.

From down the hall, I heard Oliver's voice raised in anger, just like I had in the hotel room the week before. The intensity of his tone sent a shiver down my spine. I strained to catch his words, but they were muffled, lost in the distance and the walls between us. His voice finally stopped, replaced by a loud bang as if he had thrown something against the wall.

Curiosity and concern gnawed at me, but I decided against interrupting him. Whatever battle he was fighting, it was one he needed to face alone. I took a deep breath, willing my racing heart to slow, and tried to push the disturbing thoughts from my mind. Turning onto my side, I pulled the covers tighter around me and forced my eyes closed, eventually succumbing to a restless sleep.

"Sweetheart, wake up," Oliver's voice was a gentle command, pulling me from the depths of my nightmare. My eyes fluttered open to see him leaning over me, his face etched with concern. My heart was pounding, my skin clammy with sweat.

"I'm... I'm sorry," I stuttered, my voice shaky.

Oliver reached for the sheet and tenderly wiped my face. I started to cry, overwhelmed by the nightmare's lingering dread.

“Shh, it’s not your fault. I was expecting it after what happened yesterday,” he murmured, his touch soothing.

“Yesterday?” I glanced at the clock and saw it was 3 a.m. in the morning. “Shit, it’s your birthday.”

“Yes, it is,” he grinned, the light from the bathroom casting a soft glow over his face. He always left it on so I wouldn’t stumble if I got up.

“Happy birthday,” I whispered, leaning in to kiss his cheek. My lips trailed down to his neck, inhaling the lingering scent of his cologne.

“Thank you. I’m glad you’re the first one to wish it to me,” he replied, his voice a warm rumble in the quiet room.

“We should go back to sleep,” I suggested, though sleep was the last thing on my mind.

“I don’t want to go back to sleep,” I admitted, my voice barely above a whisper.

“Oh? What would you like to do?” he asked, a curious eyebrow raised.

“Something for you,” I said, a mischievous smile playing on my lips.

He raised his eyebrows, “Such as?”

“I want to suck you,” I said huskily.

“No. Go to sleep. You can do that tomorrow.”

“It is tomorrow. Why do you always deny me? I like to do it and you taste good,” I insisted, my hand slipping between us to touch him.

Oliver groaned, his body responding instantly. “Fuck, Ryleigh, you’re going to keep pushing me.”

“I want to do it. Lie on your back,” I commanded, the need to please him driving me.

He moved to his back, and I pushed the covers off us, releasing him from his pants. By the time I had him free, his penis was rock hard, and my mouth watered with anticipation. Oliver lifted his hips so I could pull his pants down further. I positioned myself between his legs, teasing his head with my tongue, swirling it around his thick crown.

I was rewarded with several beads of precum bubbling to the top. I lapped at it before taking him into my mouth, sliding down as far as I could go without choking. He moaned, his hands grasping at my hair, gathering it in a bunch which he held firmly.

"Ryleigh," he groaned, his voice thick with desire. The sound of his pleasure spurred me on, and I knew there was no place I'd rather be than right here, making him feel this way.

I sucked him hard, pulling on his hot flesh. I loved Oliver’s taste and knew when he was getting close to his release when he tugged too tightly at my hair. A few more hard sucks and a squeeze of his base had him exploding down my throat. When he released my hair and went slack, I cleaned him with my tongue before I moved up beside him.

“How was that?” I said with a grin.

“Jesus Christ, you’re going to be the death of me,” he panted out.

He kicked off his pants, discarding them on the floor before he sat up to pull the covers over us. Down below, my clit throbbed with desire but Oliver was already asleep when I snuggled against his chest. It would have to wait until we woke up for work.

~

“Come for me, Ryleigh,” Oliver commanded, his voice a husky whisper.

Two hours later, I awoke to the sensation of his lips trailing kisses across my body. His hand slipped into my white lace boy shorts, skillfully bringing me to a fast orgasm. Before I could catch my breath, he yanked my panties down and buried his tongue between my legs, paying me back for earlier in the morning.

Now, he had me on all fours, hammering into me with his long, hot cock. His fingers curled around my hips, and he rocked against my ass with a relentless rhythm. I was so close.

. . .

"Come on, baby, I can't hold on much longer," he urged, his voice strained with need.

I let out a howl as I began to come, my body convulsing with pleasure. Oliver pounded into me, his climax hitting hard as he spurted deep inside, filling me with his hot semen. I collapsed onto the bed, sliding off his still hard penis. The intense satisfaction made me wish we could stay home all day and make love.

"Want to shower with me?" he asked, his breath still heavy.

"I need time to recover," I replied, my body trembling with aftershocks.

He crawled over me and pulled me against him, his warmth soothing. It was still early, and we could afford to doze for a little while longer.

"I have a gift for you," I mumbled into the pillow.

"Your love is all I need," he murmured, his voice soft and sincere.

"That might be true, but I still wanted to get you something," I insisted.

I went to move, but he held me tightly, refusing to let go. "Oliver, let me go."

"It can wait for a few minutes. I want to hold you," he said, his voice filled with a quiet intensity.

I indulged him because it was his birthday. He kissed me several times before I tucked my head under his chin, our bodies entwined. The next time we woke, it was nearing 6:30 a.m.

“Shower with me,” Oliver mumbled.

I ran my fingers over his chest. “Can I make you breakfast?”

He stretched. “If you want to. It’s not necessary. I’d like some Eggs Benedict with a side of Canadian bacon.”

I raised my eyebrows. “Seriously? Pick something normal.”

“That is normal, I love it.”

I felt stupid. We’d been together for a few months and there was still so much we didn’t know about each other.

I bit my lip. “You never said anything.”

“You can make it for me tomorrow.”

“So, shower?” he asked.

“Will you behave?”

“It’s my birthday. Shouldn’t I be able to do whatever I want?”

“Is that a no?”

“Do you want me to behave?” he asked seductively.

I chuckled. “No.”

Chapter 3

After a breakfast of scrambled eggs and mini bagels, we headed for the office. I kept the gift for Oliver tucked in my purse along with a card, planning to give it to him at lunchtime. Our day was a whirlwind of phone calls, reports, and meetings with his internal staff. Everyone was polite, but I could sense a few people might create problems for me.

By the time lunch rolled around, I was both starving and eager to give Oliver his birthday present.

“Would you like to go out to lunch?” he asked, his eyes twinkling with anticipation.

“It’s your birthday, it’s entirely up to you,” I replied with a smile.

“Let’s go out.”

I went to my office to grab my black wool coat while Oliver straightened his desk. A few minutes later, he showed up at my door. My new furniture had finally arrived, making the space feel cozy and welcoming.

"I like everything you chose," Oliver said, plopping down on the champagne-colored microsuede couch and bouncing up and down.

I watched him with a mix of amusement and fascination. "What exactly are you doing?"

"I'm checking to see the bounceability of the cushions," he replied, grinning like a mischievous child.

"Is bounceability even a word?" I asked, raising an eyebrow.

"Probably not, but these are springy," he said, bouncing again for emphasis.

"And why exactly would I need them to be springy?" I inquired, trying to suppress a laugh.

`"For after-curricular activities," he said with a wink.

I softly cursed under my breath. "This is a professional environment, not exactly suited for what you're implying."

"Do you think you'll be fired?" he teased, a playful glint in his eye.

"Not if you keep it professional," I shot back, shaking my head with a smile.

Oliver stood up, offering me his arm. “Shall we, Ms. Stewart?”

“We shall, Mr. Fox,” I replied, linking my arm with his.

As we walked to the elevator, I felt a surge of excitement for the day ahead. This man, with his mix of childlike enthusiasm and steely determination, had a way of making even the most mundane days feel special. I couldn’t wait to see his reaction to the gift I had carefully chosen, a token of my love and appreciation for everything he had brought into my life.

“Where are we going for lunch?” I asked, curiosity piqued.

“You’ll see,” Oliver replied, a mysterious smile playing on his lips.

I frowned slightly, hating when he kept things from me. It should've been me taking him to lunch, but Oliver always did things his own way, even on his birthday. He led me to the elevator, and we squeezed in with the lunch crowd. As we moved to the back, he held my hand, stroking the back of it with his thumb, a soothing gesture that calmed my mild irritation.

When we exited the building, Vlad was waiting for us with the limo. The weather had turned unseasonably warm, much warmer than it had been in the morning. I shrugged out of my coat before getting into the car. Once inside, Oliver pulled me onto his lap, capturing my lips in a bruising kiss. His hand fisted in my hair, preventing me from pulling away. When he finally released me, I was breathless.

“What was that for?” I asked, dazed and flushed.

“I love you. I love you so much,” he said, his voice thick with emotion.

His statement almost sounded like a cry, and I couldn’t help but wonder what was wrong. He hadn’t told me about the phone call he had taken the night before, and I wondered if that had anything to do with his sudden intensity.

“I love you too. Where are we going?” I asked, trying to read the emotions flickering in his eyes.

“Upstate,” he answered, his voice softening.

“Excuse me?”

"Upstate," Oliver announced, his eyes gleaming with mischief.

“But we’ll be late getting back to work. Don’t you have a conference call with the Ryders at 2:00 p.m.?” I protested, my brow furrowing.

“Canceled. We’re taking the rest of the day off,” he replied, his tone leaving no room for argument.

“Where are we going?” I pressed, curiosity gnawing at me.

“Get changed,” he instructed.

“Changed into what?” I asked, puzzled.

Oliver tugged at his light blue tie, pulling it over his head and then gesturing to the black duffel bag sitting on the bench seat opposite us.

“What are you up to, Mr. Fox?” I queried, suspicion lacing my voice.

“Don’t worry about it,” he said with a smirk, his eyes dancing with amusement.

He shifted to grab the duffel bag, opening it and handing me a pair of my favorite worn blue jeans, a pale yellow t-shirt, and a forest green cashmere sweater. I watched as he began to strip, neatly folding his clothes and placing them on the seat beside him.

He was wearing my favorite hip-hugging gray boxer shorts, which framed all the delicious parts of Oliver. Heat flooded my cheeks as I stared, unable to tear my eyes away.

“Aren’t you getting dressed? Stop staring,” he teased.

“Shut up. You’re gorgeous, and you know it,” I retorted, feeling a smile tug at my lips.

Just to tease me, he leaned back against the seat and began to check his emails, feigning nonchalance. He knew exactly what he was doing. I pulled my skirt over my head and removed my blouse, sitting there in just a blood-red lace bra and thong set. Oliver pretended he wasn’t affected, but the growing bulge between his legs betrayed him.

"You're creating problems, Ryleigh," he said, his voice low and strained.

"You started it," I shot back, a teasing lilt in my voice.

"And I want to finish it," he growled.

In a flash, he tossed his phone onto the opposite seat and pulled me underneath him. He hovered above me, his gaze locking onto my hazel eyes. I reached up and traced the slight stubble on his jaw, enjoying the rough texture against my fingertips.

"So, am I your birthday present?" I whispered, my voice trembling with anticipation.

"If you are, it's my birthday every day," he murmured, his lips brushing against mine.

The intensity in his eyes made my heart race. This spontaneous, passionate side of Oliver always left me breathless.

He shucked off his boxers before he lowered himself onto me, our bodies pressing together, I felt the world outside the limo fade away. Whatever he had planned upstate, I knew it would be unforgettable.

"I want you naked."

I giggled. "I guess it's only fair since you are."

I unclasped my bra and wiggled out of my panties, handing them too him as they dangled from my finger. He put them to his nose and inhaled, closing his eyes before he rolled me under him.

"You always smell so good. I'll never forget your scent."

He extracted a condom from his coat pocket and handed it to me. I unfurled it on his shaft as I sat on his thick thighs then straddled him, positioning his latex covered cock between my slick folds. When I sank down, he closed his eyes and wrapped his arms around me. We rocked together as he pressed my body against his. I sucked on his earlobe as I softly sang happy birthday to him.

"That's such a turn on," he said.

"What is?" I panted.

"You, singing in my ear while we make love."

"You find that a turn on?"

"Anything you do is a turn on."

"How about when I come?" I said, gasping. "Because I'm going to right now."

My core exploded with white hot heat as I came. I squeezed Oliver inside me, and he held me as he thrust his hips upward until he came with a loud groan. After we finished, we stayed locked together even when Vlad called back on the intercom to say we were leaving the city.

Fifteen minutes later, we were dressed for our visit upstate. Oliver was wearing a pair of black jeans and a gray V-neck sweater that showed a hint of his beautiful well-muscled chest. I leaned my head against his shoulder while he checked his phone for a few incoming emails.

“You’re not telling me where we’re going?” I asked.

Oliver shook his head. “No.”

I slowly licked my lips. “I’d like to give you the gift I got for your birthday.”

“You didn’t need to get me anything.”

“I know I didn’t need to get you anything, I wanted to.”

I grabbed my purse and opened it to take out the card and small black velvet box that held the sapphire and gold ring. Oliver read the card and he sniffled a little at the sentiment. I could swear I saw tears in his eyes as I handed him the box.

“What is it?” he asked.

“Open it,” I said with anticipation.

He popped the box open and shook his head when he saw what was inside.

“This is too expensive.”

I swallowed back the emotion clogging my throat. “Shut up, Oliver. I have an inheritance I can spend.”

“This is exquisite.”

He slipped the ring on his finger and held his hand out. I pulled it off and turned it at an angle so he could see the inscription inside. This time I saw him wipe his eyes with his thumb.

“Ryleigh....” he whispered.

“I love you, Oliver, and I want you to know how much. You can always have me with you as long as you wear this.”

He took it from me and put it back on. “I'm never taking it off.”

“The sapphires remind me of your eyes.”

Oliver held my hand until we pulled off the highway in lower Westchester County. I recognized the signs as we drove through the city of Pleasantville. A few minutes later, Vlad turned into the Bianchi Winery. We traveled down a long driveway until we came to the main winery and restaurant.

“We're having lunch here?” I squealed.

"Not in the restaurant."

I looked at him, puzzled. “Where, then?”

“You'll see. Be patient. You would think it was your birthday.”

I frowned. “I should've planned this.”

“It doesn't matter who planned it as long as we're together.”

As Vlad parked in the main driveway and opened the door for us, we stepped out and approached what looked like a rustic barn. We walked through two thick double wooden doors, each adorned with a rectangular piece of colorful stained glass. Inside, a small man with thinning black hair and a large bulbous nose greeted us.

He hugged Oliver warmly, then turned to me. "I'm Vittorio Bianchi," he said with a slight Italian accent.

"Vittorio, this is my fiancée, Ryleigh Stewart," Oliver introduced.

"She is bellissima," Vittorio declared.

I felt my face heat up. "Th-thank you," I stuttered, glancing at Oliver, who had a smirk on his face.

Vittorio led us through a large store and tasting area, lined with wooden crates and shelves filled with wine bottles. We continued through a dusty storeroom and out to the vineyard, where a battered green golf cart awaited us. Vittorio took the front seat, while Oliver and I settled into the back.

The cart bumped along a narrow path through the tangled grapevines, eventually stopping at a small clearing where a table was set up. It was beautifully arranged with several crystal wine glasses, white china, and silverware on top of a red linen tablecloth. As soon as we sat down, a light-haired man in a waiter's uniform appeared, carrying a thick wooden charcuterie board.

My mouth watered as I took in the sight of the food: an assortment of cheeses cut into slices, pieces of thick crusty Italian bread, salty green and black olives, dried apricots and almonds, hummus, homemade pickles, and pieces of hard salami, sopressata, mortadella, and capicola.

"This looks fantastic," I said, my stomach growling in anticipation.

"I'm glad the day warmed up," Oliver remarked, pouring us each a glass of wine.

"Suppose it didn't?" I asked, raising an eyebrow.

"Then we would have found somewhere cozy inside," he replied, clinking his glass against mine.

Vittorio reappeared with a knowing smile. "Enjoy your meal. If you need anything, just call for me."

As we settled into our meal, the flavors burst in my mouth, each bite more delicious than the last. The sun filtered through the grapevines, casting a warm, dappled light over us. I looked at Oliver, his eyes sparkling with happiness.

"Thank you for this," I said, my voice filled with emotion. "It's perfect."

He reached across the table, taking my hand in his. "You're perfect," he said softly. "And I wanted to make today special for you."

I felt a lump in my throat, overwhelmed by his thoughtfulness. As we continued to eat and laugh, I couldn't help but feel a deep sense of contentment.

Whatever challenges lay ahead, I knew we could face them together. Today was a reminder of the love and joy we shared, and I was grateful for every moment.

"How do you know Vittorio?" I asked, curiosity piqued as I glanced around the vineyard.

"I'm part owner of this place. A silent partner," Oliver replied casually.

I took a sip of wine. "You own this place?"

"Part of it," Oliver said, popping a green olive in his mouth.

I marveled at the beautiful surroundings, the lush grapevines, and the rustic charm of the barn. "Maybe we should get married here."

"I thought you wanted The Garden Room?"

"I do, but this place is beautiful," I said, feeling torn.

Oliver rolled his sapphire eyes playfully, making me laugh. "Make up your mind, sweetheart."

"The Garden Room," I decided with a smile.

"Are you sure?"

"Positive. Have you spoken to Rachel Vicaria?" I asked, referring to the wedding planner I had my heart set on.

"It's on my list. I haven't gotten a chance, but we have plenty of time. Frankly, I wish we were getting married sooner."

. . .

“I know you do, but we don’t need a piece of paper, you know that.”

“I do, but I prefer it,” he said, his voice softening with emotion.

I leaned closer, a mischievous glint in my eyes. “Well, it’s your birthday, so why don’t you sweep me off to a justice of the peace and we’ll be married right now?”

Oliver dropped the piece of sharp cheddar he was eating, his eyes widening in surprise. “Excuse me?”

“Let’s get married right now,” I repeated, more seriously this time.

He stared at me, a mixture of shock and love in his gaze. “As much as I would love to make you Mrs. Fox this very minute, I wouldn’t spoil your fun. I know you want all the things that go along with the festivities of a wedding.”

My heart swelled at his consideration. “You know me too well,” I said softly.

Oliver glanced up from his plate. "By the way, Serena Putnam should be phoning you on Monday," he said, tapping his pen on the desk.

I looked up. "Who’s she?"

"The wedding planner," Oliver replied with a small smile. "You’ll have a much easier time with help."

I nodded thoughtfully. "How are the preparations for the house on the island coming?"

"They already started breaking ground," Oliver said, leaning back in his chair.

"Already?" my eyes widened. "You said it was in the planning phase."

Oliver chuckled. "Money talks, my dear fiancée. I have several crews out there."

I tilted her head, skeptical. "But how do you know?"

"One of my project managers is overseeing the entire project," Oliver explained confidently. "Nothing will be done half-assed."

I crossed her arms, a playful smile on my lips. "Don't you think we should name the island? We can't keep calling it 'the island.'"

He looked thoughtful for a moment. "Why don't we call it Ryleigh Island?"

I laughed, shaking my head. "No. That would be embarrassing."

"Why?" Oliver asked, feigning innocence. "Of course, everything pales in comparison to you."

I rolled my eyes, still smiling. "Think of something else. How about Fox Island?"

Oliver nodded, considering it. "That could work."

"Do you think it will be ready by the time we get married?" I asked, a hint of hope in my voice.

"I'm sure gonna try," Oliver said, reaching out to take my hand. "I want you to be happy."

I squeezed his hand, my eyes softening. "I'll be happy staying in a grass hut as long as I have you to myself."

After finishing our meal, I felt slightly tipsy from consuming too much wine. Oliver suggested a tour of the vineyard in one of the battered green golf carts. As we cruised through the lush rows of vines, the warm, golden light of the setting sun bathed everything in a dreamy glow.

By the time we returned, the sky had begun to blush with the approach of dusk. We said our goodbyes to Vittorio, who enveloped me in a warm hug, and then set off for home.

Once we were settled in the limo and on the highway, Oliver reached into his back pocket and pulled out his wallet. He extracted a credit card and handed it to me, causing me to frown.

“What's this?” I asked, eyeing the card with suspicion.

“It's for any expenses for the wedding and anything else you want,” he said, pressing the sleek black American Express card into my hand.

I looked at it, running my thumbnail over the raised lettering of my name. “I don't need this. I can use my own money.”

“Nonsense,” Oliver replied with a dismissive wave. “I

won't have you spending your own money on our wedding."

"Oliver, it's our wedding, not just yours," I insisted, my voice firm.

He leaned closer. "Can you indulge me, please? It's my birthday. You love to argue with me."

"It's healthy to argue," I countered. "You should worry if I just bend to you."

Oliver chuckled, shaking his head. "I doubt that will ever happen."

"More than likely, you're right," I conceded, feeling a yawn creeping up on me. "I think I need a nap."

"Are you feeling okay?" he asked, concern lacing his voice.

"A little too much wine and good food," I admitted.

"Take a nap on the seat. I have a little work to do," he suggested, patting the seat beside him.

I stretched out on the bench seat and rested my head on his thigh. The gentle motion of the limo combined with Oliver's occasional strokes through my hair lulled me into a peaceful state. As I drifted off, the rhythm of his typing on his phone provided a comforting background sound.

When we got home, we settled on the patio on the white loungers. It was a beautiful fall afternoon, and I was grateful we didn't need to go back to the office. The sun's warmth lingered for a while, but once it disappeared behind the taller buildings, the temperature dropped rapidly. I shivered slightly.

"Want to go inside?" Oliver asked, noticing my discomfort.

"I think so. I don't like the cold weather," I admitted, rubbing my arms.

"I could schedule some meetings in warmer places," he suggested. "Would you like to go to Miami or Los Angeles?"

"That would be lovely but not necessary. Stop spoiling me," I said, smiling at his thoughtfulness.

"Sweetheart, I went thirty-six years without having someone to spoil. I want to spoil you," he insisted, his eyes twinkling with sincerity.

"You're making me lazy," I teased, though I felt a warmth spread through me at his words.

"I'm sure that's not true," he said with a chuckle. He rose from his lounger and offered me his hand, helping me out of mine. A gentle breeze began to blow, further chilling me as we headed inside. Oliver yanked the handle on the heavy slider and pushed me gently inside, his concern evident. I was happy to escape the cold.

Without warning, he scooped me up in his arms, and I wrapped my legs around him, feeling the solid warmth of his body as he cupped my ass.

“What would you like to do for dinner?” he asked, his breath warm against my ear.

“I’m still full from lunch. Besides, it’s your birthday. Shouldn’t I be asking you that?” I replied, feeling a playful smile tug at my lips.

“We could just eat the cake,” he suggested, his tone conspiratorial.

I scowled, pretending to be annoyed. “What cake?”

“Ryleigh, you can’t hide anything from me. I know you got me a cake,” he said, a mischievous grin spreading across his face.

“You looked in the refrigerator? It was a surprise. Everything is ruined,” I said, feigning distress.

“No, it’s not. I don’t need presents or surprises from you,” he said, his voice tender and reassuring.

I planted a hard kiss on his lips, my frustration melting away. He set me on the cold white granite counter and buried his hot tongue in my mouth. I skimmed the planes of his back, stroking the strong muscles that rippled beneath his sweater. The intensity of our kiss deepened, the chill of the countertop contrasting with the heat between us.

"I'd like to take you on this counter," Oliver murmured, his voice low and rough with desire.

I ran my hands over the smooth surface, a shiver running through me. "It's too cold."

"I didn't mean now," he said, his eyes glinting with mischief. "But I think we should go on a vacation soon."

I sighed, torn between the temptation of his offer and my sense of responsibility. "I just started at Fox. I can't do that. How would it look?"

"I really don't give a shit how it looks," he replied, his tone firm. "I can do anything I want. You don't answer to anyone but me."

"But I don't want the other employees to think I'm just another pretty face," I argued, my frustration bubbling to the surface.

"They won't when they get to know you," he insisted, his eyes locking onto mine. "You're highly capable of doing what you are and more."

"Yeah, fucking my way to the top," I mumbled, the bitterness in my voice unmistakable.

Oliver's eyes flashed with blue fire. "Don't you ever say that," he snapped.

"I'm just repeating what others have said," I said, feeling a lump form in my throat.

"Who? I'll fucking fire them right now," he growled, his protective instincts flaring up.

"No one in particular, but I'm sure it's been said before," I said, trying to keep my voice steady.

He let go of me and ran his hand through his thick hair, tousling it into a bit of a mess. "My executives have commented on your competency several times. They think you're doing a wonderful job."

Despite his reassurances, I was filled with self-doubt about my position, and it was coming through at the worst possible time. "Because you're the boss. They're not going to tell you I suck."

Oliver smirked as he stood between my legs, his expression turning playful. "And how would they know you suck? That's personal."

I felt my core clench at the thought of pleasing Oliver. It made me want to drop to my knees and repeat our earlier morning encounter. "Did I remind you of something?" he asked, his voice dripping with seductive promise.

"Would you like me to do it again?" I whispered, my breath hitching in anticipation.

His eyes darkened with desire, and he leaned in, his lips brushing against my ear. "Maybe later."

I raised my eyebrows. "Am I wearing you out, Mr. Fox?"

"I've had more sex with you than I've had in the past two or three years."

I'm surprised to hear this. Oliver was so handsome, I'm sure women were throwing themselves at his feet to share his bed.

"I find it hard to believe," I said, skepticism clear in my voice.

"Don't," Oliver replied firmly. "I'm particular about who I sleep with."

"How many partners have you had?" I asked, unable to keep the curiosity out of my tone.

"Is that relevant to our relationship?" He raised an eyebrow, clearly deflecting.

I twisted a strand of hair around my finger.

"I'm just asking," I insisted, wanting a straightforward answer.

"How many have you had?" he countered, a small smile playing on his lips.

"Oh, answering a question with a question? If you must know, I've slept with four men, all of whom I dated."

"When was your first?" he asked, leaning in closer, his eyes searching mine.

"That's a very personal question," I said, feeling my cheeks heat up.

"We're engaged. I think it's a legitimate question," he replied, his tone soft but insistent.

“When was your first?” I shot back, trying to divert the conversation.

Oliver nuzzled my ear, licking the rim. He was trying to distract me from my line of questioning.

“Now who’s answering a question with a question?” he teased.

I clung to his sweater as he moved from my ear to my neck, planting kisses along my pulse. My heart rate picked up and I clenched my hands into the fine cashmere.

“You still haven’t answered my question about how many women you’ve slept with,” I pointed out, not letting him off the hook.

“Several,” he said with a nonchalant shrug.

“How many is several? I want a number,” I insisted, my curiosity now tinged with irritation.

He stepped back and I let his sweater go as he stared at me.

“Let it go, Ryleigh. It’s not important,” he said, a hint of frustration creeping into his voice.

“Then tell me how many,” I pressed, not backing down.

He sighed, running a hand through his hair. “I don’t know the exact number, maybe thirty.”

“Excuse me?” I frowned, my lips pursed in disbelief.

“About thirty or so. Why is it a big deal? Most of my sleeping around was done in college. I think I can count on two hands how many women I slept with after that, maybe one hand.”

“That’s still a lot of women,” I said, unable to hide my discomfort.

“Why does it bother you? None of them claimed my heart the way you have,” he said, his voice softening as he looked into my eyes.

“Were you ever in love before me?” I asked, needing to understand his past better.

Oliver stroked his chin thoughtfully. “Infatuated, maybe—but that was a long time ago. Were you?”

“Yes, several times but nothing as intense as our relationship. You’re like the blood in my veins, I need you,” I admitted, my voice trembling with the intensity of my feelings.

He cupped my face in his hands, his eyes searching mine. “And you’re everything I never knew I needed,” he said, his voice filled with sincerity and love.

“I feel the same way. You’ve made me want something I thought I would never want.”

“What’s that?”

“A wife, a family. My life was my company until you came along. Now I have to balance out my work and relationship with you.”

"Does that bother you?"

"Not in the least. The results are well worth it. I'm not letting you get away."

I pulled him toward me. "I feel the same way."

"My sweet tooth is kicking in. I was wondering if we could share a slice of cake?"

"Nope."

He raised his eyebrows. "You don't want cake?"

"Not yet. I'd rather you take me to bed."

"Sweetheart, my balls are in no condition for a repeat. I promise to make it up to you unless you would like to be my cake."

"I wanted to do something for you."

"You have, over and over again."

I giggled because I had more sex with Oliver than I did when I was with men my own age. He was a machine even at thirty-seven. I placed my hand on his chest to push him away so I could slide off the counter. Hidden in the back of the oversized stainless steel refrigerator was a white pastry box tied with candy cane striped string.

I removed it and got a knife from the drawer, slicing through the string before I slid the box over to Oliver. He slowly pulled the flaps open before he lifted the top. Inside was a white butter cream iced cake with blue flowers on the edges. In the middle I had them write

"Happy Birthday Oliver" in sapphire colored icing, the same as his ring.

"This looks delicious. What's inside?"

"Why don't you cut it and find out?"

I watched as Oliver removed the cake, getting icing on his thumb. I grabbed his hand and took the finger in my mouth, licking it clean with my tongue. He groaned and quickly removed it from between my lips.

"Christ, Ryleigh, you're killing me here."

"Slice it."

He made one cut, then another to make a thick slice, grabbing a spatula from the drawer to lift the piece up. The cake in the middle was chiffon with the same butter cream filling as the icing on top of the cake. I got a dessert plate from the cabinet, placing it on the counter in front of Oliver before I retrieved a fork from the drawer near the refrigerator. He placed the slice on the plate then picked it up and inhaled deeply.

"This smells delicious."

"Taste it."

He took a small piece on his fork, and I watched as he placed it between his thick sensual lips. I knew I was in trouble because he was making me hot just by eating. Oliver slowly chewed, closing his eyes before he swallowed.

“This is fantastic. It reminds me of a cake my mother used to make.”

“I’m sorry. I didn’t mean to bring up painful memories.”

“It was a good memory. Do you want to taste?”

“Just a little.”

He took a piece, and I held my mouth open for him to slip it inside. It was as he said, fantastic. Oliver took a swipe of icing on his finger and placed it against my lips. I once again sucked it inside my mouth, swirling my tongue over the pad. I watched his eyes grow dark and he noisily sighed.

“Forget dessert.”

He put down his fork and scooped me up in his arms, carrying me to the bedroom.

Chapter 4

I slept in Oliver's embrace throughout the night. Our lovemaking was a perfect end to a perfect day. By the time I fell asleep, I was exhausted and now as dawn peeked into the uncovered slider, I could feel how sore my body was. Oliver pushed me to the edge again and again using his tongue, mouth and penis to give me pleasure I never thought I would experience.

I shifted against him, and he grumbled in his sleep, tightening his hold on me as if he thought I would disappear. I didn't mind. I loved feeling his hard muscles against my body. I was glad it was Saturday, and we could sleep later. I dozed off again, waking to the sound of the shower.

The sun was fully up, warming the room with its golden rays. I snuggled deeper under the covers, my hands sliding beneath the pillow. A few minutes later, I opened my eyes to see Oliver exiting the bathroom, a thick ivory towel wrapped around his waist. It was the perfect vision for a lazy Saturday morning.

“You’re awake? Did I make too much noise?” he asked, noticing my gaze.

“Doing what? I only heard the shower,” I replied, stretching languidly.

“I worked out this morning,” he said, running a hand through his damp hair.

“When did you leave bed?” I asked, glancing at the clock on the bedside table. It was shortly after 9 a.m.

“Around 7:30,” he answered casually.

“Why did you get up so early?” I frowned, not understanding why he would leave our cozy bed.

“Because my gorgeous fiancée is corrupting me, and I’m missing my daily workouts. I might have to start going in the afternoons again,” he teased, his eyes twinkling.

“Maybe we should go together after work. I haven’t worked out much since we’ve been together. With all the food you feed me, I’m going to gain weight,” I said, poking at my belly playfully.

“You’re beautiful, and you could use a few more pounds,” he replied, smiling softly.

“Says you. So, can we work out together?” I asked, sitting up slightly.

"Sure. Do you have a gym you like to go to?" he asked, leaning against the closet door.

"I used to work out at the college and then a gym near it," I said, thinking back.

"You can come to mine, but Bronson is out. Find another trainer," he said firmly.

"I don't need a trainer," I protested.

"You should try Brad. He's the owner of the gym," Oliver suggested.

"Is he handsome?" I teased, raising an eyebrow.

"As a matter of fact, he is, but he's also gay, so you'll get nowhere," Oliver retorted with a grin.

"As long as he's nice to look at," I quipped, winking.

"You are sounding quite superficial, Miss Stewart," he said, crossing his arms and giving me a mock stern look.

"Well, if you must know, Mr. Fox, I only have eyes for your hard body," I replied, my voice dripping with playful seduction.

Oliver whipped off his towel, revealing his gloriously naked body. "You just love to tease me," he said, his tone challenging.

"You're pretty good at it yourself," I shot back.

He went to the closet, and I heard drawers opening and closing. I remained in bed, snuggled under the comfortable soft sheets and dark blue quilt. When Oliver finally emerged, he was dressed casually in a pair of gray sweatpants and a black short-sleeved t-shirt. The mattress dipped as he sat down next to me, and my eyes fluttered open.

“Did you have any plans for today?” he asked, brushing a strand of hair from my face.

“Not really. I thought we could just relax,” I said, smiling up at him.

“That sounds perfect,” he said, leaning down to press a tender kiss to my lips before he got up and left the bedroom. I didn’t feel like getting up even though it was now close to 9:30. It was Saturday and I wanted to sleep some more. Often in college, we would stay up until 4:00 a.m. and sleep until the midafternoon, only to do it again the next night.

I turned over onto my side and curled the quilt around my body, falling back into a deep sleep. I was startled awake by Oliver’s loud voice. This time it was not only his that I heard. I jumped up and pulled on Oliver’s white terry cloth robe that was hanging on the back of the bathroom door. I cinched the waist as I hurried down the hall, my feet slapping against the wood floor.

I got there just as Jonah pushed Oliver in the chest, making him slide on the floor in his socks. If I didn’t stop them, there would be all out war. Both men’s faces were bright red and as soon as Oliver recovered, he charged Jonah, screaming curses at him.

"Stop it!" I screamed as my fiancé barreled into the slightly smaller man. They both went sprawling to the floor with a loud thud. Oliver was on top of Jonah and getting ready to punch him when I dug my nails into his muscular forearm. That gave his brother the chance to spin his body, knocking Oliver off and sending him back into me. I was pushed to the floor as his body landed on mine.

My hand was bent and sandwiched between us causing me to howl in pain. The sparring men stopped to pay attention to me as I cradled my wrist in my other hand.

"Fuck, you see what you did?" Oliver screamed at Jonah.

"Me? Why can't you just listen?"

"Stop fighting," I cried out, tears rolling down my cheeks. The pain was intense, and I wondered if my wrist was broken.

"I'm sorry, sweetheart."

"Is she all right?" Jonah asked.

"You get the fuck away from her," Oliver growled.

"Oliver...." I said, hoping he would turn his attention back to me. I felt him arranging his robe over my legs, not realizing I was exposed from the fall. My face began to heat that Jonah had seen my intimate parts. Oliver helped me up and took me into the kitchen, checking my wrist while his brother stood there with a worried look on his face. Oliver palpated my wrist, holding it in his hand and gently rotating it. I winced and he stopped.

“I don’t think it’s broken. Let me get you some ice.”

He got a bag from the pantry and filled it with ice, taking the dishtowel that was hanging on the stove handle and wrapping it inside. Jonah came and sat on the stool next to me even though Oliver gave him a hard look.

“I’m sorry, Ryleigh,” Jonah said.

“What were you two fighting about?” I asked.

“Jonah has gotten himself into a bunch of shit as usual. He wants me to bail him out,” Oliver growled.

“He’s your brother. You should help him.”

“Ryleigh,” Oliver cautioned.

“You should listen to your fiancée,” Jonah said.

Oliver pointed at his brother. “Shut the fuck up. You don’t tell me what to do.”

“What’s the problem?” I asked.

“I’m being hunted,” Jonah said.

“You don’t need to fill her ears with your bullshit. Haven’t you done enough?” Oliver yelled.

I bit my lip, worried that the last relation of the Fox bloodline to my husband would be gone if my fiancé didn’t offer his assistance.

"Help him," I croaked.

"You're going to Fox Island." Oliver said.

"Why doesn't it surprise me that you have an island?" Jonah sneered.

Oliver's jaw ticked with tension. "It shouldn't. You'll help with the construction of the new house."

Jonah raised his eyebrows. "How? I don't have construction experience."

Oliver placed his palms on the counter and leaned forward, his brow furrowed. "You need to get away from whatever crap you're involved in. The company jet will take you to St. Croix and you'll be brought to the island by boat. This is your last chance, Jonah. I'm not helping you again. You keep your nose clean for the duration."

"What the fuck am I supposed to do for entertainment?" he yelled.

Oliver didn't take the bait, keeping his voice steady.

"Go swimming and run on the beach. I own many acres. Plenty of outdoor stuff to do."

"This sucks. Do I have to live in a cave?"

"No. There's a couple of buildings that the construction crews are living in. I'm warning you, don't start trouble. Maybe when you come back, I can find a spot for you back with society."

“Don’t do me any favors,” Jonah mumbled. I shot him a dirty look and he gave me a weak smile.

“You can thank my fiancée for your reprieve.”

Oliver’s cell rang and he walked toward the hallway to answer the call, leaving me with Jonah. It gave me time to look the man over. He had the same sapphire blue eyes as Oliver but wasn’t quite as muscular. His hair was a shade darker than his brother’s, and he had a scar near his left ear.

“What kind of trouble are you in and why were you fighting with Oliver?”

He ducked his head. “You’ll have to ask him. I don’t think he wants you involved.”

Somehow, I felt that I was involved and that’s what the fight was about. Oliver rarely raised his voice except where I was concerned. He was highly protective of me, and I doubted that would change in the future. I moved the ice bag on my wrist and winced.

“I’m sorry,” Jonah said as he rubbed the back of his neck. It had taken me until now to notice the clothing he was wearing, a pair of dirty blue jeans and torn faded gray t-shirt which made him look like he was living on the street. I wondered if he really was. Oliver came back a few minutes later.

“Vlad will be here in a little while to take you to the airport.”

Jonah pursed his lips. “Huh? I’m leaving right now?”

"Yes. I'm not letting you get into any more trouble. Get your life together, Jonah. You'll be thirty-four soon. Time to grow up."

"What about my stuff?"

Oliver looked his brother up and down. "You can buy new clothes. It doesn't look like you're dressing too swanky these days."

Jonah shrugged. "Yeah, well when you live in a fucking fleabag hotel. If you helped me before, I wouldn't be in this situation."

"Don't worry about it. You're done with your old life or I leave you on the side of the road. Promise me Jonah."

"What about my problem?" He asked.

I sawed my teeth over my bottom lip. I think his problem was a problem that I was involved in but Oliver wouldn't say. I hated when he kept me in the dark.

"It's being handled."

"And the other problem?"

"It's not your concern. You disappear and the other problem goes away."

Jonah frowned, which told me the second problem wasn't going away with his disappearance. Oliver turned his attention to me.

"How is your wrist?"

"It hurts, but the ice makes it feel better."

“I’m sorry you got hurt.”

“You have some making up to do.”

He nodded. “I know.”

Oliver’s phone chirped and he glanced at the message. “Vlad is here. Time to go, dear brother. Let this be a new start for you. Ryleigh, I’ll be right back.”

Jonah looked over his shoulder as he walked away. “Goodbye, Ryleigh. I wish this meeting was under better circumstances.”

“Maybe you can join us for our wedding,” I called.

“That would be nice.”

“We’ll see,” Oliver said tersely. “Let’s go.”

Oliver led Jonah out of the penthouse. I took the ice bag off my wrist and moved it around. It felt better but it was slightly black and blue. I hoped I didn’t break a bone. Oliver came back a few minutes later.

“Everything go all right?” I asked.

“As good as can be expected.”

“What was that all about?”

Oliver ran his knuckles gently over my cheek, his touch a mix of comfort and concern. “Nothing you should worry about. I have my security team looking into everything,” he said, his voice steady.

I looked up at him, searching for reassurance. “Vlad?”

“No,” he replied, shaking his head slightly. “This is my IT security team. They need to clear up a few things for Jonah.”

I bit my lip, a habit I hadn’t quite managed to break when I was nervous. “And the other problem?”

“Again, none of your concern,” he said firmly, but not unkindly. “Do you want to shower?”

I shook my head, needing more than just a quick rinse. “I’d rather take a bath.”

Oliver’s eyes softened. “Do you want me to join you?”

I hesitated, then nodded. “Would you?”

“Of course,” he said immediately. “I feel guilty about what happened.”

I brushed off his concern, though my wrist still throbbed. “I’m fine. My wrist will be okay.”

“It’s not just about today. I should have shipped Jonah off sooner. The island is remote. No one would know he was there,” he said, his voice tinged with regret.

“It’s not your fault. He’s been disappointing you forever,” I reminded him, hoping to ease his guilt.

“I know, but he’s still my brother. This situation has escalated, and I can’t let it go any longer. I needed to intervene,” he said, his tone resolute.

He kissed me on the cheek and gently tucked my hair behind my ear.

"I look horrible," I murmured.

"You're always beautiful. Jonah said I was very lucky," he replied, his eyes locking onto mine.

"He looks like you," I noted, trying to lighten the mood.

"Yes, he does. I wish he acted like me too," he sighed.

"Maybe this will be his chance to get it together. I know you want a relationship with him," I said softly.

"I have one," he corrected me. "A volatile one."

"It could change. Aren't you worried he'll head to St. Croix and get into trouble?"

"My staff has strict instructions not to transport him off the island without my permission. If he wants to go to St. Croix, he has a long swim ahead of him," Oliver said, a hint of a smile playing at his lips.

I took a deep breath, feeling the weight of the day's events pressing down on me. "I want to take my bath now."

Oliver took the ice bag from my hand and dropped it into the sink, placing the black checkered dish towel on the counter. He led me into the bathroom and sat me gently on thc vanity, turning on the water.

"Which bath beads do you want?" he asked, already moving towards the closet.

“Lime basil if you have it,” I replied, craving the soothing scent.

He found the container and added some to the water. Within moments, the fragrance filled the bathroom, a welcome distraction. Oliver planted soft kisses on my face, whispering apologies about my wrist. When the tub was filled, he undressed quickly and helped me in first, then slipped in behind me, holding me close.

"Sweetheart, how are you feeling?" Oliver's voice was tender, filled with concern.

"Oliver, stop feeling guilty. It happened. I’m more worried that I was exposed to your brother," I replied, trying to make him understand that my embarrassment was the real issue.

"Exposed?" he asked, raising an eyebrow.

"My robe opened. I’m sure he got a good eyeful," I explained, feeling a flush of humiliation creep up my neck.

Oliver's expression hardened slightly. "If he did, he’ll be the last man to see you naked."

"That’s not funny. It’s embarrassing," I said, wishing I could forget the whole ordeal.

“That should be the least of your worries," he said, trying to downplay the incident.

I turned to my side, curling up and placing my head on Oliver’s chest. He wrapped his arms around me, his fingers tracing soothing patterns along my spine. A minute later, he began to sing softly.

"You sing?" I asked, surprised.

"Sometimes," he admitted with a small smile.

"You have a nice voice," I told him, genuinely impressed.

"Thank you. Not too many people know I can sing."

"Do your friends?" I asked, curious about this hidden talent.

"Of course. We used to go to karaoke bars as a joke when we were younger," he said, chuckling at the memory.

"I guess the joke was on them," I teased.

"They're all horrible. Dax is tone-deaf and Wilmer always tries to sing songs that his voice isn't suited for," he said, shaking his head.

"Sing some more," I requested, closing my eyes to better absorb the richness of his voice as he sang a love ballad. His voice was smooth and rich, a balm to my frazzled nerves.

We stayed in the tub until the water started to cool. Oliver slipped out first, quickly wiping away the leftover bubbles and excess water. He lifted me out and wrapped me in his robe, the warmth and scent of him enveloping me.

It was well after 3 p.m. by the time we emerged from the bathroom, and my stomach growled, reminding me that I hadn't eaten since the night before. The container of crab salad that was almost a constant in Oliver's refrigerator was calling my name. I pulled on a pair of socks and padded down the hall to the kitchen, leaving Oliver as he got dressed.

I opened the refrigerator, located the crab salad, grabbed a fork, and struggled with the top. Oliver came to my rescue, popping it off with ease so I could dig into the delicious seafood.

"I guess the day kind of got away from us," he remarked, watching me with amusement.

"I only woke up a few hours ago—abruptly, might I add," I said, reminding him of the chaotic morning.

Oliver sheepishly grinned. "I can't apologize enough."

"Don't sweat it, babe," I said with a grin.

He returned my smile and busied himself making a thick roast beef sandwich on rye bread, then we headed to the living room to watch television. It was just another lazy Saturday, aside from the earlier drama.

~

I started the work week with an ace bandage wrapped around my wrist. It had stiffened up when I went to sleep on Saturday evening, which hampered our lovemaking. Oliver insisted we pass for the night and did the same on Sunday, making me grouchy. Sex with him was like a drug to me—the more we had it, the more I craved it.

Monday brought a cascade of problems. First, there was an issue with the permits for the project in Los Angeles with the Ryders. If they were delayed, money would be wasted. Oliver placed a few calls and managed to get them pulled, keeping the project on schedule.

Next, a shipment of parts from an overseas factory was held at customs. These parts were crucial for completing machinery at one of his plants. Again, a phone call from Oliver seemed to smooth things over. His influence extended far and wide and watching him navigate these challenges was a turn-on.

By late afternoon, my core was swollen and wanting. My clit ached and throbbed. I tried to think of other things, but two days without sex and watching Oliver conduct business was just too much to bear. I felt like a bitch in heat, and I wanted him. I had been sitting in my office, reading through some reports, when I decided I couldn't take it any longer.

I went to Oliver's office, finding him pacing with his earpiece attached as he conducted a conference call. I quietly closed the door and began to disrobe. He glanced up at me, frowned, but kept talking as if nothing unusual was happening.

I watched his smooth hands move through the air as he spoke, his sapphire eyes locked onto me as I removed my ivory blouse, then my black skirt. I was down to my powder blue bra and thong when he concluded his call.

He ripped out the earpiece, throwing it onto the desk. It skidded underneath some papers. "What are you doing?" he demanded, his voice low and strained.

"You're going to fuck me right now. I can't take it anymore," I said, my voice shaking with need.

He crossed his arms, muscles straining against the blue oxford cloth. "Take what?"

"We haven't had sex in two days, and watching you all day is just too much," I confessed, my eyes pleading with his.

"What you're asking for is very inappropriate for the office," he said, his tone stern.

I reached back and unclasped my bra, yanking it off my arms. My breasts tumbled out of the lace, and my nipples hardened to peaked rosebuds. Oliver's eyes traveled up my body, settling there.

"Take it all off. I want you naked," he commanded, his voice thick with desire.

"I thought this was inappropriate for the office," I teased, a smirk playing at my lips.

"It is, but you started it," he growled, striding to the door. He flicked the lock and then opened his black leather belt. The bulge in his pants was begging for release. I slid my panties down my legs, kicking them toward him. Oliver caught them in his hand, put them to his nose, then shoved them in the back pocket of his gray slacks.

The air between us crackled with tension as he closed the distance, his hands moving to my hips, lifting me onto the edge of his desk. Finally, we would satisfy this burning need.

"I'm naked, now what?"

He didn't say anything as he opened his slacks, revealing his black boxers. His cock was pressing against the fabric. I held my breath until he tugged them down, letting his shaft spring free. We stood there looking at each other. I wanted him so badly, but I didn't want to be the one to make the first move. As if reading my mind, Oliver came to me, took my good hand and placed it on the hot velvet skin of his penis.

"Stoke."

I wrapped my hand around him and gently moved my hand up and down while he fondled and kissed my breasts.

"I need you," I whispered.

His blue eyes darkened. "And you'll have me but on my terms."

"My wrist hurts," I whined.

Olive smiled wickedly. "Trying to manipulate me, Miss Stewart?"

"Is it working?" I asked with hope.

"Not in the least."

I knew he was full of shit because I could hear his respiration pick up as I stroked him. I bent my head down to lick the head of his cock, but he stopped me.

"Do that and we won't be having sex."

"What? Why?"

"I have exactly twenty minutes before my next call."

I smirked. "Wouldn't it be fun for me to suck you off while you're on it?"

"No, it wouldn't be fun since I need to concentrate."

I raised my eyebrows. "You seemed to do fine while I was undressing."

"That's a bit different than my dick in your mouth."

"Then fuck me before I get myself off."

Oliver smirked and crossed his arms. I kept stroking him and it was a battle of wills. When he made no moves, I let him go, moved to the couch and lifted my legs so my heels were balanced on the edge. I could see Oliver's eyes widen as his pupils dilated. I was open and exposed when I placed my fingers on my clit and began to rub.

He just stood there as if frozen to where he stood. His cock bobbed when he shifted his hips, and it made me wonder if he was experiencing the same ache in his balls that I had in my core. I closed my eyes as I grew close to release. Oliver had other ideas and just before I came, he approached, pushing my hand away causing me to mewl in protest.

"Fuck. I was ready to come."

"You're not coming unless my cock is inside you," he growled.

He knelt, placed his shaft at my entrance and thrust into me. I let out a loud groan as he filled me, stretching my walls with his organ. Oliver grabbed my knees with his hands and fucked me hard, slapping his balls against my ass. It felt so good, especially when he latched onto my left nipple and sucked.

"Oliver," I moaned.

"That's it. Come for me."

He didn't need to ask because I was there and a few seconds later, I let out a squeal as I began to come. He didn't stop, hammering me like I was the head of a nail.

"You just keep pushing me until you get what you want," he hissed.

"You don't have to give in," I said, panting loudly.

"I do because I love you so much."

Oliver ground his teeth, grunting as the first spurt of hot semen hit deep inside me followed by several others. He continued to move even after he completed, gently rubbing my clit.

“You don’t have to.”

“Shut up, Ryleigh. I want to.”

I sagged against the back of the couch until my second orgasm went off like fireworks. When I finished, Oliver leaned over to kiss me before he pulled out. He once again became the CEO of Fox Asset Corporation, washing himself in the bathroom and closing his pants. Five minutes later he was sitting at his desk preparing for his conference call while I was like a boneless bowl of jelly.

“Sweetheart, get dressed,” Oliver prodded.

“I’m numb.”

He chuckled. “I can’t have you distracting me, and I need you to listen in on this call.”

I reluctantly rose, gathering my clothes from the floor and heading into the bathroom to right myself. I would have loved to take a shower, but there was no time, so I settled for cleaning myself with a washcloth. As I looked in the mirror, I tried to straighten my hair back into a tight ponytail, wishing I had more time to freshen up.

. . .

When I emerged, Oliver was already dialing the phone. He gestured for me to sit in one of the gray cushioned chairs in front of his desk. I smoothed my skirt and sat down, listening intently to the conversation.

The discussion was about the software company Oliver had purchased a few months back. Employees were threatening to quit due to unbearable working conditions. He was speaking with the plant manager, Gabe Locke.

“What exactly is the issue?” Oliver asked, his voice steady, but I could see the muscle in his jaw tighten.

“They want higher wages and a better working environment,” Gabe replied, his tone fraught with tension.

“And what did you say?” Oliver pressed.

“I told them I would have to speak with you.”

Oliver exhaled loudly. “Gabe, I put you in charge to handle situations like this.”

“I understand, but I can’t authorize wage increases without your say so.”

Oliver's frustration was palpable. “I’d like to see the books.”

“Everything is under control as far as capital expenditures,” Gabe stammered.

“I still want to review the books. I can have my audit team there tomorrow.”

“It will take some time to get the accounting together.”

“It shouldn’t. That’s what Accountware is for.”

Gabe stumbled over his words, but Oliver kept pressing until he reluctantly agreed. Oliver's face reddened with anger as he curtly disconnected the call, jabbing his finger on the button to end it.

“Fucker,” he muttered under his breath.

“Oliver?” I ventured, sensing the storm brewing within him.

He looked up at me, his deep frown darkening his features. “I already know the irregularities with the plant. I’ve had my auditors keeping an eye on the situation for a few weeks now. The books aren’t balanced as they should be. I had our IT team log into the system so my accountants could figure out the issue. Nearest I can tell, Mr. Locke is embezzling.”

I put my hand over my mouth in shock. “Why are you letting it go on?”

“Evidence,” he said simply. “Are you up for a trip to Seattle this evening?”

“We’re flying out tonight?” I asked, surprised.

“I’d like to give Gabe a surprise when he comes in tomorrow,” Oliver explained, his eyes hard with determination.

“Suppose he takes off tonight?” I questioned, worried about the potential escape.

“That won’t happen. I have a security team out there watching him. He hasn’t been running the plant very well. The employees dislike him, but it’s only based on his recent behavior. I have two employees funneling me information. Something is off. Mr. Locke has two choices: either he pays back the money he’s stolen, or I have him arrested and jailed for his crimes.”

I nodded, feeling a mixture of excitement and apprehension. This trip was going to be more than just a business visit—it was a mission to bring justice.

“Who will you put in his place?” I asked.

“A long-time employee. The man knows the company well and is quite capable of handling Mr. Locke’s job. I guess he thought I was far across the country and wouldn’t find out. I always find out or I wouldn’t be where I am.”

I licked my lips. “I’m impressed and a little aroused.”

Oliver leaned back in his chair. “You’ll have to hold that thought until we’re in the air.”

“We’re taking the jet with the bedroom?”

“Yes. Would you like to join the six mile high club? You couldn’t last time we flew.”

“I might be convinced,” I said with a smirk.

He quirked an eyebrow. “You’ve become insatiable lately.”

“Because of you. You make me crazy.”

Oliver chuckled. “No, I make you horny, Miss Stewart. You’ll need to learn to control that fire. I can’t interrupt my day to service you all the time.”

I snorted. “You make it seem as if I’m a nymphomaniac.”

“Close to it. Eventually, I’ll have to hide from you.”

I crossed my arms over my chest. “Is that a joke?”

“Of course it is.”

I laughed and rose from the chair to head back to my office. I wanted to check my emails even though most of what I got was from Oliver.

Chapter 5

"You want more?" Oliver asked, sweat beading at his temples.

"No—I can't, no more." I was breathless, my body trembling from the intensity of it all.

Oliver kissed me on the forehead and pulled me against his damp, naked body. We had been in the air for two hours, and during that time, he had given me four orgasms. I was spent and exhausted. In four hours, we would be landing at Sea-Tac Airport, and I desperately needed to get some sleep.

"Sleep," he whispered, his voice tender.

I yawned. "I plan on it."

He kissed me again and then gently removed his arms from around me. I didn't have the energy to ask what he was doing as I faded off to sleep.

When I woke, Oliver was fully dressed in a gray suit, minus his jacket, which hung on the chair at the small desk he was working at with his laptop. He tapped away at the keys, focused, until I called his name.

"Yes, sweetheart," he responded, looking up from his screen.

"Where are we?"

"About a half hour out of Seattle. You should get dressed," he said, his eyes softening as they met mine.

"I slept well. This bed is very soft," I remarked, stretching languidly.

"We hit some turbulence about two hours ago, but you didn't stir."

"I was tired. I'm still tired."

"We're staying in one of my hotels in Seattle. The beds are very comfortable," he said, a hint of pride in his voice.

"You own hotels?" I asked, surprised.

"Ryleigh, you're going to need to fully familiarize yourself with Fox Asset Corporation's portfolio. I own hotels, restaurants, a few golf clubs, real estate, resorts, and many other interests here and overseas."

"What's the name of the hotel in Seattle?" I inquired, intrigued by this new piece of information.

He smiled, a glint of amusement in his eyes. "The Diamond Square. It's one of our flagship properties. You'll love it."

I nodded, feeling a mix of excitement and curiosity. Oliver's world was vast and intricate, and I was only just beginning to unravel its layers. The Diamond Square, I mused. There was one in Manhattan. It was upscale and elegant. I wondered why he didn't tell me he owned the hotel line.

“You own those? You have one in Manhattan. Why didn't you say something? We could've been married there.”

He shrugged. “I didn't want to influence your decision.”

I furrowed my brow. “Seriously? That makes no sense. How many hotels do you have?”

Oliver didn't look at me while he typed. “We have four names under Fox Asset Corporation totaling about one hundred forty-four properties.”

“Oliver, exactly how rich are you?”

Now, he gave me his full attention, his eyes meeting mine. “I'm wealthy enough to keep you in the lap of luxury for the rest of your life and beyond.”

I propped my upper body on my elbows. “So, I could choose to sit home and have babies if I want?”

“Would you be satisfied with that?”

“Maybe but not too soon. I enjoy working.”

"I enjoy you working too. It's a pleasure to have you near me all day."

I shoved the sheet off me and went to freshen up in the bathroom. I heard the captain's voice come over the intercom alerting us we would be landing soon. I washed my face in the small porcelain basin and cleaned as best I could. I would need a nice hot shower when I got to the hotel.

Oliver was back typing when I came out of the bathroom. He continued as I pulled on my clothing. I fixed the sheets on the bed but he told me not to.

"We have staff for that. They'll clean the jet and change the sheets."

"I could get used to being catered to."

"I'm sure you can."

He closed his laptop and slid it into a soft black briefcase at his feet then stood up and came over to where I sat on the corner of the bed.

"You're beautiful," Oliver said as he stroked his knuckles over my face.

"How are we getting to the hotel?"

"I have a limo waiting. Let's get buckled in. We should be landing shortly."

~

I had never been to the Diamond Square Hotel before, and it was magnificent. The dark marble floors, inlaid with lighter tiles in a zigzag pattern, gleamed under the light of massive crystal chandeliers hanging from soaring tray ceilings. The décor epitomized opulence: rich mahogany-colored wood with gold accents lined the walls, and an entire bank of gold elevators dominated one wall.

Oliver walked up to the front desk and retrieved our keycards without needing to check in. The young woman in a blue uniform addressed him as Mr. Fox with a respectful nod. A bellboy, also in a matching uniform, took our bags, loading the two dark blue suitcases onto a cart. He escorted us to our room, navigating a long hallway lined with thick black carpet featuring a floral design.

Our suite spanned two floors, and I was immediately taken by the panoramic view of Seattle. Even through the fog, the city lights sparkled in the night. I pressed my hands against the thick glass windows, mesmerized, until Oliver's voice called me back to reality.

He stood at the granite bar, which was fully stocked with top-shelf liquor. Pouring himself a half glass of vodka, he dropped in some ice cubes from the freezer.

“What's wrong?” I asked, noting the unusual choice of hard alcohol.

“I hate firing people,” he admitted, his expression troubled. “It's part of the business, but I hate it.”

“Gabe deserves it. He’s stealing from you to the detriment of your employees,” I reminded him gently.

“I know,” Oliver sighed, swirling the ice in his glass. “I should be spitting mad, but Gabe’s worked for me for a while. Something must be wrong if he resorted to embezzlement.”

I walked over to him, placing a hand on his arm. “You’re a good man, Oliver. You care about your employees. That’s why this is hard for you.”

He gave me a small, grateful smile. “Thanks. It’s just… I thought I knew him. This betrayal stings.”

"So, what are you thinking?" I asked, watching the tension in Oliver's jaw as he swirled the vodka in his glass.

"I know he's stealing. That's a given. I want to know why," Oliver replied, his voice firm but thoughtful.

"Does Mr. Fox have a soft spot?" I teased, grinning. His empathy was one of the things I loved most about him.

He took a sip of his vodka and loosened his red tie. "I'm not a cold-hearted bastard. You should know that by now."

"What will you do?" I asked, genuinely curious about his next move.

"I want to talk to him privately," he said, setting his glass down with a decisive thud.

"If that's what your gut is telling you, then do it."

"It is. I want to know the reason."

"Does that mean arrest is off the table?" I asked.

"That depends on what he has to tell me. I'll know if he's lying," Oliver replied, his eyes hardening with resolve.

I moved closer and slid my arms inside his jacket, hugging him tightly.

"I like having you with me. It's soothing," he said.

"Does that mean if I wasn't, you would be a bastard?" I teased.

"Possibly," he said, a smile breaking through his stern expression. He kissed me on the top of my head and took another sip of his vodka.

"I need a shower and something to eat," I said.

"The food here is superb. Pick anything you want," he offered, gesturing to the lacquered wood dining table with twelve chairs around it to where a tablet lay on the table.

"Does this have a menu on it?" I asked.

I went to retrieve the tablet, picking it up.

"Yes, among other information. Press the on button."

I pressed it, and the tablet came to life. A minute later, I was scrolling through the extensive menu. Everything was high-end, but I was in the mood for something simple.

"I want the Wagyu beef burger with Gruyere and black truffles."

"That sounds good. They have pomme frites," Oliver said, trying to sound sophisticated.

I smirked. "Oh, you mean French fries?"

"Yes, Miss Smarty-pants."

"Can you call? I want to shower," I said.

"What do I get in return?" he asked, a playful glint in his eye.

"I think what you got while we were flying here is enough of a reward."

"You think so?"

"Yes, I do. Please order."

I headed to the bathroom in the primary bedroom. The bed was bigger than a king with a beige satin cover and thick white sheets. Six pillows leaned against the beige padded headboard. The bathroom was even more impressive. It was as big as my apartment.

An oversized oval tub sat on light gray porcelain tile. The vanity was several feet long with dove gray granite and double square white vessel sinks. I ran my hand over the curved chrome faucet before turning my attention to the shower.

It was as large as my bedroom with thick frameless glass doors. The tiles were white mosaic on the side that held the rain shower head and back wall while the other two sides were thick glass. I couldn't wait to step inside and let the hot water wash away the stress of the day.

"It's impressive, isn't it?" Oliver's voice startled me. I turned to see him leaning against the doorjamb, stripped down to his black boxers.

"Very impressive," I admitted, taking in the sight of him. "But aren't you supposed to be ordering food?"

"I did," he said, walking towards me. "Now, I thought I'd join you in that shower."

I couldn't help but smile. "Really? You think you can keep up?"

"Oh, I know I can," he said, his voice low and confident as he closed the distance between us.

“Oliver, if you come in here with me, we won’t just be showering.”

“Sex is not on my mind but I would like to wash you.”

I groaned because his idea of washing me was to seduce me with his hands. It turned me on when he massaged shampoo into my long mahogany locks.

He held up his hands. “I promise, I’ll just wash you.”

“Uh huh.”

He ignored me and went to turn on the shower while I undressed. A few minutes later, we were both under the water and he was holding me against his hard body, cupping my ass in his big hands.

"Oliver...."

"Shh, I like this very much," he said.

"You're not playing fair. You said you would only wash me," I whined.

"And I will. I want to hold you."

"Did you order dinner?"

"No. They know I'm here. Whatever I order will be up to our room in fifteen minutes."

"I'm starving."

He let me go and grabbed a small bottle of shampoo and squirted some in his hand. The hotel provided toiletries. Oliver massaged my hair with his hands until my hair was nice and lathered then he moved me under the water. Next, he retrieved one of the washcloths stacked in a built-in shelf and put on a dollop of body wash, cleaning me from head to toe. He lingered between my legs as he cleansed me and I pushed his hand away.

He smirked. "What? I want to make sure you're clean."

"You're trying to arouse me."

"I'm doing no such thing," he protested.

“Liar,” I mumbled.

Oliver said nothing as he helped me wash the soap off.

“My turn.”

“I can do it myself.”

“Oh no. I want to assist.”

He smirked as I washed his hair, bending his knees so I could reach the top of his head. I used my hands rather than a washcloth to clean his skin and when I got to his cock, I began to stroke him.

“Ryleigh, what are you doing?”

“You know what I’m doing.”

He hardened against my fist as I continued pumping. Oliver gripped my shoulders and closed his eyes as I made him come in great creamy spurts. His chest heaved and he leaned against me as he caught his breath.

“I think I’m done for the evening.”

“I bet.”

"Oh my God, these are so good," I exclaimed, dabbing at the burger juice running down my chin.

"They better be. I expect excellence in my hotels," Oliver replied with a satisfied smirk.

"If the rest of the food is this good...." I trailed off, savoring another bite.

We were seated at the large dining table, enjoying a late dinner. It was nearing 10:00 p.m., and I could feel the fatigue settling in. Oliver took a large bite of his burger, following it with a few pomme frites dipped in ketchup.

"Slob," I teased, laughing as he wiped his mouth.

"You're right, these are delicious," he agreed, ignoring my jab.

"I like this hotel. Let's move into the one in New York," I suggested, half-joking.

"You don't like the penthouse?" he asked, raising an eyebrow.

"I love the penthouse, but come on, these burgers are fantastic."

"My chef can make them anytime you want. We don't need to move to the hotel."

"You're corrupting me. I don't know if I can ever go back to ramen noodles and fast food."

"That stuff is salty and full of chemicals. You shouldn't be eating it anyway," he said, adopting a mock stern tone.

"Thanks, Dad," I replied, rolling my eyes.

"I'm not old enough to be your father."

"If you became a teen dad you would be," I joked, unable to resist.

Oliver put down his burger and wiped his mouth. "That's not funny. You make me sound like some older creepy guy."

"You're anything but," I assured him, smiling warmly.

"Finish dinner. We need to get an early start tomorrow," he said, his tone shifting to a more serious one.

Oliver looked lost in thought, so I let him be, focusing on finishing my meal. The brioche bun was delicious, but I only ate half before giving up on the carbs and savoring the truffles, meat, and cheese. By the time I raised the white flag, I was stuffed.

"Done?" he asked, glancing up from his thoughts.

"Yes. I'm sleepy now."

"Get ready for bed. I need to do a few things before I join you."

"Oliver, is everything all right?" I asked, sensing his distraction.

I'm just thinking about my game plan for tomorrow. It's nothing you should worry about."

"Are you sure?" I pressed, not entirely convinced.

"Positive."

I piled my plate on the cart the waiter had brought and headed to the bathroom to brush and floss my teeth. I was naked under my robe and decided to slip into bed that way, leaving the light on. I didn't know when Oliver joined me, but I felt his arms slip around me as he held me close and whispered that he loved me.

I piled my plate on the cart the waiter brought and went to the bathroom to brush and floss my teeth. I was naked under my robe and decided to go to bed that way, slipping under the covers but leaving the light on. I don't know when Oliver joined me, but I felt his arms slip around me as he held me close and told me he loved me.

~

For once, I was awake before Oliver. He slumbered next to me, softly snoring. I slipped from his grasp and donned my pink robe, heading to windows to watch the sun rise over the city. What a beautiful sight. At least it wasn't raining today though I did see several clouds in the sky. I don't think I could live here with all the precipitation the Pacific Northwest received.

"Sweetheart?" Oliver mumbled.

I looked back to see my fiancé turned toward me.

"Yes?"

"I was just wondering where you were."

"I just wanted to watch the sun rise. This view is incredible."

"The view I see is incredible."

I blushed. "What time are we leaving?"

He sat up in bed. “I think I prefer you to stay here.”

I frowned. “What? Why? I thought I was going to be involved.”

“Gabe can be volatile at times.”

I felt a bolt of fear go through me. “Volatile?”

“Don’t worry; his bark is worse than his bite. I’m afraid he’ll blow up when I confront him.”

“Will you have security with you?”

If this man was volatile, it was possible he could hurt Oliver especially if he suspected he was about to lose his job or be arrested for his theft.

He nodded. “My team will accompany me. You need not worry about my safety.”

“As your fiancée, that’s my job, to worry.”

He held his arms out to me. I climbed into his lap as he bent his head to press a kiss to my lips.

“I’ll be fine.”

“What am I to do while you’re away?” I asked.

I was hoping we would visit Seattle together but with nothing to do while he was away, I might be on my own.

“Go shopping or something. You have the credit card to use.”

“I thought you wanted me to have security?”

"You will. Brenda is here. She'll travel wherever you go."

"How did she get here?"

"Ahead of us."

"I can use my own money," I said defiantly.

"If you must but the card is there for you if you need it."

I rolled my eyes. "I don't need or want your money. I'm not with you because you're rich."

Oliver nuzzled my cheek with his nose. "Good. I don't think I could tolerate a gold digger."

I slapped his chest. "Jerk. You know I don't care."

"So if I was poor, you would still date me?"

"I might even marry you. As long as you keep me entertained in bed, I don't care about your bank account."

He chuckled. "Good to know. Maybe I'll sell it all and give it away to charity."

"Except for Fox Island," I said, trying to sound casual but failing to hide my excitement.

Oliver raised his eyebrows. "You would live there?"

"Sure. It's quiet, and the weather is lovely," I replied, smiling at the thought.

"What about hurricanes?" he asked, his brow furrowing in concern.

"We could ride it out in one of the caves on the island," I suggested with a shrug.

"How do you know there's a cave?" He tilted his head, intrigued.

"I'm just guessing. Is there?" I asked, my curiosity piqued.

"Two, in fact," he confirmed with a nod.

"Will you take me to see them?" I asked, leaning in closer.

"Possibly. I was thinking of a two to three-week honeymoon," he said thoughtfully.

"On the island?" I asked, my excitement growing.

"Of course, unless you want to go somewhere else after a week," he said, his eyes twinkling.

"I'd like to be alone with you," I said softly, feeling the warmth of his gaze.

"Then the island it is," he decided, his voice firm.

"If it's ready," I added, a hint of doubt in my voice.

"I'll make sure it's ready. I want you to myself too," he assured me, his hand resting on my cheek.

"What about the staff?" I asked, practical as always.

"Only when we need them, and they'll reside in another

building," he explained, his fingers brushing my hair back.

"I love you," I whispered, my heart swelling with affection.

"I know," he said confidently, adding a wink.

"Ass," I muttered, shaking my head with a smile.

"You know it. Let me take a shower. I want to get to the plant before Gabe gets in," he said, standing up and stretching.

I moved off Oliver's lap, feeling the warmth of his body leave mine, and he flipped the sheet off him to reveal his nudity. A part of me wished we could stay in bed all day. We had talked about it, but it never seemed to happen. Maybe I could talk him into staying in bed when it got colder.

As Oliver headed to the shower, I watched him, my mind already wandering to our secluded paradise on Fox Island. It was going to be our little haven, away from the chaos, just the two of us.

~

I waited until Oliver left for the production plant to take a shower and prepare for the day. When I came out, I selected a pair of black jeans and a burgundy V-neck sweater from my suitcase. The bra and panty set I chose was pink and basically scraps of cloth held together by elastic and lace. Brenda arrived at my room just after I pulled on a pair of socks.

"Miss Stewart, I'm to escort you if you go out."

"Yes, I know. Can you please call me Ryleigh?"

She smiled. "I prefer to call you Miss Stewart."

"Is that because you feel comfortable, or it's a requirement?" I asked.

"It's part of the protocol."

"I'm changing the protocol. Call me Ryleigh."

She nodded and sat on the couch while I secured my sneakers. I wasn't sure when Oliver would be back, but he told me I had one of the hotel limos at my disposal. I spent most of the late morning going in and out of luxury stores looking for a gift for Oliver. I found what I wanted in the second to last place I stopped, Yorkshire Jewelers. I had the clerk wrap my purchase in a small white gift bag.

The last store I entered and shopped around in was a lingerie place much like Boudoir Fashions in New York. I bought a few pairs of panties and bras before I headed back to the hotel. Oliver wasn't there and I hadn't heard from him since he walked out of the room this morning. My stomach churned as I texted him.

Is everything all right? I'm worried.

Please don't. Everything is fine. We'll
talk when I come home.

I breathed a sigh of relief and asked Brenda is she wanted to join me for lunch. She declined saying if I didn't need her any longer, she would head back to her room. After she was gone, I placed the gift bag on the large dining table so Oliver would see it when he got here. He arrived a half hour later. I jumped up from the couch as soon as I heard the door open. He looked exhausted, like he went ten rounds in the ring.

"What happened?" I asked.

"Let me change and we can talk."

I left him alone as he went to the bedroom to change, paging through the complimentary Seattle Times. Oliver came back dressed in a pair of blue jeans and a white polo shirt. He plopped down next to me and kissed me on the cheek.

"You seem tired," I said.

"I am. What Gabe told me was horrible. His wife and daughter both have cancer. His wife has breast, and daughter leukemia. "

I put my hand over my mouth as I sharply inhaled. "Jesus Christ, that poor man."

Oliver grasped my hand, gently squeezing. "I was right, he was embezzling but for a good reason. He couldn't afford the medical bills. He was stealing because he didn't want to go bankrupt. He has two young sons also."

"Did he tell you immediately?" I asked.

His jaw ticked with tension. "No. In front of the accounting team he tried to play it like it was a glitch in the software. They knew better and so did I. I took him into a private room, and he broke down, telling me everything that was going on. He didn't know what else to do."

I put my other hand over his. "How are you handling it?"

He sighed. "I put him on leave with full salary."

"And the money he embezzled?" I asked.

Oliver pursed his lips. "He would get that much in a yearly bonus. He won't get one this year in order to replace what he took."

This was a lesson for me. Sometimes you had to make the hard choices but it wasn't always what it looked like on the surface.

"Can you trust him?"

"I told him if he has financial issues due to his family's illnesses, he's to come to me. I don't condone what he did but I'm giving him a pass this time. He's a good employee and this is the only blemish on his record."

I kept his gaze. "It's a pretty big blemish."

"Sometimes you need to look deeper. I'm not always in it to make money. There's the human factor in business. You're dealing with people not objects."

"You're a good man."

"I have so much. I can afford to help others when they need it."

"Do you donate to charities?"

"All the time and all over the world. We're working on projects to bring fresh water to millions of people in Africa and Asia along with solar power for electricity. Fox Asset Corporation funds several programs to feed and house the impoverished. I believe in giving back."

"I know. You give so much to me."

Oliver glanced at the bag on the table. "Speaking of which, what's in the bag on the table?"

"Why don't you check and see," I said, a smile playing at my lips.

He raised an eyebrow but went to retrieve the bag, bringing it to the couch. "What are you up to?"

"Just open it and stop being suspicious," I teased, leaning back to watch his reaction.

He carefully pulled out the white tissue paper, balling it up and placing it on the coffee table. His eyes widened when he removed the black box with "Vacheron Constantin" engraved in gold on the top.

He looked up at me, curiosity and surprise mingling in his gaze, before opening the box to reveal the watch I had bought for him. Made of eighteen-carat white gold with a black alligator band, it was a statement of elegance and opulence. And a test.

“This is gorgeous,” he breathed, his voice filled with awe.

He took off the yellow gold Rolex he was wearing and replaced it with the Vacheron Constantin, admiring the way it looked on his wrist. “I love it. Thank you for this gift.”

“It was expensive,” I said, testing the waters.

“So, what’s the problem?” He looked at me, his brow furrowing slightly.

“I thought you would be angry I spent so much.”

“Ryleigh, I probably make the cost of this watch every minute of the day. I don’t care if you want to spend money.”

“I was testing you,” I admitted, my voice softening.

“Why? I told you to spend whatever you’d like.” His tone was gentle but probing.

He sat on the couch next to me. The watch looked beautiful on his strong wrist and I was glad to have purchased it for him.

“So, I can go on a shopping spree on Fifth Avenue?” I asked, half-joking.

“Sure. Get used to spending money,” he said, a playful glint in his eyes.

“You spoil me,” I said, feeling a warm flutter in my chest.

“I’m just glad to have someone to spoil,” he replied, his expression sincere.

“Were you lonely before me?” I asked, suddenly serious.

“I was in denial before you. I kept thinking I was fulfilled by work. I wasn’t. It wasn’t until you that I realized I wasn’t living.”

“Even with all the social events and women on your arm?” I pressed, needing to understand.

“Once again, they were part of keeping me busy,” he said, shaking his head.

“Why haven’t we attended an event together?” I wondered aloud.

“Do you want to? You know I prefer to stay home and have you all to myself,” he said, his eyes locking onto mine with a tenderness that made my heart skip a beat.

In that moment, I realized the depth of his feelings for me and the life we were beginning to build together.

"I’d like to go to at least one," I said, trying to keep my voice light.

Oliver's expression darkened slightly. "I do it for security reasons. I don't want you to be exposed."

My stomach tightened, a knot of anxiety forming. What wasn't he telling me about the threats against my life?

"If it's not safe, then forget it," I conceded.

"It's safe as long as you listen to our security team," he assured me, his tone firm.

"I do," I insisted, but I could hear the defensiveness in my own voice.

"Sometimes you can be stubborn," he said, his eyes softening. "You still haven't decided what you want to do with your apartment."

"I want to move in with you full-time, but I need to have space sometimes," I admitted.

"That would mean spending time away, and I hate that," he replied, a hint of frustration creeping in.

"I don't mean sleeping somewhere else. I mean going out with friends," I clarified.

"Why can't we go out together?" he asked, clearly not understanding.

"Because space is good. It doesn't mean I love you any less," I explained gently.

"I hope not," he said, though there was a vulnerability in his eyes that tugged at my heart.

"Don't be silly. You own my heart as much as I own yours," I reassured him, reaching out to squeeze his hand.

"Where would you like to go?" he asked, his voice softening.

"My friends from home would like to come down for a night in the city," I said, excitement bubbling up.

"A night where?" he asked, suspicion already creeping into his tone.

"At a club."

I hadn't been out for a night on the town in so long. In college, I used to go out with Sadie or some of my friends from the dorm almost every Friday and Saturday. Now that I was with Oliver, I'd become a homebody.

"Which club are you referring to? Clubs are hard as far as security. They're crowded and full of men with grabby hands," he said, his protective instincts flaring.

"I've never had a problem before," I pointed out.

"You've never been engaged to a man in the public eye," he countered.

I rolled my eyes. "Wow, conceited much?" I teased, trying to lighten the mood.

"It's true. I want you safe. If you want to go to a club, then go to one of mine," he suggested, his tone firm but caring.

"Why doesn't it surprise me that you own clubs around the city?" I said, teasing playfully.

He straightened up as if puffing with pride and stroked his hand over the stubble on his chin.

"Not just Manhattan," he replied, a smirk playing on his lips.

"Where else?"

"Los Angeles, Miami, Las Vegas, Vancouver, London, Rome, and Chicago," he listed casually.

I giggled. "Maybe we should take the company jet and hit all of them."

"That could take a while," he said, his smirk turning into a full grin. "I own eighteen of them."

I snorted. "What don't you own?" I asked, genuinely curious about the extent of his empire.

"I'm not sure what you mean," he said, tilting his head.

"You're quite diversified," I said, marveling at the man before me.

Oliver shrugged as if it was no big deal but it was a huge deal for someone who basically started from scratch was now a billionaire at thirty seven. I'm not sure if he even understood how admirable what he did was.

"I told you my portfolio is quite expansive. I suggest you familiarize yourself with it if you plan to be my wife and protégé," Oliver said, his eyes twinkling with a mix of challenge and affection.

I laughed softly. "That could take months, if not years."

"We have time. The rest of our lives," he replied, his voice warm and reassuring.

"So, what about the club? Which ones do you own?" I asked, curiosity getting the better of me.

"Ice, Pinnacle, Bamboo, Club Inc., Rooftop, and Show Me Yours," he listed.

"I've only been to Bamboo," I admitted.

"I also own some bars," he added, a hint of pride in his voice.

"When can I go?" I asked excitedly.

"Whenever you want, but I insist on security. You'll stay in the VIP section," he said firmly. I saw a fleeting look of worry cross his face before he masked it with a confident smile.

"I want to go this upcoming weekend. Can my friends stay at the penthouse?" I asked, feeling a flutter of excitement.

"How many friends are we talking about?" he inquired, his tone cautious.

"Three. Benny, Diane, and Lisa."

"Who are these friends?" he asked suspiciously.

"I went to high school with them, and we've kept in touch."

"Is Benny an old boyfriend?" he asked, his voice tightening.

I couldn't resist teasing him. "He was my first."

He wasn't but it was refreshing to see how jealous Oliver got at the mention of another man in my life, even if it was years ago.

He raised his eyebrows, a mix of surprise and concern. "I'm not sure I feel comfortable with you hanging out with your first lover."

"Why not? There's obviously nothing going on between us now."

"I'd certainly hope not. He's seen you naked," Oliver said, his tone a mix of protectiveness and jealousy.

"But it's long over. There's no spark between us," I reassured him.

"I don't want to say no, but I don't think I want him around you."

"I'm kidding. Benny is only a friend. He's dating Lisa," I clarified, grinning at his relief.

"Who was your first and when? We never finished our discussion," he asked, leaning back and regarding me intently.

"High school. I was sixteen, and his name was David. We dated for several months, and I thought I was in love."

"How did it end?" he asked, genuinely interested.

"Amicably. The chemistry just disappeared. I think our love was infatuation. He was my real first steady boyfriend. I broke it off," I explained.

"Do you still see him?"

In a fit of possessiveness, Oliver pressed a kiss to my neck, moving to my ear and nuzzling it. His warm breath against my skin sent chills down my spine.

"I did, but he moved to Little Rock after college. You have no competition, Oliver. None," I said, my voice softening.

"I'm well aware," he said, a satisfied smile tugging at his lips.

"Who was your first and when?" I asked, curious about his past.

I clasped his hand, playing with his fingers.

"Fifteen. We were too young to enjoy what we were doing. Her name was Kayla, and she was my girlfriend for a time."

"Were you in love with her?"

"Like you, it was infatuation. I'd never had a girlfriend before her. We were so wrapped up in each other, but it faded after a while. Our relationship became a chore. It was too emotional for us," he explained, a nostalgic look in his eyes.

As we talked, I felt a deeper connection forming between us, our pasts blending into the present, shaping our future together. I wanted to know everything about him because there was so much to tell.

"You never had a girlfriend before you were fifteen?"

"Why does that surprise you?"

"You're gorgeous. How could the girls resist you?" I asked, my curiosity piqued by Oliver's easy confidence.

He chuckled, a hint of nostalgia in his eyes. "I was gangly and awkward at the time. It took another year before women were climbing over themselves to date me."

I raised an eyebrow, incredulous. "That's a really arrogant thing to say. What the fuck, Oliver?"

He shrugged, unbothered by my reaction. "I don't make the rules. It's true. I just filled out the summer between my junior and senior years. I started working out, and the next school year, they wouldn't leave me alone."

I tilted my head, scrutinizing him. "And no one's caught you since?"

His gaze softened, and he reached out to gently touch my cheek. "Not until you."

A warmth spread through me at his words, but my stomach chose that moment to rumble loudly. I laughed, breaking the tension. "I'm hungry. I need some lunch."

Oliver's eyes darkened with desire. "Well, I need some you."

I smirked, teasing him. "You haven't had enough of me?"

"Nope," he said, his voice low and husky.

Before I could protest, he stood and scooped me into his arms, carrying me to the bedroom. We spent the afternoon making love, the world outside forgotten as we lost ourselves in each other. My stomach growled in protest, but I didn't care.

Later, after we showered, I ordered a ridiculous amount of food off the menu—things I knew would make me sleepy from too many carbs, sugar, and salt. Oliver watched me with amusement as I ate, his laptop open beside him.

When I finished, he tucked me in, his touch tender. He sat on the bed next to me, going over some reports on his laptop. The clicking of his nails on the keyboard was a strangely comforting sound, and I dozed off, feeling safe and content.

Chapter 6

I couldn't sit still. My excitement buzzed under my skin, making it impossible to focus on the magazine article in my lap. Any minute now, my friends would arrive, and the anticipation was driving me mad.

Across the room, Oliver sat on the couch, sipping brandy and bouncing his knee—a telltale sign of his growing nerves. I noticed he had been drinking more lately, and I hoped it wasn't because of me. He always got anxious when I went out, but Trevor and Brenda would be with us tonight.

"When will Wilmer and Ivan be here?" I asked, trying to break the silence.

"After you leave," he replied, his voice calm but his eyes betraying his unease.

"What are you doing tonight?" I probed further, hoping to distract him from his worries.

"Heading to Zapata to play a few rounds of pool," he said, taking another sip of his drink.

I smirked, teasing him. "Let me guess, you own that too?"

He chuckled. "Half of it—Jordan Grayson owns the other."

"And another piece of the puzzle falls into place," I said, shaking my head in amusement.

"Puzzle?" he asked, raising an eyebrow.

"How many collaborations do you have with other companies?"

"A lot. It's good business to work with others. Jordan is an upstanding guy. We should go out to dinner with him and his wife, Emma. I think you'll get along well with her."

"Why?" I asked, curious.

"Why should we go out or why would you get along with Emma?" he clarified.

"Why would I get along with Emma?"

He took another sip of his drink. "Because you have the same type of thinking. Strong and independent with a touch of fire."

I grinned, feeling a spark of intrigue. "Touch of fire, huh?"

"Come here," he said, his voice low and inviting.

I slid over to him, adjusting my form-fitting black dress as it rode up to reveal my black lace thong.

"I hope that's not going to happen in the club," he murmured, his eyes darkening with desire.

"Don't worry," I whispered, leaning in close. "No one will see my goodies but you."

His hand slid up my thigh, sending shivers through me and I pulled away reluctantly, smoothing my dress back down. We didn't have sex last night or today because Oliver was exhausted from an intense negotiation for a piece of property in Palm Springs. He wanted to build a Diamond Square Resort. So, he was fired up but so was I.

"Behave," I demanded.

He groaned. "I can't. I should have fucked you in the shower."

"You were still on the phone when I went in."

He reached for me again, but I backed away. "I mean I should've pulled you in when I went."

"I already did my hair."

"Please?" he begged.

I loved to bring him to his knees, but this wasn't the appropriate time to roll around the bed. There was no time.

"Oliver, my friends will be here in a few minutes," I protested.

"I won't last until you get home."

"I doubt I'll have energy when I get home. Even if I did, we'll have to be quiet since the guest rooms will be occupied."

Oliver groaned and shifted his position when my cell buzzed.

I swiped the screen to see who it was. "They're downstairs. Think of something horrible because I doubt it would be appropriate for them to see your erection."

Oliver looked down at his cock pressing against his black jeans. He closed his eyes as I stood up and called the lobby to tell them to let my friends up to the penthouse. Oliver stood up and adjusted his pants as his erection subsided. He straightened his gray sweater and downed the rest of his brandy, taking the glass to the kitchen.

I waited eagerly by the door, my heart pounding with excitement, until the knock came. Without hesitation, I yanked it open to reveal all three of my friends standing there, each with small suitcases in tow.

Benny, tall and thin with unruly blond hair and bright blue eyes, grinned as he took in the penthouse. Lisa stood beside him, her black hair a stark contrast to his, her porcelain skin glowing in the soft light. Diana, closer to my coloring with her auburn hair, smiled warmly at me.

"Damn, this place is awesome," Benny whistled as he looked around.

We hugged tightly, the energy between us palpable. As I let go, I introduced them to Oliver, who greeted them with a million-dollar smile that I knew was already winning them over.

"Glad to meet some of Ryleigh's friends. Can I show you to your rooms?" Oliver offered politely.

We followed him down the hall to the guest rooms, arranging who would stay where. Diana would be closest to the primary, while Lisa and Benny would be next to Oliver's office. After dropping off their bags, we showed them the hall bathroom, stocked with fluffy white towels.

"Want a tour?" I suggested as we regrouped in the hallway.

They all agreed eagerly, and Oliver excused himself with a quick call on his cell. I led my friends to the patio, where the city lights twinkled below us.

"Damn, Ryleigh, you really scored with Oliver," Diana remarked, her eyes wide with awe.

"I don't care about the surroundings, just Oliver," I replied, smiling at the thought of him.

"You've got to admit it's a great perk," Lisa chimed in.

"Yes, it is. I love this place, so spacious," I agreed.

"What about your apartment?" Benny asked, curious.

"It's sitting vacant. Sadie is living with Finley," I explained.

"Excuse me," Lisa interrupted. "Is that the same workaholic Finley who has no time for a social life?"

"Apparently, he has time for Sadie, and I'm happy for them," I replied, feeling genuinely pleased for my brother and best friend.

After the quick tour, we settled on the couch to catch up.

"How's work?" Lisa asked, breaking the silence.

"It's good though my boss can be a hard ass," I joked.

"I heard that," Oliver's voice floated down the hall, and we turned to see him approaching.

"You were supposed to. Everything all right?" I asked, concern flashing in my eyes.

"Just a call from my attorney. Everything is fine. Can I offer anyone a drink?" Oliver offered, his voice casual and reassuring.

"I think we can wait until we get to the club since the owner has so graciously offered free drinks as well as entry," Benny replied with a grin.

"He's a good guy, isn't he?" Lisa chimed in, her eyes sparkling with excitement.

"I think so," I agreed, a warm feeling spreading through me.

Oliver settled himself next to me, his arm wrapping around my shoulders in a comforting gesture.

"You're all dressed very nicely," he observed, his eyes lingering appreciatively on each of us.

Diana's dress, a deep blue shade, mirrored mine, while Lisa looked chic in a black skirt and sleeveless burgundy blouse. Benny's black dress shirt and dark blue jeans completed the ensemble, perfect for a night out.

I couldn't help but smile at the thought of dancing with my friends, knowing that by the end of the night, my makeup would be smudged and my hair tousled, but right now, I felt confident and ready for whatever the evening had in store.

~

"Show Me Yours" was an experience unlike any other. The ambiance was both seductive and sophisticated, with soft blues and beiges adorning the space. As we entered, my eyes widened at the sight of the staff. The hostess, in a skimpy light blue dress, seemed conservative compared to the waitresses, who wore black leather micro skirts and halter tops that left little to the imagination.

The waiters, clad in skin-hugging leather pants with no shirts, exuded confidence and allure. It was as if every person I laid eyes on was sculpted from marble, beautiful and well-muscled.

The pulsating beats of Nathaniel Heaton, the renowned DJ, filled the air as he worked his magic behind the turntables. Lights danced across the high ceilings, casting a kaleidoscope of colors over the packed dance floor.

Trevor and Brenda led us to the VIP area, where a private space awaited us with bottle service. I settled onto the beige banquette, tucking my purse beside me, as a tall blonde waitress swiftly took our drink orders.

Usually a wine enthusiast, tonight I opted for something stronger and ordered rum and Coke. Lisa, Benny, and Diana stuck with beer as we settled in, soaking in the electrifying atmosphere. Halfway through my drink, the urge to dance became irresistible. Trevor joined us on the dance floor, while Brenda stayed behind to keep an eye on our belongings.

Surrounded by my friends, I felt a surge of happiness as we claimed our spot on the dance floor. Despite the chill of October lingering outside, the air conditioning inside barely kept up with the heat generated by the crowd. Sweat glistened on my skin as I moved to the rhythm of the music, my loose hair clinging to me.

Trevor, ever vigilant, subtly positioned himself nearby, ready to intervene if needed. When a man bumped into me, Trevor quickly stepped in, creating a barrier between me and the intruder. Undeterred, I continued to dance until I was drenched in sweat. Gesturing to my friends, we made our way upstairs.

Upstairs, a pitcher of ice water awaited us, a welcome relief from the heat of the dance floor. When the waitress returned to take our drink orders, I ordered another rum and Coke, while my friends opted for water.

Sipping my drink, I couldn't shake the feeling that Oliver was keeping an eye on me, ensuring I didn't overindulge. It should have bothered me, his interference, but instead, it comforted me to know he cared so deeply.

“Are you having a good time?” Benny asked.

“Awesome. I’m so glad you could come.”

He hugged me tightly, planting a kiss on my cheek. Benny and I had known each other since elementary school, when he moved to Hudson Brook in fifth grade. We’d been friends ever since, and I considered him one of my best friends.

Clinging to his sweaty shirt, I hugged him back, feeling a sense of comfort in his embrace. When I let go, I turned as Brenda tapped me on the shoulder, holding out her phone. I frowned as I took it from her hand and put it to my ear.

“Yes?” I answered, curious about the unexpected call.

“Come downstairs,” Oliver growled, his voice low and commanding.

“Downstairs where?” I questioned, puzzled by his request.

“Below the VIP deck is a hidden door near the stairs. Let Trevor escort you,” he instructed firmly.

“What’s your problem?” I couldn’t help but feel a pang of annoyance at his tone.

“Humor me, Ryleigh,” Oliver insisted, his voice stern.

Reluctantly, I handed the phone back to Brenda and glanced at Trevor, who nodded in confirmation. It seemed Oliver had given him advance notice of his request. Not wanting to cause a scene in front of my friends, I told them I had to check with club security. If I said I needed the bathroom, Lisa and Diane might want to join me.

Trevor led me down the stairs, and I felt the curious gazes of several people as I descended. The panel under the stairs popped open, and I was pulled into a darkened room before the door shut behind me. In the dim light, I could make out Oliver’s silhouette and catch the familiar scent of his cologne. He wrapped his arms around me, latching onto my neck and leaving a trail of kisses.

“Oliver, what are you doing here?” I whispered, feeling a mix of surprise and desire.

“I’m going crazy thinking about you,” he confessed, his breath hot against my skin.

“Are you sure it wasn’t because another man had his hands on me?” I teased gently, trying to lighten the mood.

“Who touched you?” Oliver’s voice was suddenly tense, and I realized he was serious.

• • •

“Benny hugged me, and you called a few seconds later. There’s nothing between us.” I reassured him, feeling a pang of guilt for unintentionally causing him distress.

“I know that. I’m not jealous,” Oliver admitted. “But I spent the last two hours with my dick as hard as steel. I need you.”

“I’m a mess. I need a shower,” I protested weakly, feeling torn between desire and practicality.

“I don’t care. I want you,” Oliver insisted, his voice husky with desire.

He moved, slowly pressing me against the wall.

“What is this place?” I asked, my voice tinged with curiosity as Oliver's hands roamed over my body.

“It’s my personal office. No one except Jordan comes in here,” he explained, his tone possessive.

I felt sweaty and disheveled from dancing, and I tried to push his hands away as he lifted my dress and slid his hands between my thighs. Despite my protests, I could feel the dampness of my panties, a clear indication of my arousal.

“Stop fighting me, Ryleigh,” Oliver commanded, his voice firm but tinged with desire.

“I’m disgusting,” I protested weakly, feeling self-conscious about my sweaty state.

“I don’t care. You’re sexy to me no matter what,” he

reassured me, his hands now roughly cupping my breasts.

With his touch igniting a fire within me, I yielded to him, allowing him to pull my dress up over my hips. Our lips met in a fervent kiss, and I ran my fingers through his hair as he explored me with his fingers, sending waves of pleasure coursing through my body. When his thumb found my clit, I couldn't contain the pleasure, whimpering into his mouth as I climaxed.

So responsive tonight," Oliver murmured.

"It's been two days," I confessed, feeling a flush of embarrassment at my lack of control.

"You want me as badly as I want you. I want to hear you scream the next time I make you come," he whispered, his breath feathering against my ear.

"But people will hear," I protested, suddenly conscious of our surroundings.

"The music is so loud, and this room is almost soundproof," he reassured me, his lips trailing kisses down my neck.

I hadn't realized it before, but the music was barely audible in our secluded spot. Lost in the moment, I hadn't paid attention to anything but Oliver and the pleasure he was giving me.

With newfound confidence, I reached down and undid his belt, opening his zipper and stroking his cock.

"How long have you been like this?" I asked, my voice barely above a whisper, my desire for him overwhelming any sense of inhibition.

"Two hours. You should've let me make love to you before your friends arrived," Oliver confessed, his voice filled with longing.

"We would've had two minutes," I countered, a hint of regret in my tone.

"It would have been enough to take the edge off until we got home tonight," he reasoned, his desire evident in his words.

"Oliver, you don't make love quickly. It's not in your DNA," I pointed out, smiling at his eagerness.

"I was so turned on by you. This little sexy dress clinging to every beautiful curve on your body," he admitted, his voice husky with desire.

I felt a rush of warmth at his words, grateful for the way he saw me. Despite the constraints of time and circumstance, the intensity of our connection remained unwavering, and I knew that our passion would only grow stronger as the night progressed.

I stroked him more vigorously as he latched onto my ear and took the diamond stud I had on my lobe into his mouth as he sucked. He moaned against me, making me even hotter. The orgasm I experienced a few minutes ago did nothing to calm me. My nipples strained against the cloth of my dress in hard peaks.

"Slow down or I'll come," he growled.

"That's the point," I muttered.

"I want to come inside you. I've been thinking about your hot little pussy all night. It's the only way."

"Unless I make you come with my mouth," I whispered.

Oliver groaned. "Another time."

He pushed my hand away, reaching into his pocket to retrieve something. I heard a tear of paper.

"What's that?" I asked.

"A condom. There's no proper place to clean up here."

"I'm surprised you don't have a private bathroom in here."

I helped him peel his underwear down and the latex made a noise as he rolled it on. He pulled my dress over my head and expertly reached back to unclasp my damp bra before he knelt to remove my panties. I slid out of my shoes so he could take them off.

"Put the shoes back on," he requested.

"Why am I naked and you're still dressed?"

"Do you want to argue, or do you want me to fuck you?" he asked.

"I want to feel your skin against mine."

He backed away as I slipped on my four-inch heels. I saw him move in front of me and heard the whisper of his sweater coming off and the jingle of change as his jeans came down. Oliver reached for my hand, placing it against his bare chest.

"Happy?"

"Very," I said, stroking his muscles. "I love feeling you like this."

He lifted me in his arms, pressing me against the smooth wall and cupping my ass with his hands. I felt his cock pressed at my entrance and he let me down slowly. I hooked my ankles around his waist and wrapped my arms around his neck as I engulfed him.

"You feel so fucking good," I moaned.

"I love to be inside you. You're so snug."

Oliver tightened his embrace, thrusting in and out so that I slid up the wall with each stroke. The muscles in his shoulders strained as his respirations grew heavy. He moved away, letting me down.

"What are you doing?" I protested at the loss of him inside me.

He led me to a couch which I could barely see. "On all fours," he demanded.

I felt around as I hunted for the cushions then moved into place and he slipped back into me, grasping my hips hard and shoving deep inside my slick channel.

"Oh God, Oliver, I'm going to come," I moaned, feeling the heat building inside me.

"Scream," he urged, his voice laced with desire.

"I can't," I admitted, my breath hitching with anticipation.

With a sudden motion, he pulled out of me, leaving me teetering on the brink of ecstasy.

"Fuck me," I begged, my voice raw with need.

"Scream for me, Ryleigh. I know you want to," Oliver insisted, his tone commanding.

"I can't," I protested, feeling frustration bubbling up within me.

"Then you don't come," he declared firmly.

I sighed in frustration, feeling the ache of desire pulsing through me. "Neither do you, then."

"My will is stronger than yours," he asserted confidently.

As I reached toward my own pleasure, Oliver grabbed my hand, holding it firmly in his grip.

"I need it," I cried out desperately.

"Then do as I ask," he replied, his voice softening slightly.

"Why, Oliver?" I questioned, feeling a mix of confusion and longing.

"I love to hear you scream when you come. I want to know I satisfy you," he confessed, his words sending a shiver of arousal down my spine.

"You do. I don't need to scream," I insisted, my voice filled with conviction.

He slipped back inside me, and as he felt my body respond, he withdrew once more. "Please," I pleaded, my body trembling with anticipation.

Oliver teased me relentlessly, each withdrawal leaving me on the edge of desperation. Tears welled in my eyes as I yearned for release, the ache of desire consuming me.

He withdrew one final time, moving us to the couch and pulling me onto his lap. As he discarded my shoes, I reached for the condom, desperate to feel him completely.

"No. I told you, there's nowhere to clean up," he reminded me, his tone firm but tender.

"I don't care. I want nothing between us," I declared, my voice filled with longing.

"You're a dirty girl," he teased, his words sending a thrill through me.

"I love you, Oliver. Make me come," I pleaded, my heart pounding with desire.

Removing the condom, I rose onto my knees, positioning his shaft at my slick entrance before lowering myself onto him. As we rocked together, our bodies moved in perfect harmony, each sensation sending waves of pleasure coursing through me.

With a primal cry, I threw my head back as ecstasy washed over me, Oliver's arms the only thing keeping me grounded as I rode out the intensity of my climax. As I collapsed against him, spent and sated, I knew that in that moment, there was nowhere else I'd rather be than in his arms.

“That was incredible,” I managed to mumble, still catching my breath.

“You’re incredible,” Oliver replied, his voice filled with admiration.

“I want to go home,” I stated, feeling a sudden desire for the comfort of our own space.

“You have guests,” he reminded me, a hint of reluctance in his tone.

“Can’t Trevor take them home? Speaking of guests, where are Ivan and Wilmer?” I inquired, curious about their whereabouts.

“I left them at Zapata with a complimentary bottle of Patron. They won’t miss me,” Oliver explained casually, his focus clearly on me.

“I want you again,” I confessed, unable to resist the pull of desire.

“That can be arranged,” he replied, his voice husky with anticipation.

Oliver latched onto my neck, leaving a trail of kisses and sucking gently.

“Stop it, I’m gross. I danced for almost an hour,” I protested weakly, feeling self-conscious about my sweaty state.

“You’re sexy and beautiful. I can’t resist you,” he whispered, his breath hot against my skin.

“Seeing how your penis is still inside me, I believe that to be true,” I teased, a hint of amusement in my voice.

He held me close for a few more minutes, his touch gentle as he caressed the sweaty skin of my back. Eventually, he shrank and slipped out of me, and I climbed off him, feeling the warmth of his semen coating my inner thighs. With a flick of a small lamp attached to the wall above the couch, Oliver illuminated the dimly lit room, casting a soft glow over us.

“Now I’m really a mess,” I sighed, feeling a mixture of embarrassment and exhaustion.

“I warned you. I have some wet wipes in the desk,” Oliver offered casually.

Turning towards the corner of the room, I spotted a large wooden desk with a computer sitting on it. I padded over and pulled open the middle drawer, finding a full package of wet wipes.

Popping open the top, I removed several wipes and began cleaning my thighs and between my legs. It wasn't a perfect solution, but it would have to do for now. Depositing the used wipes in a small black plastic garbage can by his desk, I turned to see Oliver lounging on the couch, watching me with a relaxed expression.

"Aren't you getting dressed?" I asked, feeling self-conscious under his gaze.

"I love the view," he replied, his eyes lingering on me appreciatively.

"I'm a sweaty mess. I bet my mascara makes me look like a raccoon," I grumbled, feeling insecure about my appearance.

"A sexy raccoon. I don't care, sweetheart. I love you no matter what," he assured me, his words melting away my insecurities.

Retrieving my panties and bra from the floor, I quickly slipped them on while Oliver lazily pulled on his boxers. We dressed in comfortable silence, and I wished there was a mirror in the room so I could check my hair.

"Ready?" Oliver asked once we were both dressed.

"I look like crap," I admitted, feeling less than confident about my appearance.

"Nonsense. It doesn't matter how you look; it matters how you feel," he countered, his voice filled with warmth and affection.

“Fantastic with all the endorphins and alcohol running through my system,” I replied with a weak smile.

Oliver took my hand and led me out through the hidden door, reaching back to flick the lock and pushing the panel closed behind us. As we walked up the stairs to the VIP lounge, I noticed a few people staring at us curiously. My friends and Brenda and Trevor were waiting for us.

“Ryleigh doesn’t feel well,” Oliver lied smoothly.

“What’s wrong?” Lisa asked, concern evident in her voice.

“My stomach. I should’ve gone easy on the rum,” I improvised, hoping my friends would buy the excuse.

“We can go with you,” Brenda offered, her concern mirrored by Trevor.

“No, stay. The limo will be at your disposal as soon as it drops us off. Trevor and Brenda will take you home,” Oliver reassured them, his tone firm but kind.

“Are you sure?” Benny asked, his brow furrowed with concern.

“Positive. We can eat breakfast together tomorrow. Oliver is having his chef come at ten,” I added, hoping to put their minds at ease.

“Sounds awesome. Feel better,” Lisa said, her words echoed by Benny and Diane as they bid us farewell.

“Thank you,” I murmured gratefully as Oliver led me down the stairs to retrieve our coats.

“You made me lie to my friends,” I whispered, feeling a twinge of guilt.

“It will be well worth it, and it wasn’t a big lie. You’ll see them tomorrow morning,” Oliver reassured me, his tone gentle but firm.

“It is tomorrow morning,” I pointed out, glancing at my watch. It was just after midnight.

“Then this morning,” he amended with a playful grin.

Vlad was waiting with the limo at the curb, and I slipped on my wool coat as we exited the club.

“Take it off,” Oliver instructed as we slid inside.

“My coat?” I questioned, confused by his sudden request.

“I’ll settle for your coat right now,” he clarified, his eyes smoldering with desire.

With a coy smile, he shucked out of his coat, and I followed suit, depositing mine on the opposite seat as he had. Oliver wasted no time in seducing me with his tongue and hands as we drove towards the penthouse. By the time we arrived, he had me on the edge of combusting, my body throbbing with need.

“You must love having a chef at your disposal,” Benny remarked between bites of French toast, his mouth full.

“It’s nice, but we don’t call on him that much,” I replied, smiling at the memory of our leisurely brunches.

“If I had a chef, I would never do my own cooking,” Lisa chimed in.

“I like to cook,” I interjected, defending my culinary skills.

“And she does a good job,” Oliver added, his tone fond.

Lisa wrinkled her nose in mock disgust. “You must have gotten better since we were kids. Remember when you burned popcorn and had to throw out the pot because you couldn’t scrub it clean?”

“I was fourteen at the time. I’ve improved since then,” I retorted with a laugh, enjoying the banter with my friends.

After breakfast, we lounged around the living room, enjoying each other’s company. As my friends prepared to leave, Oliver arranged for Vlad to shuttle them home in the limo.

“We should do this again,” I suggested as they gathered their things, and they all agreed enthusiastically.

Still feeling lazy, I opened up the paper and rested my head on Oliver’s sweatpants-clad thigh while he stroked my hair tenderly.

"Thank you for last night," I said softly, feeling a surge of affection for him.

"You mean this morning?" he teased, a playful twinkle in his eyes.

"That too," I replied, smiling up at him.

"What's gotten into you?" I asked, curiosity piqued by his unusually tender demeanor.

"You don't know?" he replied, his gaze intense.

"No. Tell me," I urged, sitting up to meet his eyes.

Christ, Ryleigh, it's you. I crave you. Last night was just an example of my need," he confessed, his words sending a shiver down my spine.

"Your love scares me sometimes. I'm afraid I might do something to break your heart," I admitted, feeling vulnerable.

"I'm sure you won't. I can feel how much you love me," he reassured me, his touch gentle.

"I do, but we're holding on so tightly to each other," I confessed, feeling the weight of our connection.

"That shouldn't scare you. It should make you happy that we're bonded," he insisted, his voice tender but firm.

"Are you mine today?" I asked, seeking reassurance.

"Yes. I have nothing going on, but I might receive a call from Carla Chan," he replied, mentioning his attorney.

“Your attorney?” I inquired, curious about his schedule.

“She’s working on some contracts,” he explained.

“Does she ever sleep?” I joked.

“You’d have to ask her, but I suspect not,” he replied with a chuckle.

“She’s worse than you,” I teased.

“I thought no one was worse than me?” he quipped back.

“I haven’t met everyone at your company,” I countered playfully.

“You will eventually. I got in touch with Rigo Vicaria. You can make an appointment with him this week,” he informed me, referring to the wedding dress designer.

I nodded, grateful for his thoughtfulness. With Oliver by my side, I felt ready to face whatever challenges lay ahead.

“I thought I was working with Rachel?” I questioned, a hint of confusion in my voice.

“Either one. They work together. I’m sure anything they design will be magnificent,” Oliver replied, his confidence unwavering.

“I have no doubt. Their designs are beautiful,” I admitted, feeling a surge of excitement for our upcoming wedding.

"Not compared to you," he insisted, his gaze filled with adoration.

"What colors should we have for the wedding?" I asked, eager to involve him in the planning process.

"It's your choice," he replied, his tone indicating his willingness to support whatever decision I made.

"It's our wedding. Shouldn't you have a choice?" I pressed, wanting him to take an active role in the decision-making.

"I'll go along with whatever you want," he assured me, his words filled with sincerity.

"Black and blood red," I suggested playfully, enjoying the banter.

"It's a summer wedding. Those colors are too heavy for the time of year," he countered, his practicality shining through.

"You see, you do have an opinion," I teased, delighted by his engagement in the conversation.

"I guess. Pick something lighter," he relented, allowing me to take the lead.

"I was thinking powder blue and sapphire, like your eyes," I proposed, a smile tugging at the corners of my lips.

"I think that's a lovely combination," he agreed, his hand reaching up to gently twirl a lock of my hair around his finger.

Oliver bent down to claim my lips in a tender kiss, and butterflies fluttered in my stomach at the sensation. As our lips met, I couldn't help but wonder: would I ever stop feeling this way? With Oliver by my side, I knew one thing for sure - our love would only continue to grow stronger with each passing day.

Chapter 7

Oliver left for London at four this morning, and I feel miserable. A bad cold has taken hold of me, likely due to the lack of sleep and the sudden change in weather. This morning, I bundled up in my heavy winter coat as the wind whipped around, sending a chill through my bones. I should've stayed home, but now, three hours later, my head is swimming, and my sinuses are filled with fluid.

For the past two weeks, I made it my mission to familiarize myself with Fox Asset Corporation's entire portfolio. Oliver left me alone as I absorbed as much information as I could. As his soon-to-be wife, he wanted me to know everything about his businesses. During that time, I discovered just how generous my fiancé truly is. He financed several projects around the world to help the less fortunate.

Oliver was a significant donor to Kids Afloat, a charity for underprivileged youth right here in the city. He was also part of a company that provided funds at low interest rates to women and minority-owned businesses. Additionally, I found information about a charity project he was working on with Jordan Grayson and Hunter Lawson to build low-income housing and make it rent-to-own.

The more I learned about Oliver Fox, the deeper I fell in love with him, if that was even possible. I was head over heels for him, enough so that I'd been neglectful of my relationships with my family and friends. I knew I would have to work on tearing myself away to spend time with them.

"Miss Stewart?"

I looked up to see Henri at my door, wincing as the fluid in my head sloshed around, causing a wave of nausea to hit me like a wall of water. I choked back a gag as I answered.

"Yes, Henri?"

"Are you feeling okay?" he asked, a look of genuine concern on his face.

"Not really," I mumbled.

I sneezed, and as I reached for the box of tissues on the corner of my desk, it fell to the floor.

"Damn," I muttered, moving to retrieve it. But before I could reach it, I collapsed onto the floor.

I woke to Henri placing me on the couch in the corner of my office.

“What happened?” I asked groggily.

He looked at me with worry. “You fainted. I think you should go to the hospital.”

“I’m fine,” I protested weakly.

I coughed, feeling a sharp ache in my chest, as the phone rang on my desk.

“Can you answer that, please?” I requested, my voice hoarse.

Henri grabbed the headset and answered the call. I heard him say, “Yes, sir,” before he held out the phone to me.

“Who is it?” I asked, still trying to gather my senses.

“Mr. Fox,” Henri replied, his tone urgent.

Oliver left for London at four this morning and I feel miserable. I have a bad cold, probably from the lack of sleep and the change in the weather. This morning, I wore my heavy winter coat as the wind swirled the chilled air around me. I should’ve stayed home because now three hours later, my head was swimming as my sinuses filled with fluid.

For the past two weeks, I made it my mission to familiarize myself with Fox Asset Corporation’s entire portfolio. Oliver left me alone as I absorbed as much as I could. As his soon to be wife, he wanted me to know everything about his businesses. During that time, I learned how generous my fiancé was. He financed several projects around the world to help the less fortunate.

He was a large donor to Kids Afloat, a charity for underprivileged youth right here in the city. He was part of a company that lent funds at low interest rates to women and minority owned businesses. I also found information about a charity he was working on with Jordan Grayson and Hunter Lawson to build low income housing and make it rent to own.

The more I found out about Oliver Fox, the more I fell in love with him, if that was even possible. I was head over heels for him enough so that I'd been neglectful of my relationships with my family and friends. I knew I would have to work on tearing myself away to spend time with them.

"Miss Stewart?"

I looked up to see Henri at my door, wincing as the fluid in my head sloshed around, causing a wave of nausea to hit me like a wall of water. I choked back a gag as I answered.

"Yes, Henri?"

"Are you feeling okay?"

"Not really."

I sneezed and as I reached for the box of tissues on the corner of my desk, it fell on the floor.

“Damn,” I said as I stood up to retrieve it. Henri was moving toward it at the same time I was except I didn’t make it as I collapsed on the floor. I woke as Henri placed me on the couch in the corner of my office.

“What happened?”

He gave me a look of concern. “You fainted. I think you should go to the hospital.”

“I’m fine.”

I coughed and my chest ached as the phone rang on my desk.

“Can you answer that please?”

Henri grabbed the headset on my desk and hit the red flashing button on the console. I heard him say “Yes, sir” and he held it out to me.

“Who is it?”

“Mr. Fox.”

“Oliver?”

“What’s the matter?” His voice sounded panicked, and I suppose I would’ve felt the same if I was in another country with no way of getting to him.

“I should've postponed this trip,” Oliver's voice crackled through the phone.

“You can't always take care of me,” I muttered, feeling guilty for being a burden.

“That doesn’t mean I don’t want to. Go to the hospital,” Oliver insisted, his concern palpable even over the phone.

“I'm fine,” I protested weakly, though the pounding headache and chills said otherwise.

“That’s not what Henri tells me. You need rest,” Oliver replied firmly.

“Maybe I’ll leave at noon,” I suggested, trying to find a compromise.

“I’m ordering you to leave now. Stop fighting with me, Ryleigh,” Oliver’s tone left no room for argument.

“I don’t want to be alone. I hate the penthouse when you’re not there,” I admitted, feeling vulnerable.

“Is that why you came to work sick?” Oliver asked, his voice softening with understanding.

“A little. It’s lonely without you,” I confessed, feeling a lump form in my throat.

“Go home. Brenda will stay in one of the guest rooms,” Oliver decided, and I felt a wave of relief wash over me.

“Where is she?” I inquired, wanting reassurance.

“Waiting downstairs with Vlad. I’m asking the pilot to turn around,” Oliver informed me, his concern evident.

I rubbed my temple with my fingers, closing my eyes. My head was pounding like a thousand drums.

"No. You need to do this," I insisted, not wanting to disrupt his plans.

"I can scout out a spot for another club when you're well. I'm only three hours into my flight," Oliver reasoned, showing his dedication even from afar.

"I'll be fine as long as Brenda stays with me," I assured him, grateful for his thoughtfulness.

"Are you sure?" Oliver double-checked, his worry lingering in his voice.

"Fine," I relented, suppressing another coughing fit.

"Christ, Ryleigh, you're making me rethink my decision," Oliver confessed, his concern bordering on exasperation.

"Go to London," I urged him, not wanting him to worry about me.

"I'll try to be home tomorrow evening," Oliver promised, his commitment to me unwavering.

"You said you would be away for four days," I reminded him, wanting to ensure he didn't sacrifice too much for my sake.

"Due to the circumstances, I can cut the trip short. Now go home, and I'll call you later," Oliver insisted, his love shining through his words.

“Thank you,” I whispered gratefully, feeling overwhelmed by his care.

“You don’t have to thank me. I love you,” Oliver said softly, his affection warming my heart.

“Love you too,” I replied.

I ended the call and turned to Henri, who was waiting patiently by my side. “Miss Stewart, do you need my assistance downstairs?”

“I’m not sure,” I admitted, feeling weak and dizzy.

Henri offered his arm, and I accepted it gratefully as we made our way out of the office. With Henri’s support, I managed to navigate to the waiting limo, where Brenda was already seated, ready to accompany me home.

“You don’t look too well,” Brenda observed with concern, her voice filled with sympathy.

She placed a cool hand on my forehead, and I shivered as the coldness seeped into my skin.

“You’re hot. You must have a fever,” she concluded, her worry deepening.

“I just want to go to bed,” I murmured, feeling drained and exhausted.

I dozed off during the ride home while Vlad expertly navigated the streets to the penthouse. When we arrived,

Brenda helped me upstairs, her steady presence a comfort.

I welcomed the warmth of the lobby as we entered, feeling a chill settle over me. I stopped at the thermostat in the hall to raise the temperature, hating the approach of November and the impending winter it signified.

Brenda guided me to the bedroom, her arm around my shoulders. "Let's get you to bed," she said softly, her voice a soothing balm to my frazzled nerves.

"I hate this time of year," I muttered, my voice barely above a whisper.

Brenda gave me a sympathetic smile as she helped me out of my coat. "I know. But you'll feel better soon, I promise."

I nodded weakly, too tired to respond. It took effort for me to change my clothing, pulling on a pair of flannel pajamas. As I crawled into bed, Brenda pulled the covers up around me and brushed a strand of hair from my forehead.

"Try to get some rest," she said gently. "I'll be right here if you need anything."

I closed my eyes; the warmth of the blankets and Brenda's reassuring presence finally allowed me to relax. The sound of her soft footsteps as she moved around the room was the last thing I heard before sleep claimed me.

I wondered if Brenda was a mother. She couldn't be more than thirty, but she was maternal in every way. She cared for me like I was her child, making me tea and checking on me throughout the day. My fever hovered at one hundred one, only decreasing with a dose of aspirin. I slept most of the time and when the room became dark as evening fell, I stayed in bed.

My appetite was non-existent, and the very thought of food turned my stomach. The next time I woke, my hair was smoothed back from my cheek.

"Mom?"

"No, sweetheart, it's Oliver."

"You're home?" I mumbled.

"Yes. I couldn't stay away," Oliver said, his voice a comforting balm in my haze of sickness.

He snapped on the lamp by my bedside, and I squinted as my eyes adjusted. Oliver was still dressed in the black pinstriped suit, white shirt, and silver tie he had left the penthouse in this morning. Worry lines creased his smooth features, and I hoped he wouldn't catch my illness.

"I'm glad you're home, but I'm sorry you cut your trip short," I said, my voice barely above a whisper.

"I did what I needed to do. My partners found the perfect site. I was back at the airport in less than two hours."

“You flew sixteen hours for me?” I asked, my heart aching at his sacrifice.

“Don’t be angry,” he said gently, sitting beside me and taking my hand. “I just care so much about you.”

“I’m not angry, but I don’t want you to get sick.”

“And I don’t want you to be sick.” He leaned down, placing a lingering kiss on my forehead. His lips were warm and comforting against my feverish skin. He stood up to get undressed, and I turned away from the light because it made my head throb. A few minutes later, he sat on the bed again, his concern palpable.

“Can I get you something? Did you eat today?” he asked, his eyes searching mine.

I felt nauseated at the thought of food. “No, nothing.”

He pressed the back of his hand to my cheek. “You feel warm. You should drink something.”

“I’ve been drinking, but that’s all. I have no appetite. Brenda was very helpful today.”

He smiled. “I sent her home when I came in. She said she hopes you feel better.”

“She’s a nice lady,” I croaked.

“She likes you very much.”

“I like her too. Does she have children?” I asked.

“Not that I know of.”

"She was very maternal."

"I'm glad to hear that. Let me get you some water at least."

The bed gave as he stood up and switched off the light. I turned onto my back, watching his retreating silhouette illuminated by the hall light. He came back a few minutes later with a large glass of water, ice cubes clinking softly. He placed it on my nightstand.

"You should drink," he said softly.

"I'm not thirsty," I protested weakly.

Oliver frowned. "Humor me, please."

With much effort, I sat up, and he handed me the glass, helping me tip it to my mouth. I drank greedily, not realizing how thirsty I really was. The cold water felt good as it soothed my tortured throat.

"Thank you," I whispered, sinking back into the pillows.

"Anything for you," he murmured, brushing a strand of hair from my forehead. He climbed into bed beside me, wrapping me in his warmth. "Try to get some rest. I'm here now."

I nestled into his embrace, feeling safe and cherished despite my fever. As fatigue pulled me under, I realized how much his presence meant to me and how grateful I was for his unwavering love.

"I mean for everything. You must be exhausted," I rasped.

"I slept on the plane."

"In the bedroom?" I asked.

The bedroom in one of his jets was very comfortable. I slept for several hours in the comfortable bed while we made a trip to Seattle.

He shook his head. "No. I didn't take that one. I'm having quarterly maintenance performed on it right now."

"So, you slept in the seat?"

"They're very comfortable."

Oliver walked around to his side of the bed and slipped under the covers. He pulled me against him, fingering my red flannel pajamas.

"These are kind of sexy," he teased.

"You think so?"

Oliver pressed his lips to my forehead. "Anything you wear is sexy because you're wearing it."

"You're in love."

"Yes, I am. Now go to sleep."

He embraced me and softly kissed my cheek as I faded off. My dreams were vivid and strange as they sometimes are when I'm sick. The man from the street who stared at me was in them. He wouldn't stop following me and I felt my heart pound in my chest.

"Ryleigh," Oliver whispered. My eyes shot open and tried to adjust to the dark room.

"What?" I mumbled.

"You were moaning."

"You should like that," I whispered.

"Not that type of moan. You sounded scared."

"I don't remember what I was dreaming about."

I cleared my throat, and the loose mucus caused a round of coughing which hurt. I had trouble catching my breath.

His eyebrows slammed together. "You don't sound good."

I groaned. "I just want to sleep."

Oliver touched my head with the heel of his hand. "You're burning up."

I was finding it hard to breathe as I tried to pull in oxygen. It felt like pulling razor blades into my lungs.

"It hurts," I whined.

"You need to go to the hospital."

"I can't."

"You're going. I should've made Brenda take you."

Oliver sprang from the bed, grabbing his phone as he ran into the closet. I heard him talking as he dressed. He came out wearing a pair of jeans and a large gray sweatshirt.

"Where are we going?"

"The hospital. Vlad will be downstairs in a few minutes. Let's get you dressed."

My stomach churned, and I felt like throwing up as I tried to sit up. The room was spinning and I fell back. From there, I don't remember much except Oliver picking me up in his arms.

The next time I woke, I was in the ER being attended by two nurses and a doctor in a white coat. My arm had a tube attached to it with a drip bag hanging on a hook above me. Oliver was leaning against the wall as the hospital staff did their job. He left when they brought in a portable X-ray machine.

I didn't want to be fussed with but I knew it was required. My face reddened when I realized I was in a hospital gown. It meant that someone had seen me naked.

"Miss Stewart, stay still while we take an X-ray," the technician said.

I waited patiently as he snapped a few shots. Oliver came back in the room after they took the machine out. He looked exhausted and worried as lines creased his forehead.

"Sweetheart, how do you feel?"

"Like shit. What's this stuff in the bag?"

"A saline drip. You need fluids and they gave you antibiotics. The doctor suspects you have pneumonia."

I moaned. "Great, not again."

Oliver raised his eyebrows. "You've had it before?"

"A couple of times. It must be why my lungs are killing me."

"Damn it," he cursed, "I should never have gone to London."

"Stop feeling guilty," I protested, before breaking into a fit of coughing.

"Relax, you need to rest."

I closed my eyes only to be disturbed by the staff entering the room. I opened my eyes to see the doctor, a tall man with sparse gray hair and a lopsided smile.

"I'm Dr. Cancro. I'm pretty sure you have pneumonia. We're waiting for the slides."

I grunted. "It feels like pneumonia."

"We're administering antibiotics in the drip. You'll need to rest until this passes."

"As long as it's not here. I hate hospitals."

He smiled before he left the room, leaving me with a hovering Oliver.

"Sit down. I'll be fine," I said, trying to muster a reassuring smile.

"I can worry about you, so stop telling me what to do," Oliver shot back, his eyes blazing with concern.

"I guess I won't be coming to work for the rest of the week," I murmured, feeling the weight of exhaustion settle over me.

"You think I give a shit about that? I won't be going to the office either. I can work from home."

"I don't want to keep you," I insisted, my voice weak.

"For fuck's sake, would you stop worrying about me?" he growled, his frustration boiling over.

"I'm sorry," I whispered, feeling a pang of guilt.

His voice softened instantly. "Don't you understand what you mean to me? Nothing compares to you, nothing."

I inhaled deeply, wincing at the sharp pain in my chest. Everything hurt, and all I wanted to do was sleep. I closed my eyes, trying to block out the discomfort. I heard the chair scrape along the floor, then felt Oliver's warm hand enveloped mine.

"Just rest," he murmured, his thumb gently stroking my knuckles. "I'm here. You're all that matters."

His presence was a balm to my aching body and troubled mind. I squeezed his hand weakly, feeling a sense of peace despite the feverish haze. With Oliver by my side, I knew I could endure anything.

"What are you doing out of bed?" Oliver said.

"My back hurts. It's been four days. I can't stay in bed any longer."

"Put on some socks at least," he insisted.

I'd been in bed for the past few days, and I was going stir crazy. Oliver waited on me hand and foot, even canceling conference calls just in case I needed him. He was the perfect nurse.

I went to the closet and opened my sock drawer on my side, taking out a pair of white ankle cut athletic socks. My feet weren't cold, but I wanted to appease Oliver. When I came out, he was cradling the phone against his ear while he prepared me a bowl of soup. I was sick of soup and wanted something more substantial. After four days of being sick, my appetite had returned with a vengeance. I tapped his shoulder before he pulled the tab on the can and shook my head.

"What do you want for lunch?" he asked.

"Not soup."

Oliver concluded his phone call. "Henri, email me the information. I'll be in touch."

He took the phone in his hand and disconnected the call before he took me in his arms.

"You feel much cooler. Did you take your next dose of antibiotics?"

"I'm not due for another hour."

"Good girl."

I hated when he patronized me because it felt more like I was his child than his fiancée. He'd been so agreeable the past few days that I let it go and pulled open the refrigerator.

"I can get you lunch. What do you want?" Oliver asked.

I shrugged. "I don't know, which is why I'm seeing what you have."

"*We* have."

"Excuse me?"

"What we have. This is your home too."

A week ago, Oliver had had his staff clean out my things from my old apartment. Finley asked Sadie to live with him permanently and we put our furniture in storage. Oliver graciously paid off the lease. I know it was a big sigh of relief for him to know I would be safe and under his roof. He still hadn't said a word about the real reason why he wanted to protect me.

"Our home. Happy?"

"Very. Now, what do you want to eat?"

I decided to bust Oliver's chops and asked for poached

eggs on English muffins. To my surprise, he started to get everything out on the counter.

“I was kidding.”

“Do you doubt I can cook?”

“Not one bit.”

“What do you really want to eat?” Oliver asked, his eyes searching mine.

I thought for a moment, savoring the idea. “Wagyu burger with sautéed mushrooms and Gruyère.”

“You haven’t eaten much in days. A burger will give you a tummy ache,” he cautioned.

“I’ll be fine. Please?” I batted my eyelashes at him, hoping to sway his decision.

“You’re impossible,” he sighed, though a smile tugged at his lips.

“That’s why you asked me to marry you. You need a challenge,” I teased.

“Why would you say that?”

“Most things come so easy for you,” I shrugged. “You need to work for this.”

“You’re right, I do,” he replied, his gaze intense and unwavering. “Because you’re the most important person in my life.”

“So, burger?” I asked, pressing my advantage.

He picked up his phone from the counter and called in my order. My mouth watered at the thought of biting into the juicy burger, imagining the melted Gruyère and tender beef. After he hung up, I wrapped my arms around his waist, resting my head against his back.

"Ryleigh, don't do that," he murmured.

"Why?" I asked innocently, sliding my hand under his black t-shirt to stroke the ridges of his muscles.

"You know why."

"Suppose I said I wanted you?" I whispered, my fingers tracing his skin.

Oliver gently unhooked my hands from around his waist and turned to face me. "I would say as much as I want you, the answer is no. You're not one hundred percent, and I suspect you got sick because of the little sleep you get."

"Another thing you're blaming yourself for?" I growled, frustrated.

"Yes. We don't need to make love three times a night."

"We don't NEED to, but we WANT to. There's a big difference," I argued.

"Be patient," he advised softly.

"Patience isn't my strong suit," I admitted.

. . .

“You don’t have to tell me that. I’m well aware,” he said, planting a kiss on the top of my head before retreating to his office.

I frowned after him, feeling the sting of his absence. It felt good to get out of the bedroom, and I plopped down on the couch, picking up a decorating magazine from the table. Oliver received several trade magazines since he was in the business, always keen to stay updated on the latest trends and discuss designs with his interior decorators.

Our meal arrived twenty minutes later, the aroma from the silver tray making my stomach growl. I didn’t wait for Oliver to sit down, taking a large bite of my burger and softly moaning as I chewed, savoring the blend of meat, cheese, and mushrooms.

“Easy. Take small bites,” Oliver advised, a hint of amusement in his voice.

“I’m starving. I’ve been eating soup for the past few days,” I mumbled between bites.

“You don’t have to make up for it in one shot,” he said, uncovering his own plate to reveal the same type of burger, accompanied by a large heaping pile of pomme frites. I reached over and took some for myself.

“Did you talk to your parents today?” he asked.

“I called my mother this morning. Anders was at work,” I replied.

“How are they doing?”

"Fine. My mother sounded closer to normal today."

The memory of my first bout with pneumonia resurfaced, a freshman in college, spending two days in the hospital and two weeks in bed. It was during Christmas break, but it was the closest I ever came to dying.

I could barely breathe and felt like I was drowning. The experience left my mother fearful, especially when I got it again in my junior year. It wasn't as severe, but I still spent a week in bed.

As I took another bite of my burger, I felt Oliver's eyes on me, full of concern and love.

"She worries about you," Oliver said, his voice gentle but firm.

"She doesn't have to. I'm not a child," I retorted.

"But you're her child."

"Yes, I know."

"Ryleigh, I don't mean to sound like your father."

"Well, sometimes you do, and it's annoying. You're not my father; you're my fiancé."

"Point taken." He paused, a frown creasing his lips. "I just... I worry about you."

"Seems like there's a lot of that going around," I muttered.

Oliver shook his head and took a massive bite of his burger, juices dribbling onto the plate. We didn't speak for the rest of the meal, and I managed to eat only half of my burger. Not eating for several days had shrunk my stomach. I placed the remainder down and leaned back against the chair, feeling a wave of fatigue wash over me.

"Full?" he asked, his eyes scanning my face with concern.

"Very, and I feel tired."

"Get into bed. I'll be in right after I finish."

I wiped my hands and slowly rose, heading to the bedroom. Exhaustion hit me hard as I slipped into bed, and in a matter of minutes, I was asleep. Oliver woke me half an hour later, gently shaking me awake.

"What's so important?" I grumbled.

"Your medication. Please take it," he urged.

I turned over and sat up in bed, taking the pills he handed me and washing them down with the glass of water he brought.

"I'm going back to bed," I mumbled, feeling groggy.

"I have to make a few calls."

"To who? It's after 6 p.m.," I questioned, knowing full well he often made calls at odd hours and to different countries. I was irritated and wanted to irritate him back.

"It's not your concern. You must be feeling better because you're getting more difficult," he remarked.

I stuck my tongue out at him, feeling a childish satisfaction. He raised his eyebrows before a smirk played on his handsome face.

"I'm filing this for later use."

"Filing what?"

"Your tongue sticking out at me. You're still sick, so I need to refrain from making any requests to use it."

I rolled my eyes, but a smile tugged at my lips. "You're impossible."

"And you love me for it," he said, bending down to kiss my forehead. "Now, rest. I'll join you soon."

I nodded, sinking back into the pillows, feeling a bit better knowing he was near. The last thing I saw before drifting off was Oliver's silhouette, the soft light from the hallway casting a halo around him. His presence was my comfort, my anchor. With him by my side, I knew I could weather anything.

I stuck my tongue at him and he raised his eyebrows before a smirk played on his handsome face.

"I'm filing this for use later."

"Filing what?"

"Your tongue sticking out at me. You're still sick, so I need to refrain from making any requests to use it."

“Sex fiend.”

“Damn right. Go back to sleep. I’ll be back in a little while.”

“Thank you.”

He grinned. “No thanks needed.”

Chapter 8

It had been three weeks since my bout with pneumonia, and December had already settled in. I had learned a lot from Oliver during my time at Fox Asset Corporation—both about the company and about him personally. He valued my opinion, even leaving me some plans for the new buildings he was working on by the waterfront in Queens to review.

I was engrossed in the plans when I heard yelling coming from Oliver's office. The last time I saw him, he was quietly typing away at his laptop. Curious, I pressed my ear against the wall we shared, catching bits and pieces of his conversation.

I only caught a minute before he stopped and cursed loudly. It sounded like Jonah was up to something. Intrigued and concerned, I headed to Oliver's office and knocked softly on the door.

"What is it?" he snapped.

"It's me," I said gently.

"Come in."

I opened the door to find Oliver sitting at his desk, his face bright red, chewing on the corner of his lip.

"What's the matter?" I asked, closing the door behind me.

"Fucking Jonah. He got into some trouble on St. Croix," he replied, running his fingers through his hair in frustration.

"I thought he didn't have access to any transportation."

"He stowed away on the transport boat that dropped off supplies. He's been working well with the crew, and the foreman gave him a job to do on the roof of the crew house. Apparently, he sneaked away, jumped on the boat with a wallet full of money from one of his coworkers, got drunk, and started a fight with a police sergeant's son at a local bar. The kid got a broken nose, and now they want to sue."

I gasped. "Damn him. What was his excuse?"

"He said he was blowing off some steam, that I can't expect him to be holed up on the island all the time."

"Doesn't he realize he's exposing himself?" I asked, feeling a mix of frustration and worry.

"I don't know what he's thinking," Oliver said, shaking his head.

"What's your next move with him?"

"I paid off the sergeant's son and he dropped the charges. The incident is now a misdemeanor. I told Jonah if I have to chain him to a freaking post, I will."

"I'm sorry," I said softly.

Oliver looked at me, his expression softening. "I want to take you to the island."

"Where would we stay? You said it's not nearly done."

"We'd stay on St. Croix. After everything that's been going on, we need a break."

I nodded, the idea of getting away sounding incredibly appealing. "Okay. When do you want to go?"

"As soon as possible. We both need to clear our heads," he said, standing up and walking around the desk to pull me into a tight embrace.

His warmth and the steady beat of his heart against my ear were soothing. "I'll start packing," I whispered, feeling a sense of anticipation and relief wash over me.

"I forgot to tell you; Ty wants to talk to me. He said they enhanced the video enough to make out features."

Ty actually had called me a week ago, but I was stalling.

Oliver frowned. "Do you want to see if you can identify the man?"

"It was seventeen years ago. I don't know if I'll remember enough and if I do, I have no idea who this man was or is. He could've disappeared for all we know or be dead. I hope he's dead. My father didn't deserve what happened to him."

"No, he didn't. And neither did you. You were an innocent child thrust into that violence."

"It fucked me up for almost a year. I lost an entire year of my life because of some stupid fender bender."

"He doesn't think you're good enough for me," I blurted.

Oliver frowned. "And who is good enough for you? Him?" he asked, his voice full of hostility.

I shrugged. "It's not like that with us. He's just protecting me."

He ground his teeth. "You don't need his protection. You have me and your family."

"Ty has always been protective of me."

"That was before you were engaged. You don't need him now."

I sighed with frustration. "He's a friend. Please don't say anything to him."

"I don't plan on it because that would create a wedge between you and him. I know how important your friends are to you."

I changed the subject to avoid an argument. "Speaking of which, Finley and Sadie want to get together this upcoming weekend for lunch. Is that possible?"

"I think we can swing it. Where?"

I smirked. "Diamond Square?"

Oliver raked his fingers through his hair. "You know I hate going there."

I snorted. "It's your freaking hotel. Why would you hate it?"

"Because I don't want my employees to think I'm spying. I have others to check on their work."

"Don't be ridiculous. It's either your hotels brunch or the SW."

"SW. I prefer it."

"And I prefer Diamond Square. I love the dessert table. They don't have those little macrons I love at SW."

Oliver rolled his eyes. "I get you a boatload of them if you want."

"Diamond Square," I insisted.

I knew if I kept pushing him, he would give in the way he usually did.

"You're being difficult again," he said.

"Good. What time?"

Oliver's shoulders slightly sagged in defeat; I loved to win at our disagreements.

"I guess noon. You know this is going to cost you," he said with a wicked grin.

I rolled my eyes. "I figured. Name your price."

"I'll have to think about it and get back to you in bed tonight."

"Is that all you think about?"

"You know it's not, but you are a good chunk of my focus."

"So, you have Ryleigh brain?"

"Yes, I do. It's not a bad brain to have. Are we working out tonight?"

I rubbed my leg. "My hamstrings are killing me. Brad worked me hard yesterday," I whined.

Oliver laughed. "You slacked off all these months and now it's time to pay the piper."

"I could just say forget the workout."

"Nope. You promise to get back to your regular workouts. I'm afraid I corrupted you all these months."

"If this is corruption, I love it."

Oliver checked the Vacheron Constantin watch I had given him a few months ago when we were in Los Angeles.

"I have a security briefing in a few minutes."

"Do you want me to stay?" I asked.

"It's boring. What do you think of the plans I gave you?"

"I'm making notes a la Oliver."

"I'd like to see them when you're done."

His desk phone rang, and he excused himself. I let myself out of his office and headed to mine. I was getting just like him, using a pencil to write notes on paper. I went to the office in the penthouse a few days ago to get a pen and found stacks and small slips of paper with handwritten notes. I wondered how he kept track of everything.

Oliver

"What are the ramifications of Jonah's fuck up?" I asked, clenching my fists.

"The report is buried and hasn't been entered in the computer system," Vlad said.

I was sitting at my desk, speaking with my head of security on the phone. I needed to find out the information he had about my brother.

“And have you been tracking the movements of Antonio Caruso?”

“Yes. We have evidence he was the one that ransacked Miss Stewart’s apartment. We have no idea what he was looking for.”

“Did he do it himself?”

Vlad let out a clipped laugh. “You expect him to do his own dirty work? We found a couple of his mugs who like to talk. They did the work.”

“And of her father’s murder?” I asked.

“The cop is close.”

I ground my teeth. “If he finds out it’s Caruso, Ryleigh’s life is even more in danger than it already is. I need you to keep your movements discreet. If Caruso finds out we’re onto him, he’ll come after Ryleigh even if he has to expose himself.”

“And what of Jonah?”

I tapped my nails on the desk. “Keep tabs on the travel of Caruso’s men. Jonah is a sitting duck on Fox Island if they find out he’s there. As much as he pisses me off, he’s still my brother. I have no choice but to protect him.”

“Suppose you didn’t?”

“If Caruso found out Jonah didn’t have any worth to me, he would kill him and continue to pursue Ryleigh. He wants what Jonah owes him, dead or alive.”

"We should have more information on his movements in a few days."

"I want to take her to the island but only if it's safe. When will you know? I'd like to make arrangements to visit before the Christmas holiday."

"Caruso is heading to Brazil in the next week with his family. The IT staff hacked his system and found the information," Vlad said.

"That doesn't mean he isn't having us watched. I need to be sure."

"I'll see to it."

"Thank you. You have forty-eight hours."

"Will do, sir."

I hung up the phone and sighed loudly. I just hoped Jonah didn't alert Caruso as to his whereabouts. It could set a whole nightmare into motion if it did. Walking around with this knowledge was torture for me and it was even worse because of the picture Ryleigh had of her father.

She didn't know that Robert Stewart was dirty and the things he did behind the scenes in his business. When and if she found out, it would devastate her. I hoped that would never happen.

How coincidental that Ryleigh's former boyfriend ran up gambling debts with one of Caruso's bookie operations. Maybe if they hadn't dated, she wouldn't be in danger.

The stupid kid mentioned her as a possible source for funds to pay his debts.

He tipped them off when he joked about her nightmares and her very name piqued their interest, setting the wheels in motion. My brother didn't help, ripping off thousands of dollars from Caruso's high end goods vending machines. He wanted Jonah to pump Ryleigh for information unless he could pay the money back with three hundred percent interest. I would have gladly paid the debt if I believed Caruso would leave Ryleigh alone, but I knew the contrary.

I dealt with Antonio Caruso before, a mean, ruthless fucker. Robert Stewart had gotten into bed with the man and when the deal went bad, he paid the ultimate price. I knew what Caruso was capable of when his way of life was threatened.

Maybe if that stupid newspaper article hadn't run about cold case files, it would have stayed buried. Tyler Barnes and a few of his fellow officers gave an interview. They each revealed what they were working on, and I guess Caruso was listening even after all these years. Little did Barnes know he put Ryleigh in danger.

Until that time, Caruso thought he got away with the murder of Robert Stewart. A drowning man will always look to take you down to save himself. It was the reason why I needed to keep Ryleigh surrounded by security. I refused to lose her.

~

I let Oliver alone to take his call. I finished up the day by making some final notes on the project in Queens. I might be a novice, but I noticed a few things that might be questioned. I hoped I was making Oliver proud with the work I was doing. Though I wouldn't admit it out loud, I looked up to him and my heart would swell each time I thought about him. He showed up at my door a few minutes before five.

"Ready to go?"

"It's before five. I don't think my boss would like me leaving early."

Oliver smirked. "Your boss can shove it. I want to take my fiancée home."

I grinned at him as he came into my office and lifted my black wool coat from the closet by the bathroom. I stood and he helped me into it, giving me a hard kiss on the mouth.

"Did you get everything finished today?" he asked.

"Yes. I made notes on the plans. Just a few ideas you should consider."

"I'll look them over tomorrow."

"I'm starving," I admitted, my stomach growling in agreement.

"You didn't eat much at lunch. Are you feeling all right?" Oliver's concern was evident.

“I just wasn’t hungry,” I replied, reaching up to smooth his sandy hair off his forehead. It was getting long, and he definitely needed a haircut. “You need a cut.”

“I know. I’ve been meaning to call the salon.”

“I could cut it for you,” I offered.

“You cut hair?” He raised an eyebrow in surprise.

“Yes, why are you so surprised?” I asked.

“Because you never said anything before.”

There were still so many things we didn’t know about each other but we were learning.

“A girl can have some secrets. Would you like me to cut it for you tonight?”

“Exactly how much training do you have?” he asked, skepticism coloring his tone.

“I’m good, I promise. Ty’s mother taught me. She’s a stylist and has been for years. I got so good I did Matthew and Finley’s hair when I was in high school. You know how those two are with their appearance,” I said with pride.

“So, I won’t look like you put a bowl on my head?” He grinned, teasing me.

“Try me.”

“Oh, I definitely plan to try you when we get home,” he said, grabbing my hand and kissing the back of it before tucking it against him.

Oliver led me to the elevator, saying goodnight to a few executives on the way out. They all seemed shocked that he was leaving at 5 p.m. We had been working long hours, and this was one of the few days we left on time.

In the limo, Oliver pulled me onto his lap and hugged me tightly. Something felt off. He didn't do what he usually did, which was to plant kisses on my throat and chest. He just held me in his arms, his grip firm yet tender.

"Is everything okay?" I asked, resting my head against his shoulder.

He sighed deeply. "I just have a lot on my mind."

"Jonah?"

"Yeah, and everything else. It's been overwhelming lately."

I hugged him back, trying to offer some comfort. "We'll get through it, Oliver. Together."

He kissed the top of my head. "I know. I just need to remind myself of that sometimes."

"Let's get married," he murmured.

"We *are* getting married."

"Now."

The word stole the breath from me. There was definitely something wrong but if I knew Oliver, he wouldn't tell me.

“Look at me.”

He seemed so vulnerable that I worried he would tell me he had something terminal. He looked up at me and his expression looked so serious.

“I want you to be my wife. I can’t wait.”

I tugged his hair, weaving my fingers in the thick strands. “It’s only seven more months.”

“Seven months too long,” he said, tugging my collar down and pressing a kiss to my skin.

“You agreed to July,” I said.

He lifted his head and nuzzled my nose with his. “I’m impatient. I want you to be Mrs. Fox.”

“I practically am. We live together like we’re married.”

His breath feathered across my lips. “My attorneys want me to have a prenuptial drawn up.”

“I think it’s a good idea,” I said without hesitation.

He met my gaze. “I don’t.”

“I’m not with you for your money or what you can do for me. I’m marrying you because I love you. I have my own money,” I reasoned.

“I think you should let me invest it for you.”

My stepfather had invested my trust fund years ago, building a comfortable nest egg for me. I didn’t need to work if I chose not to, but I would rather save my money for something important or retirement, which ever came first.

"Anders does a fine job," I said, trying to keep my tone light.

"I've seen your portfolio. I think I can do better," Oliver countered.

"When did you see my portfolio?" I asked, surprise evident in my voice.

"A couple of months back. You left your statement on the counter. And you're right, Anders has done a fine job, but I can do better."

"Does it matter? That money is chump change compared to what my fiancé has," I pointed out.

"Yes, it is, but I'd feel better having it under my control," he insisted.

"No. Anders is my stepfather. How would it look if I took it out of his control?" I asked, frustration creeping into my voice.

"Like you're making an adult decision," he replied smoothly.

I untangled myself from his arms and slipped off his lap, staring out the window. "Thank you for the offer, but I'll leave it where it is."

Oliver's frown deepened, his eyes growing dark with confusion.

"Ryleigh, what did I say wrong?" he asked, his tone softening.

"I don't want everything under your control. Is that so horrible?" I snapped, my annoyance flaring.

"No, but I want you to be secure," he explained, his voice gentle.

"Are you planning on going bankrupt?" I challenged.

"Well, no. It would take a lot for that to happen," he admitted.

"Then stop worrying about my money unless you plan to divorce me," I said sharply.

"That's not even a consideration," he replied, sounding hurt.

"Then let this go."

"I'm sorry," he murmured.

"Drop it," I snapped again. Oliver said nothing else, and I could hear him tapping on his phone. I was irritated, not just because he wanted to control my money, but because he thought he could do it better. Maybe he could, but I trusted Anders to take care of my funds.

My inheritance had grown to almost three million dollars since Anders had handled the investments for the last fourteen years. If I ever broke up with Oliver, I would have a comfortable nest egg for retirement.

“Ryleigh?”

I sighed and turned to look at Oliver. “What?”

His face was passive. “Don’t be angry at me. I only want what’s best for you.”

“I know you do but I sometimes feel you want to control everything.”

“That’s not true.”

I wrung my hands. “This goes along the lines of holding on too tightly. We should probably take a night off from each other.”

“What the fuck does that mean?” he growled.

“It means we should do things separately for a night. Matthew needs me to take care of Blackie on Friday. It would be easier if I stay there.”

“NO! Why do you need to stay at his place?” he asked angrily.

I let out a frustrated breath. “Because I need a break.”

“You can’t leave me.”

I threw my hands up. “Oh my God, Oliver, I’m not leaving you. We’re spending one night apart.”

“That’s how it starts.”

I was thankful when Vlad pulled up to the building. I quickly opened the door and slipped out onto the sidewalk before Oliver, moving toward the lobby before he exited. The elevator was open, having just let off a few of the residents and I stepped inside. Oliver was right behind me, and he punched in the code for the penthouse with such force I could see his finger turning white.

He said nothing to me, just stood there glowering as we ascended up. I had a feeling our evening would be awkward. He stepped out ahead of me and jammed his key in the lock, pushing the door open. When I came through, he pushed me to the wall, kicking the door closed.

“Oliver, please,” I pleaded.

He pressed his body against me and latched his mouth onto mine. It didn’t take long for me to give in, and I kissed him back, nipping his lip with my teeth. The sexual tension between us was palpable and he pushed off my coat, then his own and reached up my dress to grasp my panties.

They were delicate lace and gave way as he tore them from my body. In seconds I was up against the wall, my legs wrapped around him and his penis thrusting hard inside me.

“I can’t lose you,” he whispered as he desperately fucked me.

“You’re not losing me.”

He slowed and came to a stop, carrying me to the couch while he was still inside me. He dropped down and held me tightly, rocking me in his arms. I silently came a few seconds before he grunted and spilled his seed into me.

"It feels that way," he panted.

I loosened his tie and kissed his neck. "It's just one night. Spend some time with your friends."

He continued to rock me. "One night feels like forever when we're apart."

"Is it the apart or the circumstance of the apart?" I asked.

I knew what Oliver was doing. He was claiming me, trying to put any doubts in my mind that I had about our relationship. But I didn't have doubts. I knew I wanted to marry and spend the rest of my life with him. That wouldn't change no matter how many arguments we had.

"Both," he said quietly.

I met his eyes with my own. "Why are you so insecure about me spending time away from you?"

"I'm not insecure. I worry," Oliver admitted.

My brow furrowed. "About what? I have security. Brenda can stay with me."

"Why don't you bring Blackie over here?" he suggested.

I raised my eyebrows. "I didn't think you would want a dog in the penthouse."

"I love dogs," he said.

"Would you consider getting one?" I asked.

"Maybe after we're married."

"I'll hold you to that. I need a shower. Do you want to come in with me?"

"How about a bath?"

I chuckled. "Baths with you are trouble."

"No more than showers are," he said with a grin.

"Oh my, this was delicious," I said as I finished off my bowl of spaghetti. After we showered, Oliver made spaghetti while I put together a salad and made some garlic bread.

"I'm glad you liked it."

I patted my full belly. "You can cook for me anytime."

"Let's clean up and relax."

"I'd like another glass of wine. This was good," I said gesturing to the bottle of merlot Oliver opened.

He poured me another glass and I got up to take my bowl and his to the sink. We worked together and within ten minutes, we were relaxing on the couch with glasses of wine. I had my back propped against the arm of the couch while Oliver massaged my feet.

"Your feet are sexy," he said.

"That's what you think are sexy?"

“The whole package is sexy but your feet are too. I like this polish,” he said as he rubbed the nail of my right big toe. I had applied two coats of black cherry polish a couple of days ago.

“I like it too.”

“You know I can have the salon come here to give you a private manicure and pedicure.”

“I usually do it myself. I only go to the salon once in a while.”

He slid his hand up my leg, stopping at the hem of my short pink satin robe.

I yawned. “I’m tired.”

“Are you sure? I bet if I used my tongue, you would find some energy.”

I rolled my eyes. “I’ve decided that you’re worse than a teenage boy. I have to call Matthew and let him know I’m taking Blackie here tomorrow. I want to make sure it’s all right with him.”

He smiled. “You decided to stay?”

I snorted. “You act like I’m leaving for good. It was one night.”

“But I love having you with me.”

I pressed a hard kiss to his lips then stood up to call my brother. I went to our bedroom and hit Matthew’s contact information.

"What's up?" my brother said as he answered.

"I want to bring Blackie here," I said, pressing the phone to my ear as I paced around the bedroom.

My brother's voice crackled through the line after a moment's hesitation. "Why? You usually stay at my place when you take care of him."

I took a deep breath, glancing out the sliders to the patio. "I wasn't living with Oliver the last time I took care of Blackie."

"Maybe my girlfriend can take care of him," he suggested, his tone casual.

"Girlfriend?" I echoed, stopping in my tracks. "You're dating someone?"

"Yeah, for a couple of weeks now. She's awesome."

I couldn't help but smile at his enthusiasm. "Does this awesome woman have a name?"

"Tova. She's a business consultant. I met her at the coffee shop near my apartment."

"Is she worthy?" I teased, recalling our old family joke.

He laughed, a sound that warmed my heart. "More than worthy. Have you spoken to Finley lately?"

I sighed, twirling a strand of hair around my finger. "No. Every time I call, he's busy. Sadie told me he's working on a big project for Jordan Grayson. We're having lunch with them on Saturday at Diamond Square."

"He's asking her tomorrow. They're going out to dinner."

I gasped, my eyes widening. He never said a word to me about thinking of proposing to my best friend. I was a little annoyed he didn't include me in picking out the ring.

"I had no idea it was that serious."

"They make me sick with their lovey-dovey crap," he said with a mock groan.

I laughed, shaking my head. "Maybe you should try it for yourself."

"I'm not sure if I'm ready for that kind of commitment," he admitted. "I'm only twenty-six. I still think you're too young to get married."

"I'll be almost twenty-four when I marry."

"I don't want to get married until I'm at least thirty."

"Does Tova know that?" I asked, raising an eyebrow even though he couldn't see me.

"I'm playing the field," he said. "I doubt this will turn into anything serious. She's busy, I'm busy."

"That's usually when it hits you out of nowhere. Bam, you're in love."

He was quiet for a moment, then changed the subject. "Is Fox treating you well?"

"He is," I replied softly, a smile tugging at my lips as I thought about Oliver. "He really is."

“Any nightmares lately?”

I wouldn’t admit to Matthew that the nightmares were still coming. When we were kids, his room was next to mine and he would climb into bed with me when I had one. His presence calmed me, and I slept through the night knowing my brother was there to save me.

"No, I’m good," I said, trying to wrap up the call.

"Glad to hear it. I’ll talk to you later. I promised I’d call Tova," my brother replied, his voice light and happy.

"Oh, you promised?" I teased, imagining his face flushing slightly on the other end of the line.

"Okay, I’m hanging up now," he said with a chuckle.

After we disconnected, I felt a mix of emotions swirling inside me. I shook them off and went to find Oliver. I found him in his office, hunched over his desk, scribbling notes with a pencil.

I watched him for a moment, fascinated by his concentration, before I spoke up. “All the technology you have, and you use a pencil and paper?”

He jumped slightly, then smiled without looking up. “I like it better. It helps me get my thoughts down more clearly.”

I watched as he folded the paper and tucked it into his desk. “Matthew is having his girlfriend take care of Blackie,” I said, leaning against the doorframe.

"Since when does he have a girlfriend?" Oliver asked, raising an eyebrow.

"Two weeks ago. He said he's not interested in getting tied down. Oh, and Finley is asking Sadie to marry him tomorrow night."

"Really?" Oliver's eyes widened in surprise.

"He better hurry because now that I know, I can't keep this from her," I said with a laugh.

"You'd better, or Finley will have a fit."

"He never even told me! I could've helped him pick out a ring. Sadie's been my best friend for five years," I ranted.

"Maybe he was afraid you'd spill the beans."

"I can keep a secret, especially one as big as this. I guess I'll see the ring when we go out to lunch on Saturday."

"I asked for a private room," Oliver said, a hint of mischief in his eyes.

"Why? I want to enjoy the buffet," I protested.

"We can still enjoy the buffet, but we'll be sitting in a private room."

"I want to sit with everyone else," I insisted, crossing my arms.

"Stop being difficult. The room is very comfortable, and we'll have our own private wait staff for drinks. I want to order a bottle of champagne for your brother and Sadie. Maybe we should get them a cake to celebrate."

"That would be nice. I'm sure they'd appreciate the sentiment."

"I'll take care of it," Oliver said, his voice gentle.

"Sadie's favorite color is green," I added.

"For the cake?"

"Yes, and she loves chocolate."

"Okay, green and chocolate. Got it," he said, scribbling the notes on a scrap of paper.

I smiled, feeling a warmth spread through me. "Thanks, Oliver. You're the best."

And he was. Not only did he take my feelings into account but those around me. He was accommodating and sweet. I never thought I would find someone like him or that someone like him even existed.

Chapter 9

Friday afternoon, Oliver ducked into my office, his long navy-blue coat buttoned up and gloves on. He looked every bit the dashing figure against the backdrop of my cluttered desk.

"Where are you going?" I asked, my fingers still poised over the keyboard.

"You mean where are we going," he corrected.

"I'm not finished entering this data."

"Your boss will forgive you. Get your coat."

I stopped typing to look up at him. I hated when he kept me in the dark but I was getting used to being the fiancée of Oliver Fox.

"Oliver, just tell me where you're taking me," I said, trying to keep my curiosity in check.

“Difficult,” he teased, a grin spreading across his face.

“I’m not. I’m just curious,” I protested.

“If you hurry, you’ll find out soon enough.”

After slipping on my coat, he led me to the elevator, and we descended to the lobby. Outside, a limo was waiting.

“What are you up to, Oliver Fox?” I narrowed my eyes at him, suspecting another one of his surprises.

“Vlad, take us back to the penthouse,” he instructed the driver, ignoring my question.

I crossed my arms and stared at him. A smile danced on his lips as he pretended to be busy reading emails on his phone. Dragging information out of him would only make him tease me more, so I kept my mouth shut.

Back at the penthouse, he told me to dress warmly.

“Warm for what?” I asked.

“Just do it.”

He went to the closet to remove his charcoal gray suit, and I couldn’t resist admiring his sculpted body as he dressed. He turned and caught me looking, making me blush and look away.

“Hurry up. You take so long,” he chided, a playful smirk on his lips.

I pulled on a pair of dark blue jeans and a thick royal blue sweater. Oliver was now in black jeans and a cashmere V-neck gray sweater. Fifteen minutes later, we were back in the limo, joined by Brenda and Trevor. I raised an eyebrow but didn't say anything as Oliver put his arm around my shoulders.

We headed toward midtown, and I tried to figure out where we were going. My suspicions were confirmed when we pulled up near Rockefeller Center. I had mentioned to Oliver that it would be fun to ice skate and walk Fifth Avenue to look at the holiday windows.

"You're taking me ice skating?" I asked, excitement bubbling up inside me.

"Yes. You said you wanted to."

I leaned in and gave him a lingering kiss on the lips, my heart swelling with affection. We skated for over an hour until my nose hurt from the cold. The sun began to set, and the wind picked up, adding a biting chill to the air. Trevor skated with us, keeping a watchful eye out, while Brenda patrolled the perimeter of the rink.

Even though it was a weekday, the rink was filled with people enjoying the ice. Oliver was a surprisingly good skater, even going backwards with ease. After we finished, we went inside to warm up with some hot chocolate.

I cradled the warm cup in my hands, feeling content and happy. "Thank you, Oliver. This was perfect."

He smiled, his eyes twinkling. "You said you wanted to

go. Work was light today so I thought we would take off early."

I scooped up some of the whipped cream from the top of my hot chocolate and held it out for Oliver. He sucked my finger into his mouth, caressing the pad with his tongue before he let it go. A bolt of heat shot through me, warming my body and making my core clench with desire.

"What are we doing tonight?" I asked huskily.

"What would you like to do?" Oliver asked, his voice rich and inviting.

"Pizza with the works," I replied, feeling a twinge of guilt.

"With the works?" he echoed, eyebrow arched.

"I know, I've been lazy this week."

He chuckled, shaking his head. "We'll go to the gym for longer next week, maybe an hour and a half."

I sighed. "I guess. I need to do some shopping, too."

"I thought you did last week."

"That was online, but some things require in-store purchases."

"Take Brenda with you, maybe Trevor too. It's busy and crowded this time of year."

"It's Manhattan, it's busy and crowded all the time."

"Finish your hot chocolate. I'd like to go home and have you all to myself."

"You really are a homebody," I teased, leaning into him.

"I spend all day talking to people and shaking hands. I want to relax and take it easy. Maybe we can have some more of that red wine from last night."

"That sounds good. Pizza and red wine."

"And you?" he asked.

"And me."

He squeezed my hand, his eyes softening. "I love you, Ryleigh."

He was about to kiss my hand when a voice pierced the moment.

"Ollie?"

Oliver turned, his expression shifting from affectionate to surprised. A stunning woman with fiery red hair and striking green eyes approached us. Her confident stride and radiant beauty instantly set me on edge.

"Ollie?" I mouthed, incredulous. Oliver shook his head slightly, standing to greet the woman. She kissed his cheek, leaving a red lipstick stain that she casually wiped away with her fingers. The familiarity in her touch made my stomach churn.

"How are you, Lara? Let me introduce you to my fiancée," he said, his tone a bit stiffer than before.

Lara's eyebrows shot up. "I thought you said you weren't the marrying type?"

"At the time I knew you, I wasn't," he replied coolly. "Lara Harvin, this is Ryleigh Stewart."

I extended my hand, trying to mask my irritation. Lara ignored it, nodding at me instead. I clenched my jaw, fighting to keep my composure. Her dismissive attitude was infuriating.

"I thought you were supposed to give me a call for drinks," she said, her eyes flicking to me for a moment.

"I've been busy," Oliver replied, his discomfort palpable.

"I bet you have," she said, her gaze lingering on me before turning back to Oliver. "We can talk another time."

Then, as if I weren't even there, she reached up and stroked his face, her eyes locked on mine as she pressed her lips to his. Oliver looked momentarily helpless before quickly pulling back.

"Lara, that's enough," he said firmly, stepping away from her.

She shrugged, a sly smile playing on her lips.

"Call me. I miss spending time with you. See you later Eileen," she said as she sauntered away, joining a group of people she'd been sitting with. I was seething with anger and Oliver gave me a sheepish look.

"What the fuck was that?" I hissed.

"Nothing. She's a friend."

"You could've fooled me. I'm tired. Let's go home."

Oliver signaled for the check as I pulled on my navy blue down coat. I was in no mood to hear his explanations and was happy that Brenda and Trevor were in the limo with us. If they weren't, I would've exploded. I sat there simmering, hoping I could hold my tongue until I got into the penthouse.

~

"You're angry, I get it."

I yanked off my coat, shoving it on a hanger and putting it in the foyer closet.

"Do you, Oliver? Do you really get it?" I whipped my head around, shooting him a glare. "How many times?"

"How many times what?" he asked with confusion.

I ground my teeth. "How many times did you fuck her?"

"A few times," he admitted, "but not in the past couple of years."

"You told me you didn't have a lot of sex before me. How close were you to her?"

"We spent time together. Why are you so upset?"

I clenched my fists. "Because she touched and kissed you like you were hers. You just stood there like an idiot. I looked like a fool," I yelled.

"I didn't want to create a scene."

I got into his face. "So if one of my exes did that to me you wouldn't have an issue as long as I didn't create a scene?"

His eyebrows slammed together. "Of course I would have a problem with it. She means nothing to me and never did like you do."

He tried to push me against the wall and go in for a kiss, but I ducked under his arm and started walking down the hall to the bedroom.

"Ryleigh, let's talk about this," he begged.

"There's nothing to talk about. How many other women will I encounter that will do the same thing? How many know your body intimately and want to be where I am?"

"Which is where," he said as he strode into the bedroom and tore off his sweater.

"Your fiancée, sharing your bed, loving you."

"There are a few but I never had any feelings for them. I never ever felt the way about them that I feel about you. We belong together. Don't let this one stupid thing drive us apart."

I sat down on the bed and ripped at my shoelaces, creating a knot because I was too hasty. I tried to open it and got frustrated, finally toeing off my sneakers and kicking them away from the bed. Oliver picked them up and began working on the knots. I said nothing as I tore off my socks then went to go the closet. He joined me a couple of minutes later, pressing his chest against my bare back as I hunted for a shirt to wear.

"Oliver," I whispered.

"I never meant to hurt you."

I turned around, leaning against him. I no longer felt like eating as my stomach churned like a washing machine on the heavy cycle. I just wanted to relax in bed even though it was barely 6:00 p.m.

"Do you still want to get pizza?" he asked softly.

I shook my head. "Maybe later."

"Are you sick? You only ate a chicken sandwich for lunch."

"I'm upset."

"Please don't be. You mean so much to me."

I backed away, taking one of Oliver's white t-shirts that was folded in one of the cubbies on his side of the closet. I slipped it over my head before I pushed my jeans down my hips and let them fall to the floor.

"You're wearing that to bed?"

"Yes, why?"

Oliver licked his lips. "It's seductive."

"It's a freaking white t-shirt."

"Yes, it's that and it's also see-through. I can see your nipples and red panties."

"Deal with it," I said as I walked out of the closet and peeled back the blue quilt on the bed.

I knew he was watching me and bent over to plump the pillows, jutting out my lace clad ass before I slid into bed. Oliver joined me a few minutes later only wearing a pair of black form fitting boxers.

We were both wound tight as a spring and it was only a matter of time before we both boiled over and I ended up naked underneath him. I switched on the flat screen television on the wall, pulling away the remote when Oliver grabbed for it.

"Can you please switch to the financial news for a minute?" he asked.

"No. It's Friday and that's work," I protested.

"Just a few minutes," Oliver begged.

"No. I don't want to deal with anything business or work related."

Just to be a brat, I switched on some reality show that I knew he hated. He propped his pillows against the headboard and crossed his arms over his chest.

"Ryleigh, please?"

I waved him away with my hand. "Next commercial."

"Now."

"Check your phone. I know you have all those stock apps on it."

He was quick but not quick enough, trying to snatch the remote out of my hand. I pulled it away, holding it over the floor so he couldn't reach. He was leaning over me and bent down to suck my nipples. I gasped as I pushed his mouth away.

"Stop that. Play fair!" I demanded.

He chuckled. "Oh, we're playing now?"

"You seem to be."

"Works for me."

He shoved the covers off, hopped between my legs and tugged at my panties.

"What the hell are you doing?"

"I'm hungry and I'd like to start with dessert first. Lift your hips."

When I didn't comply, he tugged harder until the lace tore, discarding the red scraps on the floor.

"Stop destroying my panties!" I yelled.

"Then honor my requests."

I kept switching the channels as he dipped down and took a long stroke of my clit with his tongue. I wanted to cry out, but I held it in. He pushed my leg to the side and inserted a finger - still I kept quiet. It was a war of wills. Oliver kept watching my face which I tried to keep passive. He circled my swollen nub with the tip of his tongue while finger fucking me. I was quickly losing control.

My belly was burning as I grew closer to orgasm and I bit my lip to hold in another moan. Oliver was trying his best to get me to make noise. He continued to lash his tongue over me until I dropped the remote, arched my back and cried out his name as my orgasm ripped through me.

“That’s my girl.”

I fell back to the bed, boneless but not sated. The only thing that would satisfy my need was his cock. As if reading my mind, he removed his hands from me, got off the bed and pushed off his boxers. His rigid penis was bobbing against his belly as he gripped it in his fist and pumped. I watched him as he climbed on the bed, opening my legs wider to accommodate him.

“Ready for me,” he said as he stroked himself.

“You know I am.”

He covered my body with his own and slammed into me. I dug my nails in his back as we fucked, mewling and whimpering under him. He nibbled at my breasts without pushing up my shirt, dampening the fabric with his saliva. Oliver kept relentlessly pounding at me, grinding his base against my clit until I released again with a loud howl. He didn’t find his own until he gave me one more orgasm then collapsed on top of me.

“You know we use sex to deal with frustration between us,” I panted.

“I know, but isn’t makeup sex so much fun?” he asked.

“Sex with you is always fun and now I’m starving.”

“Pizza with the works?” he said as he kissed the tip of my nose.

“And fried calamari.”

“You’re working out extra hard next week.”

“I promise.”

He pulled out of me and helped me up so we could take a quick shower together. Any anger I had melted away with the endorphins coursing through my system. This wouldn’t always work, and it was probably not healthy to handle disagreements between us in this way, but it was how we dealt with them for the time being.

"Shit," I muttered as a piece of sausage slipped off my slice and landed on the table. We had ordered a pizza with the works, and it was hitting the spot perfectly. The calamari was slightly crunchy but not rubbery, and the tomato dipping sauce had just the right balance of acidity and sweetness.

Oliver chuckled, shaking his head. "You're eating like you haven't had food for two days."

"I'm hungry. Don't piss in my cornflakes," I shot back, grinning.

Oliver almost spat out his sip of wine, coughing a few times. "What did you just say?"

"Don't piss in my cornflakes. You've never heard it before?" I asked.

"No. I must be out of the loop."

"Well, you are old," I teased, my eyes twinkling.

He leaned back, a smirk playing on his lips. "I'm sure there are plenty of young men who can't do what I do in bed. There's something to be said for experience."

I laughed, feeling the tension from earlier melting away. “Oh, is that what you call it?” I smirked before I took another bite of pizza.

“Would you prefer someone younger with less experience?” he asked.

I shrugged. “Maybe I could find someone my age with the same experience as you.”

He quirked an eyebrow. “Would you want to?”

I shook my head. “No. I found my prince.”

“So, I'm a prince and not an old king.”

“A little of both but it doesn't matter to me because you're special.”

Oliver leaned over and kissed me on the lips, leaving me with the taste of the red wine he was drinking. I took another large bite of my pizza before setting it down, feeling satisfyingly full.

"Finally done?" he teased, eyeing my half-eaten slice.

"I think two slices is plenty. You ate quite a bit yourself," I replied, gesturing to the large pizza that now had only three slices left.

"I was hungry too. Our little tiff spurned on my appetite."

"Just our tiff and not the sex we had?" I asked, raising an eyebrow.

"That too," he admitted with a grin. "I'm getting up early tomorrow to work out. Do you want to join me?"

"No," I said, shaking my head. "I decided this week is a wash. I'll be lazy for another couple of days and then get back on the wagon."

His eyes twinkled. "Does that mean you'll be sleeping late?"

"Probably. We don't need to meet Finley and Sadie until noon."

"I placed an order for a cake."

I pressed a kiss to his temple. "You're sweet."

"It's not every day someone gets engaged."

"I'm sure most people hope it's the last time they get engaged."

"I hope you enjoyed your engagement because it's the last time you're getting engaged," he said, a playful but possessive glint in his eyes.

"Possessive asshole," I muttered, though I couldn't help but smile.

"I'm not possessive, I'm straightforward. You're not leaving me at any time during our marriage."

"Oliver, you can't predict the future."

"I can predict the future, and you're not leaving me. Promise me, Ryleigh."

His face grew serious, his sapphire eyes pleading with me. I sighed, feeling the weight of his gaze.

"I promise," I said softly.

He relaxed, a satisfied smile curling his lips. "What do you want to do tonight?"

"I already said I was being lazy."

"Does that mean I'll be forced to watch those horrible shows you like?" Oliver asked.

"It's part of a relationship. You don't always watch what I want to watch."

"I watch the news to keep up on what's going on in the world. Let's clean up. I have a couple of emails to answer and I'll meet you in the bedroom"

He stood up, gathering the plates and leftovers. I watched him for a moment, appreciating the way he moved with purpose, even in the small act of cleaning up. He headed to his office, quickly answering his emails that couldn't wait.

When he entered the bedroom, I was already lounging on the bed, remote in hand. He climbed in beside me and I snuggled into his warmth as he wrapped an arm around me.

"Ready for some terrible TV?" I asked, grinning.

"Ready as I'll ever be," he replied, kissing the top of my head.

We settled in, the comfort of routine wrapping around us like a warm blanket. Despite the chaos and interruptions of the day, moments like this made everything worthwhile.

~

After a lazy night of kissing and watching television, I slept until almost 9 a.m. in the morning when Oliver slipped back into the bedroom from his workout.

Oliver pulled off his white sweatshirt, damp with sweat, revealing a gray t-shirt clinging to his muscular torso. I watched, yawning loudly as he disrobed.

"Where did you go?" I asked, stretching out on the bed.

"Downstairs. It's chilly out today," he replied, ruffling his damp hair.

I groaned, burying my face in my pillow. "I hate winter."

"Then you'll like my surprise," he said with a playful grin.

"What surprise?"

Another surprise. He was making me insane with surprise.

"We're heading to Fox Island on Monday for a few days."

"We're staying there?" I asked, my interest piqued.

"For a day or two. I want to see the progress and check on Jonah. He's been behaving himself."

"I hope so. He's caused enough headaches."

"There was a delay with some of the materials, so the schedule is a little off," he admitted, slipping out of his red sweatpants.

"Off enough to make us go somewhere else for our honeymoon?"

I hoped not. I'd been anticipating a stay on our own island without the interference of cameras in our face and prying eyes. I wanted to be just us to explore not only the island but each other.

"No. The schedule was set for the beginning of June, so a few days here and there won't disrupt our honeymoon."

"Where are we staying?" I asked.

"More than likely St. Croix, unless you want to bunk with the construction crews."

Oliver continued stripping, leaving him in a pair of boxers which he shoved down his hips. My eyes traveled over his body, distracting me from our discussion for just a moment.

"I thought you were housing me in a grass hut on the beach," I teased, eyeing his now naked form.

"Would you like that?"

"I don't mind roughing it. Could you stand it?"

"I can stand anything you can," he said confidently.

I watched him for a few moments longer, appreciating his form and knowing it wouldn't take much for him to become aroused. "Can I shower with you?"

"We have time," he said, a glint in his eye.

"We have three hours to shower. I doubt we'll be in there that long."

"I misunderstood," he said with a smirk.

"Oh, you mean you thought I meant sex?" I grinned.

"Didn't you?"

"No. Stop putting words in my mouth and head."

Oliver scooped up his clothing, dropping it into the hamper in the closet before padding naked into the bathroom. As soon as I heard the shower turn on, I got up and stripped. I slipped in behind him, hugging his body and pressing my face against his back as rivulets of soap rolled down him.

"I thought we weren't having sex?" he said, his voice a low rumble.

"Can't I hug you?" I replied, feeling the heat of his skin against mine.

"I'd rather do something else. All I could think of was you as I worked out," he confessed, turning to face me, his eyes dark with desire.

"Then take me," I whispered, meeting his gaze.

With a low growl, Oliver pulled me close, our bodies melding together under the hot spray. The water cascaded over us, washing away the world outside as we lost ourselves in each other.

~

The room Oliver rented at Diamond Square was spacious, almost too big for just the four of us, but I didn't complain. Soft lighting illuminated the elegant space, casting a warm glow over the large round dark wood table and the four matching cushioned chairs arranged around it. Finley and Sadie arrived a few minutes after us, led into the room by a waiter dressed impeccably in black slacks and a crisp dress shirt.

My gaze immediately fell on the hand Sadie had wrapped around my brother's arm, and my heart swelled with joy as I caught sight of the ring he had given her the night before. The large round diamond with its halo of smaller stones sparkled under the soft light, a testament to their love. I couldn't contain my excitement as I stood up to hug them both.

Sadie looked radiant in a burgundy long-sleeved jersey dress, while Finley appeared dashing in light slacks, a tweed sports jacket, and a matching burgundy tie. It was clear that Sadie was taming him from his usual torn jeans and rock and roll t-shirts.

"We're engaged," Sadie announced, holding out her hand with a dazzling smile. I squealed with delight and enveloped her in another hug, feeling elated. My brother playfully pressed his hands to his ears and shook his head.

"I can't believe you're going to be my sister," I exclaimed, beaming at them both.

Finley and Oliver chuckled as we hugged, their conversation turning to business while Sadie and I excitedly discussed our plans for the future. A waiter soon arrived with a bottle of Dom Perignon, prompting us to raise our glasses in a toast to the happy couple, the clinking of glasses breaking up our chatter.

"So, when are you two thinking of getting married?" Oliver inquired, his curiosity evident.

"Not sure. I still have a few big projects coming up," Finley replied thoughtfully.

"Sadie, when do you want to get married? Because if you wait for my brother to make up his mind, it will be five years from now," I teased, earning a playful glare from Finley.

"I resent that," he retorted, though his eyes twinkled with amusement.

"It's true, dear brother. You get involved with things and lose yourself in them," I persisted, smirking.

"Still see that Oliver hasn't tamed that sharp tongue of yours," Finley remarked, turning to Oliver with a grin.

"That is impossible. Ryleigh is her own woman," Oliver replied, his voice filled with pride.

"That she is," Finley agreed, reaching over to give my hand a reassuring squeeze.

"I'm starving, can we go eat?" I interjected, eager to continue celebrating.

"Sure. Let's go," Finley replied, leading the way out of the room with Sadie on his arm, and Oliver and I following close behind. As we made our way to the restaurant, I couldn't help but feel a surge of happiness for my brother and his soon-to-be wife, grateful to share in their joyous moment.

Chapter 10

"What's the matter?" Oliver asked.

"I ate too much."

I was lying on the couch rubbing my stomach with my hand. I loved the buffet at Diamond Square and took a little of everything. They had a carve bar where the chefs were slicing tender roast beef, juicy turkey, pork roast and other meats.

The seafood section contained several raw selections along with cooked. I filled a separate plate up with crab legs and took a small bowl with clarified butter. I took several spoons of pasta salads and vegetables, but I made sure to save room for the dessert table.

Oliver chuckled. "You ate enough crab legs to turn into one."

"You know I love crab."

“That’s a given. You also ate too many macrons.”

I hummed. “They had blueberry and key lime. Why didn’t we take some home?”

“You had them on top of the cake for Finley and Sadie.”

He smiled. “And don’t forget the champagne.”

Oliver sat down next to me and gently pushed my hand away so he could take over rubbing my belly. He pushed up my white t-shirt and rubbed his smooth hand over my skin. The pads of his fingers brushed the undersides of my breasts and before long, he was palming them.

“My breasts don’t hurt, my stomach does.”

"I like them better than your stomach," Oliver murmured, his fingers trailing lightly over my skin.

"I know you do, but I'm in no condition for sex right now," I replied, feeling exhausted.

He frowned. "I'm not asking for sex."

"Then stop playing with my breasts," I said, gently pushing his hand away.

Oliver withdrew and caressed my stomach instead. "Are you packing tomorrow?"

"What time are we leaving?" I asked, shifting slightly to get more comfortable.

"I'd say 8. You can sleep on the plane if you're tired."

`"I won't be if you leave me alone," I joked, though a hint of seriousness lingered in my tone.

"Don't blame me for our nocturnal activities. I seem to remember you starting it last night when I was ready for bed," he teased.

"Aww, poor baby," I teased back, earning a playful glare from him.

"Just for that, we aren't having sex tonight," he declared, though I could see the hint of a smirk playing on his lips.

"You're putting your foot down?" I raised an eyebrow, amused by his sudden resolve.

"I am," he affirmed, crossing his arms.

"That doesn't mean I have to listen. Even Finley knows I'm stubborn," I countered, a smirk tugging at the corner of my lips.

"You're difficult, but I can melt you," he said confidently, leaning in to kiss my cheek.

"At least I'll get a good sleep tonight," I quipped, snuggling closer to him.

~

"Oh God, I thought you said no sex tonight," I panted.

"I lied," Oliver said, before thrusting into me again. I wrapped my legs around his back and pulled him closer. I was trying to hold on because it felt so good, but each time he hit that spot deep inside me, I wanted to explode. I rippled around him before I shattered into a million pieces, my chest heaving and heart pounding.

Oliver kept moving and it amazed me his staying power. I shuddered as he grazed the root of his cock against my ultrasensitive clit, and he stopped moving to let me rest.

“You can continue,” I panted.

He ground his teeth. “If I continue, I’ll come.”

“That’s the point.”

“No, the point is for me to make you come.”

“And I have.”

He kissed my neck and bit into my earlobe. “I want more. I love to feel you come on my cock.”

I reached up to push a lock of hair from his sweaty forehead. “I think I’m way ahead of you in the orgasm department. You’ve given me so many.”

“I’m not keeping count.”

He lifted himself off me and pulled out. His penis glistening with my juices.

“On your knees,” he commanded.

“I don’t have the strength.”

Oliver flipped me over onto my stomach, slipped a pillow under my hips then laid on top of me, thrusting his cock inside my slick channel. He sandwiched me to the bed as he fucked me. With each stroke, my clit rubbed against the soft fabric of the pillowcase causing delicious waves of electricity to course through me.

“Shit, I’m gonna come again.”

“This time I’m joining you,” he grunted. I squeezed him as I detonated and he followed, slamming into me until he was spent.

“Jesus Christ Ryleigh, I’m not sure I’ll ever get enough of you.”

I was weak, boneless and fully sated. “I think I’m done for the evening. You wore me out.”

Oliver slipped out of me and climbed out of bed. I heard the water running as I laid there, unable to move as I waited for the numbness to wear away. He came back a few minutes later and gently rolled me over, wiping between my legs with a warm cloth then drying me. He removed the pillow and pulled the covers over me.

“Sleep, sweetheart.”

Oliver didn’t have to ask me twice. I fell into a deep sleep, dreaming about our wedding day. It was a beautiful event with lots of white flowers and champagne toasts but as the festivities wound down, I found myself hiding in the darkness from a man who was pursuing me. I couldn’t escape and when I thought I was safe, he found me, dragging me out and pointing a gun in my face.

"Ryleigh, wake up!"

My eyes fluttered open to see Oliver's worried expression.

"What happened?" I mumbled.

"You don't remember?" he asked.

"It was our wedding day. A man."

"A man what?"

"A man with dark hair was following me. I tried to hide but he found me and pointed a gun in my face. It felt so real."

Oliver's expression darkened. "That's never going to happen. We'll have security the entire day."

"I know that, but I can't stop my subconscious from what I dream about."

"You don't have to worry. You're safe."

He hugged me to his bare chest, burying his head in my hair. I love Oliver so much, but I had my doubts that even he could protect me if someone wanted to get to me.

~

The next morning, I felt groggy as shit. I could feel the start of a headache behind my eyes as I shifted in bed. Oliver was draped around me, and his body heat was stifling. I tried to wiggle out of his grasp.

“Where are you going?”

“You’re too hot.”

“So are you.”

“Not that kind of hot.”

“You don’t think I’m hot?”

“Sexy, yes and temperature which is why you need to get off me. You’re making me sweat.”

“You didn’t seem to mind me making you sweat last night.”

“That was different. I expect to sweat when we have sex.”

He loosened his grip and I moved away from him but stayed in bed. Oliver stroked my hair and ran his fingers over the outside of my ear.

“Such delicate ears.”

“You’re sweet. What do you want to do today? It looks like snow.”

I looked out the patio window at the gray day that was just starting to dawn. I was glad we were leaving for St. Croix on Monday. A little time on the beach and some bright sunshine would do me good. I was excited to see the progress of our home on Fox Island.

Oliver leaned back against the sofa, his expression thoughtful. "I need to do some shopping," he said.

I raised an eyebrow, intrigued. "You? I'm surprised you weren't done weeks ago."

"I have more people to buy for this year," he explained.

"Who did you buy for last year?" I asked, curious.

"A few friends and Jonah," he replied casually.

"Friends? Female friends?" I couldn't help but ask.

"Don't start. You weren't in the picture back then. You can't expect me to feel guilty for buying gifts for female friends," he defended himself.

"You gave Lara a gift?" I questioned further, feeling a pang of jealousy.

"We were spending time together. I didn't want to be rude," he explained, though his tone was defensive.

"What did she buy you?" I pressed, unable to contain my curiosity.

"Why is this conversation relevant?" he sighed, seeming slightly annoyed.

"I just want to know what she bought you," I insisted.

Oliver hesitated before finally admitting, "Cuff links."

My expression darkened. He always wore a certain pair of cufflinks, and if they were the ones from her, I wanted him to stop.

. . .

"The monogrammed ones you always wear?" I asked, my voice tinged with hostility.

"Yes. I like them. It's not because I feel anything for her," he assured me.

"I don't want you to wear them anymore," I stated firmly, my jealousy bubbling to the surface.

"Your green streak is showing," he remarked, though there was a hint of amusement in his tone.

"I'm not jealous. She's a bitch, and you shouldn't wear anything from another woman," I retorted, my tone firm.

"I'll put them away," he relented.

"You'll give them away," I insisted, determined.

"That's rude. They're gold," he protested.

"So?" I countered.

"Ryleigh, do you have gifts from Ty?" he asked, shifting the focus of the conversation.

"A few. Ty is different. I haven't slept with him, and he's just a friend," I explained, feeling the need to clarify.

"But he's a man. Isn't it the same thing?" he challenged.

"No, it's not. You had an intimate relationship with Lara," I insisted, feeling a surge of frustration.

"I didn't. We fucked, and she escorted me to functions," he clarified, his tone defensive.

"You fucked her, that's intimate," I countered, my voice rising slightly.

"Why does it bother you so much?" he questioned, genuinely curious.

"Because she touched you like you were hers. You're mine," I admitted, my jealousy laid bare.

"I am yours, and this conversation is ridiculous. I'll put the cuff links away," he conceded, seeming tired of the argument.

"Thank you," I said, feeling a sense of relief.

"Stop worrying about Lara. She means nothing to me," he reassured me.

"I hope not," I replied honestly, still feeling uneasy.

"You doubt me," he observed, his tone tinged with hurt.

"No. I'm just saying I hope she doesn't mean anything to you," I clarified, wanting to reassure him.

"She's a friend and that's all, just like Ty is to you," he said, attempting to ease the tension.

"Point taken. Let's move on," I agreed, eager to change the subject.

"So, as I was saying, I'd like to do some shopping," Oliver continued, shifting the conversation.

"I'd like to do some shopping too. Can I come with you?" I asked, hoping to spend time together.

"No. I have to get things I don't want you to see," he replied, his expression serious.

"Then I'll go by myself," I stated, determined.

"You'll take Brenda. I can have Vlad escort me," he suggested, his tone firm.

"Fine. Works for me," I acquiesced, though a part of me still felt unsettled.

After three hours of shopping, my feet were killing me. I made the mistake of wearing a pair of boots that were new. I sat down on a pink padded bench in Boudoir Fashions. One of my gifts to Oliver would be a long beige satin nightgown with spaghetti straps. I was looking through their website a few weeks ago and he commented about this very nightgown. I had no idea he had a preference.

This was the last store I stopped in for the day. I had already missed lunch and my stomach growled in protest. All I wanted to do was go home, take off these boots and have a sandwich. I hadn't heard from Oliver in a few hours, and I suspected he was just as tired as I was from fighting the crowds of Christmas shoppers.

“I think it's time to go,” I told Brenda who was sitting next to me.

"Let me call Trevor," she said. Trevor had the black sedan while Oliver took the limo with Vlad. At least I didn't have to lug around packages like other shoppers. Each time I finished at one store; we dropped off the bags with Trevor.

Outside, Fifth Avenue was teeming with visitors looking at the Christmas windows. I fought through the crowd with Brenda behind me and was thankful when we got into the car.

"I love and hate Christmas in Manhattan," I said.

Brenda smiled. "I know what you mean."

"You never told me if you have any family."

"I have two sisters. They live in New Jersey," she said.

"Are you seeing them for the holiday?"

"I'll be working. We all will."

"We're going to my parents for the holiday. I don't think it's necessary that you come."

"Mr. Fox wants us on duty."

I frowned, unzipping my boot and rubbing my right foot. I could feel a blister on my heel. I wondered why Oliver wanted the entire staff on duty. Oliver wasn't home for me to ask when I got into the penthouse. I looked around for spots to hide things since I didn't want him to discover anything.

I used the credit card he gave me for purchases and went a little overboard. Matthew told me a while back that he wanted silk shirts with French cuffs, and I bought him two. They were soft and I picked them out a powder blue and ivory.

Finley was easy since he'd been talking about tickets to Cygnus. They were sold out and even his contacts couldn't get him seats. With one phone call, Oliver got him seats on the stage and passes to meet the band after. Finley would be so surprised. I bought Sadie a pair of diamond earrings. She admired mine and I wanted to get her a pair ever since.

My fiancé was harder to buy for. What do you get the man that has almost everything? The lingerie was just one gift I knew he would appreciate. The rest took some thinking. I hoped he would like whatever I bought.

When Oliver finally came home, I was sitting in the tub full of fragrant lime basil bubbles, sipping a glass of chilled white wine. He called for me as he came down the hall to the bedroom.

"In the bathroom."

He ducked his head in, and I smiled at his handsome face. "You were gone a long time."

"When did you get home?" he asked.

"About an hour and a half ago. I have a blister from my boots," I said as I held my foot up for him to see.

"Did you finish shopping?"

I nodded, spreading my arms out on the rim of the tub. “Almost. I used the card.”

Oliver leaned against the doorjamb. “That’s what I gave it to you for.”

“I got Matthew those silk shirts he wanted.”

He smirked. “He is becoming quite the dapper man.”

“He always was so particular.”

Oliver removed his green wool hat, and I sucked in my breath.

“You got your hair cut?”

He ran his hand through his sandy hair. “You like it?”

“It looks good, but the hat flattened it. I thought you wanted me to cut it for you?”

“I was near the salon, so I went in. Alfonso did a good job.”

Oliver had gotten a short fade, and his hair was thick and slicked back in the middle. He looked sexy and I couldn’t wait to see it when it wasn’t disturbed by a hat.

“Yes, he did. Want to join me?”

He nodded. “I think that would be fun. Let me get undressed.”

I held my almost empty wine glass to him. “Can you refill my wine before you come in?”

He entered the bathroom after he shucked off his navy-blue wool pea coat and took the glass I held out to him, gently tugging on my hair so he could give me a kiss. As he walked away, I thought I caught the scent of another woman's perfume.

It probably was nothing since I was sure he had probably been sandwiched against people all day the way I had. Anyone's scent could've transferred to him. Oliver came back a few minutes later with my wine then removed his clothes.

"Want to move forward?" he asked.

"No. Why don't you sit in front of me?"

He raised an eyebrow. "Okay, sure."

He sat on the edge of the tub and slipped in then got between my legs and leaned back against my chest.

"I like this," I said.

"I'm not too heavy?"

"You're fine."

I took a sip of my wine and placed it on the small white porcelain shelf over the tub. I stroked Oliver's hair with my wet hands, plastering it down on his head.

"There's not as much for me to pull."

He chuckled. "We're you planning on pulling my hair?"

I wiggled my legs around him. "You know what I mean."

“It will grow back in no time. This is neater. My hair was getting out of hand.”

I began to massage his strong shoulders, running my wet hands over his muscles. “Was it busy today?”

“It was. I was getting pushed around in the stores. I love the holidays but not some of the stuff that goes along with it.”

“We have to pack.”

Oliver ran his fingers over my legs. Despite the warm water, goosebumps peppered my skin. “I know. I hope we can get out before the snow comes in.”

“How much is expected?” I asked.

“A few inches but I prefer to be in the air before it starts.”

“I hope we have time to go to the beach,” I said with anticipation.

“We will and you’re going to love Fox Island.”

“I can’t believe you own an island,” I said excitedly.

“We own an island.”

“Does Jonah know you’re coming?” I asked.

“No. I’d rather surprise him and see what he’s up to.”

I planted kisses on Oliver’s shoulder and stroked my hand down his belly, stopping just above his pubic area.

I was tempted to touch him lower, but I kept my hand still, fingering the ridges of his stomach.

“Can I help you with something?” he asked.

I nuzzled his ear. “No. I like touching you.”

“No kidding.”

I moved my hand further and wasn’t surprised to find him partially erect. I stroked Oliver’s shaft with soapy hands, and he softly moaned as he grew to full staff.

“It didn’t take long,” I whispered.

I moved faster, fisting him tightly as I pumped up and down. Oliver bucked his hips, groaning my name. He dug his nails into my thighs then grabbed my hand to stop me, but I persisted until he gave in and released me. I changed speed, pumping slowly. The water rippled as his hips moved in rhythm.

“Come for me, baby,” I whispered.

His body tensed and he grunted loudly as he climaxed. I continued to stroke until he stopped me.

“That was so good, but I prefer to come somewhere else.”

“I think we should get out of the tub. I’m tired. I think I have a bruise on my arm. Some lady in Macy’s elbowed me when I was looking at cookware.”

“Cookware? Why were you looking at pots and pans?”

“My mother wants the copper-bottomed set and an iron frying pan.”

“Did you buy them for her?”

“The frying pan. I think Anders is buying her the set. He didn’t answer his phone so I took a pass. It would be embarrassing if I gave her the same gift as him.”

“Not embarrassing. She would have twice as much to cook with.”

Oliver stood up and stepped out of the tub. Bubbles lingered on his body and he entered the shower stall to wash them off. I followed, hitting the plunger so the water drained from the tub. We took a quick shower and dressed in our robes.

“What about a tree?” I asked as we headed for the kitchen.

“You want one? I never had one. They’re a bit messy.”

“We need a tree,” I insisted.

“We’ll get one when we come back from St. Croix.”

“I might just want to stay there if the weather is nice.”

“It will be nice. It’s almost always nice.”

Oliver retrieved my wine glass from the bathroom and refreshed it then poured himself a glass of the same fruity white wine. We sat on the couch, and he gently massaged the blister on my heel.

"Does it hurt?" Oliver asked, concern etched across his features.

I winced slightly. "A little. It'll go away. I just can't wear those boots for a while."

He nodded, relief washing over his face. "You won't need to for at least a few days."

I sighed, shifting to a more comfortable position. "We should pack. What time is Vlad picking us up?"

"6:00 a.m. sharp, so don't be dragging around in the morning," he teased, a playful glint in his eyes.

I snorted, rolling my eyes. "I don't always do that. I've been tired lately, probably from the interrupted sleep courtesy of my fiancé."

Oliver gasped dramatically. "Don't blame me. You wake me up just as much as I do you."

"Keep telling yourself that if it makes you feel better," I retorted, giving him a playful shove. "Are we taking the larger Fox jet?"

His eyes twinkled mischievously. "You mean the one with the bedroom?"

I nodded eagerly. "Yes, that one."

"We are. Maintenance is finished, and it passed with flying colors," he said, his arm wrapping around me as I snuggled deeper into his side.

"I like that jet," I murmured, closing my eyes for a moment.

"I bet you do. So many naughty memories in it," he chuckled, his fingers tracing patterns on my shoulder.

"I like being naughty six miles up. You've given me so many new experiences," I admitted, a smile playing on my lips.

"We should pack before it gets too late," he suggested, glancing at the clock.

"Are we sharing a suitcase?" I asked, looking up at him.

"That depends," he replied, a smirk tugging at his lips.

"On what?" I pressed, curious.

"If you don't overpack. You have a tendency to do that. We're only going for three days. You don't need to go crazy," he teased, poking my side.

"I never know what you want to do. Suppose you take me out to a fancy restaurant and I didn't bring a dress?" I countered, pouting slightly.

"That's what stores are for. They do have them on St. Croix," he replied with a chuckle.

"I know they do, silly," I said, rolling my eyes.

"Pack light and whatever we need, we'll buy," he assured me, pressing a kiss to my forehead.

"I'm excited," I confessed, feeling a flutter of anticipation.

"Me too," he said softly, his eyes meeting mine with a warmth that made my heart skip a beat.

~

I yawned, stretching slightly in the plush seat. "When will we be landing?"

Oliver checked his watch, glancing at me with a small smile. "Probably in a half hour. Did you have a good nap?"

"Yes," I nodded, sinking back into the butter-soft tan leather. "These seats are so comfortable, like first class."

"Better than first class," he corrected with a wink.

I had fallen asleep the minute we took off, the flurries outside doing little to unsettle me. Oliver had reassured me not to worry about the weather. My sleep had been disturbed last night by a nightmare—not loud enough to wake Oliver but scary enough to disrupt my rest. I had tossed and turned until the alarm went off.

"Did you have a nightmare?" he asked, his voice soft.

"When? Now?" I blinked, trying to shake off the remnants of sleep.

"Last night. I felt you moving around."

"I'm sorry. I didn't mean to wake you. It's the stress of the trip," I explained, biting my lip.

Oliver sighed, a hint of concern in his eyes. "I still think you should see a therapist."

"I'm not interested. They couldn't help me before," I replied, my tone defensive.

"You were six. Things change, and your brain matures."

"I don't want to get involved. I have too many things on my plate."

"Will you at least think about it?" he pressed gently.

"Yes. If I decide to go, you'll be the first to know," I answered curtly, turning to look out the window. We were flying over a few clouds, but I was sure it would be sunny when we got to St. Croix. The weather app on my phone had promised sunny and warm in the eighties.

Sensing I didn't want to discuss it any longer, Oliver returned to his laptop, tapping away until a female flight attendant, dressed in black slacks and a white blouse, came out to tell us to prepare for landing. Oliver packed up his silver laptop, stowing it in his brown soft leather briefcase.

A few minutes later, we began our descent, and the sun's rays blasted through the window as we exited the cloudbank. I squinted, pulling down the built-in white shade, relieved to see the weather prediction was correct. Once we landed, the captain exited the cabin to open the door.

I stood up, adjusting my yellow sweater and smoothing my blue jeans with my hands. From my purse, I took out my sunglasses and slipped them on to ward off the bright sunlight as we left the plane. A blast of heat hit me, immediately causing sweat to bloom on my skin.

Oliver had discarded his sweater before he stood up from his seat, and I wished I had done the same. A black SUV was waiting on the tarmac, and our large Louis Vuitton suitcase was loaded into the back while we slipped inside. Vlad and Brenda, our security detail, took the seat behind us.

Our driver, a large man with a pug nose and ice-blue eyes, sat up front. His bulging muscles strained at his gray sports jacket, making me wonder how many of them he'd torn. We were driven to a marina where a small boat was waiting to transport us to Fox Island.

"We forgot the suitcase," I said, a hint of panic in my voice, as Oliver helped me onto the deck of the small white boat. He chuckled, a low, soothing sound.

"We're not staying on the island. The suitcase will be taken to our room at Diamond Square St. Croix."

"You own a hotel here?" I asked, my eyebrows shooting up in surprise.

"A resort, really. Plenty to do there, and I'm sure you'll enjoy the beach," he replied with a knowing smile.

I tore at my sweater, yanking it over my head and tying it around my waist as the captain fired up the motor on the boat. The breeze felt incredible against my skin as we stood on the deck, the boat chugging through the turquoise water. I tilted my head upward, soaking in the sun on my face.

“You should put on sunscreen. The sun is fiercer than in New York,” Oliver advised, his tone gentle but insistent.

“I don’t burn that easily,” I protested, waving a dismissive hand.

“You have fair skin,” he reminded me.

“Stop being a mother hen,” I teased, rolling my eyes.

I glanced over at Vlad, who was trying to stifle a smile, and then back at Oliver. He just shook his head and grabbed my hand, kissing the back tenderly. The island came into view a few minutes later, a long stretch of sandy beach disappearing into a grove of leafy palm trees. Two boats loaded with supplies sat anchored on the dock that jutted out into the water.

The heat was getting to me, and I wished we had stopped at the hotel so I could have changed into shorts. I wiped at a trickle of sweat as it leaked down my cheek, feeling sticky and uncomfortable. Oliver, on the other hand, looked cool and composed, his shirt barely showing any signs of sweat.

“I need air conditioning, stat,” I muttered, more to myself than anyone else.

Chapter 11

After the boat was secured on the new wooden dock, we disembarked, stepping onto the hot sand. Even though I was wearing sneakers, I could feel the heat seeping through the rubber and leather. In the distance, the beeping of equipment and the banging of tools filled the air.

As we approached the construction site, I was awed by the progress. Concrete walls were being put into place, and the entire foundation, as well as most of the outer walls, were complete. Men worked diligently on the roof, laying orange clay tiles. Oliver introduced me to the foreman, Charles Hennigan. He was a small man with a bald head, but it was clear he commanded respect. When a worker tried to give him a hard time, he stared him down with unwavering authority.

“How is everything, Charles?” Oliver asked, his voice carrying over the noise.

"On schedule," Charles replied. "We made up some time with the walls. The pours went well and dried fast, thanks to the lack of rain."

"How's Jonah? And where is he?"

"I sent him to the bunkhouse. He didn't seem to be feeling well. I think he might be a little dehydrated."

"Thanks. I'd like to see him."

Oliver shook Charles's hand before heading toward a large concrete house painted white with gray shutters. We walked along the hot sand until we reached a sturdy steel door.

"What will you do with this house when ours is built?" I asked, curiosity piqued.

"It will be turned into employee quarters," Oliver explained.

"No one will be in the house with us?"

"Do you want them to be?" he asked.

"No. I want to be alone with you."

I reached up and smoothed my hair back, feeling the sweat on my scalp. I couldn't wait to get inside and out of the sun. Oliver pushed open the gray steel door, and I raised my eyebrows in surprise. From the outside, the house looked stark and boring; however, that was not the case inside.

Cool air rushed over my skin as we stepped into a large, open room. It housed a modern kitchen with stainless steel appliances, including an oversized refrigerator and a six-burner stove. White quartz counters gleamed, and the island accommodated eight black iron stools. A long wooden rectangular table was surrounded by twelve chairs.

On the other side of the room was a large conversation area with three overstuffed brown couches and a flat-screen television mounted on the wall. Gray tile swept through the rooms, leading down a long hallway where several doors hinted at bedrooms and bathrooms. The ceilings were open rafters, and large windows covered with closed white Venetian blinds kept the sun at bay. The walls were painted a basic white, with no décor yet adorning them.

I sighed with relief as the air conditioning soothed my overheated skin. "This is amazing," I said, turning to Oliver. "I had no idea it would be so nice inside."

Oliver smiled, pleased with my reaction. "I wanted to make sure everyone was comfortable. The main house will be even better."

"I can't wait to see it finished," I said, genuinely excited.

"Neither can I," he replied, his voice warm. He squeezed my hand gently. "Let's go check on Jonah."

Oliver called out for Jonah, and we heard a voice from one of the rooms at the end. We found his brother lying in the bottom bed of one of the two wooden bunk beds in the room. He was wearing a white tank top and blue plaid boxer shorts. A blush started to creep up my face and I looked down at the floor, embarrassed by his state of undress. Jonah sat up then flopped back on his pillow.

He groaned. “What are you doing here?”

“What’s wrong?” I could hear the worry in Oliver’s voice.

“Dizzy. I’m not sure what’s wrong. Charles told me to drink but I have and it’s not going away.”

Oliver sat down on the edge of the bed and touched Jonah’s forehead. He pushed his hand away.

“I don’t have a fever. I’m just dizzy.”

“You need to go to the hospital. You might be too dehydrated, and drinking won’t help. You need fluids intravenously.”

“You said I couldn’t leave the island.”

“You can leave for a medical emergency. Get some shorts on. We’re heading back to St. Croix and can drop you off.”

I stepped out of the room while Oliver helped Jonah get dressed. When Jonah tried to stand, he stumbled, and Oliver made him sit down.

“You need help to the boat. You’re not going to make it by yourself,” Oliver said.

“I have to throw up.”

Oliver grabbed a small plastic garbage can near the door and handed it to Jonah just in time. He purged his stomach and the smell that hit me was revolting. I pushed back a gag and stepped out of the room.

"I'm sorry. If I stay here, I'll be the next one to throw up," I said.

"Go wait in the kitchen. I called Vlad and Brenda to come up here to help me."

I gladly did as Oliver asked, sitting on one of the stools at the counter before my curiosity got the best of me. The refrigerator was four times the size of a regular one and I yanked open the door to look inside. It was well stocked with drinks, frozen foods, dishes covered in tin foil, cold cuts, fruit and other items.

"Being nosy?" Oliver said.

I whirled around. "This refrigerator is huge! You could store a dead body in here."

He raised his eyebrows. "Wow, that's morbid."

"You really could, just look," I said, yanking open the doors.

"I've seen it. I plan to put the same one in the new house."

I grinned. "Seriously? It's just the two of us."

"I don't want to run out of food while we're here. I was thinking we need at least a couple of weeks for our honeymoon."

“I’ll have you all to myself?” I asked.

I was going to kiss Oliver, but we were interrupted by a knock on the door. Vlad and Brenda were standing there, each wiping sweat from their faces. It was humid here and I felt the rush of warm air as they came inside the house.

“Where is he?” Vlad asked.

“Down the hall.”

I hugged Oliver, feeling the dampness of his t-shirt sticking to his back. A minute later, Jonah was being escorted out of the house. He seemed shaky and pale. I hoped he would be all right.

~

After we got Jonah settled at the Christiansted Medical Center, we said our goodbyes and headed to the hotel. I was exhausted and desperate for a shower. Oliver left Vlad with Jonah, while Brenda accompanied us. She had her own room two doors down from our suite.

“We didn’t need a suite. It’s too big,” I said, looking around at the spacious floor plan that included a small kitchen, dining area, living area, and a wet bar. The bedroom rivaled the one in the penthouse, and I couldn’t resist jumping onto the white satin cover, sliding against the padded headboard and six oversized pillows.

“You’re like a little kid,” Oliver remarked with a chuckle, joining me on the bed and mimicking my jump.

"I need a shower," I declared, getting off the bed and gazing out the windows that faced the ocean. Dots in the distance through the turquoise water hinted at Fox Island. With seven months before our wedding, I was confident the house would be finished on time.

"Charles said we're on schedule to finish by June. We should pick out furniture while we're here," Oliver said, his tone businesslike.

I turned to him with a frown. "I thought this was a vacation?"

"A working vacation," he corrected. "I want everything perfect when we get down here for our honeymoon."

"You can only do that if we actually come here before we get married," I pointed out, raising an eyebrow.

"Then we will," he said, shrugging.

"No, I want it to be a surprise," I insisted.

"You've already seen it. Besides, you always yell at me for surprising you. Are you going to let me see the design of your dress?" he teased.

My mouth dropped open as I untucked my shirt from my jeans. "No. It's bad luck to see the dress."

A few weeks ago, I had sat down with the Vicarias to discuss what I wanted in a wedding dress. They emailed the design to me a couple of days later, and I was in love. Oliver would cry when he saw it on me.

"That's a myth," he said, smirking.

. . .

"Be patient. You'll love it. We need to discuss your tux," I reminded him.

"We have plenty of time for that. I can buy one."

"What about the groomsmen?" I asked, folding my arms.

"I can buy their tuxes too," he said nonchalantly.

"Big spender," I mumbled.

Just then, my cell phone rang, and I slid it out of my back pocket to answer. "Hello, Ty. How are you?"

"I'm good. I miss you. I sent you a few texts, but you never answered me," Ty said, his voice warm.

"I'm sorry, things have been crazy," I explained.

"Can we go out for drinks one day this week?" he asked.

"Drinks?" I repeated, glancing at Oliver, who narrowed his eyes and crossed his arms. I looked away from his intense stare.

"I'm not in New York," I continued.

"Where are you?" Ty sounded surprised.

"St. Croix. Oliver wanted to show me the home he's having built on Fox Island," I explained.

"Must be nice to have money," Ty said, his voice dripping with bitterness.

"It's not everything," I replied softly.

"But it helps. He got everything. Money, success, and the girl," Ty shot back.

"Stop it, Ty. We can go out on the weekend. How about lunch?"

"I'm busy. I do have a life outside of you." Ty's tone was glacial.

"I know you do. Does this have anything to do with my father?" I asked, my voice trembling slightly.

"Yes, it does, but you don't seem to care. I want you to look at the video we enhanced," Ty demanded.

"And what? Identify him? I don't know who it was," I replied, feeling a knot form in my stomach.

"I want you to look at some pictures. Maybe we can match it," he insisted.

"Why can't you believe me when I tell you I don't remember anything?" I said, frustration edging into my voice.

"You're suppressing. I know it was a long time ago, but don't you want your father's case solved? He deserves it," Ty pressed.

"I want it solved, but not at the risk of my sanity. I still have nightmares. You want to dredge that shit up for me and make it worse," I countered, my voice breaking.

"No, but maybe they'll go away if the man responsible goes to jail," Ty argued.

"Or maybe not," I said, tears welling up in my eyes.

"Say you'll think about it," Ty pleaded.

"I have to go. Oliver is taking me to dinner," I said, trying to end the conversation.

"Have a wonderful time," he said sarcastically and hung up. I stood there with the phone to my ear as the line went dead.

"Sweetheart?" Oliver's voice broke through my daze.

My bottom lip trembled. "He won't let it go. I can't do it. I just want it to go away," I cried, the tears finally spilling over.

Oliver came to me, wrapping his arms around me. I buried my face in his chest, sobbing.

"You don't have to do anything you don't want to do," he murmured, stroking my hair.

"I want my father's murder solved, but I can't see the man that killed him. I just can't," I whispered, my voice muffled against his chest.

"We'll find another way. You're not alone in this," Oliver said firmly, holding me tighter.

he said, his expression softening slightly. "Let's take that shower."

I nodded and we headed to the bathroom. As the hot water cascaded over us, I felt the tension of the day start to melt away. Oliver wrapped his arms around me, and I leaned into his embrace.

We had a wonderful time in St. Croix. The next day, Oliver took me back to Fox Island to drop off Jonah, who was feeling much better. We explored the two miles of land, and he led me to a waterfall and a small lagoon about half a mile from where the house was being built. I had plans for that spot when we went on our honeymoon.

We drove around in a golf cart with extra-large tires so it could handle the sand and rough terrain. The island was beautiful, and I couldn't wait to do more exploring when we were there for two weeks.

I dreaded going home because New York was in the throes of a polar cold front. It was freezing, and Sadie told me not to come back. I wished we could stay for another few days. I spent one full day browning my skin on the beach and ended up with a nice golden tan. Oliver made sure to slather me with suntan lotion every two hours so I wouldn't get burned.

On the plane, I slept while Oliver worked. He even took a conference call as we hiked through some of the wooded areas of the island. I was amazed he got any connection at all. I was so fascinated with the vegetation and the coconuts that fell from the palm trees that I wasn't even annoyed he was working.

"Ryleigh, we're landing in a few minutes," Oliver said as he gently shook me awake.

"I'm not ready. Can't we just fly to California or something? I want warm weather," I whined, still half-asleep.

"You wouldn't want to miss Christmas, would you?" he asked, raising an eyebrow.

"Of course not, but we could celebrate anywhere," I replied, my voice filled with longing.

"What about a tree?" he asked, smirking.

"Yes, what about a tree? You said we could get one," I reminded him, sitting up.

"Tomorrow after work, we can pick one up," he promised.

"Can't wait," I said, grinning.

"As long as you have no problem cleaning up after it," he teased.

"Oliver, it's not a baby or a pet," I laughed.

"They drop needles all over," he argued.

"Not if you make sure there's water in the stand. When I was a kid, we used to have a real tree all the time," I countered.

“What was your favorite Christmas?” he asked, his tone softening.

“The last one my father was alive. He bought me a dollhouse and made some of the furniture in his workshop. I think it’s still in my parents' attic. What was yours?” I asked, curious.

Oliver thought for a moment, a smile playing on his lips.

"The year I got a ten-speed bike," Oliver said, a nostalgic smile on his face. "I was twelve. There was snow on the ground, but I insisted on going out. I was scared because I slipped on an ice patch and dinged a chunk of paint off the frame. I thought my parents would be upset, but they were just happy I didn’t hurt myself."

"What color was the bike?" I asked, intrigued by this glimpse into his childhood.

"Red. It was a Schwinn. I loved that bike. I gave it to my brother after my parents died," he replied, his voice tinged with a hint of sadness.

"What did he do with it?" I asked gently.

"Lost it in a card game. Even at sixteen, I couldn’t control him," Oliver said, shaking his head slightly.

"Are you asking Jonah to be in our wedding?" I inquired, curious about his plans.

"I’ve been thinking about it, but that little stunt he pulled did not put him in my good graces," Oliver admitted, his brow furrowing.

"He seemed to be on the straight and narrow when we saw him," I said, trying to sound hopeful.

"That's because he was sick," Oliver replied, a touch of skepticism in his tone.

"He's trying to change," I insisted.

"He could've created problems with the assault. I'm glad it didn't make it into the system," Oliver said, his voice growing stern.

The flight attendant came back and told us to prepare for landing. Oliver put away his laptop and strapped his belt as we began to descend. I followed suit, my mind still lingering on our conversation about Jonah and the upcoming wedding.

As the plane descended, I turned to Oliver. "You know, maybe involving Jonah in the wedding could be the push he needs to stay on the right path."

Oliver looked thoughtful, then nodded slowly. I'll think about it. Now, let's get ready to land and face the cold."

I sighed, but his warmth and optimism made the prospect of returning to the freezing weather a bit more bearable.

~

Oliver's words echoed in my mind as I stared up at the ceiling, contemplating his insistence on going to work. It wasn't that I minded working, but the idea of spending a day at home, cocooned in warmth and comfort, was undeniably appealing.

"Can't we just go in on Monday?" I pleaded, rolling over to face him.

He raised an eyebrow, his lips twitching with amusement. "And do what? Bake cookies all day?"

I grinned. "That actually sounds pretty good."

He chuckled, shaking his head. "As much as I'd love to indulge in cookie-baking bliss with you, we have responsibilities. Plus, we're meeting with the Ryders tonight."

My curiosity piqued. "Which Ryders?"

"All four of them."

I furrowed my brow. "Why? The project is on schedule, and you just talked to them last week."

"We're discussing a collaboration here in New York."

I hesitated, unsure of how to voice my concerns without causing friction. Finally, I settled on a vague response. "You don't need me."

His gaze softened, sensing my unease. "What's your problem with them?"

"You know what my problem is with them. They're disrespectful and rude. I prefer not to be around them," I snapped.

He reached out to tuck a strand of hair behind my ear. "Don't worry, you're with me. I've already spoken to James and Callan. I'm sure their sons will behave this time."

I nodded, grateful for his reassurance, even though the knot of discomfort still lingered in my stomach. "That still doesn't make me comfortable."

"Ryleigh, please just come with me," he said gently, his eyes searching mine for understanding. "If they say anything, I want you to tell me, and we'll address it immediately. I want you to know that this won't be the only time you will face this type of behavior I'm sorry to say."

With a sigh, I relented, knowing that arguing further would only prolong the inevitable. As much as I wanted to avoid the situation, I trusted Oliver's judgment and knew that he had our best interests at heart.

I took a quick shower, relishing the warm water cascading over my skin. As I stepped out, I wrapped myself in a plush white towel, the soft fabric cocooning me in comfort.

Oliver emerged from the shower stall, steam billowing around him. I watched him shave, admiring the way his strong jawline moved with precision. I couldn't help but feel a pang of disappointment as he rid himself of the rugged stubble I had grown fond of.

"What's your problem?" he asked, catching my gaze in the mirror as he wiped shaving cream from his neck.

I smiled, shaking my head. “I have no problem. I just want to look at my handsome fiancé.”

He rolled his eyes playfully. “Looks get us in trouble. I have a conference call at 8:30 so get a move on.”

“Hmm, all business today?” I teased, letting the towel fall to the floor in a heap as I padded out of the bathroom, naked.

I glanced back over my shoulder, catching the look of surprise on Oliver's face before I disappeared into the closet. I heard his footsteps behind me, then suddenly he was wrapping his arms around me, his naked body pressing against mine.

“Fucking tease,” he growled in my ear, sending shivers down my spine.

“I’m not teasing you,” I protested, turning to face him. “I was dry and didn’t need my towel.”

He smirked, his hands wandering over my skin. “You said you're sore, but your actions say something else.”

I laughed, pushing him away gently. “And you said you have a meeting this morning. We should get dressed so you’re not late.”

His response was to cup my left breast and latch his mouth onto my ear, licking around the outside. My body began to bloom with heat and my core clenched as he moved his hand toward my cleft.

“I’m sorry Mr. Fox but you’re going to make me late and the boss hates that.”

“The boss wants to screw you,” Oliver murmured, his voice low and teasing.

“That’s sexual harassment,” I retorted, trying to sound firm despite the fluttering excitement in my stomach.

My breath hitched as his finger brushed over my clit, igniting a rush of pleasure that made me tremble.

“Not if you ask me to do it,” he countered, his touch growing more insistent.

“Sexual harassment? I would never ask for that,” I protested weakly, my resolve melting away under his skilled touch.

He intensified his movements, coaxing soft moans from my lips before abruptly pulling away, leaving me achingly needy. Oliver turned to rummage through his drawer, but I seized the opportunity to press myself against him, my hand slipping down to stroke his throbbing cock.

“Unhand me, Miss Stewart,” he teased, his breath catching as I nibbled on his biceps.

“Two can play that game,” I replied huskily.

“Fuck, Ryleigh,” he groaned, unable to resist my touch.

“That’s exactly what I want,” I purred, my desire growing with each passing moment.

With a swift motion, he pushed my hand away, lifting me effortlessly and placing me on the cold granite of the vanity. I shivered at the sensation, anticipation coursing through my veins.

"You ready for me?" he asked, his voice thick with desire.

"I always am," I whispered, spreading my legs eagerly.

He positioned himself between my thighs, his hardness pressing against my entrance before plunging deep inside me. I gasped as he lifted me from the counter, pressing me against the wall as he thrust into me with unrestrained passion.

"Yes, yes," I moaned, my body responding to his every touch.

"You're a naughty girl," he breathed against my ear, his words sending shivers down my spine. "You push me until you get what you want."

"Fuck me harder," I pleaded, surrendering to the intoxicating pleasure of his embrace.

"Hold onto my neck," Oliver murmured, his voice thick with desire.

I clung to him, feeling the intensity of our connection as he drove into me with relentless passion. With each thrust, a wave of pleasure surged through me, building towards an explosive climax. It hadn't been long since our last encounter, but the craving for intimacy drove me to new heights of ecstasy.

"I love you so fucking much. Do you even know how much?" he whispered in my ear, his words sending shivers down my spine.

"I know, because I feel the same way," I gasped, my voice trembling with my impending release.

"Come for me," he urged, his breath hot against my skin.

I surrendered to the overwhelming sensation, my body trembling as waves of pleasure washed over me. As my orgasm crashed over me, I clung to him, my nails digging into his skin as he pounded into me with primal intensity. Seconds later, he found his own release, grunting as he filled me with his hot semen.

"Oh God, that was so good," I mumbled, my body still trembling with aftershocks.

"We need to hurry, or we're going to be late," Oliver reminded me, his voice filled with urgency.

"Why can't you have your conference call here?" I suggested, reluctant to leave the warmth of our embrace.

"I could," he admitted, considering the idea.

"It would make life so much easier," I pointed out, hopeful that he would agree.

"Are you showering again?" he asked as he lowered me to the floor, his gaze lingering on me with affection.

"I think I have to. You came a lot, and a washcloth wouldn't do the job," I replied with a teasing smile.

"Then you'll find me in my office. I'll take the call here, and we can go in right after," he decided, his tone filled with determination.

"I knew you'd see it my way," I teased, a playful glint in my eye.

"You're a pain in the ass," he chuckled, leaning in to press a kiss against my lips.

"But you love me anyway, so what does it matter?" I quipped, returning his affection with a smile.

"I've been trying to figure that out," he admitted, his gaze softening with affection.

I scowled at him which made him laugh. He cleaned up at the bathroom sink while I took a quick shower, careful not to wet my already styled hair. He wasn't in the closet when I finished drying myself. I stood there deciding on what to wear. It was frigid out which was so unlike December. A polar front had moved down from Canada while we were vacationing, and it wouldn't leave.

I chose a pair of black slacks and matched them with a purple wool sweater. There was no way I would be wearing a dress or skirt in this weather. After I got dressed, I went to look for Oliver. He was sitting at his desk wearing a navy pinstriped suit, pink shirt and dark blue tie. He looked up at me when I entered the room and stopped taking notes on a piece of paper.

“Why don’t you join the twenty-first century and use your laptop?” I teased Oliver as he scribbled something more on his sheet of paper.

“I prefer to make notes the old-fashioned way. Please don’t pick on me,” he replied with a good-natured smile.

I couldn’t help but grin. “Do you want some coffee before your call?”

“Not enough time. I’ll have a cup at the office,” he declined, checking his watch.

“Do you want me to stay?” I offered, wanting to be supportive.

“It’s not necessary. This is about a deal with a Chinese supplier,” he explained.

“Shouldn’t I know?” I asked, feeling a twinge of exclusion.

“Another time. I want you to get up to speed with the real estate dealings for Fox. After that, we can branch out,” he reassured me.

“Fine,” I acquiesced, though I couldn’t shake the slight disappointment.

“Ryleigh, don’t get upset. You’re doing a great job, but there’s plenty for you to learn. It will take time,” he comforted me.

“I get it. I’ll leave you to your call,” I replied, trying to mask my feelings.

As he turned his attention to the ringing phone, I headed to the kitchen, craving the comforting embrace of caffeine. As the coffee maker hummed to life, I felt a pang of frustration. Oliver was right; there was so much I still needed to learn about Fox Asset Corporation’s dealings.

Rubbing at my temples, I waited impatiently for the machine to produce my salvation. This state-of-the-art contraption could conjure up any coffee concoction imaginable, from lattes to cold brews. Lost in my thoughts, I scrolled through my emails until Oliver emerged from his office, signaling the end of his call.

“Sweetheart, ready to go?” Oliver's voice pulled me from my thoughts.

“I guess,” I replied, still feeling a tad sullen.

“Still angry at me?” he asked, concern evident in his tone.

“No. I understand. Your company is big and there’s a lot to learn,” I conceded, trying to let go of my lingering frustration.

“I want you to concentrate on the real estate side and a few other things before we get you involved in my overseas business,” he explained, his arms enveloping me from behind as I washed my coffee cup. “You’re a smart woman. I know in a few more months, you’ll be up to speed on everything," he reassured me, planting a kiss on my temple.

"Suppose I don't want to be?" I challenged lightly, turning to face him.

He released me, allowing me to finish drying the cup before responding. "You don't want to learn the rest of my business?"

"I do. I want to know all there is to know," I clarified, placing the cup in the cabinet.

"Then stop giving me a hard time," he retorted with a playful grin.

"It's fun. You get riled up so easily," I teased, brushing past him.

"You're impossible," he sighed, following me into the closet.

"I aim to be. Who would keep you on your toes if it wasn't for me?" I quipped as I selected a pair of black ankle boots.

"I can think of a few people," he replied with a smirk.

"But not like me," I insisted, slipping on the boots.

"Ready?" he asked, changing the subject.

"Ready. I hope this day goes fast," I replied, mentally preparing for the day ahead.

"Are you wearing that outfit to dinner?" he inquired, eyeing my attire.

"Is it more formal?" I questioned, considering a change.

"Not really. I had Henri secure a table at Diamond Square," he revealed.

"That is a bit dressy. Maybe I should change unless we come back here before we go to dinner," I mused, scanning my wardrobe for alternatives.

"You're dressed fine," he assured me.

"You sure?" I sought confirmation.

"Positive. I think you look great. Purple suits you," he complimented, his gaze softening.

"What was that about Henri securing you a table at Diamond Square?" I probed, intrigued.

"I had him make a reservation," he explained casually.

"That's not what I mean. You own the damn place. Those people would bend over backward to accommodate the boss," I pointed out, a hint of amusement in my tone.

"You just love sticking that in my face, don't you? Eventually, you'll be their boss too," he countered, a playful glint in his eyes.

"Good. I plan to make use of that fact by stocking up on those delicious macarons," I grinned mischievously.

"I feel sorry for Mariah," he chuckled.

“Who’s that?” I asked, genuinely curious.

“The pastry chef. Macarons are her specialty,” he explained, amusement dancing in his eyes.

“Then I must thank her because those things are incredible,” I said appreciatively, reminiscing about the delectable treats.

“You promised to go to the gym and work extra hard,” Oliver reminded me gently, concern etched on his face.

“Afraid I’ll get fat, Fox?” I teased, trying to lighten the mood.

“Fat, thin, I don’t care because I love you either way,” he reassured me, sincerity lacing his words.

“Yeah, we’ll see when I gain thirty pounds during a pregnancy,” I quipped, a hint of sarcasm in my voice.

“I can deal with it because you’ll be carrying our baby. It doesn’t matter to me. I’ll help you lose it,” he responded earnestly, his eyes filled with love.

“Let’s get to the office. I want to get this day over with,” I suggested, eager to shift focus back to our daily routine.

Chapter 12

I reached under the table and dug my nails into Dillon's hand as it traveled up my leg. Oliver was engaged in conversation with James Ryder, seated on the opposite side. I found myself sandwiched between Dillon and Rick; the older men seemingly unaware of the situation. Dillon let out a yelp, hastily covering it up with a cough.

As he pulled his hand away, I noticed the marks my nails had left on his skin. He rubbed at them, avoiding my gaze as he took a long sip of his scotch. If anything, his alcohol consumption seemed to embolden him. Meanwhile, Rick appeared more interested in the discussion between James and Oliver, leaving Dillon free to persist.

"Why did you do that?" Dillon whispered, his voice laced with confusion.

"Are you kidding me?" I retorted, incredulous.

"No, I'm just being friendly," he insisted, his tone unconvincing.

"You're a pervert," I hissed, irritation evident in my voice.

"Something you two can bring to the conversation?" James interjected, casting a curious glance in our direction.

I looked up to see Oliver's stare fixed on Dillon's hand. One of the fading marks had started to ooze blood.

"No," Dillon said.

"I need to use the restroom; would you like to powder your nose?" Oliver said to me.

"Yes, as a matter of fact, I would."

I grabbed my purse and Callan and James stood as I got up. They were polite; I wish their sons had the same respect. Oliver placed his hand on my back and navigated me to a hallway that held the bathrooms as well as another door that led into a large office. This is where he brought me. His face was bright red and I knew he figured out what happened between Dillon and me.

"That motherfucker put his hands on you?" Oliver growled, his eyes dark with anger.

I nodded, feeling a mix of frustration and discomfort. "He's an asshole. He put his hand on my leg."

"I have to say something to Callan and James. Their sons are out of control, and I won't have them disrespecting you. I told you if they did anything, I would handle it immediately," he said, his tone firm and resolute.

"You have a good relationship with Callan and James. I don't want to get in the middle," I protested.

"I don't give a shit. You come first," he declared, his protective instincts kicking in.

"What are you going to do?" I asked, feeling a bit anxious about the potential fallout.

"I'll tell them you're not feeling well and let them finish dinner," he replied, his jaw clenched with determination. "But I'll speak with Callan and James privately tomorrow. No one touches my fiancée and gets away with it."

"I'm sorry to cause trouble," I sniffled, feeling guilty for the conflict.

"It's not your fault. You need to be assertive in business, or these guys will eat you alive," he reassured me, his hand gentle on my shoulder.

"Maybe you should put me in the PR department. I'm not cut out for this cutthroat stuff," I suggested, feeling a bit defeated.

"It comes with experience. Let's go home," he said, his voice softening as he guided me away from the table.

We returned to the table, and Oliver informed the Ryders that I wasn't feeling well. Dillon scowled when I glanced at him, as if I had done something wrong. I couldn't wait to get away from him. Oliver didn't bother to shake his or Rick's hand, instead telling Callan and James, he would see them in his office the next morning.

I felt nauseous when I got home and went to the bedroom to undress. Oliver was paging through his mail before he came into the closet.

“Sweetheart, are you all right?”

“I'm fine. I just want to take it easy.”

Oliver removed his suit and placed it in the dry-cleaning bag to give to the concierge. It was nice not to need to go to the dry cleaner, yet another thing I liked about living in a full-service building. After I got settled in bed, my cell vibrated with an incoming call.

As I collapsed onto the bed, trying to quell the nausea roiling in my stomach, my phone buzzed. Seeing Sadie's name flash on the screen, I quickly answered.

"Sadie, how are you?" I asked, forcing cheerfulness into my voice.

A soft sniffle came from the other end, making my stomach twist even tighter. "What's wrong?"

"I had a fight with Finley," she said, her voice shaky and full of tears.

"About what?"

"He's angry with me," her voice broke.

"That's obvious. Over what?"

"I'm pregnant."

I bolted upright so fast that I startled Oliver, who had just slipped into bed beside me. He stared at me, wide-eyed, as I gripped the phone tighter.

"What? When? How many months?"

"Three."

I bit my lip. "Three, and you're just telling me now? You were pregnant when we saw you for lunch. Why didn't you say anything then?"

Sadie sniffled. "We were engaged. You think I wanted to spring it on you all at once?"

"Is that why you didn't drink?"

"Yes. I found out when I was two months pregnant. And before you ask, Finley already purchased the ring before I told him. He wanted to marry me."

"What's his problem?"

"He's angry because he didn't want to do things this way. He wanted to spend time with me before we had a baby."

"Do you want me to talk to him?"

She was silent for a moment. "No. I think we'll be fine."

I let out a breath with frustration. "I think I should. Finley can be a stubborn ass. What about your wedding?"

"We decided to have a civil service and a small reception."

"Is that what you want?"

"It's what Finley wants."

I frowned. "You don't get a say? I thought you wanted a big wedding?"

"I do but I got pregnant."

"Uh, excuse me but it takes two to tango. You didn't make that baby yourself."

Oliver was staring at me the entire time I was talking. I wondered if he worried I would get pregnant before we got married. I had no intention and took my birth control pills religiously. I spoke to Sadie a few minutes more before I heard my brother in the background, and she said goodbye and hung up.

Oliver reached out, resting a hand on my arm, his eyes filled with a mix of curiosity and concern. "Is everything okay?"

“Sadie's pregnant?”

“Yes. Three months,” I said, my voice still tinged with disbelief.

Oliver's brow furrowed as he processed the news. "I knew something was up with your brother when I mentioned children."

"He's getting used to the idea, but he wanted to be married first," I explained, sighing softly.

"They had a fight?" Oliver asked, concern deepening his voice.

"Uh, huh," I confirmed, nodding. "And she's emotional because of the hormones. I'm going to be an aunt. How exciting."

Oliver cleared his throat, a small smile forming. "I'm going to be an uncle."

"You are." I grinned back. "When was the last time you were around kids?"

"Not recently," he admitted, rubbing the back of his neck. "I can understand Finley's hesitation to being a father. Running a company and having children is hard."

I chuckled, trying to lighten the mood. "How would you know? Do you have some floating around out there?"

Oliver didn't seem amused. "I was kidding," I added quickly.

"I know, but it's nothing to kid about. I'm sure Finley is scared," Oliver said, his expression serious.

"If you think so, then you don't know Finley. He always deals with things head-on, and he will with this too," I asserted, crossing my arms.

"Maybe not. Knowing you're having a child changes you," Oliver said, his tone reflective.

"You act like you know. Is this how you're going to act when I get pregnant?" I asked, raising an eyebrow.

"No, because we won't have children until after we're married," he replied, his voice firm.

"That's true since our wedding is seven months away. If I got pregnant now, I would still be pregnant in July," I said, half-joking.

"Is that supposed to be a joke?" Oliver asked, his irritation evident.

"Jesus Christ, Oliver, why so sensitive?" I snapped, feeling my frustration rise.

"I'm just feeling for your brother," he said, his voice softening.

"I'll talk to him later this week. I know he's stressed about his company," I said, trying to shift the focus.

"Why?" Oliver asked, curiosity piqued.

"He's working on several projects at once for clients, and a couple of the apps are giving him issues," I explained.

"So, he doesn't need the added stress of a baby," Oliver concluded.

"You men act like you have it so hard. We're the ones that have to carry the baby, gain weight, have our hormones all messed up, and breastfeed," I said, rolling my eyes.

"And we're right there with you. The good ones are anyway," Oliver responded, his eyes softening as he reached for my hand.

"I hope so," I said, squeezing his hand, feeling a bit more reassured.

I settled back into bed and turned on the television. The next day I planned to call my brother and give him a piece of my mind. I hated to see Sadie upset.

"I'm not ready to be a father," Finley said, his voice tight with strain.

I had finally managed to get him to answer after four attempts. "Stop being a dick. You're twenty-eight."

"I'm so busy with work, and there's no need for name-calling," he growled.

His voice sounded more strained than usual, and my instincts told me there was more to this. "Finley, is there anything else wrong?"

"Why would you think that?"

I laughed lightly. "I've known you my entire life. I know when something is wrong."

He hesitated, then sighed. “Finances. I know Sadie needs stability, but I’m not sure I can afford my apartment. I put almost my entire inheritance into my business.”

“What about the contracts and VC money you received?”

“Contracts don’t pay until I finish the applications. The VC money went to expanding the business. I spread myself too thin.”

Are you afraid of losing the business? What about a loan?”

“Loans are maxed out. I can’t borrow anymore. If I sell my apartment, that would give me several hundred thousand dollars to bolster the company, but we would have to move to a smaller place. I don’t want to do that to Sadie.”

“So, this really isn’t about not being ready to be a father. You’re worried you’ll disappoint Sadie?”

“You told me enough about what she had when she grew up. Her family is nice, but I know they struggle. Sadie talks about helping them. Their house needs work, and her parents are hoping the triplets get some type of scholarships.”

“What about Matthew?” I asked.

“I’ve borrowed from him and Anders. I can’t ask for more.”

“You never asked me. I could lend you.”

He exhaled loudly. "I was keeping you in my back pocket, hoping to work this out without asking."

"And Oliver. He could help you. Maybe you need some assistance with the books; he's great at finding money."

Finley's voice went up an octave. "Would he lend me money?"

"I would have to speak to him, and you know how he is. He would need to examine your books to see if it's a sound investment."

"Would it help if I used the brother-in-law card?"

I bit my bottom lip. "He might show you some sympathy, but don't bet on it."

Finley hesitated for a moment, the line crackling with silence. "Could you speak to him? I feel like a jerk getting in this position. I don't want to sell my apartment or lose my company."

My stomach churned, knowing that all the work my brother put into his company over the past few years could go down the toilet. "I'll talk to Oliver after I get off with you. I'm sure we can work something out."

"That would be wonderful. You're a lifesaver," Finley gushed.

"Don't thank me yet. I still need to talk to Oliver."

"Call me back."

"He might call you back."

"I'll be waiting. Thanks, Ry."

We hung up, and I sat for a few seconds, absorbing the weight of our conversation. Then I pushed my chair back and headed over to Oliver's office. I found my fiancé engrossed in reports on his laptop, taking meticulous notes on a piece of paper. He looked up and smiled when I entered. I shut the door before going to sit in front of his desk.

"Hey," he said, putting his pen down. "What's up? I heard you talking on the phone."

"Finley."

"Don't tell me you chewed him out because of what he said to Sadie," Oliver said, raising an eyebrow.

"I did, but I found out that's not the real reason he's upset," I replied, my tone softening.

Oliver stopped writing and leaned back in his black leather office chair, giving me his full attention. "What is?"

"His company is stretched thin financially," I said, watching his expression carefully.

Oliver stroked his chin thoughtfully. "And you thought I could help him out?"

"Either you or me. I can dip into my inheritance."

"No."

"No, you won't help him out? He said if he doesn't get a fresh infusion of cash, he'll have to sell his apartment. He doesn't want to put Sadie through a move. You know she needs financial stability," I pressed, feeling the tension rise.

"I meant no, I won't allow you to spend your inheritance," Oliver clarified, his tone firm.

"Does that mean you'll help him?" I asked, hope creeping into my voice.

"I need to see his books. I'm sure there's some waste," Oliver said, leaning forward, his eyes sharp with determination.

"And if there is?" I asked, my heart pounding.

"We'll trim it and discuss an investment. I can't invest in something that's not solid, but I might make an exception because he's family," he said, a small smile playing on his lips.

"I was hoping you would say that. He really needs our help," I said, relief washing over me.

"It's going to cost you," Oliver said, his eyes twinkling with mischief.

I rolled my eyes. "Sexual favors?"

"What kind of man do you take me for? I would never ask that of you," he said, feigning innocence.

I smirked. "Bullshit. You have before."

"When?" Oliver challenged, leaning back with a grin.

"Several times. You're a horrible boss. I should report you to HR," I teased, crossing my arms.

"What would you say?" he asked.

"I'd tell them how you try to seduce me while in the office. You've created a sexually charged atmosphere," I replied, matching his playful tone.

Oliver laughed, shaking his head. "Guilty as charged. But seriously, we'll help Finley. He's family, and that means something to me too."

I leaned over the desk and kissed him. "Thank you, Oliver. It means a lot to me."

He began to scribble a few more notes on his pad. "I have a few things to do before we leave."

"I meant to ask, how did your meeting go with James and Callan?" I asked, leaning against the doorframe.

Oliver sighed, rubbing his temples. "I had a few choice words about their sons. They were none too happy about their behavior and apologized."

"I'm sorry I put you in a bad position," I said, feeling a twinge of guilt.

"You didn't put me in a bad position. Their sons put them in a bad position," he corrected, his eyes softening as he looked at me.

"I guess it's something I'll have to get used to," I said, shrugging.

"Are you kidding me? You don't have to be sexually harassed to make a deal," Oliver said, his voice firm and protective.

"I know, but it's a common occurrence in business. Women get harassed and treated like second-class citizens with lower salaries and fewer promotions. We had a discussion in my business administration class," I explained, frustration evident in my tone.

"It does go on, but it doesn't go on here. If you're worthy, you get the salary and the promotion, no matter what your gender may be," Oliver said, his conviction clear.

"That's because you're a great boss," I said, smiling.

A grin danced on Oliver's lips. "You said I was a horrible boss not five minutes ago."

"Shut up. I have some things to finish," I retorted, rolling my eyes.

I heard him chuckling to himself as I exited his office, the sound following me down the hallway.

~

Vlad brought the limo to pick us up from work, and we couldn't keep our hands off each other. One night without sex was one night too long. Oliver bitched because I chose to wear slacks again, grumbling about how hard it was to get his hand in my panties.

"Deal with it," I murmured in his ear.

"In one minute, I'm going to strip you bare and fuck you until you scream," he growled, his breath hot against my neck.

"Promises, promises."

Oliver grasped the hem of my green cashmere sweater and pulled it up. My head got caught inside, and I struggled to get it off until he helped me.

"I love when you wear these innocent white bras," he murmured, his eyes dark with desire.

"Oh, does my virginal appearance turn you on?" I teased, arching an eyebrow.

"It does because it's so opposite."

"I'm a whore?" I asked, half-joking, half-curious.

"No, why would you say that?" he replied, looking genuinely puzzled.

"Isn't the opposite of a virgin a whore?"

"Not at all. I prefer to call it sexually adventurous."

I pulled my sweater back on, smirking. "What are you doing?"

"We're almost home. I'd rather spend time in bed than here in the limo."

"That sounds good to me," I agreed, feeling the anticipation build.

Vlad pulled up to our building two minutes later, double parking so we didn't have to spend too long in the frigid air. The wind was blowing fiercely, and it wouldn't surprise me if it was below zero. We hurried to the elevator, and I was relieved when it opened before we even hit the button. After the passengers got out, Oliver pulled me in and punched in the code for the penthouse.

"If there weren't cameras in here, I would do unspeakable things to you," he whispered, his voice full of promise.

"I thought you were a gentleman," I replied, teasing him.

"Have I ever claimed to be?"

"No, you haven't, but you did restore my honor today."

"I'd like to throttle those two for putting their hands on you," he said, his jaw tightening with anger.

"It's over," I reassured him, placing a hand on his chest.

"I told them I don't want their sons to come with them when we meet. What they did is the utmost disrespect, and they agreed," Oliver said, his eyes softening as he looked at me.

I nodded, grateful for his support. "Thank you, Oliver."

"Anything for you," he murmured.

He practically dragged me down the hall when the elevator opened, shoving his key in the lock and pushing me inside. He held onto my hand, slamming the door with his foot before he threw me over his shoulder and carried me down to our bedroom.

Oliver placed me next to the bed and began to undress me, dropping everything on the floor, including my coat. He left me in my underwear while he made the heap of clothing grow higher with his own piled on top.

"Get into bed."

I went to remove my bra.

"What are you doing?"

I frowned. "Taking off my underwear."

"Leave it on," I growled.

"Yes, sir."

I yanked the covers down and climbed onto the bed. Oliver's cock was pressing against his blue boxers, and my mouth watered as I thought about sucking him. I reached for him, but he backed away.

"No," he said firmly.

"I want to suck you. Why the hell do I have to beg?" I protested, frustration bubbling up.

"Because I'd rather be inside you," he replied, his voice husky with desire.

"Let me suck you, and then you can be inside me," I countered, determined.

"If you suck me, then I'll want to come in your mouth," he explained, his gaze intense.

"It's not like you don't recover quickly. I wonder when you'll slow down," I teased, a mischievous grin playing on my lips.

"Never, as long as I have you by my side. I'll be eighty and getting a hard-on for you," he said, a hint of amusement in his voice.

"I'll be sixty-six and probably all wrinkly. You might not want me," I joked, trying to lighten the mood.

"I'll always want you. Now stop giving me a hard time and lie down," he commanded, his tone firm yet loving.

I giggled as I laid back, slipping my hands under the pillow. Oliver prowled over my body like a panther, his kisses igniting a fire within me. My core clenched several times as his lips touched me, and I moaned softly as he latched onto my neck and sucked.

"Don't mark me," I murmured, my breath hitching with pleasure.

"Stop worrying," he whispered against my skin, his hands trailing down my body.

He kissed down my chest, teasing my nipples with his mouth before liberating my breasts from my bra.

Nibbling at my nipples, he continued his descent, his teeth tugging at the waistband of my panties.

"I'd like to tear these off you with my mouth," he murmured, his voice laced with desire.

"You might as well. You seem to like destroying my panties," I replied, a playful smirk on my lips.

"You can get whatever you want to replace them," he said, his fingers inching closer to my core.

"Good. I saw some six-hundred-dollar panties at Boudoir Fashions," I teased, enjoying the banter.

"Get them, use the card," he said, his tone playful yet commanding.

"You're crazy. I'm not spending that amount of money on panties," I protested, unable to suppress a laugh.

"Your whining is killing the mood. Stop talking," he declared, his voice tinged with amusement.

He wrenched down my panties, and I lifted my hips eagerly before he tore them off. I continued to tease him, but he silenced me with a passionate kiss before plunging his tongue inside me.

"Fuck! Oh God, Oliver, that feels so good," I moaned, my body writhing with pleasure.

He lapped at me, teasing my clit with his mouth, sending waves of pleasure coursing through me. I felt a massive orgasm building, but then he stopped, pulling out his penis and sliding it inside me. I squeezed my walls around him as he pumped into me, his hips slapping against mine.

“I’m gonna...” I gasped, my words trailing off as ecstasy washed over me.

I let out a loud scream as my orgasm ripped through me, my body trembling with pleasure. Oliver kept stroking inside me until I heard him grunt and release. He collapsed on top of me, and I wrapped my arms around him, feeling utterly satisfied and content in his embrace.

I let out a loud scream as my orgasm ripped through me. I closed my eyes, thrust my head back and Oliver kept stroking inside me until I heard him grunt and release. He collapsed on top of me, and I wrapped my arms around him.

“That was good,” Oliver whispered against my chest.

“Only good?” I teased, running my fingers through his hair.

“Did I say good? I meant great,” he corrected, a smirk playing on his lips.

“I’m hungry,” I announced, feeling the rumble of my stomach.

“We have crab salad,” Oliver suggested, beginning to shift off of me.

“Okay, get off me,” I joked, nudging him playfully.

“I want to lay here for a few more minutes. You smell good,” he admitted, his voice softening.

“So do you. I love your cologne,” I confessed, feeling a surge of affection for him.

“I love you,” Oliver said, his gaze warm as he looked into my eyes.

“I know that,” I replied confidently, snuggling closer to him.

“You’re very confident,” he remarked, a hint of amusement in his tone.

“I know I’m right. You do love me, and I love you,” I said, smiling up at him.

Oliver moved off my body, rolling to my side. I turned to face him and rested my head on his chest. He stroked my hair gently, tucking a strand behind my ear.

“I’m glad tomorrow is Saturday. I’m tired.” I admitted, feeling the exhaustion from the busy week settling in.

“We had a busy week. Next time we go to St. Croix, we spend a week,” Oliver suggested, his voice tinged with excitement.

“The next time we go will be in July. I want to be surprised,” I replied, feeling a sense of anticipation.

“Then I need to take a couple of days to check on the house in June,” Oliver said, his expression serious.

"No. I hate when you leave me," I protested, tightening my grip on him.

"Christ, Ryleigh, you can't have it both ways. I want to inspect the house and make sure it's to spec. Everything is made to withstand two-hundred-mile winds if we have a hurricane. I want to make sure it was built properly," he explained, his tone firm yet gentle.

"Then I'll go with you, but I won't accompany you to Fox Island," I compromised, trying to find a middle ground.

"Fine. You've gotten very attached to me," Oliver teased, a playful smirk on his lips.

"Don't flatter yourself, Fox. I just like your warm body next to me," I retorted, poking him in the side.

"I'll bet," he chuckled, his eyes sparkling with amusement. "Now, let's clean up and get some dinner."

Chapter 13

"Well?" I asked, hands on my hips, as Oliver walked through the door after spending four hours with Finley going over his books. He placed his brown briefcase on the floor and shook his head.

"It's not good," he replied, his expression grave.

A sharp twinge shot through my stomach as I stared at him, searching his face for any sign of reassurance. His sapphire eyes remained impassive, revealing nothing. I groaned in frustration.

"He can't lose the company. It's so important to him. I'm giving him the money," I declared, feeling the urgency of the situation.

"You'll do no such thing," Oliver countered, his tone firm.

I felt irritation rising within me. "Fuck you, Oliver. Don't you dare tell me I can't give my brother help. He has a baby on the way," I snapped, my emotions running high.

"Calm down, sweetheart. I'm giving him the investment. I was kidding, but you jumped so quickly that I didn't have a chance to explain," Oliver said, his voice steady.

My mouth dropped open in disbelief. "You were playing a joke?"

"Yes. Even if his books were a mess, I would've given him the loan. He has several contracts he's working on, and once finished, the funds will help bolster the business. Finley took on too much and exhausted his liquid cash. He had more going out than coming in because he needed to hire more programmers. That's a dangerous mix," Oliver explained, his words bringing a sense of relief.

"But his business is all right?" I asked, feeling the tension in my shoulders ease.

"Yes. Stewart Applications will be fine," Oliver confirmed.

A sigh of relief escaped me, and I pulled him into a big bear hug. My anxiety melted away in his embrace.

"You were gone a long time," I remarked, pulling back slightly to look at him.

"I took one of my accountants with me. We needed to examine Finley's books. He has little waste, but Jerold found a few areas he can tighten up," Oliver explained.

“How much interest are you charging him?” I inquired, curious about the terms of the agreement.

“None. The deal is that I obtain five percent of the company,” Oliver replied.

“And Finley was okay with that?” I asked, raising an eyebrow.

“He’s fine because we discussed how he can recover the five percent. I don’t mean to sound like an ass, but my attachment to his company can bring him more business,” Oliver admitted, a hint of self-awareness in his tone.

“You are an ass. I’ve told you many times,” I teased, unable to resist a playful jab.

“Yes, you have,” Oliver acknowledged with a chuckle.

“But this time I love you for being an ass. Thank you,” I said, sincerity in my voice.

“It’s business and family. I wouldn’t let your brother sink. I understand how important his company and Sadie are to him,” Oliver replied, his gaze softening.

“You made his security a reality,” I said, gratitude swelling within me.

“He made me promise not to say anything to Sadie about the investment. He doesn’t want her to know how close he came to selling their apartment. From what I see, even the funds from the proceeds wouldn’t cover his expenses," Oliver revealed, a sense of protectiveness in his tone.

"When are you giving him the money?" I inquired.

"It's already handled. I had my banker transfer the funds into his account," Oliver replied casually.

"On a Saturday?" I raised an eyebrow, impressed by his efficiency.

"I'm Oliver Fox," he said with a smirk.

"Dick," I muttered under my breath.

"Damn, Ryleigh, you're really hitting me hard today," Oliver teased.

"Stop being an arrogant ass," I retorted, though there was a hint of affection in my tone.

"It's part of my charm and the reason why you love me so much. What did you do while I was gone?" Oliver changed the subject, his curiosity evident.

"Made phone calls to Lisa, Benny, and Diane. I also spoke with Rachel Vicaria. My dress is coming along," I replied, excitement lacing my words.

"I'd still like to see it," Oliver said, a playful gleam in his eye.

"Dream on, Fox. You'll see it on July thirtieth. I also wrapped some gifts," I informed him, recalling my afternoon activities.

“Not my favorite activity,” Oliver admitted with a grin.

“If I know you, you had Henri do it,” I accused, knowing his penchant for delegating tasks.

Oliver bit his sensual bottom lip and smiled knowingly.

“No way. You made him do it?” I exclaimed, both amused and incredulous.

“He has style,” Oliver defended his choice.

“You’re unbelievable,” I shook my head in mock disbelief.

“Can I show you how unbelievable I am?” Oliver suggested with a mischievous glint in his eyes.

“How so?” I asked, playing along.

Without waiting for a response, Oliver scooped me up into his arms, planting kisses on my face as he carried me to the bedroom, our laughter filling the air.

~

On Monday, I woke up feeling grouchy. Oliver and I had a small argument about a Christmas tree, and his indecision was getting on my nerves. If he kept dragging his feet, there wouldn't be any trees left by the time he made up his mind. I stomped off to my office, plopping down in my chair and flicking open my laptop. With a jab of my black-painted nail, I powered it on.

. . .

As I logged into my email, I noticed one from Oliver. He had left me in the lobby that morning since he had a meeting in the financial district, which didn't involve me. I was on my own for the day, which suited me just fine. I clicked on his email, the subject line reading: "I'm sorry."

Sweetheart,

Don't be angry at me. Holidays are not my thing. I'm used to spending them alone or working. This is all new to me. We can discuss it when I see you this evening.

I love you with all my heart,

Oliver (Possessive Ass)

No kidding he was. I understood his reluctance to get a tree, but Christmas was one of my favorite holidays, and he was ruining it by not giving in. I knew he was trying, so I could at least give him that.

Throughout the day, I found myself snapping at Henri a couple of times, my bad mood refusing to abate. I apologized the second time; there was no reason to take it out on him. Henri was used to handling Oliver's demands, not mine.

He shouldn't have to deal with my mood swings since he wasn't my assistant. I didn't have one, and he was only helping me out by shuffling files back and forth from the recording room.

By the time Oliver returned, my mood had only worsened. The only silver lining was the slightly warmer weather, at least by mid-December standards. When Oliver knocked on my door, I called him inside, admiring his sharp suit — light gray with a dark purple tie and white shirt, a combination that framed his sexy body perfectly.

“Are you feeling better?” he asked.

“No. I’m still a bitch. I yelled at Henri,” I confessed, my frustration still evident.

A smirk played on Oliver's lips. “He can take it. I pay him well enough.”

“I apologized. He probably hates me and thinks of me as your side dish,” I grumbled.

Oliver inhaled sharply, his words slicing through the air with a sharp edge. "Don’t say that," he implored, his voice tight with a mix of frustration and hurt. "You’re my fiancée, not my side dish. Soon you’ll be my wife."

I felt a knot tighten in my stomach, a familiar ache that seemed to grow heavier with each passing day. "And that’s why I command respect around here," I retorted, my voice tinged with bitterness. "Not because of my Columbia education or qualifications. Because I’m Oliver Fox’s fiancée."

His suggestion to leave came as a relief, a chance to escape the suffocating atmosphere of the office.

"It's only 4:30," I protested weakly, but his gaze was imploring, urging me to relent.

"You can call it a day," he persisted, his tone softening. "Let's go home and order truffle burgers for dinner."

"I'm not hungry," I murmured, my voice barely audible as I struggled to meet his gaze.

“Why is it that you always have to be difficult?” Oliver's frustration bubbled to the surface, his words cutting through the tension like a knife.

A heavy silence hung between us, thick with unspoken words and unresolved tension. "You know why," I replied softly, my voice barely above a whisper.

Oliver rose from the chair in front of my desk, his movements tense and controlled. He retrieved my black wool coat; his actions deliberate as he waited for me to shut down my laptop. As I finally rose from my chair, he moved to kiss my lips, but I turned my cheek, a silent refusal that drew a sharp narrowing of his eyes.

As Oliver helped me on with my coat, his words hung heavy in the air, a tense cloud between us. "I hope you won't be like this all evening," he murmured, his voice tinged with a mixture of frustration and concern.

I couldn't help but let out a bitter laugh. "Afraid you won't get sex tonight?" My retort was sharp, laced with the bitterness that had become all too familiar in our exchanges.

His response was a resigned sigh. "I won't even attempt. I'm afraid you might bite my dick off."

A small smirk tugged at my lips despite my mood. "That would not serve me well. I rather like your dick."

"I think you more than like my dick," Oliver quipped, a hint of humor in his voice, "but I'll keep it to myself until you're in a better mood."

"Jerk," I muttered under my breath, turning away from him as he shook his head and helped me on with my coat.

Vlad was waiting downstairs with the black sedan, a silent witness to the tension that crackled between us. I slipped into the car, ignoring Oliver's presence beside me as we headed home. My thoughts churned with bitterness, knowing that the penthouse would be devoid of any Christmas cheer.

“Sweetheart?” Oliver's voice broke through my reverie, his concern evident even as I stared blankly out the window.

"What?" I snapped, my gaze fixed on the passing lights of the city adorned with festive decorations.

“Are you going to be angry at me all night?”

"Maybe. Maybe not." My response was curt, devoid of any

warmth as I continued to stare out the window, refusing to meet his gaze.

I heard him sigh beside me, the sound heavy with resignation, before he started tapping away on his phone. When we finally arrived at our building, I wished to escape his presence. I didn't want to touch him or speak to him, my mood darkened by the thought of returning to a Christmas-less penthouse.

Oliver waited for me, offering his hand which I waved away dismissively. Pulling my coat tighter around me, I made my way to the door, my steps heavy with the weight of my emotions. In the elevator, I stared down at my shoes, trying to block out the world around me.

We were nearly to the apartment when Oliver suddenly remembered the mail. He told me to go ahead as he headed back to the elevator. With a heavy heart, I unlocked the door with the key he had given me and pushed it open, only to freeze in astonishment.

The entire place was transformed, bathed in the warm glow of Christmas lights. A towering ten-foot tree dominated the living room, its branches adorned with an array of colorful ornaments. Red garland twirled around its length, and a festive tree skirt sat beneath, proclaiming "Merry Christmas" in cheerful green letters. Lights twinkled around the windows, casting a soft glow across the room, and festive decorations adorned every surface.

For a moment, I stood there, stunned into silence by the unexpected sight. Then, slowly, a small smile crept across my face, thawing the bitterness that had settled in my heart.

"I was busy today," Oliver's voice came from behind me, and I turned to face him, my eyes brimming with tears as I took in the sight of our transformed home. He had done this for me, despite his discomfort, and the realization flooded me with a mixture of gratitude and love. Without hesitation, I wrapped my arms around his neck, pulling him close as I planted a fervent kiss on his lips.

"You did this for me?" I sniffled, overcome with emotion.

"I'd do anything for you," he replied softly, his arms encircling me in a tight embrace. "All by yourself?" I asked, feeling a surge of wonder.

"I can't take all the credit. Anna helped me decorate," he admitted, his eyes twinkling with mischief.

Anna, one of Oliver's assistants, was known for her love of Christmas, and the thought of her lending a hand filled me with warmth.

"I don't know what to say," I admitted, feeling a lump form in my throat.

"An apology would be nice," he teased, a playful grin tugging at his lips.

"You're incredible, and I'm sorry," I replied earnestly, feeling a weight lift off my shoulders.

"Do you know what you're apologizing for?" he quipped, raising an eyebrow.

"Being a grouch and calling you names," I admitted sheepishly, feeling a flush of embarrassment.

"That would sum it up. Check out the patio," he urged, gesturing towards the sliding glass door.

Stepping closer, I peered outside and gasped in delight. The patio was adorned with twinkling lights and a smaller Christmas tree stood near the door, mirroring the festive display inside.

"You really went all out," I murmured, feeling overwhelmed by his thoughtfulness.

"I wanted you to be happy. I have a big surprise for you on Christmas Eve," he confessed, his eyes sparkling with anticipation.

"You know I hate surprises," I protested weakly, but he only grinned in response.

"Too bad. Get used to it. Wasn't this a surprise?" he teased, his tone laced with amusement.

"Yes, but what surprises me more is that you did this on your own. You could've hired someone," I pointed out, touched by his sincerity.

"I know, but then it wouldn't have been personal. My time is valuable, but it was well worth seeing the smile on your face," he replied earnestly, his gaze softening.

"I love you," I whispered, feeling a rush of warmth flood my chest.

"I know," he replied confidently, a smirk playing at his lips.

"Arrogant jerk," I teased, unable to hide the affection in my voice.

“There’s the name calling that I love so much.”

I shucked out of my coat and Oliver hung it in the foyer closet. We went to the closet to change, and I so wanted to do something for him. His gesture made me wet. Then again, he always made me wet by just being in his presence. I unzipped my dress, pulling it over my head and standing there in a pair of mauve lace underwear.

Oliver was unaware of my state of nakedness as he removed his suit coat and began working on his tie. I just leaned against the cold granite counter waiting for him to notice me and when he did, his eyebrows raised. My nipples were beaded, and my breasts ached for Oliver’s touch. He just stood there and stared.

"Do you need something?" Oliver's voice cut through the tension that hung heavy in the air.

"Would it surprise you if I said I needed to be fucked?" My words were laced with a mixture of desire and defiance, a challenge thrown into the charged atmosphere.

• • •

"With your appetite, not in the least," he replied, his tone tinged with amusement and a hint of longing.

"My appetite? What about yours?" I countered, feeling the heat of frustration rising between us.

"Do you want me to make love to you or do you want to argue?" His words were a low growl, thick with desire.

"Arguing makes for good makeup sex," I teased, a small smile playing at my lips as I watched the desire darken his eyes.

Oliver rolled his eyes, a silent acknowledgment of the familiar dance we found ourselves in. He reached down, his hand brushing against the fabric of his slacks as he stroked himself through the material. Without hesitation, I dropped down to my knees in front of him, my fingers deftly working at his zipper.

He gathered my loose hair in his hand, holding it gently as I released him from the confines of his clothing. I inhaled deeply, savoring his scent - a heady mix of clean musk and Oliver - as I tugged at his pants, bringing them down along with his black silk boxers.

He stood before me, his gaze locked on mine as I fisted his thick penis, licking the head with the tip of my tongue. A deep, guttural groan escaped his lips as I took him halfway into my mouth, relishing the taste of him.

Oliver's hips gently rocked back and forth, setting a rhythm as he fucked my mouth with a steady, controlled pace. I eagerly lapped up the precum that flowed from him, savoring every drop.

"Shit, Ry, that feels great. You know just what to do," he moaned, his voice thick with pleasure.

I hollowed my cheeks, applying more pressure as I sucked hard at his shaft, driving him closer to the edge. With a loud moan, he released himself into my mouth, the warmth of his cum filling me as I continued to work him until he finished.

When I finally released him and stood up, he kicked off his remaining clothing and scooped me into his arms, carrying me to our bed. In the soft glow of the blinking lights from the patio tree, Oliver made love to me, our bodies moving together in perfect harmony as the world outside faded away.

~

"Can these burgers get any better?" I said, taking a hulking bite and savoring the rich flavors.

"I doubt it," Oliver replied with a satisfied smile.

"Thank you for everything," I said, my gratitude spilling over.

"Sweetheart, you don't need to keep thanking me," he insisted, reaching across the table to touch my hand.

"I took you out of your comfort zone. I feel I do," I replied, squeezing his hand gently.

"I need to get used to celebrating holidays with family," he admitted, a thoughtful look in his eyes.

"Yes, you do. My family loves you," I assured him, feeling a warm glow of happiness.

"I'm glad," he said, his smile softening.

"If they knew what you did for Finley," I added, feeling a surge of pride.

"I'm not asking for praise. He has a stable business and just needed a hand," Oliver replied, his modesty evident.

"You didn't have to give it to him," I pointed out, knowing how much his support meant to my brother.

"I wanted to, and he was a sound investment," he said simply.

I leaned over and kissed him, tasting the red wine on his lips. The kiss deepened as I gently pushed my tongue into his mouth, feeling the heat between us flare. Oliver pulled me onto his lap, his hands roaming my body, cupping my breast and pushing my pink silk robe open. Desire curled through me like a hot wire, but I pulled away reluctantly.

"We're like two magnets," he said, his voice husky with desire.

"I agree, but I'm hungry," I replied with a laugh.

Oliver chuckled, moving me back to my seat so I could finish dinner. We capped our meal by feeding each other spoonfuls of chocolate chunk ice cream, the sweetness a perfect end to the night. After we finished, we snuggled in bed together, watching the first flurries of snow blanket the patio as we turned out the lights.

"Are you happy?" he asked, his arms wrapped around me.

"Very," I replied, feeling a deep sense of contentment.

"I'm glad. That's my goal," he murmured, his voice soft and tender.

"You've achieved that," I said, nestling closer to him.

As I dozed off in his arms, I fell into a deep, dreamless sleep, feeling safe and loved.

Chapter 14

Our lives grew hectic over the next couple of weeks leading up to the Christmas holiday. I barely saw Oliver during the day as I immersed myself in his company, discovering the vast array of his holdings. It was amazing how he kept up to date on almost all of them, juggling numerous responsibilities with ease.

As Christmas Eve approached, I sensed that Oliver was up to something. He had a certain gleam in his eye that hinted at a surprise, probably a gift for me. He planned to close the offices at noon that day, and the employees were hardly working, enjoying a catered holiday breakfast and exchanging Secret Santa gifts instead.

"Ready to go?" Oliver asked, ducking his head into my office with a smile.

"Yes, just shutting down my laptop," I replied, quickly wrapping up my work.

"Do we need to pick up anything for tomorrow?" he asked, his tone casual but his eyes twinkling.

"Only Matthew, Finley, and Sadie," I said, excitement bubbling within me.

Christmas at my parents' house promised to be special. Sadie and Finley would be announcing her pregnancy, and I knew my mother would be overjoyed at the prospect of a grandchild, even though she would be a young grandmother at forty-nine. She adored babies.

"I know them, but anything for dessert?" Oliver teased.

"You already sent pies and pastries. Give it a rest," I laughed, shaking my head at his generosity.

Oliver smirked, clearly pleased with himself. The day before, while we were at work, he had arranged for Vlad to drive the desserts up to Westchester and drop them off at my parents' home. My mother called to tell me we had sent too much; more than seven people could possibly eat. I told her to talk to Oliver since it was all his idea.

As we made our way to the elevator, we said our goodbyes to everyone we passed. The elevator was crowded, and Oliver sought out my hand, holding it firmly as we moved to the back of the car. He kept hold of my hand all the way to the limo, and during the drive to his penthouse, his grip never wavered.

When we arrived, Oliver turned to me with a mysterious smile. "Go upstairs by yourself," he instructed.

Curious and slightly puzzled, I nodded. "Okay, but what's going on?"

"You'll see," he said, his smile widening. "Just go upstairs, and I'll join you in a bit."

I couldn't help but smile back, my anticipation growing as I made my way to the elevator and headed up to the penthouse. Whatever Oliver had planned, I knew it was going to be something special.

“Why?”

He pinched the bridge of his nose and closed his eyes, “Does everything have to be a test? Just do as I ask for once.”

“I’m going.”

He waited until I was safely in the elevator and the doors closed to walk to the concierge desk. I wondered what he was up to. I went inside and changed into a pair of dark blue sweats and a gray Columbia t-shirt. Oliver strolled through the door about ten minutes later.

“What’s going on?” I asked with suspicion in my voice.

“Nothing. I had to get the mail,” he said as he held up a few envelopes then shucked out of his coat. I settled on the couch and picked up a magazine when I heard whining coming from outside the door.

“Oliver?” I called him but didn’t answer me and I listened closely, tossed the magazine on the coffee table and edged to the door. It was a soft whine and I yanked it open to find a blue hard-shell carrier with a red bow on the top. A card was attached that read “Merry Christmas, Mommy.”

Inside was a small black and white French bulldog, who looked strikingly similar to Blackie. I knelt on the floor and popped open the wire door, gently taking the pup into my arms. Instantly in love, I pressed my nose to the top of his head, cooing softly and cradling him.

"Do you like him?" Oliver’s voice came from behind me, filled with excitement.

I looked up to see him standing there, a huge smile lighting up his face. "He’s beautiful. How did you know I wanted a dog?"

"Come on, sweetheart. You think I don’t hear you? You talk about how much you love Blackie," he said, his smile growing even wider.

"How old is he?" I asked, marveling at the little bundle of joy.

"Ten weeks. He’s had his check-up and shots," Oliver informed me, his eyes twinkling with pride.

"We have nothing to feed him. We have to go out," I fretted, already planning a list in my head.

Oliver scowled playfully. "On Christmas Eve? Not a chance. Everything is taken care of. I have toys, training pads, a bed, bowls, puppy chow, and a leash. I wanted to get you a collar, but you need to pick out his name first."

"I can't believe you did this," I said, my voice full of wonder.

"Merry Christmas," he said warmly.

I stood up with the puppy in my arms and went to Oliver. His sapphire eyes shone with affection, and I stood on my tiptoes to give him a kiss on his sensual lips.

"I guess I'll be taking a back seat to this little fellow," he teased.

"Not a chance, but you are very high on my list," I replied with a smirk.

I carried the puppy inside, and Oliver took the carrier, placing it in the foyer. I put the puppy on the floor and sat down with him. He walked around, sniffing and stopping every few seconds to look around, unsure of his surroundings.

"What shall I name him?" I mused aloud.

"It's up to you. He's yours," Oliver said, watching us with a contented expression.

The puppy eyed the tree and made a beeline for the many presents stacked under it. Before I could grab him, he was hidden in a sea of red, green, silver, and white gift bags of different sizes, moving further underneath. I shoved them out of the way and grabbed him before he got lost.

"I should call him Mischief or Trouble. He's already getting into some," I said, laughing.

Oliver disappeared into his office and came back with a doggy bed, bowls, and training pads. I wondered if he got some cleaning solution for dog urine, remembering Blackie's accidents on Matthew's carpets. Our home had expensive furniture and carpets, and I was sure Oliver wouldn't be pleased if the dog used any of them as his toilet.

I put the puppy down again, and once more he made a beeline for the tree. I managed to grab him before he burrowed in and out of reach.

"Definitely Trouble," I declared.

"Then Trouble Fox it is," Oliver said with a chuckle.

"Where was he?" I asked, curious about how he had kept the surprise.

"With the concierge. I had my security staff taking care of him," he replied nonchalantly.

I rolled my eyes. "Really? That's not their job."

"They were guarding him. He is part of the family," Oliver said, his tone serious but his eyes twinkling with amusement.

Trouble ended up falling asleep on his doggy bed after we played with him for a little while. He was utterly pooped. We ordered Chinese food, and had it delivered, setting up a cozy dinner as we watched him doze on his bed near the terrace doors.

“He’s so sweet. Thank you for a wonderful gift,” I said, glancing lovingly at the little pup.

“There’s plenty more where that came from,” Oliver replied with a grin.

“I know. For you too.”

“Would you like to open some up tonight?”

“Maybe after dinner. It’s weird not being with my parents,” I admitted, feeling a pang of homesickness.

“We could go if you want to. I’m sure Vlad won’t mind the drive,” Oliver offered.

“Absolutely not. I dragged it out of him that he was spending the night with his girlfriend. How does he even have time to date with the schedule you keep him on?” I asked, half-teasing, half-serious.

“I’m not that bad. Besides, I’m sure he’s more than happy to do it with the bonus I gave him.”

“How much?”

“Let’s just say it’s a lot. He does a lot for me,” Oliver said, nonchalantly.

“For us. Did you call Jonah?” I asked, changing the subject.

“He’s doing fine. As long as he’s behaving himself.”

"Did the crew go home for the holiday?"

"I suspect most of them did. I gave them off for a few days. I think Charles stayed, and Jonah's not going anywhere. I bet a few others stayed also."

I dug my chopsticks into a container of sesame chicken, putting a small piece into my mouth. "Do you miss not sharing holidays with anyone?" I asked, curiosity mingled with concern.

"I never took time to think about it. I occasionally went on trips with Dax or Wilmer. Ivan was playing hockey, so we almost never saw him during the holidays."

"It hurts me to think you were alone," I said, my heart aching for him.

"Don't be hurt. I chose to be alone. I was busy with my business. Holidays were just ordinary days until you came along. If I had business overseas, Japan, China, or Australia, it was the next day already and business as usual."

"That still makes me sad," I murmured.

"You changed all that. Thanksgiving was the first holiday in a long time that I spent with family."

He plucked a piece of fried shrimp from the white cardboard container and held it to my mouth. I gently bit into it as he pulled the tail away and dropped it on a napkin.

"You're sexy," he said, his voice low and husky.

I licked my lips. "So are you."

He grinned at me with a wink and popped another piece of shrimp in his mouth. God, I loved him.

We finished our dinner, savoring the last bites of our meal, and I felt a warm sense of contentment. The flickering lights from the Christmas tree cast a cozy glow over the room, and Trouble snored softly from his bed, his tiny body rising and falling with each breath. This Christmas was already shaping up to be the most special one yet.

The crackling of the wrapping paper proved irresistible to Trouble. As we opened gifts and pulled tissue paper from the colorful bags, the puppy rolled around, trying to chew on the wadded balls until Oliver grabbed a bag and started shoving the garbage inside.

My fiancé had been incredibly generous with his gifts. I unwrapped several pairs of precious stone earrings, sexy lingerie—which I suspected was more for his benefit than mine—cashmere sweaters in various shades of blue, Christian Louboutin heels and boots, a gift certificate to La Roma Day Spa, a Cartier watch, and a gold bracelet. And that was just the beginning; there were still several bags with my name on them under the tree.

Oliver, on the other hand, was notoriously difficult to shop for. What do you buy for a man who has everything?

I had opted for several silk shirts with his monogram, silk boxers, and chocolate paints, which made his eyes light up when he opened them. I also chose some unusual gifts for his desk at work—stress relievers and a personal vibrating massager for his neck. When he took it out of the bag, he raised an eyebrow at me.

"What exactly is this used for?" he asked, a mischievous glint in his eyes.

"It's for all the knots in your neck when you're tense," I explained, trying to keep a straight face.

"When I'm tense, I just walk next door to your office. There are other things I can do to relieve stress," he said, his voice low and suggestive.

I felt heat creep up from my neck as I remembered what we did in my office during lunch a week ago. Oliver had come in after a particularly difficult negotiation for a piece of property, ranting about what a bastard the former owner was. I had ended up riding him until the tension melted away and his bark simmered to a whisper.

"Don't remind me," I said, feeling the blush spread across my cheeks.

"Oh, I won't let you forget," he teased, pulling me close for a kiss. His lips were warm and insistent, and I melted into his embrace.

"There are rules," I said, trying to keep my voice steady.

"My company, my rules," he said smugly.

I leaned back, crossing my arms. "I knew you would say that. It still doesn't make it ethical just because it's your company."

"I'm not screwing just anyone. I'm making love to my fiancée."

I smirked. "Doesn't make it right. I'm sure human resources would agree."

"Will you tell them?" he asked, raising an eyebrow.

"Why would I do that? I'd have to admit to my bad behavior."

"That means you condone that type of behavior," he said, moving closer, feeling the heat rise between us.

"As long as the behavior is aimed toward me by only you."

"I hope so, or else I'll fire the offender's ass."

"Hypocrite," I mumbled, the word slipping out before I could stop it.

Oliver chuckled. "Thank you."

I rolled my eyes. "Open more of your gifts."

By the time we opened half our gifts, I was ready for bed, exhaustion pulling at my limbs. I knew I'd sleep tonight. Oliver would just have to behave. I placed a few towels in the large carrier and gently put Trouble inside, bringing him into the bedroom.

I wanted him to be close. After changing and brushing my teeth, I settled into bed. Oliver left the Christmas lights on outside on the patio, their soft glow casting a warm ambiance. I loved watching them while we lay together. He took me in his arms and kissed the top of my head, and I stroked his bare chest.

"Thank you for a lovely evening," he said, his voice a soothing rumble.

"Ditto. I still can't believe you got me a puppy."

"Hopefully he won't make noise during the night."

We weren't so lucky. A couple of hours later, Trouble was whining and crying in the carrier. I shook the grogginess from my head, slipped out of bed, and opened the carrier.

"Is he okay?" Oliver asked, his voice thick with sleep.

"Yes. He's probably just lonely. Blackie was the same way." I cradled the puppy in my arms, his tiny body warm and soft against me. He fell back to sleep, and I carefully placed him back into the carrier. He gave us another couple of hours before he stirred again. This time, I felt one of the towels in his crate was wet. He must have had to pee. I changed it and slipped him back inside, where he quickly fell back to sleep.

Returning to bed, I felt Oliver's arms wrap around me again, pulling me close. "You're amazing, you know that?" he murmured into my hair.

I smiled, snuggling into his warmth. "I try."

"Goodnight, Ryleigh."

"Goodnight, Oliver."

Christmas was my favorite holiday, but I was slow to get up. Trouble had woken me once more, and I didn't want to get out of bed. Oliver, ever chipper, got up before me and took the carrier out of the room. I assumed he was feeding the puppy and starting to train him to pee on the pads or outside on the patio. I fell back to sleep and was next awakened by Oliver as he pushed up my t-shirt to place kisses on my back.

"Merry Christmas," I mumbled, my voice thick with sleep.

"Merry Christmas to you. Are you planning to get up?" Oliver's voice was warm, playful.

"What time is it?" I asked, trying to shake off the remnants of sleep.

"A little after eight. Trouble is fed and napping on his doggy bed."

"Did he pee?" I asked, my maternal instincts kicking in even as I remained buried in the sheets.

"Yes, and poop. He's smart," Oliver replied, a hint of pride in his voice.

"I hope he won't soil any of the carpets," I said, finally opening my eyes.

"I didn't get him without expecting such. He's a puppy. Accidents will happen. We can have the carpets cleaned."

"You're very agreeable this morning," I noted, smiling at his optimism.

He moved the covers off my behind and gently bit into my ass cheek. "You have to admit you're the only one I'm agreeable with, and that's all the time."

"Not always," I teased, turning to look at him.

"But most of the time." He continued to rain kisses on my body, heating me and making my core flood with desire. I knew my panties were probably soaked when he came up for air.

"I'd like to make love to you before we shower. Is that possible?" he asked, his eyes darkening with want.

"You're negotiating?" I arched an eyebrow, half-amused, half-aroused.

"Will it work?"

"Why don't we do it in the shower? Kill two birds with one stone."

"Now that sounds like a negotiation." Oliver scooped me up against his body, and it was then I realized he was wearing a sweat-soaked gray t-shirt.

"You worked out?" I asked, surprised.

"Yes. You said I'm getting older, so I need to keep in shape."

"You're ridiculous."

"And you're gorgeous."

I was sure I wasn't. My hair was probably a matted mess, and I didn't wash my mascara off last night, leaving me with raccoon eyes. It was confirmed when Oliver put me down to undress in front of the vanity mirror.

"Ugh, look at me," I said, cringing at my reflection.

"I have, and I am," he said, pulling off his shirt and discarding it in a hamper at the bottom of the linen closet.

"I think you need glasses."

"I have them."

"For reading. I think you need them all the time."

"What kind of superficial ass do you take me for? I love all of you, no matter what you look like on the outside at a particular time."

I turned to face him, his sincerity melting away any lingering insecurity. "You always know the right thing to say."

"It's because I mean it," he replied, taking my hand and leading me toward the shower.

"I love you," I said huskily.

"I know."

"Jerk."

He chuckled. "There's the sass I can't get enough of."

I giggled as he pushed me under the water and massaged shampoo in my hair. By the time we came out of the shower, our skin was like prunes. Oliver made sure to work me over with his tongue before he penetrated me against the tiled wall. We did this twice before we came out and dried each other.

"Thank you for a fun Christmas morning."

"No, thank you, Miss Stewart."

We stayed away from each other as we dressed for the day. There was an electrical charge in the air and if we ignited it again, we would never get out of here. I chose to wear a pair of jeans and a light blue cashmere V-neck sweater that Oliver had given me for Christmas. I topped it off by inserting beautiful sapphire studs in my ears, another gift from him. They reminded me of his gorgeous eyes.

Oliver chose a pair of black slacks and a gray cowl neck sweater. He looked handsome and almost boyish with his hair slightly tousled. By the time we left, it would be neatly styled. I went to him, rubbing at the scruff that lined his jawline.

“I like when you don’t shave.”

“You want me to grow a beard?”

“Not a beard but I like this,” I said as I rubbed his face.

I took my hand away as I saw his eyes grow dark. It was a look I knew well and signaled he was aroused.

“I think we should have a light breakfast,” he said.

“I’m starved but light is right because my mother will go crazy like every year. Prepare to be stuffed.”

Oliver puffed his chest out. “If she serves like she did on Thanksgiving, I’m ready.”

He took my hand, and we walked out to the kitchen where I found Trouble sleeping in his oversized dog bed. He raised his head when he saw us. I went to him, and he whined as I petted his soft baby fur, crooning about what a good boy he was. I let him get settled before I stood up and turned to see a spread of bagels, muffins and pastries on a tray.

“What’s this?” I asked, my eyes widening as I took in the spread on the table.

“Breakfast. Do you want a latte?” Oliver asked, already moving toward the coffee machine.

“Yes, please. When did you get these?” I picked up a cranberry muffin, my favorite.

“I ordered them and picked them up when I went downstairs to work out,” he replied, his back to me as he set up the machine.

“Why didn’t you have them delivered?”

“Because you’re nosy and I wanted it to be a surprise.”

I scowled at him, crossing my arms. “I’m not nosy. I’m curious.”

“That’s what you’re calling it?”

“It’s more appropriate.”

“Uh, huh,” he said with a smirk.

I couldn’t help but smile at his back as he busied himself with the latte. Taking a napkin, I bit into the muffin, savoring the tartness of the cranberries. We enjoyed a leisurely breakfast while Oliver occasionally checked his phone for emails. It was a workday overseas, and I knew he was waiting for some information from a Japanese company relating to machinery for one of his factories.

A half hour later, we were ready to begin our drive to my parents' house after picking everyone up. It was chilly, but we wouldn’t be outside long. Anders usually liked to get a game of touch football together in the backyard, but I doubted many people would participate. I didn’t like football, and Sadie was pregnant, which my parents and Sadie’s family didn’t know but would find out today.

Vlad was waiting in front of the building with the limo, and he took Trouble's carrier from me, setting it inside. The puppy was whining, so I moved to where he was and took him out, setting him on my lap. He quieted and put his head down on my leg. I was already in love with my little boy. I looked up at Oliver, who shook his head.

"Keep that up, and he's going to be one spoiled dog," Oliver said, a teasing glint in his eyes.

"You should talk about spoiling."

"It's my pleasure."

"Hypocrite," I whispered, a playful grin tugging at my lips.

Oliver grinned as we headed toward Matthew's building. When we pulled up, he came out with his doorman, Martin. Matthew was carrying Blackie's carrier while Martin was loaded down with colorfully wrapped presents. Vlad exited the vehicle to place them in the trunk while Matthew slid into the seat beside Oliver. Blackie immediately barked, and Trouble raised his head, then stood up on my lap.

"Shit, is that a puppy?" Matthew asked as he smoothed his perfectly coiffed hair.

"Yes, it is. My fiancé got me a puppy. His name is Trouble."

Matthew chuckled as Blackie continued to bark and he opened the carrier to let him out.

“I’m not sure that’s a good idea,” Oliver said.

“Blackie is a sweetheart. He won’t hurt Trouble.”

Blackie came over to my lap and climbed up on the seat. Trouble was curious and sniffed at the older dog then plopped down on my lap again with disinterest. I petted Blackie and he sat down next to me, occasionally sniffing at Trouble.

“Looks like they’ll be buddies,” Matthew said.

By the time we got to Finley and Sadie’s building, the dogs were asleep, and I couldn’t stop petting either one of them. The same procedure was repeated as my brother and soon to be sister-in-law came down with their arms loaded with presents. Oliver and I escaped the ritual by having Vlad drop our presents off the day before with the desserts. Sadie sat on the other side of me, cooing over the puppy as we drove toward Hudson Brook.

“When are you springing the news on Mom and Anders,” I heard Matthew ask my brother. I looked up at Sadie.

“You told him too?” I asked.

“Finley did. Everyone knows except your parents and my family so act surprised.”

Sadie’s parents, Kristen and Mark, and her triplet brothers, Paul, Peter and Perry would be sharing Christmas with us. It would be joyful as well as tension filled because Mark had just been laid off from his job as a budget analyst and their financial situation was precarious. It was especially so since the triplets would be going off to college next year. I was hesitant to ask Oliver if he could help.

“I can do surprised, I had plenty of practice.”

Oliver raised his eyebrows. “You should be used to it and if you’re not, you should adjust. I plan to surprise you often for the rest of your life.”

“Surprises aren’t necessary.”

“But they keep life interesting so humor me please.”

Sadie and I giggled and chattered on about our weddings while Matthew, Finley and Oliver discussed the financial markets. It was a subject I found boring and argumentative.

Chapter 15

We pulled up to my parent's white colonial with gray shutters just before noon, the familiar sight triggering a rush of memories. Each of us piled out of the car, carrying gifts and anticipation. My mother, true to form, had gone all out for Christmas.

As we greeted everyone, the atmosphere was festive, but I couldn't shake the sense that something was off. Sadie's parents wore smiles, but their eyes betrayed worry. My best friend had confided in me that Finley had stepped in to help them financially until Mark found a new job. It was a gesture of kindness, but it spoke volumes about their struggles. Her mother's job as an office manager barely covered the bills.

Amidst the chatter and laughter, I excused myself, feeling a headache building behind my eyes. The room was suffocatingly loud, and I needed a moment of respite. As I stepped out of the bathroom, Oliver was waiting, a determined look in his eyes. Before I could protest, he pushed me back inside, locking the door behind him.

"What are you doing?" I asked, my voice a mix of surprise and amusement.

"You're too sexy for me to ignore," Oliver replied, his eyes smoldering with desire.

"You weren't ignoring me. You were socializing, which surprises me," I pointed out, raising an eyebrow.

"Why?" he asked, stepping closer, his gaze intense.

"Because you're usually more subdued," I said, feeling a flutter of anticipation in my chest.

"I'm trying. I want a family again," he confessed, his voice low and vulnerable.

"You have one," I reminded him, reaching up to brush his cheek with my fingertips.

He leaned in, pressing his mouth to mine, a soft sigh escaping him as he deepened the kiss. I melted into his embrace, my hands tangling in his hair as he cradled the back of my head.

"That familiar flutter began in my stomach and moved its way down." I whispered, feeling the heat building between us.

“Stop. You’re getting me hot,” I murmured against his lips, my breath coming in shallow gasps.

“Good. Then I haven’t lost my edge,” he whispered back, his voice husky with desire.

“Seriously? You’re very sexy and mine,” I teased.

“I see the way Sadie’s brothers are looking at you,” he said, his sapphire eyes flashing with jealousy.

“They’re seventeen. You’re jealous of teenagers?” I laughed, shaking my head.

“I’m jealous of anyone who thinks they have your attention,” he confessed, his tone serious.

“They don’t. I’m not into teenagers,” I assured him, wrapping my arms around his neck.

“Who are you into?” he asked, his voice dropping to a seductive whisper.

“Sexy titans of the world,” I replied with a smirk, running my fingers through his hair.

“Titans?” he repeated, raising an eyebrow in amusement.

“Do you not own everything?” I teased, tracing the outline of his jaw with my fingertip.

“Not quite,” Oliver replied, a hint of mystery in his tone.

“But close enough,” I said with a small smile, feeling a surge of affection for him.

I had seen much of the accounting for Fox Asset Corporation and its subsidiaries. I knew Oliver was a billionaire, but I never felt compelled to check where he fell in relation to his counterparts. He wasn't the type to discuss his finances, but he would if I asked.

"If you say so," I said, letting the topic drop for now.

"Oliver, do you think you can do something for Mark?" I asked, changing the subject.

"I'm not sure. What does he do?" Oliver inquired, his brow furrowing in thought.

"Talk to him. I'm sure you'll find he's quite knowledgeable. He's a budget analyst," I explained.

"Do you have any idea why he was laid off?" Oliver asked, concern flickering in his eyes.

"He worked for Colson Electronics. They were downsizing," I replied, a hint of frustration creeping into my voice.

"I'm well aware of their financial issues. Poor management is the problem with that company," Oliver commented, shaking his head.

"Do you think you can help?" I pressed, hopeful.

"Why Miss Stewart, if I didn't know better I would think you were asking me to give your sister-in-law's father a job," Oliver teased, a twinkle in his eye.

"First off, she'll be your sister-in-law too, and he would

be like a father-in-law once removed, which means family," I retorted, matching his playful tone.

Oliver chuckled, "You would spin it that way. No promises, but I'll talk to him."

"We better get back before everyone thinks we're up to something in here," I said, feeling a surge of warmth at his promise to help.

"I'd like to be," Oliver whispered, his voice low and suggestive.

"What is with you lately?" I asked, raising an eyebrow in amusement.

"I enjoy your body," Oliver replied, his gaze lingering on me.

"I think you more than enjoy it, you're obsessed," I said, feeling a blush rise to my cheeks.

"No, not obsessed. In love," Oliver said softly, pressing a gentle kiss to my cheek.

We made our way back to the living room, where Oliver immediately engaged Mark in conversation. At first, the man was reluctant, but as Oliver asked probing questions, a discussion began to unfold.

Meanwhile, I headed to the kitchen to help, where I found my mother speaking in hushed tones to Kristen, who was sniffling and dabbing at her cheeks. Sensing their need for privacy, I quietly backed out of the room, not wanting to intrude.

"Who wants to play touch football?" Anders called out, his voice carrying through the house.

I groaned playfully. "Go play your Neanderthal sport."

"Come on, Ryleigh, play with us," Perry urged, his voice cheerful and inviting.

He, like his brothers, was tall, lean, and rangy, with a mop of sandy brown hair and light gray eyes. Despite being triplets, each had their own distinct personality, and I found Perry to be the most endearing. He was always full of fun and told the silliest jokes. Peter and Paul were more reserved. Sadie had told me they were battling for the valedictorian spot of their graduating class. Both had received early acceptance to several Ivy League schools with almost full scholarships, which I was sure was a relief for Kristen and Mark.

Sadie and I followed the men out to the backyard, where the grass had turned straw-colored from the onset of winter. I bundled my coat around my neck as we settled into folding chairs to watch them play.

"Why are we out here?" I asked, pulling my coat tighter around me against the chill.

"To watch them play some ridiculous game with an oblong ball," Sadie replied with a smirk.

"At least they're not tackling each other. I worry about Finley," I remarked, my gaze flickering to where Oliver was joining the game.

“Oliver is older,” Sadie pointed out. “Do you worry that he’s so much older than you?”

“No. He’s healthy and takes care of himself,” I responded confidently.

“But when he’s fifty, you’ll still be in your thirties,” she said.

“Age doesn’t matter to me. I love Oliver.”

She shrugged. “I was just wondering.”

Sadie and I were chatting absentmindedly when a scream pierced the air. I looked up to see Oliver clutching his hand, his pinkie bent at an odd angle. My heart lurched, and I immediately jumped up and ran to him.

“Fuck!” Oliver growled through clenched teeth, his face contorted in pain.

Mark, who was a volunteer fireman, approached Oliver. “It’s dislocated. You have two choices. Let me put it back or sit in the hospital for four hours to have them do the same thing.”

“I think I can take my chances with you,” Oliver replied grimly, his jaw set in determination.

Tears welled in my eyes as Oliver braced himself, and Mark prepared to reset the finger. Unable to watch, both Sadie and I turned our backs, but the men around us were fascinated by the process. I winced as I heard Oliver grunt in pain as Mark completed the procedure.

. . .

With the game over, everyone retreated inside the house so Mark could splint Oliver's finger to the one next to it, which happened to be his ring finger. It held the sapphire ring I had bought for his birthday a few months ago.

"Are you okay?" I asked.

"I'm fine. It stings."

"You should take your ring off."

"Stop worrying about me," he growled.

I contorted my face. It stung and my heart hurt that he wouldn't let me show him the same type of care that he always showed me when I didn't feel well. I walked ahead of him and slipped through the sliding glass door, hurrying upstairs to my old bedroom. He couldn't pursue me since Mark was splinting his finger. I shut the door and looked around.

It had been a while since I stepped into this room, but my mother's meticulousness kept it unchanged. Everything was exactly as I remembered from the summer before my senior year. My queen-sized bed was neatly made, adorned with a powder blue comforter. Matching curtains adorned the windows, offering a glimpse into the backyard. Above my small desk hung a full collage of pictures, each one a cherished memory.

I went to the closet and retrieved a shoebox-sized plastic container. Inside lay stacks of pictures and mementos from my childhood. Seating myself on the royal blue carpet, I delved into the box, lost in memories.

A few minutes later, the door creaked open, and Oliver stood there. Ignoring his presence, I continued sorting through the box. He entered the room and closed the door, sitting down beside me. When he reached out, I recoiled.

“Don’t touch me,” I said sharply, my voice tinged with frustration.

“I’m sorry,” Oliver murmured, his expression contrite.

“Fuck you, Oliver. Why can’t I care for you? Why can’t I worry about you?” I demanded, my anger bubbling to the surface.

“That’s not your job. It’s mine to worry about you,” he replied softly, his eyes searching mine.

“Why? Because you’re so bulletproof that nothing can hurt you?” I retorted, my tone laced with bitterness.

“No. I don’t need you to upset yourself,” Oliver said gently, reaching out again.

“Tough. If you don’t like it, then don’t be with me. I can’t change the way I do things. I worry about you just like I do anyone I love,” I snapped, my voice cracking with emotion.

I picked up a pile of pictures, attempting to distract myself. Oliver tucked a strand of hair behind my ear, and I felt a flicker of annoyance. His chuckle grated on my nerves as I stumbled upon a Halloween picture from fourth grade, dressed in a pumpkin costume with a green hat and face paint.

“Look how adorable you are,” Oliver remarked, his voice filled with fondness.

“I looked ridiculous,” I replied, feeling a flush of embarrassment at the sight of my childhood costume.

“I want to have a little girl just like you were,” Oliver confessed, his eyes softening with emotion.

His words caught me off guard. We had discussed children before, but this was the first time he had expressed such a specific desire.

“You want a little girl?” I asked, feeling a flutter of excitement mingled with apprehension.

“One just like her mama,” he affirmed, his gaze unwavering.

“Suppose I have boys?” I queried, curiosity tingeing my voice.

“I’ll love them just as much,” he replied without hesitation, his sincerity evident. He sat down next to me.

Leaning over, he gently licked around the rim of my ear, sending shivers down my spine.

"Don't be upset with me," he whispered, his breath warm against my skin.

I reached out, gently taking the hand with the dislocated finger and kissed his palm. My heart twinged as I noticed he had removed his ring, placing it on his other hand.

"You took off your ring," I observed, a pang of sadness creeping into my voice.

"Mark advised me to. He said I might have some swelling. This ring is precious to me because of who it's from," Oliver explained, his tone tender.

Resting my head on his shoulder, I felt his arm slip around me, drawing me closer. Despite our recent disagreement, I couldn't help but crave his warmth and comfort.

"You hurt me," I murmured, unable to suppress the hurt in my voice.

"I know. I feel like all I do lately is apologize to you," Oliver admitted, his voice tinged with remorse.

"Then stop being an ass," I replied, unable to resist a hint of teasing.

"I might be an ass, but I love you. Remember that when I stick my foot in my mouth," Oliver said.

Before we could dwell on our conversation any further, we heard footsteps approaching. Matthew poked his head in the door, announcing that it was time for dinner.

"Time for dinner. What are you reliving your childhood?" Matthew teased, gesturing to the box I had next to me on the floor.

"A little," I admitted with a smile.

"She was a creepy kid, Oliver. She liked to play with worms and spiders," Matthew added, teasing me further.

"Shut up. I did not. I didn't want to hurt them," I protested, rolling my eyes.

"They were her friends. She used to keep the worms in a box with dirt in her room," Matthew continued, his grin widening.

I grabbed a small pink rubber ball that had *Hudson Brook Seniors* written on it in black print and threw it at him. He ducked and I heard it bounce against the wall behind him. He chuckled as he walked way.

"My brother is an idiot. I was just fascinated with crawly things when I was a kid."

"Are you still? Will I find you with a box of worms in our closet?" Oliver asked.

"No, of course not. The dirt would mess up my manicure."

He gave a kiss to my temple. "Let's head down for dinner. I'm starved."

I fixed the items in the box and Oliver stood up to retrieve the ball from the hallway. After I put the box back into the closet, we went downstairs together.

Sadie and Finley managed to keep their secret until coffee and dessert were served. As Finley stood up to make a toast, he announced to everyone that Sadie was pregnant. Astonished looks were shared around the table, and those of us who were already in the know tried our best to feign surprise. Sadie's parents didn't appear thrilled, but they knew their daughter was an adult and ultimately couldn't dictate her decisions.

Perhaps their concern stemmed from Mark and Kristen's situation. Mark and Kristen had tied the knot when Kristen was several months pregnant, much like my own parents.

Kristen, like my mother, was only twenty-one at the time, but my father, being older and well-established in his career, had provided a stable foundation. Sadie's parents might have worried about Finley's fledgling company and the potential financial strain it could place on them.

Later in the evening, as I made my way to the bathroom, I overheard Sadie arguing with her mother in Anders' study about her perceived poor decisions. My heart went out to my best friend, understanding the weight of familial expectations. While her mother was only expressing concern, she likely had no idea that Oliver's intervention had secured Finley's company with a fresh infusion of funds.

Returning to the living room, I found Oliver engaged in conversation with Mark while everyone else played with the dogs. I joined them, holding Trouble in my arms as he licked my hand affectionately. Gratitude swelled within me for Oliver's thoughtful gift of a puppy.

By the time we were ready to leave around 7 p.m., I was yawning, feeling the weight of the long day settling in. We still had presents to open, but exhaustion crept over me. Vlad arrived promptly to take us home, and thankfully, we had fewer items to transport back than we had brought. My mother had prepared an abundance of food, and we all departed with containers of leftovers.

As we were chauffeured home, I dozed against Oliver, feeling content and secure in his embrace. The effects of the hearty meal weighed heavily on everyone, inducing a sense of drowsiness. Despite feeling full long after dessert, Oliver pulled me onto his lap, peppering kisses along my neck as we headed home, cherishing the quiet intimacy of the moment.

"Still mad at me?" Oliver's voice broke through the quiet hum of the car.

"I'm over it. I don't hold a grudge. You know that," I replied, my tone softening.

"I offered Mark a job," Oliver announced, his words sparking my full attention.

"You did?" I exclaimed, suddenly wide awake.

"He's qualified, and we could use help with budgeting," Oliver explained.

“Oliver, that’s the best Christmas gift you could ever give,” I said, feeling a swell of gratitude.

“Colson wasn’t paying him well. He’s worth twice what they gave him,” Oliver continued.

“Are you making up that difference?” I asked, my curiosity piqued.

“I told him we can negotiate, but what I offer will be market. He was intrigued when I mentioned performance bonuses. He could triple his Colson salary just based on those,” Oliver revealed.

“When does he start?” I inquired, eager for the details.

“He’ll be at the office on Monday for a breakfast meeting. I want to introduce him to Tim Burrows in the Budget department. After that, he’ll head down to Human Resources to fill out paperwork,” Oliver explained, his voice tinged with satisfaction.

“You’re wonderful,” I said, unable to contain my admiration.

“He’s qualified. I couldn’t say no,” Oliver replied modestly.

“And he’s family,” I added, acknowledging the deeper significance.

“That’s beside the point. You’re just spreading the love,” Oliver remarked, a hint of playfulness in his voice.

“Contrary to my ruthless businessman persona, I’m

anything but. You know that," Oliver said, his tone softening.

"Yes, I do. I get to see your tender side," I teased gently.

"Don't spread that around," he joked, though I could hear the affection in his voice.

"How's your finger?" I asked, shifting the focus.

"It aches," Oliver admitted.

"You should ice it," I suggested, concerned for his well-being.

"When we get in. How's Trouble?" Oliver inquired, redirecting the conversation.

Glancing into the carrier at my sleeping puppy, I smiled. "Sleeping. My mother wanted to give him turkey, but I told her no. He's too young for that. If Blackie throws up tonight, I wouldn't be surprised. He was given quite a few treats."

Vlad pulled up to our building and double parked so he could help us inside with the packages, Trouble and leftovers my mother gave us. Before he left, Oliver reached into his coat and handed him a thick envelope, shaking the man's hand before he got in the car. I questioned him in the elevator.

"What was that?" I asked, my curiosity piqued.

"Bonus. I give cash," Oliver replied, a smirk playing at his lips.

“How much?” I asked.

Oliver took the carrier with Trouble from me which I was thankful for since my arm was getting tired.

“A lot. Vlad works hard and he deserves it.”

“You won’t tell me how much?”

Oliver shook his head. “Does it matter? I give all my employees bonuses.”

I laughed. “Funny, I didn’t get one.”

He leaned in closer, his eyes glinting with amusement. “You need one?”

“Oh, so I’m special and get excluded.”

“You get me. Now stop fussing.”

Once we were in the penthouse, I switched on the tree lights and put out a training pad for Trouble. Oliver was right; Trouble was smart and knew what to do. After he finished, I cleaned up and put him in his bed where he promptly fell asleep. He had eaten puppy chow at my mother’s house, and I would feed him again later.

I found Oliver in the bedroom, changing. His muscular back came into view as he slipped on a t-shirt. I couldn't help but admire his physique.

“Do you want me to make you an ice pack?” I offered.

“I’d rather sit in bed and kiss you until you beg me to stop,” he said, his voice low and enticing.

"Can I change first?"

He smirked. "Sure. Skip the panties."

I put my hands on my hips. "You said kiss."

Oliver cleared his throat. "I might have other things in mind."

"I'm sure you do."

"Forgive me for wanting to touch my fiancée. What a horrible man I am."

"You said it," I teased, giggling as I headed to the closet. I changed into one of his white t-shirts and nothing else. It hung just below my ass.

Oliver was flipping channels when I returned. He held his arms open, inviting me onto his lap. I obliged, and he immediately dropped the remote, his hands and mouth claiming me. He gently licked my lips before pressing his tongue against them, seeking entry.

I was stubborn, making him work for it. He tickled my ribs, and when I laughed, he took the opportunity to thrust his tongue inside. Oliver kissed me deeply, his tongue probing and teasing until my core ached with need. He was intuitive, his hand roaming down my belly to the hem of my t-shirt. I spread my legs, giving him better access, and the pad of his finger skated over my clit.

I gasped into his mouth as he repeated the motion, again and again, until I was panting. Silently, I begged him to make me come. When he slipped two fingers inside me, I exploded instantly, clenching around him until my body went lax. My head lolled back against his arm as he claimed my neck, sucking at my pounding pulse before diving in for round two.

He was hard, like hot steel against my hip. I didn't want his fingers; I wanted his cock. I protested when he started again, craving more.

"Let me do this," he whispered.

"I need you."

"After this. Come for me once more."

Oliver was faster this time, slicking my swollen tissue with my juices as he rubbed in fast tight circles. I came within seconds as my body went rigid and I spiraled through my second orgasm.

"Your turn," I said as I moved off his lap and clawed at the waistband of his black silk pajama pants. I couldn't release him fast enough. I didn't want him inside me, I wanted to suck him. I knelt in front of him to lick his thick crown

"Ryleigh, what are you doing?"

"Sucking you."

"I thought you wanted something else."

"That will be your second time."

He smirked, leaned back and gave into my will. I took him deep, almost to the back of my throat and he let out a loud guttural moan as he shifted his hips. I bobbed hard on him and massaged his balls. I loved everything about Oliver, his scent, his taste, him. I heard his breathing pick up and I knew he was close when he gathered up my hair and held it from my face so he could watch what I was doing.

"Shit, shit," he groaned as the first splash of cum hit the back of my throat. I kept moving; milking him dry before I cleaned him with my tongue then released him. He was leaning against the headboard with his eyes closed and a silly little grin on his face. I stroked his cheek with my knuckles and his eyes fluttered open.

"You're special," he said.

"So are you," I whispered.

His gaze met mine. "I still can't believe I found you."

"You just needed to look."

"I did look, for years. I almost turned down the graduation speech."

"I'm glad you didn't."

"My heart would still be empty if I hadn't found you."

I moved beside him and placed my head against his chest. My heart would've been empty too if I hadn't found him. He filled my soul and made me complete.

Chapter 16

"You look fabulous in that dress," Oliver said.

It was New Year's Eve and we were heading to a party thrown by Wilmer Hermann, one of Oliver's best friends, at his brownstone in Greenwich Village. I chose one of Rachel Vicaria's originals. She and her husband were branching out into evening wear for both men and women.

My dress was a long slinky dark blue sequined gown with an open back, sweetheart neckline and short sleeves. I paired it with matching five inch heels and clutch. Earlier in the day, I went to have my hair styled in an elegant chignon and my nails polished. Oliver looked stunningly handsome in a black Vicaria tuxedo, white shirt and bowtie. His recently cut hair perfectly coiffed and combed back. I wasn't averse to messing it up on the way to the party.

"Look who's talking. You're breathtaking. I'm glad you didn't shave."

"I take your requests seriously."

He smiled and I loved how his eyes crinkled in the corners.

"You think Trouble will be all right with Finley and Sadie?"

We dropped the puppy off at their apartment a few hours before. I didn't want to leave Trouble by himself for too long and we would be away for several hours. Since Sadie was pregnant, they decided to celebrate the holiday at home.

"He'll be fine."

Oliver ran his hand over my ass, gently squeezing it in his big hand. His pinkie finger was now in a splint. He went to the doctor the day after Christmas to get it checked. I hated the silver splint but I loved that it freed up his ring finger so he could wear his sapphire ring.

"Don't get me started. Hands off," I said pushing his hand from me.

He nuzzled my ear. "Let's stay home."

"No. I want to go out. This will be my first event with you."

He nibbled my neck. "This isn't an event. It's a party."

"Then my first party with you. Stop being a spoiled sport," I demanded.

"I just want you to myself."

"You have me to yourself most of the time. It's me who has to share you with the world."

He shook his head with a wry smile. "Not true. No one cares about me now that I'm off the most eligible bachelor list. Just ask Jordan Grayson. Ever since he got married, no one cares."

I snorted, rolling my eyes. "That's bullshit. I just read an article about him in The Wall Street Journal."

"Okay, so he's not totally off the radar," he conceded, shrugging.

"And neither will you be. I bet if we attend an event, we'll land in the paper," I challenged, crossing my arms.

"Maybe. When we open the new complex on the waterfront, I want you with me," he said, his tone softening as he looked at me.

"It's almost finished, right?"

"Yes, another few weeks. We have over seventy percent occupancy already. I'm hoping to have at least ninety by the time we open."

"I didn't realize you were already taking on tenants," I said, raising an eyebrow.

“It’s how the real estate business works. You can’t wait until you’re open when you still have expenses attached to the property,” he explained, adjusting his cufflinks.

“Are we ready to go?” I asked, stepping closer to fix his slightly crooked bowtie.

He caught my hands and kissed each one tenderly, his fingers lingering over my engagement ring. “I’m going to have to keep you close tonight.”

I frowned, puzzled. “Why?”

“There will be plenty of drink. People get grabby when they’re inebriated,” he replied, his eyes darkening.

“And you don’t want anyone’s hands on me?”

“Of course not. You’re mine. No one should touch you but me,” he said possessively.

“Possessive asshole,” I muttered, slipping on my shoes with a smirk.

Oliver grinned, unfazed by my comment. He enjoyed it when I called him possessive because it was true. Shaking my head, I grabbed my clutch and walked out of the bedroom.

He followed closely, helping me into my long black wool coat. He texted Vlad, and a few minutes later, we were downstairs in the limo on our way to Wilmer’s. As Vlad pulled into traffic, Oliver reached over and stroked my cheek with his knuckles.

“Last chance to stay home,” he murmured, his voice low and inviting.

“No way. I didn’t get my hair and nails done just to sit at home all evening,” I replied firmly.

“Things you didn’t need. I like your hair down and your nails were fine,” he said, his eyes twinkling.

“Says the man who gets his nails manicured every week. They were not fine. I needed it done. My cuticles were a mess,” I countered, laughing.

“You’re getting used to my lifestyle,” he observed, a hint of pride in his voice.

“But I’ll never forget my modest upbringing,” I reminded him gently.

“I had a modest upbringing too,” he said, his tone turning serious.

“Your family was better off than mine. Anders makes a great salary, but not as much as my father,” I pointed out.

“Well, you upgraded,” he teased, leaning in to kiss my lips.

I pulled back, making him scowl. “What the hell was that?”

“I just did my gloss,” I said with a playful grin.

“Shut up, Ryleigh,” he growled, his hand circling the back of my neck as he gently pulled me to his mouth.

His tongue teased mine, and after two minutes, I was rethinking the party. My core started to flood, and I was sure my nude La Perla lace panties were sodden. He broke away, leaving me breathless. I reached up to wipe the gloss from his sexy lips, feeling my heart race.

"Ready?" he asked, his voice husky.

"Let's go," I whispered, still tingling from his kiss. "You really know how to get a girl going."

"If we had more time, you would be naked right now."

I shivered at the thought of Oliver taking me here in the limo. It wouldn't be the first time, but it was exciting to have sex with the only thing separating us from Vlad and the world was a thin piece of glass. No one knew what was going on in our little compartment.

"No. We have plenty of time for that."

Oliver grumbled and moved a few inches away while I retrieved a mirror and lip gloss from my clutch. He fiddled with his phone, checking a few emails and when I was finished, I grabbed for his hand.

"I hope you'll enjoy tonight," he said.

"I'm excited."

The truth was, I was a big ball of anxiety. I hadn't met many of Oliver's friends except for Wilmer, Dax, and Ivan. They were kind and accepting, but I was sure there would be fewer of their type and more of Lara Harvin's type at this party. I wasn't stupid—I could read what was said on social media. Women could be petty and catty. I was sure I would encounter more of what I got from Lara.

"They'll love you. What's not to love?" Oliver reassured, sensing my unease.

~

We arrived twenty minutes later and took our place behind a line of sleek, black limos. This party was clearly drawing the city's elite, which didn't surprise me. Wilmer was quite wealthy—not as much as Oliver, but he did well for himself and had a trust fund besides. I couldn't help but wonder why he hosted the party at his home rather than a high-end venue.

A male attendant in a black uniform and white gloves opened the door and offered his hand to help me out of the car. Oliver quickly followed, thanking the attendant and taking my hand.

We ascended a set of stairs, where another attendant opened the double front doors, welcoming us into a grand foyer illuminated by a huge crystal chandelier. Our coats were taken, and we were given tickets in exchange.

The brownstone was elegantly decorated with walls adorned with art that, to my untrained eye, looked authentic. Jazz music filled the air, and Oliver tucked my arm under his, leading me further inside. Waitstaff dressed in black circulated with silver trays of appetizers and champagne.

The floors were made of dark, rich wood, and above us were ivory-colored pressed tin ceilings. A curving staircase with iron railings led to the second floor, which Oliver had mentioned housed eight bedrooms. But we weren't going upstairs. The open floor plan was crowded with partygoers dressed in fashionable dresses and tuxedos.

Oliver grabbed two flutes of champagne off a passing tray and handed me one. I drank half the glass in one gulp.

"Sweetheart, calm down," he murmured, his voice soothing.

"These are your friends," I said, feeling the nerves creep in.

He leaned into my ear, his breath warm. "Do I have to take you upstairs?"

My face reddened at the thought of Oliver and I sneaking away for a tryst while the party continued below. "God no. That would be embarrassing."

"We'll see," he said with a mischievous grin, taking a sip of his champagne. It was clear he was considering using one of those eight bedrooms before the night was over.

"No," I said firmly, though my resolve wavered under his playful gaze.

Our conversation was interrupted when Dax approached with his date. He was dressed in a white tuxedo with black lapels, and his date, a redhead with what I suspected were fake breasts, wore a skimpy black gown that showed off the top of her ass.

"Hey, you two."

Dax leaned in to kiss my cheek, then backed away to shake Oliver's hand. He introduced us to his date, Candy. I could have guessed her name. We exchanged pleasantries for a few minutes before Dax put his arm around her waist and pulled her away to meet some other friends. The last time I saw them, his hand was sliding down her back.

"That's quite a dress," I remarked, raising an eyebrow.

Oliver leaned in, his breath warm against my ear. "It makes her look cheap, but Dax likes them easy. It wouldn't surprise me if he disappears upstairs with her."

We circulated the party, and as Oliver introduced me to some of his friends, my nerves began to ease. I even felt comfortable enough to nibble on some of the appetizers being circulated.

An hour later, we were sitting on a moss green velvet sofa talking with Ivan and his date, a former model. She was stunning with long, flowing honey-colored hair, statuesque and down-to-earth. We shared a conversation about the Vicarias since she had modeled for them before.

As midnight approached, I was feeling tipsy from the several glasses of champagne I had drunk. I also had to use the restroom. I interrupted Oliver's conversation with a business associate to ask where it was.

"Do you want me to go with you?" he offered, his concern evident.

"I can manage. Just point me in the right direction."

Once I had an idea where I was going, I headed there, only to run into the one person I didn't wish to see—Lara. She was elegantly dressed in a short gold sequined dress, much like mine. She narrowed her eyes as I approached.

"Well, Oliver's little fiancée. I didn't think you would be here," she sneered.

I stood up straighter and looked her right in her green eyes. "Why not?"

"Oliver told me you're a homebody. It seems you've turned him into one too. Boring."

"Excuse me?" I snapped, my voice sharper than intended.

"Boring. He used to be a party boy, but you've changed him for the worse," Lara repeated, a smug smile playing on her lips.

"Why would he need to go out when he has me?" I shot back, trying to keep my voice steady.

"I'm sure you're not as exciting as he needs. You'll see. Eventually, he'll tire of you. I don't give your marriage long," she taunted, her eyes gleaming with malice.

My blood began to boil, and I felt a fierce urge to scratch her eyes out. "Your jealousy is showing. You had your chance, but he didn't want you."

"We had something together. I'm surprised he didn't tell you, but then again, Oliver likes his secrets. You'll find out." She walked away, cackling, leaving my stomach churning with unease.

Oliver was always honest with me, and I was sure what she said was just to get a rise out of me. But the seeds of doubt had been planted. I found the bathroom and slipped inside, telling myself Lara didn't get to me. My eyes stung, and I forced back the tears. She was a jealous bitch, but her words gnawed at me.

I took a few moments to compose myself, dabbing at my eyes and freshening up my makeup before stepping back out. Oliver was waiting for me, leaning against the wall opposite the bathroom.

"Are you okay?" he asked, his concern evident.

"I'm fine. Why would you think different?" I forced a smile, hoping it looked genuine.

"You took a few minutes. I got worried." He put his hand on my bare back, stroking the skin with his thumb. The touch seared into my flesh, not because he was hot, but because I loved when he touched me.

As we walked by the stairs, I paused. "What's the matter?" he asked, his eyes searching mine.

"Can you take me on a tour?" I asked, needing a distraction.

"I don't see why not." He led me up the stairs, the plush cream-colored carpet soft under my feet. I felt an urge to take my shoes off and feel it more intimately. Oliver steered me down a wide hallway with several doors, our steps echoing on the dark hardwood.

He showed me each of the bedrooms behind solid light wood doors. They all had the same elegant tin ceilings as the first floor. When we came to the last room at the end of the hall, Oliver gave me a gentle push and closed the door behind us. He took my clutch out of my hand and placed it on the cherry wood dresser.

"What are you doing?" I asked, breathless.

Oliver didn't respond. Instead, he bent down and kissed my exposed décolletage, his lips warm and insistent. I ran my hands through his hair, feeling the soft strands between my fingers. His tongue traced my cleavage, sending shivers down my spine.

"Oliver...." I whispered, my voice a mix of desire and hesitation.

"Shh. I can't resist," he murmured against my skin.

"It's almost midnight."

"Do you care?" he asked, his eyes dark with need.

I didn't care. I just wanted him, and if we made love through the turn of the year, so be it. He reached back to unzip my dress, and it slipped off my shoulders, pooling at my feet. I stepped out of it, and Oliver picked it up, draping it over the back of a dark blue wingback chair. I clawed at his jacket, and he shrugged out of it, placing it over my dress.

I stood there in nothing but my nude panties, and he latched onto my nipple with his lips, suckling it into his mouth. I moaned softly, hoping no one was upstairs to hear me.

"Where shall I fuck you? The dresser would be nice."

"Why not the bed?" I suggested, my voice trembling with anticipation.

I stroked him through his pants, and he gritted his teeth, gently biting my other nipple and tugging. The sensation sent shockwaves to my soaking core. He lifted me onto the dresser, causing a floral vase and a small crystal box to rattle. Oliver knelt down and removed my heels, caressing my calves before bending my knees and balancing my heels on the dresser's edge.

I almost expected him to tear my expensive panties, but instead, he wrenched the crotch aside and thrust his tongue into me. I had to hold on because he was making me weak, and as my orgasm came hurtling forward, I fell apart, shattering under his skillful mouth.

"You're so wet and delicious. We should've stayed home," he growled.

"This is more fun and dangerous," I muttered.

"No one will bother us here."

"How do you know that?"

"I just do." Oliver stood up as I regained my composure, opening his pants to release his cock. He bent down to pick up my shoes, sliding them back on my feet before reaching into his pocket and pulling out a condom.

"I hate those. You know that," I protested.

"You can't take a shower, and this bedroom doesn't have a bathroom."

"Oh."

I watched as he unfurled the latex over his shaft, anticipation building inside me. He lifted me in his arms and carried me to the bed, laying me on my back. Oliver grabbed the waistband of my panties and pulled them down my legs. I lifted my hips, somehow managing to remove them without taking off my shoes.

He placed a soft kiss on my mouth, and my body heated to the point of bursting into flame. Oliver teased me with the head of his cock, lubricating it with my juices before sliding inside me.

I gasped, wrapping my legs around his waist as he filled me completely. His movements were slow and deliberate at first, building the tension between us. I arched my back, pressing my breasts against his chest, my nails digging into his shoulders.

. . .

"Oliver," I moaned, my voice a plea.

"Yes, love?" he whispered, his breath hot against my ear.

"Don't stop," I begged, my body trembling with need.

He increased his pace, thrusting deeper, harder. Each movement pushed me closer to the edge. The room around us faded, leaving only the two of us in a world of our own creation. His hands roamed my body, exploring every inch, igniting every nerve ending. I could feel the tension coiling tighter and tighter within me until it finally snapped

“Fuck, you always feel so good. Wrap your legs around me.”

I hooked my ankles at the small of his back and he started to thrust, getting into a steady rhythm. He ground the root of his penis against my sensitive clit with each stroke, pushing me closer to another orgasm each time.

“I love you, Ryleigh. I love you so much. There’s never been anyone else for me but you.”

I was involved in our act of love but movement by the now slightly opened door caught my eye. I looked and saw Lara watching us, her face was stoic, and I smiled just before I closed my eyes as I came. When I looked again, she was gone and the door was once again closed.

After my release, Oliver moved me onto my knees and pounded me until he came with a loud grunt. He gently moved for a couple of minutes until he grew semi hard and pulled out, joining me on the bed where I collapsed. He stroked my hair as we heard horns blowing and people cheering. I checked his watch to see it was a few seconds after midnight.

"Happy New Year," I said.

"Happy New Year," Oliver echoed before he placed a firm kiss on my lips.

~

We went downstairs fifteen minutes later, rejoining the party in full swing. Oliver kept his arm around me as we floated from one group to another. Everyone was polite, and many engaged me in conversation. I was in a great mood, my body full of champagne and endorphins. Nothing could ruin my high, or so I thought, until I once again encountered Lara on my way to the bathroom.

There were few people in the hallway since Wilmer had the caterers put out trays of hot food.

"That's the only way you might keep him," Lara's voice cut through the air, dripping with disdain.

I whirled around, my hand poised on the door handle. "Excuse me?"

"To fuck him. Oliver likes sex, and as long as you give it

to him, he'll keep sniffing around. Once you cut him off, it's over."

"What the hell do you know about our relationship?"

She smirked. "I've known Oliver for years. He's like a dog in heat. You should think about what will happen when you get pregnant. He'll lose interest. I know."

My stomach started to churn. "How do you know?"

"Why don't you ask him?"

I crossed my arms. "Why don't you tell me yourself?"

"I'm not helping you," she sneered, turning on her heel and walking away.

I watched her round the corner and sagged against the door. I no longer wanted to spend any more time here. Forgetting the bathroom, I went to find Oliver. When I did, he was engaged in a conversation with Ivan and another man with a shaved head and long platinum-dyed goatee.

"I'd like to go home. I'm tired," I said, my voice trembling.

"Sure. Give me a few minutes," he replied, concern flashing in his eyes.

"Now, Oliver." I turned before he could answer and walked toward the foyer where our coats were. Oliver followed and gently grabbed my elbow.

"What happened in the last fifteen minutes?"

"I don't want to discuss this here," I hissed, trying to keep my voice steady.

"Ryleigh, talk to me."

I looked around for a room to duck into, noticing a pair of French doors. I grabbed Oliver's hand and pulled him inside. I felt around for a light switch and found one near the door. The room was furnished with dark leather couches and walls of bookcases, some of them empty.

"What happened?" he asked, his voice low and urgent.

"Lara."

He gritted his teeth. "What did that vapid bitch say to you?"

"She said as long as we kept having sex, you would stay interested in me. And that once I got pregnant, it was over. Why would she say that?"

Oliver's face tightened, and he began chewing on the corner of his lip. "I have no idea," he said, but there was a flicker of something in his eyes—guilt, perhaps.

"Oliver," I pressed, stepping closer. "Is there any truth to it?"

"No, of course not. You know how careful I am."

"Then why?"

"I have no idea why she would say that. She's trying to get under your skin and it's working."

I pinched the bridge of my nose and closed my eyes. It was the start of a new year, and I was already fucking up. But Lara had me curious. What did she know about my soon to be husband that I did not?

"I'm sorry. Can we just go home?"

"Yes. I'd like to spend some time alone with you."

Oliver led me to get our coats, handing the attendant the ticket he was given at the beginning of the night.

"Aren't you saying goodbye to your friends?"

"It's not necessary. Wilmer is surrounded by a few ladies and I'm sure he won't miss us."

Vlad came to pick us up a few minutes later which made me wonder where he was. It seemed that he never had time off.

Chapter 17

Oliver

"What the fuck do you mean he disappeared?" I barked into the phone, frustration simmering beneath the surface.

"He just did. He's not on St. Croix and we haven't heard from him," Vlad's voice crackled through the speaker.

I paced my office, tension coiling in my muscles as I listened to the update. Two of Vlad's security agents were supposed to be keeping a close eye on Jonah after his bar brawl incident. I thought we had nipped his reckless behavior in the bud, but clearly, I was wrong.

This time, Jonah had gone further, stealing thousands in cash from his fellow workers before vanishing into the night on a supply boat bound for St. Croix. Security had searched, but he was nowhere to be found.

"Dammit! I don't need this shit right now," I muttered to myself, feeling the weight of impending deadlines and my looming wedding press in on me. "Have you checked the airlines?" I demanded.

"Jonah doesn't have ID. Charles took his wallet when he arrived on Fox Island," Vlad replied.

"Then he found some other transportation. Keep looking, and I want a report in the next twenty-four hours," I ordered before abruptly ending the call.

Anxiety clawed at my stomach, a sensation I hadn't felt in years. Ryleigh was usually the one calming me down, not the other way around. With Jonah missing, Caruso would undoubtedly exploit the situation to get to her.

Tyler Barnes was another headache I didn't need. His relentless pursuit of Ryleigh's father's murderer was putting her in danger, and I couldn't let that happen. I escorted her to view a grainy video Tyler had enhanced, watching her break down as she failed to recognize the man.

I recognized him, though, despite the poor quality. Raphael Caruso, Antonio's younger brother, a ruthless thug I'd encountered years before. I'd saved Jonah from him once, but it had come at a cost.

The Carusos were a threat that couldn't be underestimated. Raphael's disappearance had lulled us into a false sense of security, but now he was back, and I had to protect Ryleigh at all costs.

There were signs of a leak within Tyler's department, a dirty cop in Caruso's pocket. If Tyler connected the dots, it could mean trouble. But for now, I had to focus on the immediate threat.

Antonio Caruso's empire loomed large, built on a foundation of crime and corruption. He was watching Ryleigh, but he didn't realize that I was the real threat. I could piece together the puzzle, and once we returned from our honeymoon, I would have a plan to end this once and for all.

Ryleigh

"More?" I asked, as he handed me a piece of paper with a few additional names scrawled on it.

"Our reception is ballooning to almost five hundred people. I need to put my foot down with you," I sighed, exasperation evident in my voice.

Oliver had been sneakily adding names to the guest list since we ordered the invitations a month ago. He probably thought I didn't notice that he'd ordered seven hundred instead of the four hundred we initially agreed upon. The Garden Room could barely accommodate five hundred fifty guests, and at Oliver's rate, we'd hit capacity fast.

"They're business associates. I don't want to say no," he reasoned, his tone pleading.

"Do you want me to say no?" I shot back, feeling the tension rising.

"I could just see that," he teased, throwing his hands up in the air.

"You're making me crazy. I'm so stressed," I confessed, feeling the weight of it all pressing down on me.

Oliver leaned back in his office chair. "I can help with that," he suggested with a suggestive smile.

"Yeah, you can. Stop adding to the list," I retorted, shutting down his advances.

"I mean in other ways. It's after hours and we're all alone," he persisted, his voice dropping to a low murmur.

"No. I'm not in the mood," I replied firmly, trying to push away the frustration and fatigue that clouded my mind.

I missed him terribly during his frequent trips over the past few weeks. Our sex life had taken a hit, and I longed for the intimacy we once shared on a nightly basis. Now, it has been reduced to just a few times a week.

"Ryleigh, tomorrow is the last trip. I just need to seal the deal," Oliver reassured me, his voice tinged with desperation.

"I hope so, or I'm calling off the wedding," I threatened, half-serious and half-teasing, knowing it would hit him hard.

With Oliver away so often, my stress levels had skyrocketed, and my nightmares had returned with a vengeance. The video Tyler had shown me of my father's killer had reignited painful memories, haunting me in my sleep. And with Oliver's absence, I found solace in the company of our pet Trouble, his warmth a comfort in the lonely nights.

Sadie was just about ready to pop and I hadn't been able to spend time with her as much as I would like. She was pretty much in the same boat as me since Finley was now twice as busy. Once it got out that Oliver had an interest in Stewart Applications, the company was flooded with orders. Finley was working fifteen-hour days and Sadie was not happy about it.

"You're not calling off shit. I swear, if you do, I'll kidnap you and take you to the justice of the peace," Oliver growled, his voice dripping with determination.

"Where the hell is there a justice of the peace? Plus, how would you get me to sign for the marriage license?" I countered, trying to hide the smirk playing on my lips.

He flashed a confident smile, his white teeth gleaming. "You forget, I'm Oliver Fox."

"Arrogant fuck," I muttered, unable to suppress a grin of my own.

"You bet your sweet ass. Now finish what you were doing when I called you in here and let me spend the rest of the night asking for forgiveness," he demanded, his tone softening slightly.

"That will take more than one night," I teased, knowing full well his persuasive abilities.

"I bet I can make you change your mind. What are you working on anyway?" he asked, shifting the conversation.

"I was reviewing budget analysis that Mark provided me. He made some suggestions for the Miami project," I explained, gesturing toward the papers scattered on the desk.

"I'd like to see them," Oliver replied, his interest piqued.

"I'm making a spreadsheet," I said, turning back to the task at hand.

"You've become quite the little protégé of mine," he remarked, pride evident in his voice.

"Give me a few more months and I'll surpass you," I retorted, feeling a surge of confidence.

Oliver snorted. "You think so?"

"My brain is younger than yours. I can absorb more," I quipped, enjoying the banter.

"But I've had fifteen years of practice and you've had only a year," he pointed out.

"With teachings by a master," I added, unable to resist a playful jab.

"In bed too," he mumbled suggestively.

"Pardon?" I feigned innocence, knowing exactly what he meant.

"Go finish up," he said, brushing off the comment.

I rose from the chair, purposely dropping a pen on the floor as I bent to pick it up, giving Oliver a tantalizing view. "Miss Stewart, you don't need to entice me with your beautiful derriere. I've already offered to relieve your stress," he remarked, unable to resist the temptation.

"I have no idea what you're talking about," I replied coyly, heading toward the door.

In a flash, Oliver was around his desk, embracing me from behind. His hands cupped my breasts through my blouse, sending shivers down my spine. I couldn't deny the desire coursing through me, the anticipation building with every touch.

"Stop it. I have to finish up," I protested weakly, trying to resist the urge pulling me towards him.

He ignored my plea, his hand creeping up my skirt, his touch sending shivers down my spine. "Jesus Christ, Oliver, the door is open," I hissed, my heart pounding in my chest.

"No one is here. I bet I can fuck you and no one would see us," he whispered, his voice thick with desire.

I strained to listen, hearing the distant hum of the vacuum approaching from the other side of the office. "The cleaning crew is here," I reminded him, trying to inject some reason into the heated moment.

"Then we better hurry up before they get here," he countered, his erection pressing insistently against me, igniting a fierce craving deep within.

I resisted his advances, knowing we couldn't risk being caught in the act. "No," I breathed, trying to steady my racing pulse.

But his touch was relentless, slipping under the lace of my panties, sending waves of pleasure coursing through me. I surrendered to the sensation, clinging to him as I succumbed to the overwhelming pleasure, my body trembling with release.

As I caught my breath, Oliver adjusted my skirt and kissed my neck tenderly. "Finish up and meet me here in three minutes," he instructed, his voice husky with desire.

"Is Vlad bringing the limo?" I asked, eager to escape the tension-filled office.

"He's already downstairs," Oliver confirmed, a smirk playing on his lips.

I hurried back to my office, saving my work and shutting down my laptop with trembling hands. Rushing back to

Oliver's office, I found him donning his suit jacket, his briefcase in hand.

"Can we go now?" I pleaded, my impatience palpable.

Oliver chuckled, his eyes gleaming with mischief. "Let's go," he agreed, leading the way to the elevator.

The journey down to the lobby was agonizing, every second feeling like an eternity. Once inside the car, Oliver feigned disinterest, but I could feel the tension crackling between us.

"Oliver?" I whispered, unable to contain my frustration.

He turned to me, his gaze intense. "Yes?" he responded, his voice low and seductive.

"Are you fucking kidding me right now?" I demanded, the desire burning hot between us.

In a flash, he was across the seat and had me underneath him. He hovered above me, staring into my hazel eyes.

“Did you want something?”

I reached down between us to run my hand over his erection. I could feel how hot he was through his slacks.

"This," I demanded, my voice thick with need.

"Where would you like it?" Oliver teased, his eyes dark with desire.

"You know."

"Why don't you tell me, then?" he prompted, enjoying the game.

I huffed, my frustration mounting. "Inside me. I want you to fuck me. I've wanted you to fuck me since you left for Tokyo."

He leaned back, shrugging off his jacket and tossing it onto the adjacent bench seat. My fingers fumbled with his pants, releasing him from the confines. The sight of his erection nearly made me come right then and there. I missed the feeling of him inside me so much. I gently stroked him, but he pushed my hand away.

"If you do that, I'll come all over you," he warned, his voice strained.

I giggled softly, "You have much more staying power than that."

"But I haven't come since the morning I left you."

"You didn't jerk off?" I asked, surprised.

"I didn't want to jerk off. I wanted to make love. I told you, it's all for you."

He pushed my skirt up and moved the crotch of my panties to the side, positioning himself over me. With a powerful thrust, he entered me, a loud groan escaping his lips. I gripped his ass, holding him still.

"Sweetheart, let me move."

"You feel so good. I want you to stay like this," I murmured, savoring the fullness.

I squeezed him, and he hissed, "Don't, or this is over before it begins."

"Fuck me," I moaned, the desperation in my voice clear.

Oliver began to furiously pump, each thrust sending waves of pleasure through me. Even though I'd had an orgasm less than fifteen minutes ago, I was sensitive and ready to explode again. He slammed into me, and on the fifth stroke, I came with a loud howl, one that even Vlad might have heard behind the smoky glass divider. Oliver followed a few strokes later, grunting and biting my nipples through my blouse, the intensity of his release matching my own.

"Christ, I missed your pussy," Oliver breathed, his voice still thick with lust.

"Just my pussy?" I teased, raising an eyebrow.

Oliver grunted. "You know better."

"I want this again, but slower."

"You have my word," he promised.

Oliver pulled out of me and sat back, leaving me feeling boneless and exposed. He tucked himself back into his slacks and reached into his jacket for a handkerchief, using it to gently clean between my legs. He fixed my panties, righted my skirt, and helped me up.

"I'm tired," I admitted, leaning against him.

"You're tired? I'm the one that flew in from Japan," he reminded me with a soft chuckle.

"I didn't sleep well last night."

Oliver looked at me with concern. "Why?"

I shrugged. "I just couldn't sleep."

"Sweetheart, are you having nightmares again?" he asked, his brow furrowing.

"A few. I slept with Trouble last night. For a little dog, he's a bed hog."

Oliver frowned. "You know I don't want him in bed with us. It spawns bad habits."

"Then stop going away," I retorted, my voice softer, almost pleading.

"Once more and I'm done for a while."

"What about next month? You have to fly to Fox Island to see everything is done properly."

"You'll be with me," he said.

I groaned. "I'm not sure I can. I have so much to do for the wedding."

"It's a few short days, maybe two or three. We can take a much-deserved mini vacation."

"We can discuss it in a few weeks."

He chuckled. "And you call me a workaholic."

I snorted. "You're a bad influence."

Oliver nodded. "I guess I am."

"I don't want phones or electronics on our honeymoon. I don't want to share you. I'm not even sure I want to leave the island. We can explore. I'd love to swim in the lagoon," I stated.

I made the decision of no electronics when I chose our wedding date. Even when he was off or we were away for a holiday, Oliver worked. Maybe it was selfish, but I wanted him all to myself on our honeymoon without distractions.

"We'll do all of that, but you might get sick of me."

I shook my head. "I doubt it. I missed you these past weeks."

"I'm here now," he said, his eyes softening.

As Vlad pulled up in front of our building and got out to open the door for me, I felt a wave of relief. I was glad to be home and even happier to have Oliver with me, at least for tonight.

~

I woke to the sound of the shower running. Oliver was already up, and it was nearing 6:30 a.m. I had hoped he would stay in bed with me a little longer since he was leaving for London this afternoon. I would be alone for another two days. Trouble heard me stir and jumped up from his dog bed near the closet.

"Come here, boy," I called softly.

Trouble trotted over, and I leaned over to pick him up. He was just under eighteen pounds now, a bit overweight because I spoiled him. Oliver would probably be annoyed to find him on the bed, but Trouble would be my sleeping companion for the next two evenings.

The dog settled next to me, and I put my head on the pillow, stroking his fur. He put his head on my stomach and closed his eyes. A few minutes later, the shower turned off, and Oliver emerged from the bathroom with a towel hanging low on his waist. I loved the cuts around his hips and the ridges in his abs.

"Ryleigh, I told you that's not a good idea," he said, nodding toward Trouble on the bed.

"Then stay home," I replied, not missing a beat.

"This trip is the last one for a while. You can still come with me," he offered, running a hand through his damp hair.

"I have a project. We have a back order on marble for the lobby of Fox Towers."

"I thought that was straightened out?" Oliver asked, a crease forming between his brows.

Fox Towers was a project downtown by the waterfront, a mix of commercial space and high-end residences. Oliver had placed it in my hands, and despite my efforts, we were behind schedule by a couple of weeks.

"So did I. I located a supplier that had enough, and now they don't."

"Who are they?"

"Salvaggio International," I said, sighing. "We have a good relationship and give them plenty of business."

"I feel they're giving me a hard time on purpose. The rep I deal with is an asshole."

Oliver bent down to give me a kiss, and despite his protests, left Trouble on the bed. He then went to get his phone, pacing the floor while waiting for the call to connect. He disappeared into the closet, and I heard him talking. A few minutes later, he came out with a smile on his face.

"Problem solved," he announced, his eyes twinkling.

"I spoke to Benito Salvaggio."

I sat up and Trouble jumped off the bed. "You make one phone call and fix it. I wanted to fix it. It's my job."

"Sweetheart, stop getting worked up."

"If they had the tiles then they were jerking me around. Why?" I asked.

"Benito is checking on that."

I had a feeling I knew exactly why the rep did it. Johnny Salvaggio, fucking punk, was giving me a hard time. I met with him two months ago to discuss flooring selections. He was one of those guys who didn't like to get his hands dirty. He wore expensive Armani suits and got his nails polished with a clear coat.

We met at his office and several times as we discussed options, I saw him staring at my breasts. It made me uncomfortable, but I had a job to do. When we were finished, he asked me for drinks even though he knew I was engaged to Oliver. I declined and ever since then, he'd been giving me a hard time, even refusing to speak with the contractor.

"The rep wants to fuck me," I said flatly, watching Oliver as he came out of the closet in a pair of gray boxers. His eyes narrowed immediately.

"Excuse me? How do you know that's the reason?" His tone was sharp, protective.

"Because he said it in so many words."

Oliver crossed his arms, a dangerous glint in his eyes. "So many words how, exactly?"

I sighed, recalling the uncomfortable meeting. "Oliver, the first time I met him, he was staring down my blouse. It made me feel dirty. At the end of our meeting, he asked me for drinks, and of course, I declined. Ever since then, he's been giving me a hard time."

"Why the fuck didn't you tell me this?" he demanded, frustration evident in his voice.

"Because I don't need my fiancé fighting my battles. If I'm going to work in this field, I need to toughen up," I replied, meeting his intense gaze.

"I'll kill that motherfucker," he muttered, fists clenched at his sides.

"Let it go. He's Benito's son, and we have to work with Salvaggio again."

"That doesn't mean he can sexually harass you."

"I agree, but I won't deal with them again. Next time, I'll have Henri handle it."

"I'm sorry," he said, his voice softening.

"It's not your fault. You think this is the first time?"

"Why don't you tell me these things?" he asked, genuine concern in his eyes.

"Because you're busy with your own stuff. As long as they keep their hands to themselves, I can deal with them."

"But you shouldn't have to."

"I agree, but this business is male-dominated, and if I want to play with the big boys, I need to take my licks."

"Uh, the only male you're taking licks from is me," he said with a smirk, trying to lighten the mood.

"You know what I mean."

"I do, but next time, tell me. This set us back a few days."

"Yes, it did, but we can make it up. We're not that far behind," I assured him, pushing the covers off me to reveal my naked body. Oliver's eyes traveled over me, desire replacing his earlier anger.

"I'm going to miss you," I said, my voice filled with the familiar ache of impending separation.

"You know the answer to that," Oliver replied, a small smile playing on his lips.

"Yes, I do. This is it for a while, except for the inspection of Fox Island."

"We won't be apart for that trip. I'm going with you," he assured me.

"A few more weeks. The furniture is coming next week, and the finishing touches are being put on the property."

"I can't wait to see it," I said excitedly.

"You can come to the inspection with me," he offered.

"No. I want to be surprised on our honeymoon."

"You will be," he promised, his eyes sparkling with anticipation.

I stood up and stretched, heading towards the bathroom. With Oliver gone tonight, I planned to work out with Brad. Over the past few months, Brad had helped me get into incredible shape. My torso was now muscular, and my legs and arms were tight and defined. Oliver loved the transformation.

After a long, hot shower, I found my fiancé in the kitchen, drinking coffee and reading The Wall Street Journal. He looked striking in a black suit, pink shirt, and dark pink tie. I loved how he could pull off feminine colors with such confidence.

“Are you coming to the office with me?” I asked.

“Of course. My flight isn’t until 4 p.m.”

“And when will you be back?”

“Friday afternoon.”

“I’m working out with Brad this evening. I skipped yesterday,” I mentioned, hoping to deter him from trying to distract me.

“Come here,” he said, beckoning me over.

I padded over to him, and he turned in his seat, pulling me between his spread legs. His hand slid inside my pink robe, fondling my breast.

“Don’t,” I said, pulling away gently.

“Why not?”

“Because you know where it will lead.”

“You won’t have me for two days—this is your last chance,” he teased.

“I’ll survive. I have for the past few weeks,” I replied, backing away to make myself a latte.

Oliver continued reading the paper until I turned toward him with my mug in hand.

"Are you upset with me?" he asked, sensing my mood.

"A little," I admitted.

"This is business, sweetheart. I wouldn't leave you otherwise."

"That makes it sound like I take a backseat to your business."

"You don't. You're first and foremost. If you want me to sell everything, I will. We can live like nomads for the rest of our lives."

"That makes no sense. It would be like cutting off your arm."

"No, losing you would be like cutting off my arm and taking my heart out. I can live without my business; I can't live without you."

I put down my mug and stared at him, emotions swirling. "Why do you always say shit like that?"

"Because it's true. You mean everything to me."

"I understand. I miss you when you're gone."

"You can still come with me. The situation with the flooring is taken care of."

"But I have other things to deal with."

"Suit yourself. It was just a suggestion."

"I need to get dressed," I said, taking my latte and heading down the hall to the bedroom.

Standing in front of my closet, I debated what to wear. It was supposed to be warm today but also rain. The clouds were already starting to gather, turning the day gray. I chose a navy-blue skirt and a sleeveless blouse in light blue. I could always wear a light raincoat if I needed to. The walk from the limo to our office would only take half a minute.

Oliver came into the closet while I was looking for a matching bra and panty set.

"What are you planning to do while I'm gone?" he asked, curiosity and a hint of jealousy in his tone.

"Hang out with my girlfriends, go drinking, and maybe hit a dance club. Why?" I replied nonchalantly.

"You're not serious, are you?" I asked, holding up a powder blue bra and panty set as I stood up.

Oliver's eyes twinkled mischievously. "Of course I'm not serious. When was the last time I went to a dance club?"

His smile turned wicked, and I could tell he was thinking about the time we had hot, frantic sex in his club, Show Me Yours. We had slipped into the hidden room while the music pounded around us.

"I know what you're thinking," I said, rolling my eyes but unable to suppress a grin.

"Maybe we should go back," he suggested, a devilish glint in his eye.

"Why?" I asked, slipping into my bra.

"I like what we did there," he said, his voice dropping to a husky whisper.

"We can do the same here. We don't need a club to have hot sex," I pointed out, slipping on my panties.

"But it was different and almost voyeuristic. Don't you agree?" he asked, leaning back against the doorframe.

A shiver ran down my spine at the memory. "It wasn't really voyeuristic until you told me that the wall behind the curtains was two-way glass."

"Next time, I should open the curtains and fuck you while we look out onto the dance floor," he teased.

I slipped into my skirt and blouse, trying to ignore the heat spreading through me at his words. "I wouldn't feel comfortable."

"Why? No one would see us," he said, crossing his arms over his chest.

"I still wouldn't feel right," I said firmly.

"We'll see," he murmured, a smirk playing on his lips.

"Uh huh," I replied, buttoning up my blouse.

Rain started to pelt against the patio window, and I glanced outside. "Shit, I thought we could beat it."

"It's no big deal. I have that golf umbrella," Oliver said, unfazed.

"I hate rain," I muttered, already dreading the short walk from the limo to the office.

"We might get some on our honeymoon," he pointed out.

"I hope just a little. I plan to bake until my skin is golden," I said, daydreaming about the sun-soaked beaches of Fox Island.

"That's if I let you out of the bedroom," he said, his eyes darkening with desire.

"Maybe for the first couple of days," I teased, enjoying the way his gaze traveled over me.

"Or the entire honeymoon," he countered, pulling me into a kiss that left me breathless.

I rolled my eyes as I brushed past Oliver. He gave my ass a small smack, making me gasp. It was humid, so I decided to put my mahogany hair into a ponytail. As I did, Oliver came over and kissed the back of my neck, showering it with soft kisses.

"Knock it off, Fox. I'm dressed," I said, trying to sound stern.

"And you can get redressed," he murmured against my skin.

"No, I'll stay dressed. You'll just have to wait until you get home on Friday night," I replied, smirking.

"I should've made love to you all night," he lamented, his voice a low rumble.

“After the first time, you fell asleep. How much sleep did you get on the plane coming home?” I asked, arching an eyebrow.

“I didn’t,” he admitted, a sheepish grin spreading across his face.

“No wonder you were so exhausted,” I said, shaking my head.

I turned to face him, pressing a kiss to his mouth. He gently tugged my ponytail, licking my lips before moving down to kiss my throat. I felt a shiver of desire but held firm.

“I’m not tired now,” he whispered, his breath hot against my skin.

“Friday,” I insisted, pushing him away gently.

He stood up straight, locking eyes with me. “You’re seriously making me wait?”

“Yes. It’s punishment for leaving me so much,” I said, trying to sound resolute.

He chuckled, his eyes darkening with amusement. “You’re also punishing yourself.”

“I can get myself off or use my vibrator,” I retorted defiantly.

“No, you can’t,” he said, a wicked smile spreading across his face.

"What do you mean?" I asked, my eyes narrowing suspiciously.

"I hid your vibrator. Nothing other than your fingers and me is getting you off. I much prefer you don't get off at all while I'm gone," he said smugly.

"If you want to suffer and not jerk off, fine. But if I want to get off, I will," I shot back.

"Suit yourself, but you know it can't compare to what I can do," he said, his confidence infuriating.

"You really are full of yourself," I muttered.

"I'd rather be full of you," he replied, his voice low and teasing.

"Don't you have something to do?" I asked, trying to change the subject.

"No. I've answered all my emails, and I'm waiting on you so we can leave," he said, settling into a chair.

"Watch the news," I suggested.

Trouble came bounding in from his bed by the terrace doors. Oliver scooped him up, placing him on his lap. He wasn't fooling me; I knew he loved the little dog as much as I did.

"You should get him in his carrier," I reminded him.

"In a few minutes," he said, cooing and petting Trouble.

I watched Oliver in the mirror as I put on my makeup. Since we got Trouble, we'd been dropping him off at

Good Doggy, a dog playground where he could spend the day playing with other dogs.

“Matthew said he would take Trouble while we’re away,” I mentioned.

“I thought your parents were taking him?” Oliver asked, slightly confused.

“Trouble loves Blackie, and they get along so well. Matthew’s dog walker can take them both out,” I explained.

“I guess,” he said, still feeling a bit uneasy.

“Are you worried?” I asked, sensing my hesitation.

“Blackie is bigger than Trouble. Suppose they get into a fight?” he said, voicing his concern.

“They don’t fight. Have you ever seen them?” I asked, raising an eyebrow.

“No. But...” he trailed off, still unsure.

“Stop worrying. He’ll be fine,” I reassured him.

As time drew closer to Oliver's departure for the airport, my mood grew darker and more irritable. The thought of sleeping in bed without him gnawed at me, a constant, unwelcome reminder of his absence. I regretted not deciding to go with him.

Just thirty minutes before he had to leave, Oliver sauntered into my office. His movements were smooth and deliberate, like a panther on the prowl.

“Sweetheart?” he called out, his voice a soft rumble that sent a shiver down my spine.

I glanced up from my laptop, trying to keep my irritation in check. “What’s up?”

“I’m leaving soon. Did you eat lunch?” he asked.

“No. I completely forgot,” I admitted, my stomach twisting as I realized how the day had slipped away.

“You should eat,” he said, stepping closer. “Everything alright?”

“No, it’s not. I noticed you added more to the guest list. Please stop doing that.”

He sighed, a look of mild exasperation crossing his face. “I’m sorry. Peyton Branford and his wife will be visiting New York the week of our wedding.”

“Who the hell is Peyton Branford?” I demanded, frustration bubbling over.

“The man I’m meeting with tomorrow,” he explained patiently. “He’s a business associate and has been for many years. I attended his wedding.”

“At this rate, we’ll be at full capacity,” I muttered, feeling the weight of the guest list pressing down on me.

"Is it a big deal?" he asked, genuinely puzzled.

"No, but you have to stop this. Two more weeks and we give the caterer the head count. You can't add any more people to the list."

"I promise, this is it," he said earnestly.

"I bet," I retorted, not entirely convinced.

"I have to leave. Can I have a kiss?" he asked, a teasing smile playing at his lips.

"Do I have a choice?" I shot back, my annoyance still simmering.

"If you want to leave poor Oliver with empty lips, you do," he replied, his tone light but his eyes intense.

"Poor and Oliver do not go together," I said, unable to resist a smile.

He came around the desk and bent down, his lips hovering over mine. I gave him a quick peck and looked back at my screen, trying to maintain some semblance of control.

"That is not an 'I'll be away for two days' kiss," he said, his voice a low growl.

"Then don't go if you want better kisses," I challenged.

"Come on, Ryleigh, don't be difficult," he pleaded, frustration and affection mingling in his eyes.

"It's my signature," I replied, tilting my head up defiantly.

He cupped my face between his hands and pressed a hard kiss to my lips, his tongue invading my mouth with a force that sent electricity shooting down to my core. My clit throbbed in response, and I knew if he kept it up, I would make him late for his flight.

Our heated moment was interrupted by a knock on the open door. Henri stood there, looking slightly uncomfortable.

"Excuse me, sir. Your car is ready," Henri said politely.

Oliver pulled back, his eyes still locked on mine. "I'll see you in two days."

"Yeah, two days," I echoed, trying to hide the longing in my voice.

As he walked away, a part of me wished I had asked him to stay.

Chapter 18

Brad Alistair, my trainer, was relentless this evening. He cranked up the speed on the treadmill, then had me pummel the heavy bag until my arms felt like jelly. By the time I was done, sweat was dripping from my shoulders and face, and I was thoroughly exhausted.

"You did good today," Brad said, handing me a towel.

"You're a sadist," I shot back, wiping the sweat off my face.

"But isn't it worth it?" He grinned, his eyes sparkling with mischief.

I couldn't help but smile. "Yes."

Over his shoulder, I noticed a couple of women eyeing him. It wasn't surprising; Brad was a sight to behold with his muscular frame, blond hair, and chiseled features. Even though he was gay and happily married, he was still a hit with the ladies. Brad was also best friends with Kat Argento, one of Oliver's business associates in the software industry.

Kat had built a dating website, One On One, before her partner pushed her out. She walked away with over half a billion dollars and went on to bigger and better things, including marriage and three kids.

Brad interrupted my thoughts. "You look great. Ready for your wedding?"

"I'm getting there," I sighed. "Oliver keeps adding people to the guest list, and it's driving me crazy."

He chuckled. "The life of a mogul."

"How's Jurgen?" I asked, changing the subject.

"He's great. Stay-at-home dad now. Our daughter Addison is so sweet."

"I'd love to meet her sometime."

"If you allowed children at the wedding, you would," he teased.

"I'm sorry. It would be so hectic with kids around."

"Ryleigh, I'm kidding," he said, placing a reassuring hand on my shoulder. "You'll do great."

"Thanks. Will you be here tomorrow?"

"I guess I could come. Oliver won't be home until Friday night. I hate when he's away."

Brad checked his watch. “I’m knocking off for the evening. My assistant manager can close up the gym tonight. Want to grab something to eat?”

“Can I have what I want?” I asked, my eyes gleaming with mischief.

Brad raised an eyebrow. “I’m not your parole officer.”

I grinned wickedly. “I feel like being naughty tonight. Maybe a grilled cheese with bacon.”

Brad scowled, but his eyes twinkled. “I’ll stick to protein and a salad.”

“You’re so good,” I said, shaking my head.

“That’s what Jurgen keeps telling me.”

“He should, considering he has his sugar daddy taking care of him,” I teased.

“More like he’s taking care of me. The gym is doing great, but Jurgen has become quite the day trader. Meet you in the lobby. I have to lock my office.”

As he walked away, I couldn’t help but feel a wave of gratitude for having someone like Brad in my life. Even on the toughest days, he had a way of making everything seem a little brighter.

I didn't bother showering, just threw on my gray sweatshirt. It was still drizzling and cooler now that evening was settling in. Brad and I headed to the American Café next door to the gym, where they served my favorite—grilled cheese on Texas toast.

We chatted over dinner; the conversation was light and easy. I told him about my wedding dress, making him swear to secrecy since he occasionally ran into Oliver at the gym. Just as we were finishing up, my cell phone rang.

"Finley, what's up?" I answered.

"Sadie's in labor. I'm at the hospital," he said, his voice tight with urgency.

"Which one?" I asked, my heart skipping a beat.

"Lenox Hill."

"How far along is she?"

"It's coming fast. She's almost at seven centimeters."

"I'll be there soon. I'm leaving now," I said, quickly ending the call and shoving my phone into my purse.

"I have to go. Sadie's in labor," I told Brad, my voice a mix of excitement and anxiety.

"Congratulations! You're about to be an aunt," Brad said, smiling.

I dug through my purse for money, but Brad stopped me. "What the hell are you doing?" he asked, frowning.

"I want to give you money for dinner," I said, trying to hand him some cash.

"Get out of here. Go," he insisted.

I planted a quick, soft kiss on Brad's cheek and dashed out of the restaurant. The street was slick from the rain, and I nearly slipped as I raised my hand to hail a cab. Thankfully, one was passing by just as I stepped outside. I jumped in, begging the driver to hurry.

While we sped through the city, I tried calling Oliver, but it kept going to voicemail. I left an urgent message, guessing he was probably still in the air.

Twenty minutes later, I was rushing through the front entrance of Lenox Hill Hospital. The bright lights and stark white walls and floors hurt my eyes, but I quickly found the front desk and got directions to maternity.

When I found Sadie's room, she was already being wheeled out to give birth. Finley stood nearby, dressed in green scrubs with a white mask over his face and a white cap covering his sandy hair. His eyes looked scared.

"Already?" I asked, breathless.

"It came fast. We were going to wait to go to the hospital, but Sadie insisted. I'm glad she did. I have to go," he said, his voice trembling.

My brother followed Sadie as her bed was pushed down to the delivery room. There was nothing I could do but wait.

~

"She's gorgeous," I murmured, stroking my new niece's soft cheek. Teagan Ivy Stewart had made her grand entrance at 8:22 p.m., arriving with a fierce scream. My brother, hands trembling, had cut her umbilical cord. Now she lay peacefully in a small crib next to Sadie's bed.

"Thank you. I can't believe we're parents," Sadie said, her voice heavy with exhaustion. Though her labor had been mercifully short, less than two hours, she looked worn out. Her hair was disheveled, and her face was pale.

"You did great," I reassured her.

"The doctor said I need to be careful because my next labor could go even faster," Sadie added, a mix of awe and concern in her eyes.

"I hope not," my brother muttered, worry creasing his brow.

"You'll just have to get her here as fast as possible. Lucky you were home," I said.

"I wasn't," he admitted. "I was just leaving the office."

"Do you need help? I could take a few days off," I offered.

"Mom is coming down to help, and your mom said she would too. I wanted to thank you for what you and Oliver did for my dad. It's made all the difference," Sadie said, her gratitude shining through her fatigue.

"He's an asset to Fox," I replied, smiling.

“He really enjoys the job.”

“I work with him at least once a week. He’s a whiz with figures,” I said.

“He always was. Perry is just like him,” Sadie said, her voice trailing off as she dozed.

I moved to the green couch next to the wall, watching my brother, who looked ready to drop from exhaustion.

“Are you happy?” I asked softly.

“Very. I was scared until Teagan came out and I cut the cord. Then I knew everything would be all right,” he said, his eyes softening with pride.

“You’ll make a great father, just be home,” I encouraged.

“I’m working from home for a while. I can run the office from there.”

“Good. Any progress on your wedding?”

“Maybe next spring. So much happened this year, we didn’t have a chance to discuss anything.”

“What about you?” he asked.

“Everything would be fine if Oliver would stop adding to the guest list. It’s exploding,” I said with a sigh.

“Sounds like Oliver. Where is he?”

“London.”

“Didn’t he just come home from Tokyo yesterday?”

“Don’t remind me. He said this is the last business trip. We still have to check Fox Island. The house is almost done, but I’ll be going with him,” I explained.

"I’m jealous. A whole island?" my brother said, shaking his head in disbelief.

"It’s only a couple of miles long. Nothing big," I replied with a shrug.

"But it’s your own island," he pointed out, his eyes twinkling with a mix of envy and admiration.

"You can visit us. The house is huge, and we have employee quarters," I offered, imagining him and his family there.

"He has spoiled you."

"Hey! I still do things for myself," I said, defending myself with a playful smirk. I yawned, exhaustion finally catching up with me. "I’m sorry, I’m tired. Not as much as you two, but I’m tired. Do you mind if I go home?"

"Not at all. I expected the parents to be here already," he replied.

"Where’s Matthew?"

"He went to San Francisco to meet a client."

"He won’t see Teagan until he comes back," I noted.

"Nope. She’ll be here," he said, a tired but content smile on his face.

I kissed my brother and went to look at the baby again. Teagan was fast asleep in her crib. I ran my finger gently over her tiny hand before leaving, feeling a surge of love and protectiveness.

As I was on my way home in a cab, my phone rang. Oliver's name flashed on the screen.

"Why don't you have security with you?" he growled the moment I answered.

"Sadie had the baby, a little girl they named Teagan. I ran out of the restaurant so fast that I didn't have time to call Vlad," I said, trying to keep my tone calm.

"He didn't know where the fuck you were. He went to the gym to talk to Brad. You can't do that. I have security for a reason," he snapped, his frustration evident.

"Why are you getting so upset?" I asked, feeling a mix of irritation and concern.

"Because I want you to be safe. Where are you?" he demanded.

"I'm almost home. Relax," I said, hoping to soothe his worry.

"This isn't a joke, Ryleigh. You should've taken Brenda with you," Oliver insisted, his voice stern and unyielding.

"I know it isn't, but I can't be held up just because security isn't with me," I retorted, frustration bubbling over.

"Two minutes and Vlad would've been there. He called me and said he couldn't find you."

"Why don't you just put a tracker on my phone? Or better yet, microchip me so you know where I am each and every day?" I snapped, sarcasm dripping from every word.

"No need to get nasty," Oliver said, his tone hardening.

"Shouldn't I though? You're ruining this for me. I'm an aunt and you're being a dick."

"If being a dick is keeping you safe, then so be it. Hate me for it."

"I'm hanging up now," I declared, my anger boiling over as I hit the power button on my phone just as the cab double-parked in front of my building.

I paid the driver and stepped out, only to see the man I had noticed several months ago lurking half a block down. Under the streetlights, his beady dark eyes were fixed on me. As he began to walk toward me, I felt a jolt of fear. I hurried inside, jamming my finger on the elevator button.

A glance back through the glass doors showed him standing right in front of them, staring at me. My heart pounded so hard I could hear it in my ears. The elevator finally arrived, and I zipped up to the penthouse. I practically ran down the hall, fumbling for my key when I stopped at the door. My hands trembled, but I finally got the key into the lock and shoved the door open, only to scream as I heard footsteps in the hall.

“Miss Stewart!”

“Shit, Brenda, you scared me,” I gasped, clutching my chest.

“Mr. Fox is not happy with you. He told me to check on you. I dropped off Trouble a couple of hours ago.”

“I spoke with him,” I replied, trying to steady my breath.

Her phone rang, and I almost knew it was Oliver. She answered and held the cell out to me. “I’ll call him on mine. Can you stay for a little while?”

“Sure, I’ll wait for you in the living room,” Brenda said, her voice calm and reassuring.

I heard her talking to Oliver as I walked down the hall. Trouble greeted me halfway, and I scooped him into my arms, pressing my face against his soft fur. I put him down on my bed along with my purse and sat on the corner to dial Oliver. He picked up on the first ring.

“Why the fuck did you hang up on me?” he demanded, his voice harsh with worry.

I sniffled, fighting back tears. “He was out there.”

His tone softened, fear evident. “Who was out there?”

“The man I saw months ago. He was waiting for me, and when I got out of the cab, he rushed down the sidewalk.”

“This is what I mean. You need security,” Oliver yelled.

"Who is he?" I asked, my voice trembling.

"I don't know. Maybe the cameras on the building can tell us."

"Should I ask the concierge?"

"I'll take care of it. Dammit, why don't you listen to me? I have your best interest at heart," he said, frustration mingling with concern.

"I know. I'm sorry," I whispered, feeling a lump form in my throat.

"Are you all right?" he asked, his voice gentler now.

"Just a little scared. I wish you were here," I admitted, feeling a pang of loneliness.

"I'll try to be back as early as possible on Friday. If you want, ask Brenda to stay with you."

"I have Trouble," I said, glancing at the tiny dog curled up on my bed.

"He's a tiny dog," Oliver replied, a hint of a smile in his voice despite the seriousness.

"Are you expecting a problem?" I asked, my voice tinged with curiosity.

"Not at all," Oliver replied confidently. "The building is secure, but it never hurts to have extra."

I nodded thoughtfully. "I'll think about it."

"Now tell me about Teagan," he prompted gently.

I couldn't help but smile. "She's beautiful and so small."

"Would you want one?" he asked, his tone softening.

"Eventually," I said, a hint of longing in my voice. "I'd like to spend time with you first."

"As long as we can have one before I'm forty," he teased, a chuckle escaping his lips.

"That's not long off, Mr. Fox," I teased back, enjoying our playful banter.

"You keep reminding me," he said, a mock sigh punctuating his words.

I yawned, feeling the weight of the day settle in. "I'm tired. Brad put me through my paces."

"How was dinner with him?" Oliver inquired, genuine interest in his tone.

"Good," I replied, leaning back against the couch. "He said Jurgen is a good house husband and Daddy."

"I'm sure. They're both very nurturing," he said, his voice warm with approval.

"I think I'm going to take a shower and get into bed," I said, my eyelids growing heavy. "It's very late there. Why are you still awake?"

"Because my fiancée doesn't listen to me," he said with a touch of exasperation.

"Go to sleep. You have a busy day tomorrow," I reminded him gently.

“I love you, sweetheart. Goodnight,” he said, his voice softening with affection.

“Goodnight, Oliver. I love you,” I replied, a warm feeling spreading through me as I ended the call.

As I hung up, I felt a sense of contentment and relief. The day had been long, but Oliver’s voice and our shared plans for the future filled me with a comforting sense of security. I headed to the bathroom for a hot shower, letting the water wash away the day’s stress.

By the time I climbed into bed, Trouble snuggled up beside me, I felt at peace. My thoughts lingered on Teagan, Oliver, and the beautiful life we were building together as I drifted off to sleep.

Oliver

After hanging up with Ryleigh, I dialed Vlad’s number, my mind racing with worry. He picked up promptly.

“Mr. Fox?”

“Check the video feed at my building. Someone approached her when she got out of a cab,” I instructed urgently, my voice clipped with tension.

"I'm sorry I wasn't there," Vlad responded with a hint of remorse.

"For now on, I don't care what she tells you. If she goes to the gym, you're right there. If she goes to the toilet, you're right outside the door," I ordered firmly, my concern for Ryleigh palpable.

"Yes, sir."

"Call me when you find the guy," I added before ending the call abruptly, not waiting for Vlad's acknowledgment. He had made a serious error tonight, and it could have endangered Ryleigh's life. I was giving him a pass this time due to his track record, but I couldn't afford any more mistakes.

I paced the room, my anxiety mounting. Despite the late hour, sleep eluded me. The combination of jet lag and worry kept me restless. I sought refuge at the wet bar in my suite, pouring myself a scotch from a crystal decanter. I rarely drank hard liquor, but tonight I needed something to take the edge off.

As I waited for Vlad's call, my thoughts were solely on Ryleigh. I couldn't focus on the business matters awaiting me in the morning. My mind kept replaying scenarios of what could have happened to her.

Amidst my anxiety, thoughts of Ryleigh's enticing figure crept into my mind, and I felt a surge of desire. But alongside that desire was the weight of the secrets I kept from her. There were things she didn't know, things that could shatter us if they ever came to light. I didn't keep them to deceive her but to protect her from the harsh realities I dealt with.

Twenty agonizing minutes later, Vlad's call finally came through. The scotch had taken the edge off but did little to ease my nerves.

I glared at Vlad through the screen. "What did you find?"

"Login and check the timestamp at 9:28 p.m. I can't be sure, but I think it's him," Vlad replied urgently.

I shuddered. Raphael Caruso, after all these years. I hoped Vlad was wrong. With a clenched jaw, I logged into the system and fast-forwarded the video to the specified time. The footage was crystal clear, unlike the grainy pictures Tyler had shown us. There was no mistaking it—Raphael Caruso had resurfaced.

My heart sank as I watched him appear on screen, approaching Ryleigh. The camera captured her fear, and it tore me apart knowing I couldn't protect her.

"It's him," I muttered grimly. "You know what you need to do. Under no circumstances is she to be left alone, even if she goes to the bathroom. Put another female agent on her detail."

"Brenda is upstairs with her now," Vlad reported.

"I'm aware. I want her to stay until I get home on Friday. And put a couple of agents on both Carusos. I want to know their movements and what they're up to. Have you located my brother?"

"He's gone. Nothing comes up. We've checked his associates, old haunts and even his old apartment. He just disappeared into thin air."

I clenched my fist. "I don't want to think what that could mean."

"I doubt it. He had a plan and he executed it."

"How can you be sure?" I asked.

"Your brother wanted to disappear. He's been doing it for years."

"But he usually surfaces and that hasn't happened."

"Caruso is looking for him, you can bet on it. He's laying low."

"I should've hidden him away somewhere, anywhere."

"And what makes you think he would stay hidden?"

"You're right. My focus now is Ryleigh. I don't want any fuck ups, Vlad."

"I'll see to it, sir."

"Goodnight."

I ended the call and sank onto the couch, draining the last of my scotch. Raphael Caruso—a name that haunted me. It surprised me that Antonio had sent him instead of a lackey. Maybe it was because Raphael had botched things with Robert Stewart's murder.

"He should've taken out Ryleigh also," I muttered aloud, processing the thought. Maybe Raphael didn't have the guts to harm an innocent child, or perhaps he didn't know she was there. Ryleigh never spoke much about it, and I never pressed.

It was past 4 a.m. in the morning, and I had a meeting at 7 a.m. I didn't feel like sleeping in bed, so I stretched out on the white contemporary couch. As I dozed off, thoughts of Ryleigh filled my mind, her safety now more critical than ever.

Ryleigh

I tried to scream as his hands closed around my throat. He wasn't going to end me swiftly like he had my father; he intended to squeeze the life from me slowly, relishing every moment.

His sneer bore into my panic-stricken eyes as he pressed harder against my windpipe. I braced for the agony of my neck snapping or the suffocation that never came, only to be startled awake by Brenda shaking me.

"What the..." My eyes shot open, catching the concern etched on her pretty face. Sweat coated my forehead, and I instinctively wiped it away.

"You were screaming," Brenda said softly.

“Nightmare,” I managed between ragged breaths, trying to steady myself. Trouble, my loyal companion, stood nearby, looking bewildered. I must have frightened him.

“Do you need me to stay?” Brenda offered.

“No, I’ll be fine. Thank you for waking me.”

“No problem. Get some sleep,” she advised before exiting, leaving the door slightly ajar as she found it. It was nearing 4:30 a.m., and I knew sleep was futile now.

“Come here, boy,” I whispered.

Trouble cautiously approached, stopping just out of my reach.

“I’m sorry I scared you.”

As if understanding, he finally joined me on the bed, where I gently petted his ears. He settled beside me, and I turned off the light, staring into the darkness. The face of the man who had killed my father haunted my dreams now, a chilling reminder that he was out there, waiting for an opportunity to strike.

I resolved to remain vigilant and rely on the security Oliver had in place to protect me. That was their job, after all. I wondered if Oliver knew this man. Months ago, when we watched the enhanced video Tyler had shown us, Oliver’s reaction was subtle but palpable; his face had drained of color. I was afraid to ask, but maybe I should.

I stayed awake, periodically soothing Trouble, who grumbled softly but settled beside me. With the dawn creeping through the curtains, I finally slipped out of bed and took a long, hot shower in an attempt to shake off the unease and slight headache that lingered. Brenda was already up, seated on the couch with a magazine when I entered the kitchen.

"Good morning," I called out as Brenda sat on the couch.

"How are you?" she asked, looking up from her magazine.

"I'm okay. Thank you for this morning," I replied sincerely.

"You're welcome."

"Would you like some coffee?" I offered, moving toward the coffee maker.

"That won't be necessary, Miss Stewart," Brenda replied politely.

I paused, my hand hovering over the coffee maker, and turned to face her. "Brenda, you don't need to call me Miss Stewart. Just Ryleigh is fine."

"That wouldn't be appropriate," Brenda insisted gently.

"Then why don't you call me Ryleigh when Oliver isn't around?" I pressed, hoping for a different response.

"It still wouldn't be appropriate," Brenda reiterated firmly.

I sighed, resigning myself to the formality, and returned to preparing my coffee. I brewed a strong cup with several spoons of sugar, needing the extra boost this morning. It was early, barely 7:30 a.m., and I didn't have to be in the office until nine. Trouble, sensing my movement, circled my legs, reminding me he needed to go out.

I led him to the patio where he promptly headed for the small patch of grass Oliver had installed for him. While he did his business, I prepared his kibble and set it out on the floor. He scratched at the door when he was done, eager to come back inside and devour his breakfast.

With Trouble settled, I took my coffee back to the bedroom and stepped into the closet to choose an outfit. The day looked promising, so I opted for a floral-patterned sleeveless dress that Oliver had always liked. I wished he were here to see it. Pairing it with white heeled sandals, I gathered my hair into a ponytail and prepared for the day ahead.

I was incredibly unproductive at the office for most of the morning. Mark came in to discuss some figures, but I found myself zoning out repeatedly, causing him to interrupt my thoughts several times.

"Let's take a break," I finally said, realizing my mind wasn't in the right place.

"What's wrong?" Mark asked, concern etched on his face.

"I've got a lot on my mind with everything going on. The

wedding is coming up so quickly. Oh, and I meant to congratulate you—grandpa!" I grinned.

Mark cringed, a mix of surprise and humor crossing his features. "God, I can't believe it. I'm only forty-six. I never expected Sadie to have a child this soon."

"She always talked about wanting to be a mom," I said, shaking my head with a chuckle. "Little did I know she'd end up being my sister-in-law."

Mark shrugged. "They don't seem to be in any rush to tie the knot."

"Finley mentioned they might do something next year. It's been a crazy year for both of them."

"I guess so." Mark paused, noticing my tired expression. "You seem like you've got a lot on your mind. Why don't I come back later?"

"I'd appreciate that," I replied gratefully.

Mark gathered his things into a folder and left. My head was too cluttered to focus on anything productive right now. When Brenda had escorted me into the building this morning, I couldn't help scanning the area, half-expecting to see the man with the piercing black eyes waiting for me. The same unease crept over me as I walked to my office.

Knowing Brenda was somewhere nearby was reassuring. I felt safe, despite my earlier annoyance at being constantly surrounded by security. Now, though, I welcomed it. I knew Oliver wanted nothing more than for me to be protected, especially with the recent unsettling developments.

I was overjoyed when Oliver snuggled his boxer-clad body against me early on Friday morning. I hadn't expected him home until that afternoon. Despite him overheating me by being so close, I welcomed his presence eagerly. He buried his nose in my hair, and I heard him inhale deeply.

"You smell so good," he murmured.

"You do too," I replied softly.

"I'm sure I don't, but I'm too exhausted to shower right now," he chuckled wearily.

I turned in his arms so I could face him and kissed the underside of his chin. His scruff scratched against my skin, but I didn't mind at all. I was simply happy to have him home. He started softly snoring, and I nestled my head against his chest, drifting back to sleep.

The sleep was fitful, though, and I found myself waking from a nightmare. It wasn't as intense as the one from the night before, thankfully. Oliver remained peacefully asleep beside me, undisturbed by my brief moment of fear.

Chapter 19

Oliver looked at me with concern. "Are you sure you don't want to come to Fox Island with me?"

I shook my head, smiling softly. "No. I'll stay right here on the beach waiting for you."

It was now the third week of June, and our home on Fox Island was finally completed. Part of me wanted to go with Oliver, but I had decided against it. In five weeks, I would see the place for myself.

"The beach?" Oliver raised an eyebrow.

"I might as well work on my tan while you're gone," I replied, trying to lighten the mood.

"You can work on your tan at the hotel."

"But I want to lie on the sand," I whined, knowing exactly what he was thinking.

He was concerned that the man from the street might have followed us down to St. Croix. He wanted me to stay where I could be easily protected and safe. Our suite had a patio with a small lap pool, perfect for cooling off after sunbathing. But I preferred the beach.

Oliver sighed as he tucked in his ivory polo shirt. "Take Brenda and Raquel."

Raquel was the new agent Vlad had brought on board. She was tall and blonde, with a striking appearance that could easily pass for a model rather than a security agent. Despite her looks, she was well-trained with a second-degree black belt in karate and impressive shooting skills. She had a friendly demeanor, often calling me by my first name when Oliver wasn't around.

"I plan to. It'll be a girl's day at the beach," I assured him.

Oliver frowned. "They're not your friends, they're your security."

"Should I have them wear their full clothes and gun holsters?" I teased.

"That won't be necessary. The point is for them to blend in," Oliver replied seriously.

I rolled my eyes at him. "Duh, obviously."

"You're feisty this morning, and dare I say, a little rude," he remarked.

"That's what happens when I go without sex," I retorted playfully.

"I'm sorry if I had a headache. I'll make it up to you when I get back this afternoon."

"Why not now?" I suggested with a mischievous grin.

"Because I have an appointment with Charles. I'm sure he doesn't want to be on Fox Island any longer than he has to."

"You're Oliver Fox. Isn't that what you always tell me?" I teased, enjoying the banter.

I opened my Louis Vuitton suitcase, searching for my favorite light blue bikini. As I dropped my pink robe to the floor, exposing my body, I heard Oliver stifle a groan with a cough. He sat on the edge of the bed, pulling on athletic socks, but his eyes never left me.

“Something wrong?” I asked.

“I can be fast.”

I raised my eyebrows. “Maybe I don’t want fast. Maybe I want slow.”

“Maybe you don’t get it at all.”

“Asshole,” I mumbled.

“Get on your knees on the bed before I change my mind.”

I stood there defiantly with my arms crossed over my naked breasts. Oliver stood up and opened his shorts, pulling them down along with his boxers. He was hard and ready. I was ready too because I'd been wet since I woke up an hour ago.

"Ryleigh?" he questioned.

I stared at his cock as he stroked it with his fist. The throbbing between my legs was getting to be almost unbearable and I gave in, getting all fours at the edge of the bed. He gave my bare cheek a slap and ran his penis through my folds, teasing me.

"When are you going to learn that I always win?"

"Never and you don't always win."

"Don't I?" Oliver asked.

Before I could answer, Oliver thrust inside me which made me gasp and bite my lip.

He chuckled. "I'm sorry, I didn't hear your answer."

"Fuck you," I hissed.

"I think it's more like I'm fucking you."

Oliver curled his hands around my hips and began pounding me. This one was going to be quick because my orgasm was building at an enormous rate.

"Slower," I begged.

"I said this had to be quick," he grunted.

It didn't matter, a few more strokes and I clenched my walls against him, falling apart as I found my release. My body weakened and the only thing holding me up was Oliver as he hammered into me.

"Fuck, I love this tight pussy," he moaned.

He kept moving, battering my tender walls until he groaned and spilled into me, filling me with his semen. He pulled out and I sank to the bed which is where he found me after he came back from the bathroom.

"I need a nap," I mumbled into the duvet cover.

"You don't need a nap. You just slept for several hours."

"You exhaust me."

I felt the bed dip as Oliver sat down on the edge of it to plant kisses on my bare back.

"Come on sweetheart, get up," he prodded.

"Why?" I asked.

"Don't you want to eat breakfast together?"

"I thought you had to go."

"I texted Charles and said I was delayed."

"Before or after?"

"After. He'll wait because he knows I have a nice fat bonus for him."

I pushed myself up and Oliver got off the bed so I could stand.

“Mmm, Belgian waffles. I love these with Nutella,” I said.

“I know. Why do you think I ordered them?”

“I didn’t see Nutella on the menu.”

“I’m...”

I cut him off. “I know, Oliver Fox. Do you ever get sick of saying that?”

“Not at all because it’s true. I worked hard to get where I am and I might as well enjoy my status.”

“Arrogant asshole,” I said under my breath.

Oliver looked up from his mushroom omelet. “Excuse me?”

“Like you didn’t know what I said.”

“Are you ever going to stop calling me that?” he asked.

I rolled my eyes. “Yeah, when you stop acting like one.”

“Then never.” He reached out and stroked my bare arm. After I got up from bed, I took a quick shower to clean myself, keeping my hair dry. I was now dressed in the blue bikini I pulled out of my suitcase before we made love. I finished a waffle, took a few sips of coffee and pushed back from the table.

“I’m full and ready for the beach.”

“I should only be a couple of hours. Charles made some modifications to the employee quarters, and I need to check those also.”

“What modifications?”

“He added an outdoor shower and a patio with a grill outside the sliding glass door. Just because they’re employees doesn’t mean they shouldn’t be comfortable.”

I nodded. “That was nice of you.”

“I try.”

He stood up, tipped my head with two fingers on my chin and gave me a coffee flavored kiss.

“Remember, stay with Brenda and Raquel.”

I crossed my arms. “What do you think I’m going to do? Run and get ice cream from the Good Humor man?”

“No. I mean if you want to use the restroom or go swimming.”

“Stop worrying. I know the drill.”

“They should be here in a few minutes. Do you want me to wait?”

“No. You can go. I’ll be fine. Don’t keep Vlad waiting.”

“Fine. Be careful and don’t forget sunscreen.”

He planted another kiss on my lips before he slipped on a white baseball cap and his sunglasses.

Chapter 20

Raphael Caruso

Antonio leaned forward, peering through the binoculars. "You see him?"

"Yeah. He's on his way out of the hotel with his security guy, big fucker. I'm not sure I can take him," Raphael replied, shaking his head.

"You don't need to worry about his size when you have a gun."

"If he's out of the hotel, she's by herself."

My brother, two of our associates and I were stationed in a modest hotel across the street from The Diamond Square Resorts. With a few bribes, I had managed to learn Oliver Fox and his fiancée's suite number and secured a room with a view of their location.

The Royal Sands might not have been as luxurious as Diamond Square, bit its rooftop deck provided a perfect vantage point for observing Fox's movements.

I fled to Italy after the incident with Roberts Stewart, hiding from Antonio's wrath. My brother was ruthless when crossed, and I knew I needed to eliminate both Oliver and the girl to earn my way back into my brother's good graces.

We had discovered Ryleigh Stewart unexpectedly, thanks to an article about cold cases that jogged her memory. I had attempted to approach her weeks ago, hoping to capture her and bring her to Antonio, bust she had escaped into Fox's heavily secured building.

Oliver Fox had clearly sensed the danger; security around the couple had tightened considerably. Eight agents now protected them, making my task more challenging. With their wedding approaching and plans for a secluded honeymoon on an island Oliver owned, we saw an opportunity to strike.

I grinned as I watched Ryleigh Stewart emerge from Diamond Square with two formidable-looking women, likely her security detail. I knew I could overpower them, despite their apparent strength.

I wished I could take care of Ryleigh now, but part of the plan was taking care of them together. No one would hear from them or the security detail for days before someone came to check. By the time they were found, the heat would bloat their dead bodies, making them grotesque and almost unrecognizable. The only loose end would be Jonah and he was still missing but eventually would surface.

Yes, the lives of Oliver Fox and his bride would be coming to an end soon. It would be one hell of a honeymoon.

The End

Book 2

To Be Continued - Check out an excerpt from When We Were US - Book 3 of The Sly Fox Series and click here to purchase

I never thought I would say it, but I despise my husband. I hate Oliver Fox so much that to simply look at him makes me sick. I want—*need*—him to answer for his secrets, but he just lies there in his hospital bed as the machines attached to him beep, registering his vitals.

Sometimes I sit by him and feel the urge to pull the plug from his ventilator. The doctors claim he'll eventually wake but as the days pass, I don't care if he ever does. All I can hang onto right now is the plan I have to divorce him and take over his business.

After that horrible night on Fox Island, I came back to claim the helm of Fox Asset Corporation, one of the youngest CEOs in corporate America. Oliver gave me power of attorney if anything happened to him. At the tender age of twenty four, I have the world in my hand. Over the past two months, I've grown bitter and angry. I know my employees hate me and I don't care.

I just want everything to be the way it used to be; before Oliver was shot, before I found the folder of handwritten notes hidden in a file marked *Leigh Ryerson*, before I found out about his life before me. And of course, before I would bear the physical and emotional scars his deceit created. I buried them deep, away from my family and friends to see. They didn't know the truth and I wouldn't tell them until the time came.

To Be Continued - Check out an excerpt from When We Were Us - Book 3 of The Sly Fox Series and click here to purchase

Printed in Great Britain
by Amazon

53377763R00260